The

Unity Hall says she has been writing for a long time. A totally undistinguished school career in Wembley was just saved by pages and pages of ill-spelt, untidy essays.

Still unable to spell, she has worked in Fleet Street as a journalist since leaving school, apart from three years of living in the United States where her jobs were more varied, including waitressing, selling and making doughnuts.

Unity Hall is woman's editor of the *News of the World*. She travels widely, including several recent trips to Hong Kong, lives in London, and spends as much time as possible at her home in the South of France.

Her two other books, *Secrets* and *But Not for Long*, are also published in Pan.

Also by Unity Hall in Pan Books

Secrets
But Not for Long

Unity Hall

The White Paper
≈ Fan ≈

Pan Original
Pan Books London and Sydney

First published 1983 by Pan Books Ltd,
Cavaye Place, London SW10 9PG
9 8 7 6 5 4 3
© Unity Hall 1983
ISBN 0 330 28088 0
Photoset by Parker Typsetting Service, Leicester
Printed and bound in Great Britain by
Collins, Glasgow

This book is sold subject to the condition that it
shall not, by way of trade or otherwise, be lent, re-sold,
hired out or otherwise circulated without the publisher's prior
consent in any form of binding or cover other than that in which
it is published and without a similar condition including this
condition being imposed on the subsequent purchaser

For Patsy Hurll

my friend and neighbour who has read the words,
voiced opinions, borne with the clatter
and never once complained

≈ *1* ≈

'Isn't lovemaking extraordinary?' she said drowsily, her words flattened by the warm air and heavy furnishings of the room.

'In what way?' he asked. He was lying on his back beside her, a sheet covered them both, and his hand rested lightly on her bare belly.

'It's ridiculous – afterwards,' she said. 'You doing all those undignified things to me. Me doing all those undignified things to you. And so engrossed; so enjoying it. We hardly know each other as people, but I know your body very well.' She was silent for a moment. 'And now I feel shy,' she added.

She was stretched beside him on the large bed and the sunlight coming through the window, diamond bright, striped the white sheet with yellow. They were not touching, but as her voice trailed into silence he took her hand and squeezed it.

'There's no need to be shy,' he said. 'Anyway, it's too late after what you call all those undignified things we've done to each other.'

She made a small sound that could have been a stifled laugh and then leaned up on her elbow to look down at him. He was tall enough for his feet to reach the very end of the bed, blond, with fair hair coating his chest and glinting in the sunlight. Even without clothes he looked very American, she thought.

'We should have pulled the curtains,' she said, her voice suddenly anxious. 'Anyone could have seen in.'

She had heard a heavy tread, hollow sounding on the narrow wooden verandah that ran along the front of the building and that led into the individual hotel rooms.

'No one can see in,' he said lazily, reaching for a cigarette. 'The sun's on the glass.'

A figure went by the window. She saw the bright blue and white striped anorak and the skis resting on a thickly padded shoulder. She wasn't sure if it was a man or a woman.

'They're coming back from the mountain,' she said.

'Only a faint heart,' he said. 'It's too early. Still sunny. Still light.'

The carpet at the foot of the bed was littered with their own discarded ski clothes. Hers deep turquoise; his bright red. Their gloves and goggles lay, grotesque, on the heavy wood dressing table, and the bedcover had been thrown on to the floor. The room was almost too warm.

He stayed with his head on the pillow as she looked down at him and then he lifted his hand to run it down the length of her body, tracing one finger between her small breasts.

'Jade,' he said. 'Beautiful Jade. Well named.' He stroked the skin over her rib cage and explored the flat stomach. 'Pale, pale Jade you are. Jade of the most expensive kind.'

'It's a stupid name,' she said. 'Pretentious.'

'No,' he said, his voice as positive as hers had been. Then he added lightly, 'But perhaps you should tell me the rest of it.'

'My name, you mean?'

'Your surname.'

She hesitated and moved uneasily under his hand.

'Names, actually. McKenzie McKenzie Martin.'

She waited for the usual reaction. At home in Britain when she was introduced, people always said: 'Anything to do with the shipping family?' but he merely looked incredulous and then grinned.

'Say again.'

'Jade McKenzie McKenzie Martin,' she told him. 'Absurd isn't it?'

'I guess you could say that,' he said, sitting up to pull more easily on his cigarette. His back was tightly muscled but she resisted the urge to touch.

'My sister's called Poppy,' she said, looking up at the ceiling. 'Poppy McKenzie McKenzie Martin. We're both adopted—' she paused waiting for some comment but none came. 'The McKenzie bit is my mother's maiden name. My grandfather – her father – had no son and insisted my parents took his name when they married. Martin is my father's surname. Put together they take an awful lot of room on passports. People complain they need very long envelopes to write to us.'

She looked at him to see if he understood the joke. He had. He chuckled.

'And I'm just plain Smith,' he said.

'How very American of you,' she said mockingly.

He laughed and leaned over her, kissing her small, dark nippled right breast.

'Hi, Miss McKenzie McKenzie Martin,' he said, 'glad to know you.'

'Hallo, Gary Smith,' she said and defensively pulled the sheet to cover her body. She was suddenly unhappy about the situation, wishing herself a million miles away from the pleasant – but very naked – young man she hardly knew. He had put out his cigarette and settled back down into the bed, one arm lazily over her. She realised he was going to fall asleep, in the abrupt and sudden way that men often did when they were satisfied in bed.

His breathing was deepening and knowing he would be vulnerable to truth with sleep so close she asked: 'Why did you keep following me. You *were* following me?'

'I was. And because you are a remarkably beautiful girl,' he said promptly but without opening his eyes.

'And you have a taste for the exotic?'

'Don't be difficult,' he said. 'I have a taste for small, slender, dark-haired and dark-eyed girls. If that's a taste for the exotic, I plead guilty. Personally I'd say it was an attraction of opposites. Right?'

'Right,' she said.

He turned his head on the pillow to look at her.

'But if you really want to know what got me,' he went on, 'it was that terribly British voice of yours and your English good manners.'

'I don't have a terribly British voice,' she said indignantly. 'I have no accent at all.'

'Well, let's say you don't sound as if you're from the Bronx,' he said. 'And I liked the way you are with people. Always polite. Always a smile.' He patted her stomach. 'Now go to sleep and stop asking questions.'

He was almost asleep himself, but she lay beside him wide awake and wondering what she was doing in bed with a man she had only really spoken to a couple of hours before.

She had wanted to tell him that it was not her habit to make love with men whose surnames she didn't know. Then she had decided that to say so would have seemed schoolgirlish, protesting too much and not really believable. It was true they had only really talked an hour or so before, but he had been hovering on the fringe of her life

9

for four days, ever since she had flown up from Los Angeles to Aspen. And she had been more attracted to him than anyone else she had ever met.

It had been an irritating trip. She had first seen him at the bar at the airport, drinking beer and deeply engrossed in a paperback book whose title she could not read. Then, once on board the Boeing, it was announced that the flight to Denver had been delayed for two hours because of an engine fault.

On the plane, while they sat on the tarmac sweating out the wait and the repair, he had been a few seats in front of her, still reading the book. She noticed that occasionally he turned to look at her and she hastily returned to her own book. She disliked being picked up. It was not her style to put out signals to strange men on aircraft.

They arrived near dusk at Denver to find light snow swirling as the plane came low to land and she could see what appeared to be a flat, ugly endless city coated in white below. The blond man was behind her as they left the plane and he was still behind her as she walked through the interminable, hard-on-the-feet spaces of the airport to the Aspen Airways Desk. Her hand luggage and the skis she had bought in Los Angeles were beginning to weigh heavy; there were no porters and no trolleys and she half hoped the man following close behind might offer to help.

He didn't.

By the time she had reached the Aspen Airways area, the blonde receptionist was announcing to a group of disgruntled passengers that there would be no more flights that night. The visibility had gone and outside the blizzard raged on. Through the half-open door to the tarmac, the world was white.

'Maybe in the morning,' the receptionist said. 'Once the light gets up.'

The blond man was just to Jade's left, listening.

'Where do I get an hotel?' she asked the receptionist. 'Is it worth going into Denver?'

'No.' The man was speaking before the receptionist could answer. 'It's not. You want to be back here first thing to get a plane. There'll be a backlog of people trying to get through and it's best to be early in line. Down the hall there you'll find a freephone to all the different hotels. Ok?'

He grinned, half saluted and turned away. He wasn't carrying anything she noticed, not even skis.

'The guy's right,' the receptionist said. 'You can leave that hand baggage here if you like. Just take what you need for the night. We'll get you through in the morning, somehow.'

As Jade went to look for the freephones she wondered why she had left the comparative warmth of Los Angeles – though even LA was not at its sunniest in January – for the dubious delights of skiing in the Rockies.

'Get you through in the morning' sounded as if flying to Aspen could be a major operation or even disaster. It was all very different from St Moritz, she decided.

To her surprise the blond man was at the same hotel as she had chosen – a vast, dimly lit echoing shell with a few sad mobiles trying to fill the yawning caverns the architect had left from floor to fourteenth ceiling.

They both ate in the downstairs restaurant, and he seated himself a few tables from her. He gave her a not unfriendly nod and went back to the interminable book. She wished he would join her. She felt lonely and somehow slighted. But other than the nod he paid her no attention. He read his book as he ate a hamburger. She sat staring into space and thinking, while she toyed with what she decided was the nastiest steak she had ever eaten.

It was her father who had suggested she go to Aspen for a few day's skiing after a dreary Christmas and New Year in Los Angeles.

'You need to get away,' he had said. 'Let Poppy take her turn.'

'But she won't,' Jade had told him. 'You know she won't help at all.'

'I'll see she does,' her father had said.

Jade had known that Poppy would not take her turn. Already Poppy had found herself a rich young American at the Chateau Marmont where they were staying, and had been sampling the excitements of Beverly Hills nightlife. She had stayed in bed sleeping late, sleeping off the night-before's champagne, while Jade and her father had tried to cope with the seemingly hopeless problem of Margaret McKenzie McKenzie Martin, wife to Ralph Martin and adoptive mother to Poppy and Jade.

She would have been better employed keeping her father company than sitting in this dreary hotel, she decided. It had been a mistake to come.

But the next morning, flying through the grey and white fortress of the Rockie Mountains, buffeted by winds in a small plane and clutching a paper mug of hot coffee in her hand, her spirits began to lift. The Rockies were close below; sometimes bordering the plane so that it seemed as if the wing-tips might just disturb the light snow that coated the granite. The young American was on the same plane sitting two seats behind. He had been at the airport before her when she arrived in the grey dawn. He had said 'Hi' and inquired of her night's sleep. Then he had moved on.

That was the point when he had begun to get under her skin.

And now she was in bed with him.

It had taken two days to happen and in the end she had made the first move. She had realised that Aspen was not a town in which to be alone. The Limelight Hotel where she had booked in had no restaurant. Eating by herself had meant no peace from ski-bum boys looking for a meal-ticket. Jade looked like a meal ticket in her lynx coat and expensive ski clothes. She had the shine of money and she was not able to dim it.

She had been offered cocaine which she did not take, sex that she did not want. Only throughout the day on the ski-slopes, where the dizzy altitude two miles above sea-level made her breathless, was she at ease. She skied well. She had skied since she was four years old.

The slopes were exhilarating and the standard of the other skiers on the mountain was high. But after she had skied, she ate at the Ute City Banquette restaurant, then in the evening when there was nothing else left to do, went back to the luxury and safety of her room at the Limelight Hotel.

She was lonely.

An Aspen free sheet newspaper had indicated that the Tippler's Bar at the foot of the mountain was the local pick-up place, and wondering if the blond young man would be there, she went one lunchtime after she had skied down the mountain.

The bar was packed with not-so-young people – Aspen was too expensive for the young, she had realised. They were straight off the slopes, and the room, looking on to the pretty town, splashed with the bright colour of anoraks, was like a children's paint box. The din from conversation, shouts from the exuberant sportier types, made her hesitate at the door. And then she saw him.

She walked straight to where he was sitting at a small table, looking too big for the wicker chair he lounged in, a whisky in his hand.

12

'Hallo,' he said.

'Hallo.' She felt herself hovering, and then made the decision. She settled herself at the table beside him. He looked at her quizzically, his wiry eyebrows raised, then offered her a cigarette which she refused.

'And where have you been for the last two days?' he asked her as if he were an old friend.

'At the Limelight Hotel, at the Ute City Banquette and on the slopes,' she said.

'I've seen you on the slopes. You ski well,' he said.

'Yes.' She could see the fine blond hairs on the back of his well-shaped hands. The nails were oval and very clean, his wrists bony but strong looking.

'Do you want a drink?'

'Yes,' she said.

'Whisky?'

'Yes.'

He had a small straight nose that could have been feminine, but his mouth was square with a self-indulgent full lower lip. He had a chin that jutted and his eyebrows met above blue eyes and below a high forehead with worry lines across it. She felt a stirring of excitement as he ordered the drink.

'So you finally deigned to speak to me?' he said.

'Yes.'

'What did the trick?'

'I just saw you there,' she said lamely.

'Was that all?'

She felt herself bite her lower lip.

'Not quite.'

'I thought not,' he said.

They had had one more drink while they talked about the skiing conditions and then he had walked her back to the Limelight where without any discussion about the matter, they had gone to bed.

And now she was wondering what on earth had come over her. She was, she decided, behaving like Poppy. But it was too late to do much about it. She looked at his sleeping face on the pillow beside her. The lines across his forehead seemed ironed out, and he was breathing very quietly, his mouth tight shut.

It was a good face, she decided. She could have done much worse. And as the sun moved away from the window, she too slept.

She woke to hear him pulling the curtains and turning on the two huge bedside lamps. For the moment she could not think where she was or who the big-boned naked man standing at her bedside could be. His face, concerned and yet smiling, reassured her.

'It's nearly seven,' he said. 'Do you feel like dressing and coming out? I think perhaps we ought to get to know each other.'

She had to laugh.

'You mean other than in the Biblical sense I presume,' she said.

'Exactly.' He was totally at ease in his nudity and good to look at, she thought. He had moved casually to the foot of the bed and was pulling on his clothing. Long Johns that outlined the tight muscles of his behind and accentuated the curves of his calves. His legs were very long and strong. In fact, she decided, he was altogether too tall and solid to be a skier.

'I didn't see you on the slopes,' she said.

She thought he hesitated for a moment before replying and then he said: 'I was going too fast.'

'Show-off,' she said.

He was still busy zipping himself into clothes.

'Listen,' he said. 'I've got to get back to my room and change. Dress up and I'll take you to the Golden Horn.'

'Where's the Golden Horn?'

'Round the corner, like everything else in Aspen,' he said. 'But I just happen to think it's the best restaurant in town.'

He was fully dressed, so quickly and neatly she had hardly seen it happen, and he stood grinning down at her where she still lay on the bed. 'You are a lazy-bones,' he said, and leaned down to pick her up bodily.

Instinctively her arms went around his neck, and he bent his head to kiss her.

'Jesus, you're little,' he said and kissed her again.

'And if you do that,' she heard herself saying, 'we won't be going anywhere.'

He laughed and dumped her upright on her feet to the floor.

'That's a nice little body,' he said, his hands stroking from under her arms down to her waist, and she found herself needlessly tucking in her stomach muscles and tightening her breasts. The stirring of sexual excitement was beginning again.

'Get out of here,' she told him. 'I'll be ready in half an hour.'

'I'll be back,' he promised.

And she was suddenly afraid that maybe he wouldn't come back, and yet she didn't know who the hell he was, except that his name was Gary Smith.

She found out over supper that he came from a small town in Tennessee, that his father was old Southern stock, a lawyer, and obviously rich.

'He sent me to a Yankee college – Harvard Business School,' he told her, 'and now I've disappointed him by not becoming a lawyer. I sell executive jets which gives me the chance to travel and make some money before I'm thirty. Once the old man got used to the idea, he financed me.'

'He sounds nice, your father,' she said, staring into the big log fire in the restaurant, a glass of wine in her hand while they waited for their table.

'He is,' Gary said. 'A bit like that lawyer in *To Kill a Mocking Bird* – a really civilised Southern gentleman, even if I say it myself.'

'Gregory Peck,' she said absently, her mind on her own father and his problems. 'I saw it on TV.'

'But anyway,' he said, 'what's a girl like you doing in a place like Aspen, all alone? You're a long way from home.'

There was a deeper question in his voice which she chose to ignore.

'My family are in Los Angeles at the moment,' she told him. 'We came because we heard there was a treatment that would help my mother—' she paused twisting the red wine in her glass. 'She's senile. Prematurely, of course.'

'I'm sorry,' he said, and he looked as if he meant it.

'Yes, it's awful. Worse for father. He tried not to let us see what was happening for a long time. He covered up for her. She forgot things, lost things, but she was always vague and we were sort of used to it. But then it got so that she couldn't tell the time and she didn't know whether it was day or night, and she was wandering about the estate in her nightgown. She had to be watched all the time.

'Father heard about this treatment in California where they feed oxygen to the brain, and in desperation we decided to come and try it. I sort of thought it might be one of those quack things, and I'm beginning to believe it is. She's no better. She gets Poppy and me mixed up all the time; she tells us the same things over and over again and my father's desperate.' She paused. 'She's only fifty

15

eight,' she said. 'It's ridiculous, and impossible for father. He's such an intelligent man. . . .'

Her voice trailed away. She suddenly realised that she had been talking too much about the problem, just as she always talked too much about the problem. Her father pretended it didn't exist; covered up, coped; tried to hide the evidence of his wife's failing mind from both those close to him and strangers. It was only to Jade and to Poppy that he had spoken of what was happening and then only very recently. He had conducted a conspiracy of silence for some years before he admitted that there was something badly wrong and that their mother truly was seriously prematurely senile.

'The treatment isn't working?' Gary asked.

'Not really. Maybe we came too late. That will be their excuse anyway,' she said. 'But don't let's talk about it. I can become a bore on the subject.'

'So what does your father do?' he asked.

'He was a judge, I'm afraid,' she said and he laughed at the note of apology in her voice.

'Outranking my old man, eh?'

'Not any more,' she said. 'My grandfather asked him to come into the family shipping business and he's been working there for years. In Scotland. We live in the Highlands, and he commutes between Clydeside and home. It's a long journey for him every day, what with everything else,' she added.

'You're fond of your father, too, aren't you?' he said.

'He's probably the best person on earth,' she said. 'You can't imagine how fantastic he's been to Poppy and me. He's given us everything material and so much love . . .'

'Well, you for one are very lovable,' he said lightly. 'Now come on, choose your meal.'

As she pored over the menu, she found that her father was very much on her mind and that she was feeling a totally unreasonable anxiety at having left him alone. The attraction she felt for Gary Smith was strong, but the uneasiness at not being in Los Angeles was stronger. She debated whether to make a phone call to the Chateau Marmont, and then, as the waiter came to take the order, put the thought out of her mind.

Gary walked her around the town after supper, saying she was in one of God's most beautiful spots. He explained how once the town had been a silver-mining centre until the lode had run out. He took

16

her and showed her the gingerbread wooden houses where the rich miners had once lived and prospered.

'Until it all went dead,' he said. 'Then this was a ghost town, like so many other mining towns in the Rockies. But a man called Paepcke realised the potential. Now, it's probably the most exclusive and expensive resort town in the States, though that's not what he intended. He wanted it to be a place for people who wanted to get away from the world.'

'Then they shouldn't have modernised it so much,' she said. 'These old houses are much nicer.'

'Come and see the Jerome Hotel,' he suggested. 'They haven't modernised that and you might see Jack Nicholson in the bargain. It's where he drinks.'

They didn't see Jack Nicholson, but they drank themselves, sitting in the bar of a crazy wooden hotel that hadn't changed since the late eighteen-hundreds.

'You see we do preserve some things in the States,' he told her as they crunched their way back through the snow-bound streets to the Limelight.

'So, are you staying there among all that nostalgia?' she asked him.

'No.'

'Then where?'

'Where else but at the Limelight,' he said. 'Hadn't you realised I was following you?'

There was a note in his voice that sent a slight frisson through her. It was a warning sense she could not quite define; another kind of uneasiness. She mentally shook herself and told herself not to be so silly; and that the altitude was making her nervous. She had never met a more respectable young man, a nicer young man who gave off such good vibes and who was a delight in bed.

But – why had he been following her?

'You were really following me?' she said impulsively.

'Not at the beginning. After Denver, yes. But you wouldn't let yourself be picked up. Then it got to be a challenge, and I admit I deliberately stayed in the same hotel as you.'

'How did you know which hotel I was staying in?'

'Easy. I asked the Mellow Yellow cab company. They just checked out with their drivers. You're very easy to describe.'

'Do you have some pull with the Mellow Yellow cab people?' she said lightly.

'None. But here in Aspen everyone is laid back and obliging. If I wanted to find a pretty lady, they weren't going to stop me.'

She nodded. His hand was holding hers, and his blond head with a red woolly hat covering his ears was towering above her. Why hadn't she seen him in the little breakfast room, she wondered? Why hadn't he been on the slopes? Why hadn't he been carrying skis at the airport?

'Shall we ski together tomorrow?' she asked him, curious as to whether or not he would agree.

'Why not,' he said. 'What time do you want to leave the hotel?'

'About eight?'

He looked down at her and grimaced.

'God – you're an early bird. Make it half-past at least.'

She felt a certain sense of relief. She skied too early, breakfasted too early. That was why she hadn't seen him. The uneasiness fled and she squeezed his hand through their thick gloves.

'Ok, half-past,' she said happily. 'Nine if you like.'

'Done,' he said promptly and bent to kiss her.

Aspen was the most romantic place, she decided, as they neared the hotel. The shopping malls were brightly lit with big globe lamps; the shop windows added to the light. People still in brightly coloured clothes moved arm in arm through the little streets; the sounds of laughter came from restaurants and the mountain loomed above, towering white into the black sky, and somewhere she could hear the sound of running water. The cold bit at her cheeks and her nose, and breath came faster in the high altitude. It was a ridiculous encounter between her and Gary Smith. He from Tennessee -- she from Scotland; they were more than worlds apart and she felt a sudden pang of disappointment that their meeting, their mating, and what she hoped would turn into their friendship, could only be of short duration.

He was telling her more Aspen history.

'The Ute Indians used to own this whole valley, you know,' he said. 'Roaring Fork it's called, but the white man drove them away.'

'Where did they go?'

'Higher into the Rockies. They cursed Aspen; said the white man would never have any luck here. It seemed it had come true when the silver ran out. But now look at it.'

His voice was sombre.

'You sound as if you don't *like* the look of it.'

18

She could only see his silhouette as they rounded a darkened corner.

'Not a lot,' he said. 'It's full of people who live too fast, have too much and don't give a damn. Being laid back and mellow as they like to call themselves means no responsibility. Have you noticed the desperate signs for hired help? They all screw each other without love, they spend a fortune on cocaine because it's the thing to do. They graduate to heroin and kill themselves. And they kick out their law enforcement officers who try to control the drugs coming in. But as the coke and amyl nitrate and the rest of it come in on private Lear jets, carried by tycoons of industry and captains of Congress, it's not easy. Just look at the line-up of private jets when you leave this place. It's kinda indecent. But good for business.'

She heard him out then asked: 'But then why do you come here if you dislike it so much?'

He sighed.

'I like the mountain. I like the Roaring Fork River and I like the scenery. You don't have to mix with the tourists.'

'I think you'd like Switzerland better,' she said. 'It's more natural.'

'I'll join you there next season,' he said and she felt her spirits surge.

They had reached the wooden walkways of the hotel that led to her room, and she heard the faint hissing of water and saw a cloud of soft, grey steam floating in the crisp air.

'Imagine! They've still got the jaccuzzi running at this time of night,' she said.

'Yeah, all ready for a midnight dip,' he said. 'Want one?'

His eyes were challenging her in the dim lighting of the pathway.

'In this cold?' she said.

'The water's hot.'

She considered, remembered him naked, and then said: 'Why not? Where do we undress?'

'In our rooms. Bring a towel and a warm robe, Ok.'

'Ok,' she said, again trying to control the breathlessness that could have been excitement, could have been the altitude, could have been the wine she had drunk, or was probably caused by all three.

She was in the steaming water of the jaccuzzi before him after a shivering run down the walkway from her room. She had just put on a pair of bikini pants under her robe, but once in the swirling warm water and in the darkness with the wooden outline of the hotel looming above, she wondered if she should take them off, but decided against it.

In the event, he did it for her. He arrived at the pool quietly, took off his robe and folded it neatly before slipping naked into the water, barely making a splash. He grunted with pleasure at the warmth. He was too tall to be completely covered and his broad shoulders and head were painted black in the faint light. He was moving purposefully towards where she stood with her back to the side of the pool. He reached her, bent down to kiss her, and delicately felt her breasts, her waist, her back, grunting again when his hands found the thin nylon of her pants. He slid them down, still without speaking, and obediently she lifted one leg, then the other as he took them off. Then he ran his hand between her legs and she felt her back arch with pleasure as she tentatively reached out to touch him, and found him ready.

He was half lifting her as he kissed her.

'Shall we?' he whispered in her ear, his hands clasped under her buttocks.

'Someone might see.'

'No one will.'

'But how can we? You're too tall.'

'Like this.' He demonstrated by lifting her bodily on to him and she gave a little cry. Instinctively her legs twined around him, her arms clasped tight around his neck, and she felt the pleasure of him moving in her. The cold night air burned her cheeks and her shoulders and all the while the warm water swirled and twisted about them, heightening the excitement as she clung to him, panting, trying to move on him but finding all the strength, all the thrust had to come from him as he stood squarely in the water. She could only receive him with small cries of pleasure and she never felt the cold of the night at all.

After, he stood her down again and only then was she aware of the freezing air. She thought she even felt snow, but it was just a light wind blowing the crust of white from the roof of the hotel. They stood, their arms around each other in the darkness, still in silence, and she remembered his words 'They screw without loving' and she shivered a little.

'Cold?' he asked, pulling her nearer to him. 'Come on. We must get out of here.'

20

He jumped out of the pool, picked up his own towel and wrapped it around him, then found hers and lifted her from the water. He wrapped her up like a baby and rubbed her back and shoulders briskly. Her teeth were beginning to chatter.

'No,' he said firmly, 'don't think about the cold. Rub yourself dry and get your robe on. We'll run around to the reception and get a cup of coffee.'

'What, in our dressing gowns!' she said.

'They're used to it,' he told her, and she thought again about screwing without loving as she slipped on her robe and furry boots. Then, taking his hand, ran in the shelter of the board-walks around to the front of the hotel.

It only took seconds to reach the lighted entrance to the hotel where hot coffee bubbled in the small breakfast room and the room clerk sat behind the desk.

'We've come for some coffee to warm us up before bed,' Gary said, but the room clerk ignored him. He came around from behind his desk, his attention all on Jade, his face half smiling, half anxious with embarrassment.

'Miss Martin,' he said. 'I'm so glad you're back. I have a very important message for you to ring your sister at the Chateau Marmont in Los Angeles as soon as you can.'

All the evening's uneasiness and sense of premonition settled into a knot in her stomach.

'Can I ring from here?' she asked, aware her voice was not steady.

'Yes, of course, I'll get the number for you.'

He looked glad to have something to do. He was not much more than a boy; a ski-bum probably, doing any kind of nightwork in order to be able to be on the mountain all day. He was dark and Italian looking and he was also very unhappy. He knew what she was going to hear from Poppy, she realised, and it could not be good news. Gary had sensed the tension, too, and without speaking had taken her hand. She was silent as the clerk punched out the telephone number in the brightly lit, cheerful room.

She heard him ask for Poppy McKenzie McKenzie Martin and the name had never seemed longer or sillier. Then, wordless, he handed her the phone.

'Jade?' It was Poppy's light trilling voice, but on the edge of hysteria. 'Jade, where have you been? I've been so frightened. I didn't know what to do. You've got to get here right away. I can't cope.'

'Poppy,' Jade had to speak loudly to break in. 'What's happened? Is Mother all right?'

'It's not Mother. It's Father. He's dead. He was killed this afternoon by a hit-and-run driver. You've got to get here right away. How long will it take you? I don't know what to do – police, everything. And Mother won't accept he's dead. When will you get here?'

Jade could see her knuckles white on the telephone receiver. She felt sick, but she held herself together.

'But what happened? How?' she asked.

'I can't tell you now. Just get here.' Poppy could barely speak.

Jade wanted to ask more questions – wanted to hear it was a Poppy bad taste joke, but she knew it must be the truth. Even Poppy was not capable of such cruel behaviour.

'All right,' she said, dully. 'I'll be there as soon as I can.'

She put down the phone without saying any more and, amazed at her own control, turned to Gary.

'My father is dead,' she said. 'I must leave immediately.'

And as she moved swiftly out of the lobby back through the crackling snow to her own room, she was conscious that he was following her.

≈ 2 ≈

'Where have you been?' Poppy's voice was hysterical. 'I thought you'd never come. It's been absolutely ghastly. I can't make Mother understand he's dead and I haven't known what to do.'

Her sister's broad, smooth face, as uncreased and unused as an unripe peach, was sharpened by petulance. Her almond eyes were spilling tears of frustration and the perfect cupid-bow mouth was turned down at the corners.

'It was difficult, Poppy,' Jade said patiently. 'I had to drive down

22

the mountains through the night to get the first plane I could from Denver.'

'You shouldn't have gone in the first place, leaving me with all the responsibility.'

Jade stared at her sister hopelessly. She was twenty-two years old, incredibly pretty and thoroughly spoilt, and Jade sometimes felt she had been taking the responsibility ever since they had been small children. Even now Poppy's mind was still totally concentrated on herself. She had no feeling for others; no sense of tragedy; only a relentless sense of personal survival.

'I'm here now,' Jade said. There seemed no point in explaining the terror of the night ride through the Rockies, over snow-bound roads and in velvet black darkness. Gary had insisted on driving her in a big hired car that he had arranged. He also put her on the plane at Denver getting her tickets and carrying her luggage. He had even helped her pack, and said he would settle her hotel bill and the car hire bill and told her he would be in touch. In her distress, she barely said goodbye to him. All she could think of as the car eased its way through the black and white night was her neglected instinct to telephone her father. Perhaps he would have been dead already, but maybe she could have had one last word with him, even delaying his departure so the accident would never have occurred.

'What happened, Poppy?' she said. 'Just tell me what happened?'

'It was frightful,' her sister said, a doll-like figure perched on the edge of the huge leather armchair in the sitting room of the Chateau Marmont bungalow they had rented. 'Father and I had decided to go down to Schwab's for a sandwich – you know this place has no restaurant,' she said, her voice aggrieved. 'We were walking down the hill to Sunset and a car came careering down the road, totally out of control. It mounted the pavement, smashed into Father. It killed him instantly, and just drove on. It only just missed me,' she wailed.

The irony was that they had chosen the Chateau so they would not need a car and so that over Christmas and New Year they could be like a family in the bungalow. So that they could walk, shop and visit restaurants independently of transport while keeping their mother's condition private from staff.

Jade was unable to speak. She walked across to the big plate-glass windows of the room and stood staring out on to the scrappy grass lawn outside. A Mexican woman came along the path by the windows, pushing a small cart filled with cleaning materials. Jade concentrated on her very hard, trying to control her anger and grief.

'Did they get the driver?' she asked, not looking at her sister.

'No.'

'Did you get the car number?'

'No. How could I?' Poppy's voice was defensive. 'It all happened so quickly.'

That might have been true. But Jade was certain she would have seen and remembered the number; and that if she had been there, the driver would have been caught and justice done.

Her head was filled with pictures of her father. He had been a small man; not good-looking, with a chubby, reddish face and a beaky nose. His hair had grown in a schoolboy quiff all his life, and the cosiness of his face and comfortable build had made him unimpressive in his red robes and wig when he sat in court. Before her mind went, her mother used to laugh and say that many a criminal's heart had lifted when they saw her husband on the bench, but his intellect was formidable and he could hand out harsh punishments for harsh deeds. He had also had the quality of mercy.

He had loved his family, and most particularly his wife, to whom he would grant anything in the world within his powers. But he had failed to give her back her mind, and Jade had watched him become thinner, more anxious, and tired as he tried to find some way to help.

His last attempt, bringing them all here, had ended in his death.

She turned abruptly.

'What are the police doing?'

'Not a lot,' Poppy said. 'At least I don't think so.'

'Where's mother?'

'In her room, resting. I locked the door so she couldn't get out.'

'Poppy! You didn't! She'll be terrified.'

'Well, she kept wandering.' The voice had taken on the defensive whine again. Their father used to say: 'Poppy, don't whine. You sound like an Arab street vendor,' but no one had ever been able to break her of the habit.

'Where was she wandering?' Jade asked, her exasperation with her sister growing.

'They found her down on Sunset. She could have been run over too. I didn't want that to happen. It could have done.'

'Not if you'd stayed with her. Where were you?'

Poppy's face had closed tight as an oyster shell.

24

'I wasn't anywhere,' she said. 'Just relaxing.'

Jade made a growl of annoyance. Relaxing meant bed, and not alone. But there was no point in quarrelling with her sister now. Without continuing the conversation she went to the room her parents had shared and turned the key in the lock.

Her mother was sitting on the bed; a small, pretty woman with a delicate retroussé nose, and a wild mop of curly black hair that had hardly changed colour. She looked years younger than fifty-eight until one looked into the hazel eyes and found them opaque and uncomprehending.

'Poppy,' she said crossly. 'How dare you lock me in!'

'It's not Poppy, Mother, it's Jade,' she said gently, 'and I didn't lock you in. Are you all right?'

'I'm bored,' her mother said.

'Hungry?'

'Hungry?' Her mother frowned and looked puzzled. 'No, I'm not hungry.'

Jade started to ask when she had last eaten but stopped. There was no point. Her mother would not remember. There had been no point in asking the question in the first place. Her mother never felt either hungry or satisfied. She could go for hours without food or drink, or would eat three meals in a row if they were put in front of her. It was as if the stomach and the brain no longer had any connection.

Margaret McKenzie McKenzie Martin still had energy, though. Too much energy. She was putting on her coat with the conviction of someone with somewhere important to go.

'I have to go and meet your father now,' she said.

'No, Mother.' Jade hesitated. 'He won't be home for a while. Don't you remember – he had to go back to London.'

She had copped out. She knew it, but she could not bring herself to say that her father was dead.

'London?' Her mother looked puzzled again. 'What's he doing there? And where is Kirsty? She hasn't been in to see me for hours.'

Kirsty was her mother's devoted servant back in Kinlochrannoch. And Jade realised that her mother's confusion had now also become geographical.

'Do you know where you are, Mother?' she asked very gently.

Her mother looked around the big room with the double bed, plate-glass windows and heavy wood furniture, so different from her bedroom in the big old hunting lodge in Scotland.

'At home of course,' she said, her voice irritable. 'Where *is* Kirsty?'

'With Father,' Jade said. It seemed easier. 'Come along. We'll go for a walk now.'

'About time,' her mother said.

Jade buttoned her mother's coat, took her arm and led her out into the sitting room where Poppy was curled into a chair, her face still sulky.

'You see,' she said. 'She's all right.' Jade did not reply, but stared at her sister, marvelling at the total commitment to self.

'Have you telephoned Grandfather?' she asked.

'No,' Poppy's voice was defiant. 'I thought it better if you did that.'

Jade sighed.

'In that case,' she said, 'take Mother for a walk around the pool, while I try to get things sorted out.'

Poppy heaved herself out of the armchair, and without speaking took her mother out through the glass doors. 'You know it's lunchtime,' she said as she left.

It *was* lunchtime and the thought of food was abhorrent. She must ring her grandfather. He should have been told immediately, but at least by now he should be home. Even at eighty, he had the energy of a man in his fifties. He still arrived at his shipping office in Glasgow twice a week to terrorise his staff, and spent two days a month in the London office making sure that every detail of the huge business he had created was known to him.

She put through the call, and his housekeeper answered, sounding as if she were no more than five miles away.

'Mary,' Jade said. 'It's bad news. Father's dead—' as she said the words the tears suddenly spilled. She was aware of Mary clucking at the other end of the phone, but she could not comprehend what the housekeeper was saying.

Then her grandfather was on the phone.

'What's happened?' he asked.

'It's Father,' she managed. 'He's dead. It was a hit-and-run driver.'

There was a long silence and then a deep sigh.

'How's your mother holding up?'

'Grandad, we can't make her realise he's gone.'

'She's no better?'

'Not really, no.'

Her grandfather, tough as nails and ruthless, had never been totally convinced that Ralph Martin was the husband for his only daughter. He blamed Ralph for the lack of a grandson; and at first had only tolerated both Poppy and Jade. Eventually he had decided that he loved them very much.

But he and Ralph Martin had had one thing in common. Both were besotted in their own way by Margaret McKenzie McKenzie, for her prettiness, her liveliness and what, as a girl, had seemed like scattiness. She lived in a state of constant disorganisation which had perhaps held the seeds of the disease that was to overcome her.

'What are the police doing?' he asked.

'I don't know yet,' Jade said, 'I wasn't here. I was in Aspen. Poppy called me last night and I've only just got here.'

'How's Poppy?'

'All right.' Jade could not bring herself to say more, and her grandfather grunted, obviously understanding the situation.

'Very well,' he said. 'I want you on the first plane out of there. Get your mother and your sister home to Glen Hind. I'll have my agent in San Diego fly up and handle everything that needs to be done. I'm not having you trying to bring your father's body back,' he said gruffly. 'But we'll bring him home, don't worry.'

She felt an enormous sense of relief. The thought of the technicalities of everything that had to be done had frightened her. She knew that she could not have faced seeing her father, perhaps disfigured, and certainly, as this was the United States, embalmed into a waxen image of himself. She wanted to remember him as he had been. She wanted to go home and mourn there.

'Thank you, Grandfather,' she said.

'Just get home,' he said. 'I'll have my agent call you immediately and he can deal with anything that wants doing. Do you have money?'

'Well, not a lot,' she said.

'Peter – he's called Peter Davison – will give you some and cope with anything. What time is it there?'

'One thirty-five. Afternoon.'

'Wait for him to call, and then get your mother to eat something. All right?'

'All right,' she said.

27

Her grandfather was not a sentimental man and his common-sense approach had been just what was needed. In ten minutes the phone rang and an American voice which introduced itself as Peter Davison asked for any details she could give and said he was on the way.

'Mr McKenzie McKenzie wants you to leave there today if possible,' he said. 'I'll get our travel section on it right away.'

'But my father's body—'

'That's my problem,' he said briskly.

Someone else whose name she never did catch appeared about half an hour later with money and tickets and a huge limousine. She and Poppy packed in a frenzy and by six o'clock they were at LA Airport, their mother demanding where on earth was Ralph, and at seven they were airborne.

As the huge plane wheeled over the brown reaches of the Sierra Nevadas, Jade, in a first-class compartment window seat, stared back at the vast sprawling mass of Los Angeles they were leaving behind. The town looked like a scatter of Monopoly houses; transient, impermanent, ugly.

But the city, and its violence, had robbed her of the person she loved most in the world.

Only then, as the Monopoly houses were lost in a vague mist below, did she remember Gary Smith, and that she owed him money and that they had never said goodbye properly. She did not know his address, nor he hers.

The affair had ended almost before it had begun.

Gary Smith left it a full day before he checked out of the Limelight Hotel. He had pondered on the right interval before following Jade down to Los Angeles. He had a great curiosity to meet the sister and though the news of the father's death had not been entirely a surprise, it had complicated the situation.

He flew down to Denver in the first Aspen Airways plane of the day having discarded with relief the ski-clothes and boots he had been wearing. He wore a dark, good suit in a lightweight fabric, just right for January in Los Angeles, and he carried a Burberry raincoat as it was the rainy season.

Denver was still encased in snow but he had no reason to leave the overheated canyons of the airport. He picked up his connection to LA and at near to two o'clock that afternoon he was paying off his taxi on Sunset Boulevard, just below the Chateau Marmont.

He picked up his small light suitcase and swung it up the hill to the entrance of the hotel. An English girl reading a book was half-heartedly manning the desk in the dark panelled hallway.

'Miss McKenzie McKenzie Martin?' he asked.

She looked up from her book and her eyes flickered over him, checking him for respectability, he decided. 'I'm afraid they've all left,' she said.

'Left?'

'There was an accident. Sir Ralph McKenzie McKenzie Martin,' she grimaced over the name, 'was killed. His wife and two daughters flew back to England last evening.'

He stood thinking for a moment. Jade leaving so soon was something he hadn't planned for.

'Do you have an address?'

'I'll look,' she said. She disappeared somewhere behind the desk as he stood there, his bag swinging loosely from his hand.

'Sorry,' she said when she came back. 'All I have is an address in San Diego – the McKenzie McKenzie Shipping Company. All the bookings were done through them, but a Mr Davison would probably be able to help you. Is it important?'

He grinned. 'They owe me money,' he said.

She looked quite shocked. 'I'm sure Mr Davison would settle the matter,' she said. 'They are not uncomfortably off, I assure you. It must be a mistake.'

'It was,' he told her. 'Not to worry.'

He asked her to call him a taxi and stood waiting in the street outside for it to arrive. The sun was shining, though a few grey clouds broke the monotony of the California sky. He did not need his Burberry.

The taxi came quickly and he directed it back to the airport. There he made a phone call and booked himself a ticket to Washington. After that, he wondered, how the hell long was it going to take to get him to the Highlands of Scotland?

≈ 3 ≈

Reading the will immediately after a funeral had to be barbaric, Jade decided as she sat with her mother, who was prattling on happily about what the family would do now it was Christmas. She was convinced this was the reason for the family gathering and kept asking where Ralph was. She had also confused and continued to confuse the lawyer, a middle-aged man with a middle-aged spread and eyes that had watched too many claret bottles being opened, with Ralph Martin's brother, George.

George, like so many people who did not understand her mother's problem, was offended.

The family were gathered in the big drawing room of the Glen Hind. There were not many present: Uncle George, a spare dry twig of a man, who had never possessed his brother's warmth and humour, her grandfather, Kirsty, and Poppy, who had at last shown some genuine grief as her father had been buried in the little private resting place on the hill above the house. Two were buried there already; a couple said to be lovers, and Jade had made the decision, along with her grandfather, that Sir Ralph should lie there also.

The countryside was wrapped in white snow as they walked from the chapel, and Jade had heard a muffled curse from the coffin bearers as they trudged up the slippery, fern-bordered path to the flat little plateau where the grave was to be. The snow had been cleared away, and someone had painfully dug the rock-hard ground and when she – not her mother, whom they had decided to leave with Kirsty at the house – had dropped the first clods of earth they had sounded hollow on the wood of the coffin.

Jade had not cried at the funeral. She knew that the tears would come when she was alone. She had hardly cried since the telephone call to her grandfather. There had been too much to do: getting home, dealing with her mother and making the funeral arrangements. They had decided that this should be a family affair, with a memorial service later in Glasgow or even London. Her father had been a popular man, with many friends, but it seemed too much to ask people to come to Glen Hind in the depth of winter. So the only other people who were not family were Kirsty and her father's secretary who had been with him for nearly twenty years, plus the lawyer, come from Edinburgh.

The lawyer was seated, half turned to face the little Queen Anne desk that stood near the window and to the right of the fireplace. Everyone else was settled in armchairs around the room. Jade and her mother shared the big sofa in front of the fire.

She barely listened to what the lawyer was reading. She was looking out over the grey loch where the trees were still clothed in autumn and white, remembering summers here – days in the boat with her father, learning to fish for trout and salmon from the bank of the swiftly flowing small river that belonged to the property. They had spent little time here in the winters. The family had vacationed somewhere warm – usually the Bahamas – and then there had been the skiing. For Easter they always went to the South of France, and it was only throughout the summer and at Christmas the family were gathered in the Lodge. Then the view outside looked much as it did today. White, russet and grey. It explained at least one facet of her mother's confusion.

There were bequests for the secretary, who cried quietly into her handkerchief when her name was mentioned with thanks for many years of faithful help and friendship. There was a sizeable amount for Kirsty, coupled with the hope that she would continue to care for Lady Margaret McKenzie McKenzie Martin. There was nothing for her grandfather, except gratitude for the gift of his daughter, and for the brother, George, there were some pieces of antique furniture, belonging to the Martin family, and a collection of rare coins, plus a watch and gold cufflinks which had belonged to his father.

Glen Hind and its contents were left outright to his wife, to become the property of his daughter, Jade, on her mother's death. The flat her father owned in Eaton Square was to belong to the two girls, Poppy and Jade, and money, stocks, shares and bonds to be divided equally between all three.

She heard the lawyer explain that death duties would take a considerable amount of the capital, but that there would still be enough left for the family to live in comfort, though perhaps not to the same standards of luxury as before – a remark that brought a hurrumph from her grandfather, a noise that said the family luxury was none of the lawyer's business and that the luxury would not cease.

The lawyer began to shuffle his papers together in small, precise

31

movements with the look of a man who needed either a drink or a private conversation with someone.

Jade was betting on the private conversation when a sudden movement from her mother took everyone's attention. Dark hair springing around her head, Lady Martin had set off in the direction of the garden door.

'Mother, where are you going?' Poppy asked in the pained, exasperated tones of one at the end of her tether.

'Home, of course,' her mother said. 'Where are my coat and handbag, darling?'

The atmosphere in the room was one of acute discomfort. Jade got to her feet, took her mother's elbow, and said soothingly: 'We are home, Mother, don't you remember?'

The older woman looked vaguely round the room and said: 'Of course, how silly of me.' It was obvious she was not entirely convinced.

'Your father's going to take you through to lunch now,' Jade told her, speaking as if to a child. She turned to the watching figure of her sentry-straight grandfather who stood waiting, his face a mixture of anger and compassion. 'Lead everyone through will you, Grandfather?'

He nodded and bent to take the arm of his daughter who came no higher than his chest. 'Come along, Margaret,' he said gruffly.

The lawyer was still at the desk when everyone else had left the room.

'Was there something else, Mr McBean?' Jade asked.

'Well.' He hesitated. 'There is a problem. Your father made this will six years ago. We've hardly been in contact since, and it's now become obvious that Lady Martin isn't in her right mind, if you'll forgive me saying so. There are some papers—'

'Papers?' she prompted him.

'Aye. Papers that were to be given to your mother and I'd strict instruction from Sir Ralph that they weren't to be given to your grandfather under any circumstances. He said at the time that your mother would know what was to be done with them.'

'I see.' In fact she did not see and was slightly alarmed to find that there seemed to be a family secret of some kind. But her face was impassive as she said: 'Perhaps you'd better give them to me. Do you know what they are about?'

'I do not,' he said firmly. 'But I am not convinced in my mind that I should give them to you.'

'Because you believe they may be concerning Poppy's and my adoption?' she suggested. 'There's no need to worry, Mr McBean. We know the truth of that. After all, our parents could hardly have pretended we were theirs now, could they?'

A ghost of a smile lifted his thin lips.

'Well, perhaps in that case . . .' he said, obviously pleased to be relieved of the problem.

The envelope he handed her was a large one in brown manilla and sealed with her father's crest in sealing wax.

She turned it over in her hands and then smiled at him.

'If it's waited so long, I think it can wait until after lunch, don't you?' she suggested. 'Shall we go in?'

The remainder of the day seemed interminable until everyone could decently go up to bed. The funeral guests were staying the night with the exception of the lawyer who was driven to Rannoch station to get the single-track train back to Glasgow. He had to be back in Edinburgh on the morrow, he had said.

She had barely spoken to her grandfather all day. He had devoted himself to Lady Martin, treating her as he must have treated her when she was four years old. Jade marvelled at his patience and kindness, as her grandfather was not noted for either. He was known to be granite tough; a man who had made a fortune in the South China Seas, building up a vast shipping empire. He had stayed in the East, regarding himself as an old China hand until he was over sixty, having persuaded his son-in-law to take care of the growing English and Scottish interests of the McKenzie McKenzie Shipping Line.

When he had come home, her mother had been anxious that the cold and damp of Britain would not suit him after so many years in the East. He had poo-pooed the suggestion. 'Try Hong Kong in the typhoon season for damp,' he said. 'I'm not coming home to die. I'm coming home to find my roots.'

Jade had been fourteen when he came back for good, and she remembered her father had not been pleased. There seemed to be antagonism between the two men and as she grew older she had put this down to the fact that her grandfather could not help interfering in the business that her father had been running in Britain for nearly thirteen years.

33

'Come and have a brandy, lass,' Ian McKenzie McKenzie said, late on the night of the funeral when the last guest had been dispatched to the upper reaches of the big draughty house. 'I want to talk to you.'

He led her into her father's small study where an open fire burned and poured her a generous measure of brandy from a crystal decanter. He then poured himself a large malt whisky.

'Do you want to stay here?' he asked abruptly.

'I haven't thought,' Jade said. 'I think I'll have to continue to stay with Mother. Someone must and I always have.'

'No, I don't think you should stay with your mother,' he said roughly, tough veined hands holding the big whisky glass a little too tightly. 'It's time you stopped playing Martha to Poppy's Mary. Your mother didn't adopt you to be a nursemaid and that's what she'll be confusing you with any minute now. She'll think you're her amah, back from when she was a child.'

Jade couldn't help the involuntary little gasp of pain.

'I know, lass, it's tough. But you're twenty-four years old. You've got a life to lead. You've wasted enough of it as it is. This family has always treated you like the nanny. You looked after your sister when she was little and you've had four years of your mother. Enough is enough. You're too intelligent to go on wet-nursing a woman who's lost her mind. Your mother is my responsibility now – not yours. Her illness is beyond help.'

'But I owe her so much—' Jade protested.

'The young owe the old absolutely nothing,' he said flatly. 'Kirsty will look after your mother, and Kirsty will have help. I'm bringing in two nurses and some extra domestic help. I'll get Chinese. Your mother's used to them. They'll understand better, too. More respect,' he added.

'But I think I *want* to look after her, Grandfather,' Jade said.

'No, you don't. You want your freedom. And you want a job. Would you like to come into the business? I'll train you to take over your father's place up here.'

'Why not the Hong Kong end?' she asked, the idea suddenly seeming appealing.

'Wouldn't work,' he said flatly. 'Poppy – there's a different kettle of fish. Best to find her a rich husband as quickly as possible to keep her out of trouble. Spoilt, that's her problem. She was so delicate they indulged her. Would have been better to toughen her up.'

'Father was the only one who could keep her in order,' Jade said. 'Now—'

'Well, she's not your responsibility, either,' he said.

'She is my sister—'

Again he gave his characteristic hurrumph, looked as if he wanted to say something, then changed his mind.

'Think about it anyway,' he said. 'It's no time for decisions. Give yourself a month or two.' He paused and then said, his voice suddenly gentle: 'I know you loved your father. He and I never really got on. There were reasons—' he sighed. 'But I'm always here. And,' he added with a sort of defiance, 'I intend to be here for a long time. Your father shouldn't have died. Not like that.'

There was something in his voice that made her want to ask questions, but he drained his whisky, slapped down the tumbler and said: 'I'm off to bed. And if you have any sense you'll do the same, young woman. Goodnight.'

His back like a guardsman's, his head scraping the door lintel with thinning but barely grey hair, he left the room abruptly, leaving her to finish her own drink and then put his glass and hers ready for the maid to take away in the morning.

Earlier, she had put the envelope in a drawer in her father's desk, and now she decided the time had come to see what it contained. The grandfather clock in the hall was striking eleven, and the small French clock on the mantelpiece tinkled a reply. The house was very quiet except for the creaks and squeaks of age, and the gentle crackling of the logs in the fireplace.

She felt a curious reluctance to open the envelope, but once she had there seemed to be a great many papers, all wrapped in another sheet of plain white foolscap. She debated whether to read them in the order in which it seemed they had been placed, or at random. The same reluctance to learn the contents made her decide to read at random. She inserted her small, slender fingers inside the sheet of foolscap and took out one piece of paper from the centre of the pack.

It was a newspaper cutting on yellowing paper. A label stuck to the top of it said in her father's precise, elegant handwriting: '*South China Morning Post*, 28 March 1959.'

She turned the piece of paper over, not sure which side to read, but the completed story was under the inscription and date.

The headline had been cut off, but it read:

Today in the High Court Yu Tai Cheung, 29, and Kwan Ming Shing, 30, both unemployed seamen, were committed to trial for the murder of Wan Yu, a stevedore, on 7 January 1959. It was alleged that Tai Cheung went to the premises where Ip Bak Fook, a moneylender, and his daughter and her child and Ip's wife, Tam Ha, lived.

She stopped reading, puzzled, and turned the paper over. Was she reading the right side of the cutting? There was nothing intelligible on the back.

She returned to the other side and continued reading.

Visiting Ip's home was Wan Yu, who had business with Ip Bak Fook. Yu Tai Cheung gained admittance to the house in Wanchai by offering a present. Later Kwan Ming Shing also knocked and was admitted.

'Then, it was alleged, Tai Cheung and Ming Shing tied up the money-lender and demanded $5,000. They then distributed four blades of scissors between them and murdered Wan Yu, Ip Bak Fook, the daughter, stabbing and seriously wounding the child and Tam Ha. Both men pleaded not guilty.

She read the cutting with increasing puzzlement. What had it to do with her father? Could he have been the judge on the case? If so, why keep a memento of this particularly sordid story? He must have sat on the bench for thousands of similar cases. Was that all that this envelope contained? A record of his work in Hong Kong?

She saw what looked like another cutting in among the papers, and she drew it out. This one was also from the *South China Morning Post*, dated 15 January 1959. The headline, obviously from the front-page story said:

Enquiry into Missing Schooner

Underneath were another two bold headlines

Fit and Seaworthy, Marine Board Told Riddle of Lone Message

It then went on to read:

A Marine Board of Enquiry opened yesterday (14 January) into the dis-appearance of the 500 ton schooner the *Brian Leigh*.

The vessel vanished on her maiden delivery voyage to Adelaide, Aus-tralia, with a crew of twelve, mostly Chinese, and an Australian skipper and first mate. Also aboard was the owner's representative who had flown to Hong Kong to take delivery of the ship which was built at the Cheoy Lee Shipyards.

The enquiry was told that the ship left port on the afternoon of 26

December 1958 and passed Waglan Lighthouse at about 5.30. At the time there was no indication of bad weather.

There was only one radio message from the vessel. That came at 8.50 a.m. the following day and gave the ship's position as ninety-five miles south east of Hong Kong. The weather was clear and fair. All was well.

That was the first, last and only message received from the *Brian Leigh*.

The next sentence began to give some clue as to why her father might have retained the document. It said:

President of the Enquiry is Mr Justice Ralph Martin. Mr Stephen Chang, Crown Counsel, is appearing for the Attorney General to assist the board.

She read that when the *Brian Leigh* left Hong Kong there was adequate food and water on board for the non-stop voyage to Adelaide. Mr Chang had told the enquiry that although unknown to the vessel at the time she left, a subsequent weather report had warned that there would be a local storm.

But one quite distinct from Typhoon Ada, then gathering in the Pacific [the report said]. The local storm, the enquiry were told, had not reached such force as to overturn a vessel under normal conditions. Mr Chang also said that the master of the vessel had been instructed to report his position daily to the owners. But those instructions had not been carried out.

By 23 October, nearly a month after the vessel sailed, the owners became anxious to find the whereabouts of their ship and enquiries were made to ports along the route.

Failing to obtain any news, the owners asked the Australian Navy to help and messages were sent to Naval ships in Manilla who were asked to keep a look-out.

The Royal Australian Airforce also joined the search.

'In fact,' said Mr Chang, 'the whole of the ship's route was combed. All these efforts were without success.'

Mr Chang had told the enquiry that they were there to decide if, assuming the ship was seaworthy, her loss was an act of God caused by the tropical storm. Referring again to the massive search, Mr Chang said that it was particularly tragic that a Shackleton aircraft combing the seas for the *Brian Leigh*, itself had failed to return. There was no Mayday call. Whatever had happened to the aircraft must have been sudden and devastating.

At one stage, hopes were raised when another Shackleton search plane – ironically it was looking for the first Shackleton and not the *Brian Leigh* – spotted a vessel with a crew of about thirteen aboard, grounded on Swallow Reef. However, the markings of this ship were definitely not those of Hong Kong.

This ship had been registered in Formosa.

She put down the cutting thoughtfully. What connection had the loss of the *Brian Leigh* to do with the murder of a moneylender in Wanchai? Perhaps there was no connection. Or perhaps there would be another clue within the papers.

The third one she chose was another 1959 newspaper cutting, no more than a snippet this time and stuck on a larger sheet of white paper. It said:

Woman Drowns

and then briefly:

A woman jumped into the harbour last night, 3 February, abandoning her baby on the waterfront.

There were no more newspaper cuttings, but a series of envelopes, addressed to Sir Ralph Martin QC, and some carbon copies of letters.

She first selected a small envelope which seemed to contain a piece of card. All that was inside, in fact, was a postcard-size, cardboard-backed black and white photograph. It showed a Chinese child, aged perhaps fifteen months, staring into the camera and clutching to her a thin, wizened baby whose skin seemed to be covered in heavy eczema. The baby's eyes were closed, as if she slept or were dead. The older child's eyes were big, black and wide open as she had been astonished by the photographer. The children had been photographed in a garden; behind them was a thick privet hedge and beyond a flight of stone steps which appeared to lead up to a large house.

Reluctantly Jade turned the picture over. On the back was written:

JADE, aged seventeen months (?) found abandoned at Sheung Shui, 22 March 1958.
POPPY, aged three months (?) abandoned Hong Kong waterfront, February 1959.

Afterwards when she analysed her emotions at the moment of discovery, she realised she had been neither as shocked nor surprised as she should have been.

With this new knowledge, it immediately occurred to her that her parent's explanations of her and Poppy's adoption had been too pat. And the next paper she took from the pile before her gave her the story behind the photograph.

It was a carbon copy of a letter to a Miss Eleanor Tibbets, the Home of Those Who Care, Fanling, New Territories. It had been written by her father on 12 January 1959. It began:

My dear Miss Tibbets,

It was indeed a pleasure to meet you and to see the admirable home you have created for your children in Fanling and I do hope that I shall be able to be of some assistance to you in the raising of funds so that you can continue your valuable work.

I do appreciate that, as you say, those orphaned and abandoned babies who come into your care have a very special place in your heart, and I can fully understand your reluctance to part with them, thus losing the pleasure and joy of seeing them grow into healthy, happy young adults.

Feeling as you do, you will understand also the loneliness and the great sense of loss that my dear wife feels as it is not possible for her to have a child of her own.

You will understand how she longs for a family of little ones to fill this great and unhappy gap in her life – and indeed, in mine – and I am hopeful that perhaps you will be able to assist her.

My wife yearns for not one, but two baby girls whom she can bring up as a complete family. Living as she has done in South East Asia all her life, she feels a very special warmth and care for the people of this part of the world. She would welcome the chance to give all the love and care – as you do – to children of this troubled area.

I feel that perhaps if we were to accept from you the gift of two of your girls, it would leave room for others in your loving home. As you will appreciate, in my position, the question of legal adoption would not be difficult.

May we meet again to discuss this further? And in the meantime, please accept the enclosed cheque, which I send, of course, as no more than a gesture towards the invaluable work that you do.

I remain, Yours very sincerely,

and there was her father's bold signature, below a letter couched in humble terms quite alien to him.

Shaken, she decided to pour herself a second brandy, and put another log on the fire as the French clock emitted a tremulous chime. Half-past eleven of a January night in 1982, and Jade was beginning to realise that all her long-held beliefs about herself might have to be changed.

The next paper was an envelope with a Hong Kong stamp and addressed to her father in bold, flowing strokes in thick black ink.

Slowly she drew out the thick sheet of writing paper.

'Dear Sir Ralph,' it read, and went on abruptly:

You may have seen the enclosed cutting in the *South China Morning Post*. I have the child. She is a perfect age to be sister to the other child you saw.

This new one is sickly and will need much care. I would imagine she is no more than three months old, though she is so small and frail it is hard to tell.

The other child, whom I have called Jade, has taken to the baby and is careful of her. It grieves me, but I will let these two leave my home. You can do more for them than I.

I am sending a photograph under separate cover for you to show your wife so that she can make her decision.

The signature was that of Eleanor Tibbets.

She put down the letter and stared into the blue flames of the fire. So Poppy was not her sister and they were not the children of her father's Chinese translator and his wife. Both were meant to have died in a classic car crash. The story they had been told was that she and Poppy had been left behind, aged eighteen months and three months respectively. Sir Ralph and Lady Margaret had adopted them both. Obviously none of this was true.

Jade had no memories of Hong Kong, though sometimes she dreamed of being with other Asiatics and of strange places beyond her experience. There had never been any question of going back to the Far East. They had left when she was very small; her father had gone to work for her grandfather, and she and Poppy had since lived an entirely European life.

It occurred to her, as she looked at the picture of herself and her sister who was not her sister, that the only Chinese she had ever met in her life had been waiters. It was almost as if her parents had tried to blot out her race, her background, everything that did not fit in with their European way of life. Or was it perhaps because they were old China hands that they never even thought about it?

Her father must have had Chinese friends, she decided, but having no knowledge of her racial background, she simply could not imagine this. Years at the Lycée in London, then Benenden – where there had been one other Chinese girl, as Europeanised as she and Poppy – and then finally finishing in Switzerland had left her unprepared for the picture of the two Chinese waifs that lay on her father's desk. It was salutary to find she had not always been so privileged.

She realised as she stared at the picture that she had always been conscious of being different and rather enjoyed the difference. Now suddenly she was actively conscious of being Chinese.

Wide-awake with curiosity, she went through the rest of the papers in the envelope before going to bed. Apart from the newspaper cuttings, everything there was self-explanatory. Letters from the Church, the governor, the adoption society. It seemed her father had been able to bend the rules and it was clear, too, that neither she nor Poppy should have been allowed to leave Hong Kong until they were eighteen months old. Poppy had most certainly been nowhere near that age when they left for England, her father having stepped down from the Hong Kong bench in order to bring her mother and their two new daughters back to Britain. There was an address book held together with a rubber band and with a few names and addresses of both Europeans and Chinese in Hong Kong. This she decided to read later.

Jade was a sensible girl. She had quickly assimilated the knowledge that she had not been told the entire truth about her birth. It was not difficult to accept, as her parents' reasons were so very obvious. She had to wrestle a little with the thought that now she had absolutely no knowledge of her real background whereas at least Poppy's mother had some slight identity by the tragic fact of having drowned herself in the harbour. One of the letters in the envelope had pointed out that there were thousands of abandoned children in Hong Kong in the 1950s. Mostly, it said, the children of illegal immigrants from China. Was she one of those? Where in China had she come from? The North? She remembered reading people were taller in the North. She was a good two inches taller than Poppy, and she had always assumed it was good health and good food that had made the difference. Thinking about it, she decided maybe she was tall for a Chinese.

Then there was the question of Poppy, who was not her sister. That, too, when she considered it was not surprising. She and Poppy were very different; and though she loved Poppy she also from time to time loathed her – though that was hardly unusual for real siblings. As it was she was uncertain as to whether she was relieved or saddened by her new knowledge of their lack of family relationship, and for a brief moment she felt very alone.

As she put the papers carefully back into the envelope the clock was striking midnight. She made sure the fire was safe, turned out the lights and went to her bedroom. She fell asleep in the big old-fashioned bed as white light came in from the moonlit snow outside, wondering what she would tell Poppy, then wondering about the newspaper cuttings.

But her last thoughts were of her father.

≈ *4* ≈

In the morning the funeral guests breakfasted and were then driven in a body in the big Rolls to Rannoch station, twelve miles away. Jade saw them go with relief, waving goodbye from the steps as the car went cautiously down the icy drive. She wanted to be alone, with time to think.

Poppy had gone upstairs to her room immediately after breakfast, and Jade found her mother wandering in the drawing room, touching ornaments and staring at pictures as if to familiarise herself with them.

On impulse Jade said: 'Mummy – do you remember how you adopted us?'

'Adopted?' Her mother's eyes turned glazed and milky as they always did in moments when her confusion was greatest. 'We didn't adopt you, did we?'

'Mother – look at me. Could I have been your real daughter?'

It was cruel, but sometimes anger and shock tactics were the only way to bring her mother back to a state barely bordering normality.

'Really, Poppy,' her mother said, 'what a thing to say. It was just because you were born in China. Such a poorly child. Always crying, always nightmares. You've always been difficult.'

'I'm Jade, Mummy, not Poppy,' she said sharply.

'Jade was no trouble. But then she'd been there longer. More settled.' She turned the opaque eyes: 'Do you know my daughter, Jade, then? How is she? She never comes to see me any more.' She stopped and stared round the room, suddenly frightened. 'Where's Kirsty?'

'I'll fetch her,' Jade said quietly. There was little point in trying to make contact. Best just to bring Kirsty, but she wondered dismally as she went down to the kitchen if her mother might just

42

have remembered her better if she had been her real child. Kirsty was the only person her mother really recognised. But Kirsty had been with her since she and Ralph Martin married.

Kirsty! It suddenly dawned that Kirsty would remember the circumstances of the adoptions. She must do. She had been their nanny for the years when Poppy's health was at its worst. She had been in Hong Kong with the family. She was one of the last of the faithful family retainers and quite content to remain so.

She was in the kitchen, helping the cook clear up after the big country-house breakfast which had been produced for the funeral guests. Small and round, with neatly waved white hair and very bright blue eyes, she was chatting away as she stood with a teacloth in her hand. Cook, a square woman of taciturn habits, hardly appeared to be listening as she stood with her hands plunged into a basin of frothy water. Jade thought how odd it was that the flat in London, which had no servants other than an efficient daily, had every labour-saving gadget known to man. Here in the Highlands, everything was done the old-fashioned way, because there was labour to do it.

'Kirsty – Mother's asking for you,' Jade said from the doorway.

Kirsty stopped her conversation in mid-stream, put down the teacloth, and turned to follow Jade.

'It's been no good, this treatment,' she said, making it a statement rather than a question.

'I don't think so. Perhaps we went too late.' She paused. 'Kirsty, *why*? I mean she was always so bright and lively. Scatty, maybe, but this – this – vegetable . . .'

'Whist!' Kirsty's voice was stern. 'You don't understand. Your mother had a lot more to put up with than you know about. And I'll thank you not to call her a vegetable.'

They were walking down the long corridor, lined with paintings appropriate to the Highland scene – stags, dead rabbits on platters, a burn, frozen more in paint than in nature, and a mountain that might have been Ben Nevis.

'What did she have to put up with?' Jade had slowed her pace.

'None of your business,' Kirsty said sharply.

'Because I'm adopted?' Jade's voice was angry, and Kirsty softened immediately.

'No, no, no,' she said. 'Of course not. It's just they're no my tales to tell. And it's all a long time ago.'

'Then you know we weren't the children of Father's translator?' Jade deliberately made her statement a shock.

Kirsty stopped dead, her round, dimpled face settling into worried lines.

'How do you know that?'

'Well, it's true, isn't it? Poppy and I aren't sisters. We were both abandoned babies.'

Kirsty had turned in the dim corridor to face Jade, and her voice was anxious, hurried. Jade realised she was thoroughly shaken.

'It wasn't like that. Not entirely. We thought you were sisters. We thought she had some reason for saying you weren't. The baby at the harbour wouldn't have gone to her. She only had children from the New Territories. We thought she had some reason for lying. We thought . . .' She stopped dead. 'You must ask your mother about all this,' she said woodenly, recollecting herself.

'Kirsty,' Jade's voice was a wail of exasperation. 'How can I ask my mother anything? She doesn't even know who I am any more. Who only had children from the New Territories?'

'Miss Tibbets,' Kirsty said, almost sullenly. 'She ran the orphanage.'

'And my father paid her a lot of money for us.'

'He just helped her a little,' Kirsty said, her mouth like a trap. 'And only because your mother wanted you both so badly.'

'And what about the ship, Kirsty? What about the *Brian Leigh*?'

'Ship? Now what are you on about, child? You're keeping me from your mother.'

Kirsty's plump little body bustled down the remainder of the corridor and into the hallway, exuding moral indignation. Or anxiety? Or what? Kirsty could talk the hind leg off a donkey and frequently did, but she was at the same time totally close-mouthed. Her chatter was inconsequential, unimportant. A secret with Kirsty might just as well have been dead and buried, Jade remembered, thinking of the times when she had told the younger, cuddly Scotswoman her secrets with enjoinders not to tell Mummy and Daddy. Kirsty never had.

But Jade wanted some answers to her questions. It would have to be her grandfather she tackled. He had decided to stay on at Glen Hind for a few days to give the girls support. With the bit between her teeth, Jade went to find him. He was in the study where she had opened the envelope the evening before. Someone had been sent into Kinlochrannoch to collect the *Financial Times* and he was reading it.

'Grandfather,' she said without any preamble, 'have you ever heard of a ship called the *Brian Leigh*?'

He gave a visible start, put down the newspaper and said: 'The *Brian Leigh*? Why do you want to know about the *Brian Leigh*?'

'Oh, I know about it already,' she said airily. 'It disappeared in the South China Sea in 1958.'

'Then why are you asking me about it?' he said grumpily, picking up his newspaper.

She moved so she could see his face.

'I was just a bit puzzled as to why Father would have kept newspaper cuttings about it.'

This time he didn't react.

'That's easy,' he said. 'He was the judge in charge of the enquiry.'

'I know. But what happened in the end?'

'Nothing.'

'Nothing?'

'Nothing.'

'You mean they never found her?'

'That's right.'

'Do you remember it well?'

He was not to be drawn.

'When a ship disappears and an aircraft searching for it disappears and you're in the shipping business in the South China seas – you remember,' he said. He seemed to be relaxing a little; as if he had decided he was dealing with her in the wrong way. 'It always puzzled your father. That's why he kept a record of it, I expect. He used to say it was the most interesting case he had ever heard.'

He got to his feet and went to the mantelpiece where he had put his tobacco and his pipe. He jammed the pipe in his mouth, under the stiff military moustache that still had a tinge of red to it, and sank back into the big leather armchair.

'It wasn't one of your ships?'

He shook his head. 'Belonged to some Australian company. They built it at the Cheoy Lee Shipyard, as I recall. Damn good shipbuilders they were. Nothing to do with them. Pirates did it, I reckon. The South China Seas were full of them in those days.'

She decided to change tactics.

'Did you know about our adoption?'

'What about it?' he said cautiously.

'About Miss Tibbets and the Home of Those Who Care?'

'Of course I knew about it. Didn't approve. But your mother wanted it and so your father went along with it. And how did you find out about that?'

'Father left all the papers.'

'And how did you get hold of them?'

'The solicitor gave them to me.'

'Damn fool. Always said that man was a damn fool. Your father liked him. Personally I'd have sooner bought wine from him than legal advice.'

'Should I tell Poppy, Grandfather?' she asked, suddenly realising that this was what had been troubling her more than anything.

He considered, puffing out smoke, taking time to play with his lighter. 'Did it upset you?' he asked. 'Finding out, I mean?'

She considered.

'I'm not sure yet. I haven't taken it in.' She hesitated. 'No, I don't think it did trouble me too much. I've always known I was adopted; I've always known I wasn't European. I suppose it doesn't matter all that much where Father found me.'

He grunted.

'That's the pragmatic Chinese in you,' he said. 'Very pragmatic people, the Chinese.'

'It's not the Chinese *in* me,' she said, surprised at the strength of the thought. 'I *am* Chinese.'

He grinned. 'I suppose you are. You and Poppy don't act much like 'em, though.'

Suddenly she was curious.

'In what way?'

'You smile too much for the Chinese. Poppy says what she's thinking; hides nothing. You're not afraid to contradict anybody. It's always fascinated me how the environment took over with both of you. Independent little good, well-brought-up British girls you've both turned out to be.' He gave a small barking laugh. 'Though I don't know about the "good" in Poppy's case.'

It seemed he knew about Poppy's indiscretions. She decided to go back to the original subject.

'So do I tell her, Grandfather?'

'Up to you,' he said. 'You're a big girl now, you must make your own decisions. And you must know her better than anyone. Sleep on it, eh? It's waited all this time. There's no hurry. Why don't you both go away somewhere for a bit? It's usually the Bahamas in January, isn't it? Take off for there.'

'I'd like to go to Hong Kong,' she said slowly, speaking a hardly formulated thought.

He gave her a sharp, spiky look.

'What for? All that roots stuff?'

'I suppose so,' she said defensively.

'Mistake,' he said positively.

'Why?'

'You'd find out if you went there.'

'I want to go.' She was aware she sounded stubborn.

His face hardened; the heavy lines accentuated as his eyes became two slits of grey.

'It's better to stay away,' he said flatly. 'I don't think you should go. You'll be neither fish, fowl nor good red herring. And besides . . .' he stopped.

'Besides what?'

'Your mother wouldn't like it.'

'Grandfather,' she said, 'Mother won't know whether I'm here or in Timbuktu. And I seem to remember you just telling me I am old enough to make my own decisions.'

'Another thing that's not Chinese about you,' he snapped. 'No regard for the elderly. Do as you damn well please.' Jamming his pipe in his mouth, he stalked out of the room while she watched him thoughtfully.

She was very certain that what was obvious perturbation at the idea of her going back to Hong Kong was nothing to do with her mother. But if not – what was it?

Poppy loathed being at Glen Hind. There was nothing to do, nowhere to go, and the house with its pall of funereal gloom scratched at her nerves like chalk on a blackboard.

She had felt a moment of sorrow at the graveside the day before, but she had never truly been able to relate to her father. She had been closer to her mother as a child, but she had no patience with the current version of Margaret McKenzie McKenzie Martin. This mindless woman with the opaque eyes and irritating habits was no one she recognised.

She needed some excitement; she was restless, wanting some

diversion, but she knew the family would be furious if she found diversion anywhere near. That was the most trying aspect of being in Scotland. It was necessary to go a long way away before any kind of privacy of action could be found.

She heard her grandfather talking to Jade in the little study and she made a decision. There was a pub in Perth she had visited before with some success. She would go there again.

Cook was in the kitchen, and she put her head through the door to announce she would not be home for lunch. She went through the servants' quarters and out to the stables which had been converted into garages. She decided to take the Volvo estate car that was normally used by the bailiff. Her own small Alfa would not be suitable for the purpose she had in mind.

She arranged the car to her satisfaction, the back seat down and covered with a thick tartan rug, then she set off. Sixty miles to drive and with luck she would arrive just when the pub was at its busiest so that she would be relatively inconspicuous. That was another problem in Scotland. A well-dressed, good-looking Chinese girl with an impeccable British accent was inclined to attract more attention than she cared for.

She drove competently and swiftly over the narrow roads, across bleak, snow-clad moorland and alongside Loch Tummel. She edged her way through the busy shopping centre of Pitlochry. From there the road improved and she was able to put her foot down. It was twelve thirty when she drove into the Gothic centre and wide windy streets of Perth.

The pub was less busy than she had hoped, and the cheerful little bar seemed to be full of men not much more than boys. Out of work, she decided. There were only two other women; a brassy blonde and a woman whose black dyed hair aged the pert Scottish face. They were drinking together at a small table and they gave her a calculating suspicious look as she came in through the door, her full-length mink wrapped tightly round her.

She hesitated for just long enough in the doorway to take stock and her pick. There were two men drinking at the far corner of the bar, one with his back to it, his elbows on the polished wood, lounging. He was about twenty at the most. A big-boned Highland lad with a shock of dark hair and square features. Stolid workman's hands held a pint of beer in a thin glass, but he looked very clean in tight dark blue jeans and a blue roll-neck sweater.

His companion was shorter with reddish hair and a squirrel face. He was half sitting, half standing, a stool under his behind. They both looked up and watched her as she walked confidently towards them. At the bar she ordered a whisky from a sour-faced barmaid, and then she turned to the bigger of the two men and said: 'I seem to have missed the road to Pitlochry. Am I very far out of my way?'

He had very dark blue eyes with girl's lashes and she stared straight at them and then at his wide but rather thin-lipped mouth while he gave her directions in a soft Highland brogue.

'That's very kind of you,' she said, smiling and holding his look. 'Can I buy you both a drink?'

He had already caught the invitation in her eyes, and the other lad was stirring, too, pushing the stool he had been leaning on towards her.

Both were grinning; anticipatory grins of men who knew they were on to a good thing.

'We'll both have a dram,' the bigger one said, and Poppy decided it would be him first.

Two drams later, the gingery one, whose name was Sean, suggested they show her the Pitlochry road.

'We'll come a wee way on it with you, if you like,' he said.

'There's another pub, just out of town on that road,' the dark one, James, said. 'We could have another dram there and send you on your way.'

'A good idea,' she said. She had told them she was driving up from London to visit friends in Pitlochry, and after a small joke about not having come all the way from China they had accepted the information without comment. But once outside the pub, she noticed how the ginger one looked at the number plate of the Volvo, and nudged James lightly to bring his attention to the Perthshire registration.

'Want to drive?' she said quickly.

It was the dark one who put his hand out for the keys, and she deliberately got into the let-down back seat, curling her legs under her while Sean climbed into the front. They were silent as James put the car into gear, gunned the engine and roared off down the road. He was genuinely heading for the A9, she realised, and wondered for an anxious moment if they had just meant to go to another pub, but she decided that couldn't be, not the way the atmosphere was tingling in the car. The dark boy's hands were gripped on the wheel, and he still had an inane, half-embarrassed grin on his face. Turning from the front seat, the other boy was pulling at her long, black hair in sharp little angry tugs.

James did not drive far along the A9. Just a few miles out of Perth, he turned sharp left and took the small road to Loch Almond. She moved herself into a more comfortable position, wrapped in her coat, her legs parting a little in anticipation. She could feel the heat generating in the pit of her stomach and she thought how easy it was to manipulate men. Show them the prospect of a fuck, and they were there with bells and a hard-on.

Bleak country was soon all they could see. The sun of the morning had gone, leaving lowering clouds on the horizon. The day was grey and dark would fall quickly. The only problem she had now was how to get rid of them both. After. It wouldn't be long now. James was turning the car into a cart-track and reversing it to turn to face the road. Ready for a quick getaway and very convenient for her.

He turned off the ignition and turned to her. He had left the key in the ignition and his blue eyes had darkened; looked red.

'You want it, don't you?' he said.

'Want what?'

'You know well what you want.'

She giggled. A trilling little sound in the closeted warmth of the car. Outside three seagulls wheeled, mewing and crying. With both men staring at her from the front seat, she knelt up and slowly opened the full mink coat. Underneath she was naked except for a black suspender belt and sheer dark stockings and long black boots.

She liked the way their mouths fell open. The mink and not much else was always a surprise, but an erotic one which seemed to spur her pick-ups on.

Provocatively she pointed to James and said: 'You first.'

As it was they both came over the back seat together, both pulling off their duffle coats and at their jeans' zips. She took James first, while the other watched, panting until it was his turn. There was no kissing, no caressing, just straightforward, uncomplicated laying which was all she wanted from them. The bonus was that the excitement of watching Sean writhe all over her, making the Volvo bounce gently beneath them, ignited James again. The red-headed one was grabbing at her as James laboured

50

but she shut her mind to his dissecting fingers and concentrated on the screwing, feeling the deep rolling waves of pleasure invading.

'You Chinese bitch . . . you bitch . . . you bitch . . . you bitch. . . .' he was gritting out. It was nearly over. She didn't care what he called her, just so long as he continued to service her for long enough, releasing the tensions, the frustrations that seemed sometimes to be strangling her.

As he collapsed inert, and it was finished for her too, she pushed him away with cool contempt. Men never realised she was using them, she thought. They never understood that it was they who were degraded, cheapened. These two had been her toys of the moment. The next thing was to discard them.

For a few seconds the three of them lay like litter on the back of the car, the only sound the mewing of the seagulls and their own panting breath steaming the windows. Then she sat up and pulled the mink back around her, belting it tightly.

'Let's get some air,' she said.

Their grins and their anticipatory excitement had gone. They were uneasy, almost embarrassed, and, she felt, perhaps about to turn ugly. Sometimes they suspected they had been used.

She smiled at them in turn.

'It's so hot in here,' she said, 'and not surprising.'

Neither spoke, but they picked up their duffle coats, zipped themselves and got out of the car. She followed them, swiftly locking all doors but the driver's as she got out. They didn't notice.

'That's better,' she said as the freezing air stung her nose and cheeks and she felt the cold of the snow through her boots. 'Shall we go and have that dram now?'

Neither spoke, but Sean had moved away to relieve himself, making the snow yellow and steaming where he stood. The other watched, waiting for him as she moved round the car to the driver's side. Very quickly she was inside, the door slamming behind her, the lock pressed down. The key still dangled gently in the ignition and she turned it, put the car into gear and, without any great hurry, took off down the road. It wasn't far back to the A9. She hoped the lads would enjoy their walk home. And that they wouldn't catch cold.

The sex-induced euphoria had begun to evaporate on the long drive back. At Tummel Bridge, light snow started to fall, and she had to ease her way over the moorlands, frightened of skidding into the dough-faced Highland sheep who strayed on to the roads, staring at her belligerently as she edged past them.

Kinlochrannoch looked like a picture postcard as the snow fell gently, but she drove through the little town without stopping and on to the road that ran along the side of the loch. A few miles ahead, stony and turreted, was Glen Hind, and she felt depressed at the prospect of returning there.

She left the car at the back of the house and, her mink pulled tightly around her, went into the house through the kitchen. Kirsty was helping Cook dish up a lunch of lamb chops and vegetables and she gave Poppy a disapproving look as she came in through the door.

'Your mam and your sister are already at table,' she said. 'You've missed the soup. Are you eating or no?'

Poppy nodded curtly.

'Put mine out,' she said. 'I'll be five minutes. Forget the soup.'

She slipped up the back stairs to her room, and it only took a second to pull on a dress over the stockings and suspender belt. Her breasts were so small she did not need to wear a bra, and giving her long black hair a quick flick through with a hairbrush, she hurried back downstairs, still tying the belt of her dress.

Her mother and Jade had begun to eat as she slipped into her seat at the big polished table set with silver, crystal and a magnificent candelabra. Expressionless, Jade reached to fill her glass with wine.

'Where have you been?' she asked as she put the bottle down.

'Only into Kinlochrannoch,' Poppy said, her face bland. 'Where's Grandpa?'

'Eating in his room,' Jade said. 'He's irritated with me.'

'With you! What have you done?'

'Said I'm going to Hong Kong.'

Poppy put down her fork. 'Whatever for?'

'I want to see where we came from.'

She was aware that Jade was watching her carefully, the long, dark eyes that looked so like her own fixed on her face. Their mother was stirring uneasily.

'Where's your father?' she asked. 'He promised to join us for lunch.'

Jade's eyes blinked in pain and she drew a deep breath. 'He's in

London, Mother,' she said. 'You remember. He'll be back in a day or two.'

'He really should have told me,' Lady Martin said crossly. 'I wanted to talk to him about your schooling.'

'That's all arranged, Mother,' Jade said. 'Don't you remember? You settled it before he went.'

'I don't remember—' The voice was puzzled. 'But if you say so.'

'It is all right, Mother. Really. Just eat your lunch.'

While the interruption had gone on, Poppy had been thinking about what Jade had said, and she felt a stirring of excitement. The idea appealed to her.

'When are you going?' she asked abruptly.

Jade turned back to look at her, uncertain for a moment, having lost the thread of what she had been saying.

'Hong Kong, you mean?'

'Yes.'

'I thought right away.'

'Can I come?'

Jade hesitated.

'Why do you want to go?'

The dining room windows looked out over the loch and for a moment Poppy was silent, staring at the grey water and the slow falling snowflakes.

Why did she want to?

'Because,' she said slowly, aware that she was about to say something important, 'I might feel at home there.'

Jade looked surprised.

'At home?'

'Umm. You're different from me, but I've never felt at home here.

'You mean at Glen Hind?'

Poppy shook her head, feeling her heavy hair swing on her shoulders.

'Not just Glen Hind. Anywhere. I mean – we're different. We don't belong, do we? Not really.'

'I've never felt like that.' Jade's voice was uncertain, and Poppy realised that this was the first time in many years that she and her sister had even begun to communicate.

'Well, I've always felt like it,' Poppy said. 'Strange. In the wrong place. Perhaps in Hong Kong they won't make jokes about us going sideways,' she added bitterly.

'Going sideways?' It was obvious Jade had no idea what she was talking about.

'You must have met politer gentlemen than I have,' Poppy said mockingly. 'Don't you know, sister dear, that Europeans have this joke that Chinese girls' cunts go sideways.'

'Poppy!' Jade gave a warning look towards their mother, but she was eating slowly, her jaws clamping uncomfortably on her food, her eyes opaque as she stared at nothing.

'Well, that's what they believe. I think half of them only go to bed with us to see if it's true. It might be fun to meet men who look and smell the same; and who don't think my cunt goes sideways.'

'If you only want to go to pick up Chinese men . . .'

'For Christ's sake, Jade! You can be amazingly pompous at times. No, that's not why I want to go. I want to go perhaps for the same reasons that you do. I just don't mind admitting it.'

Her sister was turning a piece of spinach over and over with her fork, inspecting it as if it were diseased. Then she said abruptly: 'We were both abandoned babies.'

'What?'

'We didn't belong to Father's translator. They got us out of a children's home.'

Poppy stared at her sister.

'So what,' she heard herself saying. 'What does it matter whose kids we were? We sure as hell didn't belong to her—' She nodded vigorously in her mother's direction. 'I never did believe that story anyway. It was far too convenient, our parents killing themselves in a car so that mother could adopt us. And besides, there were the dreams . . .' She stopped short. She didn't want to talk about the dreams. 'When shall we leave?' she said abruptly.

'I was going down to London tonight.'

'Great! I can't stand this place.' She was beginning to feel excited. 'I'll pack right after lunch.'

Jade was still playing with the spinach and she did not look up as she said: 'Grandfather thinks it's a bad idea. He says I'll regret it. Maybe you will, too.'

'So what,' Poppy said again, sure now that the only thing she wanted to do in the world was to go to Hong Kong. 'I'm collecting regrets.'

Jade's face looked very sad and suddenly older.

'I think we ought to go,' she said. 'It's where we come from. But are we going to fit in, Poppy? Will it be all right?'

Her sadness communicated itself.

'I don't know,' Poppy said quietly. 'But if we don't fit in there – where do we belong?'

The job had its advantages, Gary Smith decided as the small train rumbled its way through the Highlands. He got to travel. And on this journey he was finding himself enchanted by the views which had begun almost immediately after leaving Glasgow and continued in a eye-bewildering white blaze of delight.

The sun had decided to shine; the broad, stately sweep of the Clyde below to the left shone blue, and the broader, softer expanse of Loch Lomond to the right shone silver. The rest of the world was in monochrome. He found himself humming that he'd take the high road if she'd take the low road and wondered where he had dredged that up out of memory.

The trees, both the dark firs and bare-branched larches, were coated with white and glistening icicles as the train, taking its time, chattered up the one-way track. There was hardly anyone aboard, but he had a timetable and a train map and he knew his stop was after the one after the Bridge of Orchy once they had run over the grim vista of Rannoch Moor. A car would be waiting for him at Rannoch station. That had been laid on, and he had the keys in his pocket. A jeep would be best in this terrain, he thought, but they'd given him a Mini, a car he had never driven, telling him cheerfully that it had front-wheel drive, could cope with most things and, more important, would be inconspicuous.

Sunshine or not, it was bitterly cold as he stepped out on to the station and stood watching while an old woman pulled the points before the train set off again. The cold stung his cheeks, reminding him of winters in New York, and he dragged his heavy overcoat around him and went looking for the Mini. It was there, a bright red one, and he grinned remembering the promise of something inconspicuous. He found, as arranged, the map in the glove compartment, with Glen Hind marked on it. About thirteen miles to drive and looking at the state of the road, snow banked on either side, some drifting across to leave treacherous icy patches, he decided he'd have to take it slowly. With the speedometer never touching over thirty, he set off, able to look at the countryside as he drove.

It was all pleasingly Scottish as if the fauna were putting on a display for him. He saw a stag on the hillside, poised still, its antlers raised as a hawk hovered high overhead. A white hare ran across his path as he rounded a corner, and a herd of ungainly Highland sheep lumbered across the road, refusing to move. All in all, it took him nearly an hour to drive the thirteen miles, and he found he was wondering if Jade would go to bed with him under her own roof. He wanted to make love to her again. He'd thought about the last time in the jaccuzzi a lot. Too much for comfort. It really wasn't wise to get emotionally involved on a job.

He could see the house for some way before he arrived; big, square and baronial with pointed turrets like a witch's castle, he decided fancifully. It wasn't unlike some of the older houses in Philadelphia, and he remembered seeing wooden copies near downtown Los Angeles. Here the architecture looked more at home.

The big wrought-iron gates were open and a cattle grid kept out the wandering, aimless sheep. The drive had been swept clear of snow and it curved around through open parkland that ran down to the loch. As he reached the front door he saw a flight of stone steps leading to it. A Mini and a Volvo had been parked outside.

He drew up behind the other Mini, got out and ran up the steps. No one seemed to be about. There was a light door at the top of the steps which opened into a small lobby, and then a larger, heavy closed wooden door. He hesitated, looking for a bell. There was none. But the light door was ajar. He went through and saw a bell-pull at the side of the heavier door. He took the iron handle and tugged.

Somewhere in the house he could hear a great jangling noise and then silence.

It took a while before the door was opened by a small, round, elderly body with crisp white hair and very blue eyes. She did not speak, just eyed him questioningly.

'Is Miss Jade McKenzie McKenzie Martin at home?' he asked.

The neat little mouth with purse lines around it opened.

56

'She's no here,' the woman said in a malt whisky voice. 'She and her sister left for Hong Kong last night.'

≈ 5 ≈

FRIDAY

Afterwards, Jade could remember little of her arrival in Hong Kong. She was aware of a blur of blue and green as the aircraft swept lower, and then buildings that seemed too close for comfort and the plane was down.

She and Poppy had drunk too much of Cathay Pacific's champagne to relieve the enforced intimacy they shared. A reluctant togetherness that they had not known since they were both children.

After the refuelling stop at Bahrain, Poppy had produced a small enamel box from her handbag.

'Still seven hours to go,' she said. 'Want a sleeping pill?'

Jade looked at her curiously.

'Where did you get them?'

'I've always got them.'

'I didn't know you took sleeping pills,' Jade said.

'Well, you wouldn't, would you?' Poppy said pertly.

As she swallowed one of the big yellow pills with the last of the champagne, since it seemed a good idea to sleep, she thought how little she really knew Poppy. After the revelations at Kinlochrannoch, Poppy had clammed up and had reverted to her usual flippant self. Jade had not told her that it seemed possible they were not sisters, and Poppy, characteristically, had not asked to see the documents their father had left. As Jade waited for the pill to work, she wondered what Poppy's reaction would be. Most likely no more than a cynical acceptance, she decided, as her sister who was not her sister flipped through a glossy Hong Kong fashion magazine.

She and Poppy were the only Chinese in the first-class compartment. In the tourist-class section of the aircraft there were many

Orientals: more than Jade had ever seen in one place in her life. She watched them with curiosity as they waited at Gatwick for the flight to be called. There were a good many European tourists and also several British family groups, a few of whom had got off at Bahrain. Mostly they were going on to Hong Kong, and they all seemed to have Chinese servants whose job it was to take care of the children and carry most of the luggage. One sturdy girl dressed in black with a heavy twist of hair that kept falling in long strands from the pins not strong enough for the weight had a child perched on each hip and a bag on her back. The young European parents carried nothing, and the Chinese girl's broad, impassive face showed only acceptance of the situation. Jade felt a finger of anger stabbing her.

But leaving the plane, she was aware of nothing. As she gathered her hand luggage together she was bemused, the effect of the unfamiliar pill slowing her down, and it was Poppy who took the lead through the Customs and into the hall where they waited for their luggage.

It was also Poppy who organised a porter when their suitcases came rolling through, and Poppy who was muttering that the Mandarin Hotel should have sent transport for them, as Jade trailed behind.

They were both standing irresolute in the arrival lounge while faces, endless Chinese faces, so like their own, their owners pushing and shoving, milled around. Someone spoke to her in a tongue that sounded like bamboo clacking, and she looked blankly into the woman's face.

'I'm sorry,' she said. 'I don't understand.'

The woman's darting eyes inspected her, then she shrugged and turned away.

'What did she want?' Poppy asked.

'I don't know. I didn't understand what she said,' Jade said, suddenly aware that the small incident would be repeated again and again while they stayed in Hong Kong.

She was pondering the implications when Poppy tugged at her arm and said: 'Listen.'

Over the airport tannoy a voice was saying: 'Will the Misses McKenzie McKenzie Martin please come to the information desk.'

'It can't be for us,' Jade said. 'No one knows we're coming here.'

'Don't be silly,' Poppy said impatiently. 'What other Misses McKenzie McKenzie Martin could there be? It must be transport from the hotel.' She turned to the porter who was waiting with their luggage.

'Where's the information desk?' she asked imperiously, and the man indicated across the hall and set off at a slight trot, pushing the luggage before him. At the desk a square short man in chauffeur's uniform was standing, his hat in his hand. As they neared him he stepped forward and half bowed.

'The Misses McKenzie McKenzie Martin?' he asked.

'Yes.' It was Poppy who answered.

'I have instructions to take you to your hotel.' He had the accent of a Chinese waiter not long in the West.

'Thank you,' Poppy said, turning to Jade and adding: 'I told you so.'

The chauffeur then broke into rapid Cantonese, speaking to the porter. His hat now under his arm, he led them through the crowds, Jade yawning and trying to get her senses back in working order.

Had she been less stupified by the champagne, the length of the flight and the sleeping pill, she might have realised earlier that the big white Rolls-Royce that awaited them was not from the Mandarin Hotel. But she was still following Poppy, who immediately entered the car as one used to the geography of a Rolls. Jade stood hesitating on the forecourt for no positive reason she could identify.

A young Chinese was already in the car. He sat in the corner on the white leather seat, his legs precisely crossed. He wore an impeccably tailored silk suit. His face had two sharp cheekbones relieving the broad ivory planes. His black hair was swept unnaturally backwards and held in place with some kind of substance that made his head glisten as if it had been polished. The gleaming hair made him faintly vulgar and a little sinister, but his intelligent face and small elegant hands dispelled the impression. He said: 'Won't you get into the car, Miss McKenzie McKenzie?'

The voice was not a waiter's. More British public school with a faint but different kind of strangulation of the vowels.

She nodded, reassured, and stepped into the car, settling herself next to Poppy so that all three of them were on the spacious back seat.

'The Mandarin, isn't it?' he asked.

'That's right,' Poppy said, and the man beside her leaned forward and clacked instructions to the chauffeur.

'Are you going to the Mandarin too?' Jade asked as the Rolls pulled smoothly away into a sunny, faintly windy morning.

'Yes – to accompany you,' he said.

'You're not a guest there?' Jade was beginning to feel slightly uneasy.

'No. Forgive me, I should explain,' he said, and produced his wallet from which he extracted a visiting card and handed it to her.

She took the stiff, gold-engraved card.

'Jimmy Lee, Managing Director, Green Butterfly Furs,' she read out loud, and turned to look at him. 'I don't understand,' she said.

'Let me explain. As you see, I am the managing director of a fur company. Perhaps the best in Hong Kong, though I say it with due modesty. It is my practice to scan the first-class passenger lists of the aircraft arriving from Europe and the United States. I decide on whom might be the most likely customers for our superb furs. Then as a little encouragement and incentive to buy from Green Butterfly above all the many furriers in the Colony, I offer the use of my Rolls and my chauffeur for the period of their stay in Hong Kong.'

'I see,' Jade said turning the card over. 'And what if those you choose are into wild-life conservation?'

'If I may say so,' he murmured, 'it is clear that you are not. At this time of year you will not be needing your beautiful lynx here, nor your sister her mink. It is a little cool in the evenings in January. I think you would find a small fur jacket would be more suitable. Perhaps I can interest you in one. We can make to our clients' specifications' – the word was not easy for him to say – 'in a very short time.' He was not smiling, but his small round eyes and the smooth eyelids above looked as if they were hiding a joke that he had no wish to share.

'I've always fancied an ocelot jacket,' Poppy was saying.

'You are most definitely not into conservation,' he said. 'But it might be possible . . .'

Jade was beginning to come awake.

'Why did you pick on us?' she asked abruptly.

'The name McKenzie McKenzie Martin is not unknown in Hong Kong,' he said gently. 'And the *South China Morning Post* carried a small paragraph announcing your arrival.'

'Did you expect us to be Orientals?'

He seemed to hesitate.

'No,' he admitted.

'Didn't you think you'd found the wrong couple?'

He pursed his lips. 'Not when I saw your coats. It was possible, but unlikely.'

'We were adopted.' Why was she explaining? she wondered.

'That seems obvious,' he said, but his tone was of the utmost politeness.

She turned to look out of the window, irritated at having been Shanghaied in such a fashion, and then smiled to herself at the aptness of the expression. Outside, the car was speeding through endless high-rise flats; washing hanging from the balconies like the coloured flags of all nations. The street was wide and seemed hilly, and outside everywhere there were people, trudging, badly dressed and seemingly all carrying too much.

'How far is the hotel?' she asked.

'It is Hong Kong side. You are Kowloon side now. We must pass under the tunnel to the island. The journey takes about twenty-five minutes.'

He was half sitting in his corner so that he could see both their faces.

'Your English is very good,' she told him.

'And yours,' he said gravely. The two words astonished, then shocked her. She turned her head to look at him to see if he were mocking, but his smooth face was expressionless. She thought she might have sounded patronising, but then was irritated again. Of course she spoke good English. Poppy was giggling behind her hand at her sister's discomfort, but she decided to continue this faintly bizarre conversation.

'Where did you learn?' she asked.

'Here in Hong Kong. And you?'

She wanted to say she had spoken it all her life. But maybe he had too.

'Benenden,' she said instead.

'Ah, a school much favoured by British royalty, I believe,' he said. 'I myself was at Queen's College here. No royalty, but Dr Sun Yat-Sen was an alumni.'

'Who was he?' Poppy asked.

He made a gentle clucking noise with his tongue.

'The Father of the Revolution in China,' he said. 'It is Chinese history.'

Jade felt rebuked while asking herself that why the hell should she know about Chinese history. But then, on the other hand, why didn't she?

'We didn't do Chinese history,' Poppy was saying cheerfully. 'Bet you don't know who Garibaldi was.'

'The Italian who did a similar job for Italy,' he said as if bored by the simplicity of the question. Then, changing the subject: 'Look, we are about to enter the Cross Harbour Tunnel – one of the miracles of Hong Kong. It is over a mile long, you know. Do you have tunnels as long in Britain?'

Jade had an uneasy feeling he knew perfectly well that they had tunnels as long in Britain, but was pretending ignorance for politeness after flooring Poppy with Garibaldi.

'Lots,' she said briefly.

Even Poppy, never noted for her sensitivity, seemed to realise that the conversation was becoming ridiculous. Briskly she returned to business.

'Are your furs cheap?' she asked, a typical Poppy question. Poppy liked money and disliked spending it. Jade suddenly remembered that both their airline tickets were on her American Express card, and that she would have considerable difficulty getting Poppy to pay up what she owed.

'Inexpensive – by European standards,' Jimmy Lee was saying. 'But I hope you will come to my show rooms in Central and see for yourself. Or it might amuse you to come to the factory and watch the coats being made. From there we can make an even more special price.'

They were speeding through a tunnel that could have been anywhere in the world, except that the drivers of all the taxis and cars passing were Chinese. But then so were she and Poppy.

'Do all Chinese tradesmen operate like you?' she asked, knowing it was a snobbish remark, but needing to regain some sense of her own identity.

'Tailors meet the planes,' he said, 'but I believe I am the only furrier to adopt the scheme. And trade, you will find, has different connotations in Hong Kong. Trade is important. To be a trader of any kind is a serious matter. We do not look down on our traders.' There was a gentle admonition in his tone, but she still felt that he was laughing at her.

'I shall come and look at your furs,' Poppy said positively. 'And can we really have the use of the Rolls and the chauffeur – even if we don't buy anything?'

'Of course. That is what I said.'

'And what will *you* do for transport?' Jade asked, stroking the white leather of the upholstery.

'I have another of these,' he said. Which, she decided, had totally floored her.

They were coming up from the tunnel now, and he was pointing out landmarks as they drove along the waterfront.

'The yacht club,' he said, pointing to a low building set well off the road. 'Maybe you will be invited, but there are few Chinese to be found there, I'm afraid. Can you see the homes of the boat people? No – maybe not. You must look at how they live. It is a great contrast to the Mandarin Hotel.'

'And to this car,' Jade said, wondering at her need to put him down.

'Indeed,' he said, 'but my origins were those of the boat people. We make our own fortune here in Hong Kong.'

For the first time he smiled, and looked rather smug.

'We are very near the hotel now,' he said, pointing ahead behind the chauffeur's shoulder. 'It is behind that tall building there, the Connaught Centre. We call it the house of a thousand orifices,' he said. 'Perhaps you can understand the description.'

Poppy, looking at the building on the waterfront with its rows of polkadot windows, giggled. 'Yes,' she said, 'but doesn't it spoil the view from the hotel?

'Only in places,' he told her. 'It has been built on reclaimed land. The road we are driving along was once much nearer the water. You will find there is much reclaimed land in Hong Kong. Many reclaimed things . . .'

Jimmy Lee was beginning to get under Jade's skin. He seemed to say nothing that hadn't a concealed double meaning, but the double meanings were impossible to decode.

The car was pulling into a curved entrance where porters in red livery waited. The chauffeur leapt out and hurried to the boot where with the help of the porters he began to unload luggage. Jade and Poppy were gathering together their hand baggage, and Jade thought Jimmy Lee was right about one thing. She was roasting in her lynx coat and wishing she hadn't worn it.

'Do you have friends here?' he was asking.

'Not really, just some contacts,' Jade said cautiously, in case he was looking for more customers.

'Perhaps then you would have dinner with me tonight. At the

Furama Hotel. It is not the best food in Hong Kong by any means, but it has the best view. It would give me pleasure to take you both.'

Ridiculously, Jade's first thought was that she could not go to dinner with a Chinese who held his black hair down with some shiny substance. What would Grandfather say? But Poppy was accepting for them both, explaining they had no plans at all and yes, they would meet in the Captain's Bar of the Mandarin at seven thirty. Jade, still feeling several degrees under, found herself on the pavement without having said a word.

The porter was speaking to her in Chinese, and she made a gesture denoting futility with her hands and said in English: 'I'm sorry, I don't understand.'

'I bring baggage in,' the porter said patiently and Jade looked for some sign of what the man was thinking, but could find none.

'Wasn't that Jimmy Lee charming?' Poppy was saying enthusiastically as they walked into the hotel. 'He might be a good contact for getting into the life here. He must be loaded with those two Rolls. And attractive, didn't you think?'

Jade hesitated. She was looking at one of the most luxurious hotel lobbies she had ever seen, and Jade had seen a great deal of luxury in her twenty-four years.

'I thought he was – well, odd,' she said. 'He never seemed to be saying what he meant.'

'I didn't notice that.' They had reached the reception desk, staffed by elegant, dark-suited young Chinese men. 'I thought he was Ok.'

'Maybe,' Jade said doubtfully.

They registered; the young man behind the desk snapped his fingers and a boy came to take their keys and escort them to their rooms. Jade had booked them a room each. She and Poppy would not have survived two days in shared quarters, and if Poppy wanted to get into mischief, Jade did not wish to know.

'It looks like a super hotel,' Poppy said as she turned the corner from the marbled hall to where the lifts were. 'A good start. Rolls-Royces and a grand hotel. I'm going to like it here.'

'It's not what I expected,' Jade said.

Poppy stared at her.

'What did you expect? A load of coolies wearing those funny hats?'

'I don't know what I expected,' Jade said crossly. 'And you

shouldn't have accepted that Chinaman's invitation.'

'Why not?' Poppy said as she moved into the lift, Jade behind her. 'We haven't anything else to do. Funny, though,' she added, 'if he thought we'd be Europeans, why did his chauffeur pick us out right away?'

'But we *are* Europeans,' Jade wanted to say, but kept silent, dismissing the thought by thinking Poppy was right. It was odd that the chauffeur had picked them out.

'What are we going to do about lunch?' Poppy asked, whose mind was always on the next meal. 'Shall we eat here?'

They were walking down a long, softly lit corridor with deep carpets and a motif discreetly painted on the walls.

Jade looked at her watch which she had changed to Hong Kong time on the plane. It was not quite eleven o'clock.

'If you like,' Jade said. The boy had stopped and was opening one of the doors and waving her in.

'Ok,' Poppy said. 'See you in that Captain's Bar place at one o'clock.' Then, following her into the room, 'I say – this is all right, isn't it?'

The room was all right. One large bed; big lamps, long windows, carved wood cupboard, a bar and fridge, furnished in Western style with the faintest scent of Oriental elegance.

But it was the view that took away the breath. The soaring tower of the house of the thousand orifices was just to the right, leaving a clear view of the harbour where a green-painted ferry boat slid across the blue water. Other fussy little craft darted in the narrow channel. Junks with beige sails moved majestically and there were dredgers, tied up in rows like sardines in a tin. Beyond was Kowloon where they had landed at Kai Tak airport, a mass of skyscrapers with a vast plane taking off, lurching below the mountains above the buildings into the sky. Sea hawks wheeled below, hovering high over the water, and beyond were misty green mountains. China maybe, Jade thought, enjoying the pale blue sky with scuttling white clouds which seemed to be racing the dinghies below.

'I hadn't expected it to be beautiful,' she said.

'Mother always said it was beautiful,' Poppy announced.

'You talked with Mother about Hong Kong?' Her voice was surprised.

'Often,' Poppy said, and tightened her lips in the way that meant she was saying no more.

Absently, Jade gave the boy far too big a tip, and he smiled and fawned.

'*Do jeh*,' he sung, bowing, and with a curious half-run left the room, pushing Poppy's luggage before him while its owner followed.

Jade pushed out her breath, let her shoulders sag at the relief of being alone and went back to the window to watch the mobile, changing view. It would have been a scene her grandfather must have watched a million times, she thought. She felt a stab of guilt when she thought about him. He had been really angry, more angry than she had ever seen him, when she had confirmed that both she and Poppy were definitely leaving for Hong Kong. 'A crackbrained scheme. Idiotic!' he had called it. 'You don't know what you're doing. You'll both be disappointed, hurt and disillusioned.'

He had refused to give them any financial help. He had refused to give them any introductions. He had been quite unreasonably against the whole idea.

'Why Grandfather?' Jade had asked him.

'Because you're going to a world where you don't belong,' he said.

'Then where do we belong?'

'Here. Where you've been brought up. What's that ridiculous modern expression – *culture shock*. Well, you're due for a bit of that, my girl, if you insist on taking yourself off East. You haven't thought it out.'

She was already discovering what he meant. So many faces like her own, and yet so different. She felt a fool that she could not speak in the tongue that came so easily from the mouths of people who were her own race and compatriots. Jimmy Lee with his obvious education, wealth and success had thrown her, too. Perhaps Poppy was right. Perhaps she had expected a lot of people in funny coolie hats. She felt a touch of resentment that Poppy and her mother had talked of Hong Kong, and that Poppy seemed to be more at ease, less disturbed by the experience than she was.

She felt she was a deep well of ignorance about her background; as if there were a part of her that had not been fed with vital information. Watching the view below, she realised that she had always felt different, but in a superior, comfortable way. Her race had been immaterial. Being young, beautiful and very rich, indulged at home, at restaurants, in shops as she had always been, made being different glamorous and pleasing.

She felt different in a different way here, but at the same time excited; on the threshold of discoveries.

Grandfather might not have given any aid, but he did not know she still had her father's Hong Kong address book. She would visit those people one by one and talk of her father and her mother; maybe even learn something about herself. She would find the orphanage and Miss Tibbets. She would try to find out more about Poppy's mother. She left the window and went to where her Gucci travelling bag lay on the bed. The address book was inside, zipped away for safety. She was taking out the shabby red leather-covered book, and beginning to remove the elastic band that held the pages together, when there was a discreet knock on her door.

'Come in,' she called.

The same porter who had brought up her luggage came into the room.

'For missy,' he said, handing her a long thin parcel wrapped in glossy white paper. She found him another coin and he sung his '*Do jeh*' again and left.

She turned the box over, puzzled. A present from the hotel? Or the attractive but obnoxious Jimmy Lee? Certainly not from Poppy.

She sat on the bed and pulled off the wrapping paper. Inside was a card and written on it in neat handwriting: 'With the compliments of Jimmy Lee.' The box was made of expensive shiny cardboard and she lifted the lid cautiously. Inside, nestling on a sheet of tissue paper, was a fan. A fan with a frame of the most beautiful carved ivory and with a small gold loop to hold it. She picked it up and splayed it out, finding, to her disappointment, that its body was made of paper. Ordinary white paper, unworthy of the workmanship of the frame.

'What a very odd gift,' she said out loud, and carefully folding the paper so it would not tear, she put it back into its box.

She sighed, a soft sound in the quiet room. The effects of Poppy's pill were with her still. She lay her head on the pillow and, slipping off her high-heeled shoes, lifted her feet on to the bed and slept.

On her right-hand side lay the red-covered address book, and on her left was the white paper fan.

'You must be careful in the hotel,' the Chinese girl whose name was Emma was saying. 'It's the Chinese New Year in a fortnight's time, and everyone is supposed to pay all their debts to ensure good luck throughout the next year. As we are pragmatic people, it doesn't effect the "good joss" if the money is stolen. So don't leave cash or traveller's cheques around. Or anything of value, come to that.'

'We saw the New Year signs,' Poppy said. 'There's a huge one out back of our hotel. Says something like Fat Choy.'

'*Kung kei fat choy*,' Jimmy Lee said. 'It's Chinese – Cantonese actually – for "wish you prosperity". Apt enough here, but not in China where there are no profits and no capitalism.'

'Bloody nuisance, Chinese New Year,' said the man called Stephen Norris, the only European at the table. 'Endless complaints of burglaries, more muggings, extortion. I wish they *wouldn't* pay their damn bills.'

'Oh come,' the girl called Emma said. 'Stop sounding like a *gweilo*.'

'What's a *gweilo*?' Jade asked, fascinated by the conversation. '*He* is,' the girl said, pointing at Stephen Norris. 'A foreign devil. A round-eyes. He can't help it, poor thing.'

Everyone around the table laughed, including Stephen Norris, and Emma's grin drew Jade into an Oriental circle.

'Don't you speak any Cantonese or Mandarin?' she was asking.

They were sitting at the round table, separated by Jimmy Lee who appeared to be Jade's partner for the evening. On her other side was Stephen Norris who was, apparently, a member of the Hong Kong police. Then came Poppy and next to her a thin-faced, extremely handsome young Chinese with girlish features and a smoothly muscular body under his impeccable dark suit. He was called Kwan Ching and his English was as perfect as that of the other Chinese who sat at the table.

Jade liked the girl best. She was asking questions in the friendliest way, with no condescension at all.

'Not a word,' Jade told her. 'You see, we were brought up in Europe. Poppy and I were adopted when we were little . . .'

'By the shipping McKenzie McKenzies?'

'That's right.'

Emma was shaking her head.

'Why on earth didn't they teach it to you? The old man speaks Cantonese, Mandarin and about a dozen other dialects better than most of us.'

'Our background was hardly mentioned,' Jade said, almost

apologetically. 'And I'm afraid I never even thought about it very much. Life was too easy.'

'Why was it too easy?' Emma asked, pushing a strand of her thick glossy hair away from her forehead. She was most beautifully dressed in a soft leather suit in the palest of beige. She wore soft leather matching shoes. As Jade and Poppy did, she exuded the scent of money.

'Well,' Jade hesitated. 'My father was killed recently, and, I don't know why, it just made me think about where I came from. Coming here has been what my grandfather described as cultural shock.'

Emma lifted her eyebrows.

'You expected us all to be coolies?'

'Poppy accused me of the same thing today,' Jade said. 'No – I didn't expect that. I don't know what I expected. But I didn't, well – I didn't expect you, let's say.'

'Me?'

'Yes. The sophistication . . .' She was stumbling, aware that everything she would say would be wrong. 'Do you work?' she asked abruptly, changing the subject.

'Indeed,' Emma said. 'As my father did before me, I import French wines, Scottish whisky and British gin. Most particularly I import expensive French brandy. We drink more of it here than anywhere else in the world. Our men think it is an aphrodisiac,' she said matter-of-factly. 'An impression those of us who import the stuff do little to dispel. Anyway, they may well be right. Would you say it has that effect on me, Stephen?' she asked across the table, her voice mocking.

The look that Stephen gave her in return was one of bafflement; a man confronted with an enigma that he was eternally perched on the brink of solving. He muttered something that Jade did not quite hear when Poppy said across the table: 'Thank you for the fan, Jimmy.'

Over lunch at the Chinese restaurant on top of the Mandarin, she and her sister had discussed the fans they had both received. Poppy had been particularly scathing about its quality, but now her tone was honeyed.

'You're welcome,' Jimmy Lee said.

'So pretty,' she purred, and opening the clasp of her black silk evening handbag, she produced the fan.

Kwan Ching and Jimmy Lee seemed mesmerised as she unfolded it and gently waved it across her face.

'Must be careful,' she said. 'It's so delicate.'

The atmosphere had changed. Only Emma and Stephen seemed unaffected by the fragile butterfly object that revealed and then concealed Poppy's enchanting little face.

'Did you like yours?' Jimmy Lee asked Jade.

'Very much,' she said hastily, her Benenden manners coming to the fore.

He didn't quite hesitate; but there was something like a fractional pause as if he had expected something more. Then he said abruptly: 'Would you like to dance?'

'Why not?' she said.

'Mind where you leave your handbag,' Emma said laughing. 'Not there . . .'

She had put her handbag on the slightly raised piece of floor beside her chair. As she looked down it had already receded a few inches from where she was standing. The restaurant, storeys high in the air, was turning. The brilliant night-lit views of Hong Kong and Kowloon beyond changed constantly and the kaleidoscope jumble of lights dimmed the stars over the South China Sea.

'More women lose their handbags that way . . .' Emma said. 'Leave it on your chair.'

Poppy had put the fan away and was getting to her feet to dance with Kwan Ching, and the four of them threaded their way through the tables walking around the circles until they came to the dance floor which remained static as the restaurant revolved around it.

'We may never find our table again,' Jimmy remarked. 'I'm sorry it's so crowded, but Friday evening is a popular night to go out.'

He led her smoothly on to the small, polished floor and put his arm around her. He danced well. Jade was amused to find that he was dancing the old-fashioned way, cheek to cheek, his shoulder muscular under her hand, though he was only an inch or two taller than she. He smelt of something lemony and expensive. She saw that his fingernails had been professionally manicured. He was very smooth. But how old was he? No more than twenty-five, she decided.

'Well,' he was saying. 'Do you feel at home here?'

'Oh, yes,' she said politely.

'You have quickly acquired one of our most noticeable characteristics,' he said.

'What's that?' The band was playing a Beatles number and the dimly lit floor was crowded.

'To say the thing you do not believe rather than offend,' he said.

'Is that Chinese?' she asked. 'It sounds like good manners to me.'

'Ah, but we carry it to extremes of hypocrisy and downright dishonesty,' he said. 'You will see.'

They danced in silence then and, making conversation, she asked if the movement of the room around them ever made people queasy.

He laughed: 'Sometimes. Why, are you?'

'No. Not at all.'

'Hungry?'

'Not particularly.' They had already selected food from the buffet that the hotel offered. It was European cooking and not very good.

'Thirsty?' He was smiling at her, his eyes narrowing even more. He was attractive, she decided, and then felt surprised that she found him so.

'Yes,' she said. 'That champagne seems to be holding jet lag at bay rather satisfactorily.'

'We'll go back to the table,' he said.

Emma and Stephen were still sitting there. He was glumly staring into the champagne glass, looking like a man who would rather be drinking Scotch. Emma looked up and smiled as they appeared.

'You found it again,' she said. 'People sometimes take hours . . .'

She had a habit of letting her sentences trail away as if her audience must know what she was talking about.

'Come and sit next to me,' she said, patting the seat where Kwan had been. 'Talk to me until he comes back. This one' – indicating Stephen – 'has gone all strong and silent. But then he . . .'

Jade settled herself and reached for her glass.

'Cultural shock, eh?' Emma mused. 'Why?'

'Because—' Jade had to think about it. 'I'm not sure who I am any more.'

'Nonsense,' Emma said briskly. 'You're whoever you've always been. This place is stiff with American Chinese, all bent on finding their cultural heritage. They don't have hang-ups . . .'

Jade longed to ask her where she had learned her English, but had no intention of falling into that trap twice.

'Perhaps they were brought up by Chinese parents,' she suggested. 'It would make it less confusing. I feel a little like the Great Dane in Thurber, was it, who believed he was a dachshund and was always trying to get on people's laps because he'd always lived with a dachshund and the dachshund could sit on laps.'

Emma laughed, then said: 'I do think you are making too much of it. Most of us here are very Westernised. Well, those of us who have been educated, that is. Look around here – in Hong Kong, East isn't entirely East and West isn't entirely West, and the twain do meet.'

'Some of the time,' Jimmy Lee said cryptically.

Kwan and Poppy were coming back from the dance floor and Jade slid into her own seat.

'Well, how's the world of crime?' Kwan was asking Stephen Norris, his tone jovial.

Norris' expression became more liverish than ever.

'Read the *South China Morning Post*,' he said. 'Unending.'

'Have they made any progress with the Peak murder?' Jimmy asked.

'I don't know.'

'You mean poor old dotty Dottie Adamson?' Emma said. 'That was particularly nasty.' She turned to Jade. 'Dottie Adamson was a local character. Very rich – an elderly Eurasian woman who worked for Caritas, the Catholic charity here. She was murdered in her home about nine days ago now. Stabbed in some sort of ritual with a pair of broken scissors.'

'Broken scissors!' Jade interrupted, suddenly alert. 'How were they broken?'

'Split in two,' Stephen grunted. 'It's a fairly common murder weapon – after the axe, the hatchet and the kitchen knife.'

'It's not the first tragedy in that house,' Jimmy Lee said. 'Years ago at one of the famous Peak parties – the Peak is the most expensive district in Hong Kong,' he said to Poppy as explanation, 'all the *gweilo* were throwing back the gin and the entire staff were murdered without the guests hearing so much as a scream.'

'It's bad *fungshui*, that's the trouble with that house,' Emma said authoritatively. 'You can feel it. Uncomfortable place. Definitely bad . . .'

'What's bad *fungshui*?' Poppy asked, and Jade noted with resignation that Kwan Ching had his hand on her thigh under the table. It was obvious from the positioning of his arm.

'When the dragon's in the wrong place,' Emma said, putting a cigarette into an ivory holder and lighting it with a gold Dunhill lighter.

'The dragon's in the wrong place?' Jade echoed.

'Umm. At the back of the house, breathing on it, instead of in front, guarding.'

'The dragon?'

'The dragon.'

Jade looked around the table.

'What is the dragon?' she demanded of all of them.

'They won't be able to tell you,' Stephen Norris said. '*Fungshui* is part of life here. It's geomancy, really. All to do with wind and water being in the right place. Man, the Chinese believe, can be influenced for good or evil by the site where he lives, works or is buried. Everything here is constructed so as not to disrupt the harmony of the mountains, the wind, the water and the spirits of the dragons.'

'Dragons?' Jade said again, hopelessly.

'The dragons use the mountains and hills as underpasses,' Emma explained. 'We have *fungshui* men who work with special compasses to examine the earth and find the dragon spirits and the direction of the wind and the water so they can discover the most favourable place to build.'

'It's all nonsense of course,' Stephen Norris said.

'Well, maybe,' Jimmy said. 'But if so, why do the big Hongs bring in the *fungshui* man before they even allocate and furnish offices? The Regent Hotel has the best story. It's by the harbour, Kowloon side. When they were constructing it, the *fungshui* man told the French company who own it that the lounge was where the dragon went to take his bathe in the harbour. They made the lounge all glass so as not to interrupt his view.'

Jade was shaking her head.

'Honestly,' she said. 'You sit there in your expensive clothes, drinking champagne and calling Europeans *gweilo* – and talk about the dragon as if it really exists. And you wonder why I'm confused.'

'Oh, I don't know,' Poppy said suddenly. 'Why should it be any more ridiculous to believe in the dragon than to believe that two people both born under the same star sign should have anything in common?'

Emma burst out laughing.

'But we believe that, too,' she said. 'Only we don't call them star signs.'

Jimmy Lee had brought her home. Poppy had gone on to an even later nightspot called the Godown with Kwan Ching, and Emma and Stephen had driven off in the direction of Causeway Bay in a smart little red MG. Jimmy Lee walked her back to the Mandarin – a stroll that took about five minutes. The Rolls had been left behind. It was a crisp, clear night, with a pale moon and a few galleons of clouds riding high.

'It may rain tomorrow,' he said, and again sounded as if it were a deeper pronouncement than the mere words. Then he added: 'In which case, you might like to come and see my factory.'

She had completely forgotten about the fur coats and his factory and she laughed softly.

'Selling a fur coat comes expensive,' she said, thinking of the amount of good champagne they had drunk that evening.

'Sometimes it is a pleasure,' he said, giving her a sideways look.

He escorted her into the hotel, suggested a drink in the bar which she declined.

'It has been rather a long day,' she said.

'And tomorrow?' he asked. His bright, intelligent eyes were watching her and he was half smiling.

She hesitated.

'I don't think so,' she said. 'There are things I have to do. Telephone me.'

'What things?' he asked.

'Just things,' she said vaguely.

He pursed his lips and nodded.

'I'll telephone you. Goodnight.' He nodded his head in what was almost a bow, and turned on his heel and left.

She found she was very tired as she took the lift to the eighth floor and her room. It was all she could do not to yawn loudly and openly.

And once in her bedroom, she showered quickly, wiped off her make-up and cleaned her teeth before slipping naked into bed.

The maid had put the white paper fan and the address book on the bedside table when the bed had been turned down, and she was thinking about Jimmy Lee as she picked up the address book. He was growing on her in spite of the curious uneasy-making effect he had occasionally.

Tomorrow, though, as much as she had been tempted to take up his offer, she would start tracking down her father's friends. And make arrangements to find the orphanage where she and Poppy had once lived.

'Start at the beginning,' she decided and she opened the book at 'A'.

For a moment she could not believe what she was reading. There was just one name on the page: Dorothy (Dottie) Adamson, and the address: White Gables, off Severn Road, The Peak, Hong Kong.

'My God!' she whispered to herself. 'It's not possible.'

But it had to be possible. The coincidence would be too great. She sat staring across the room at the big mirror on the wall opposite. The appalling thought struck her that if Emma was correct and Dorothy Adamson had died eight days ago, it was the same day that her father's life had ended, too.

'And what was the purpose of asking us there?' Emma asked. She was in the big double bed that dominated the small bedroom of her apartment. Scarlet sheets were pulled up under her chin, and her long hair was spread against scarlet pillows.

'He wanted people who spoke English and at least one *gweilo* about to make them feel at home,' Stephen said. His shirt was off revealing a small pot belly – caused by addiction to English beer – which he patted absently, looking at himself in the mirror. 'I ought to get back on to active duty,' he said.

'Giving out licences must be far more lucrative,' she said mockingly. 'And what do Jimmy Lee and Kwan Ching require licences for?'

'Nothing as far as I know,' he said, glaring at her as he slid down his trousers. He walked towards the bathroom in his jockey shorts, bright orange and green striped, and Emma thought again how tasteless he was, but how, for her, indispensible. For the moment.

'You mean they're not planning to start a *mah jong* school?'

'No,' he shouted.

'Nor a massage parlour, restaurant, or gymnasium specialising in the martial arts?' she said. 'I can see they aren't lion or dragon dancers, so why would a crook like Kwan Ching be cultivating a good honest policeman like you, whose only value is that you can hand out licences?'

'Maybe they are planning on becoming lion dancers,' he said sarcastically, emerging from the bathroom. 'I can just see them all dressed up leading the parade.'

'Let's hope that's all they're planning on becoming,' she said. 'Be careful, sweetheart, or you'll have the ICAC after you.'

There was a short silence, then he muttered:

'The ICAC can fuck themselves.'

'More likely they'll fuck you up,' she said.

He ignored this.

'Anyway,' he said. 'Kwan Ching is not a crook. He is a very successful businessman.'

'That's right,' she said. 'A crook.'

She was silent, thinking, as he wandered around the apartment, turning out lights, putting the chain and bolts on the front door. In the street far below, the day and night hubbub of Causeway Bay revelled on. Even double glazing could not keep out the noise, but she was used to the din. Like most Chinese who lived in the built-up parts of the Island, she never heard noise; it was as if the inhabitants grew invisible mufflers. It was only the Europeans, usually visitors, who complained; though Stephen never stopped grumbling about the noise.

Finding herself at dinner with Kwan Ching had been a surprise. His reputation was seemingly good, but Emma's business took her into clubs and restaurants that were not always as respectable as she might have wished. But business was business. She had heard talk of Kwan Ching – most of it bad.

She was puzzled as to how Stephen had met the man. And her threat about the ICAC was not idle. Since the Independent Commission Against Corruption – know locally as Interference in Chinese Ancient Customs – had arrived in Hong Kong, cleverer coppers than Stephen Norris had bitten the dust, disappeared inside the island's gaols, but mostly with their profits from bribery intact in a foreign bank. Stephen wouldn't be that smart.

She had no evidence that he was up to mischief, but it irked him

76

to live in her apartment and be subsidised by her money. He could be trying to improve his situation, and in his job it would be the easiest thing in the world.

'Anyway,' he said, as he came back into the room. 'It was Jimmy Lee who invited us. I've known him for years. His factory's on my old patch in Kowloon. And he's as straight as they come.'

'What does he do?' she asked.

'Makes furs. Green Butterfly's the company.'

'Is it now? I bought my mink there. I'd have asked for a discount if I'd known he was a friend of yours.'

'You wouldn't have got it,' he said. 'He's as tough as nails.'

'And what's he up to with the McKenzie McKenzie girls?'

'How the hell should I know? He just asked us to dinner.'

He was getting into bed, the jockey shorts left on the floor. She liked his body, even with the pot. He had strong shoulders and tough arms. His back view narrowed to a neat waist and tight-muscled buttocks. Sexually, she had never met anyone as well endowed and she found his body hair, thick, curly and light brown, exciting. Chinese men were smooth of body and straight of hair, and she even enjoyed his smell which was strong and animal-like, particularly when they were making love.

He teased her that in their hottest moments she smelled of overripe tropical fruit.

In bed, he lay flat on his back, staring at the ornate ceiling above before twisting to turn out the lamp with the dragon base. Normally he would have turned to her, taken her hand and placed it on him while he felt for her small breasts. He would have been erect and urging her to stroke him.

Tonight he did not move.

'What's the matter?' she asked. She had been anticipating the moment and was disappointed.

'Nothing.'

'In that case—' She leaned over to touch him herself. For the first few seconds he remained acquiescent, and then almost immediately he was ready. He groaned, rolled over so he could nestle at her breasts while her small fingers teased him.

What he really liked was mouth contact. He loved to bury his head between her thighs and bite and kiss her until her back was arched and she was begging him to take her properly. Curiously, he rarely kissed her mouth. She would have to ask him and only then

77

would he excite her by kissing her expertly and roughly, bruising her lips. It was having to ask him that made it arousing.

Sometimes she thought that the lovemaking was all that held them together. He was such a difficult and strange man. They had met at a cocktail party where she had gone with one of her business partners. She had left with Stephen Norris, he had taken her to dinner at a Chiu Chow restaurant where she noticed he had not paid the bill. Charitably she decided that he must have an account there, but her common sense and the reputation of the Hong Kong police told her this was unlikely.

He rarely smiled. He had a brooding quality and he was, she realised, deeply unhappy. It took time before he told her why. A year after his parents' marriage had broken he had joined the Hong Kong police as a cadet, aged eighteen, and unable to think of anything else to do.

He disliked being a policeman, but there were other misfits like himself in the force and he'd rubbed along reasonably well.

Four years later he'd gone back to the UK on leave and met a girl who had agreed to marry him and go to Hong Kong.

'I'd had a few Wanchai chickens and the odd *yu daan* massage,' he had told her, 'but I was pretty inexperienced sexually.'

'*Yu daan*?' she had said, puzzled. *Yu daan* was a fish dumpling, for soup, made by hand in the markets. He had hesitated to reply and then realisation dawned on her. 'Ah, yes,' she said, remembering how the manufacturing process resembled the petting act.

'My wife, I discovered, was a lot more experienced than I was,' he told her. 'She was four years older for a start.

'And then I discovered her affairs. Lots of them. She even went off with one of the Chinese station sergeants and got herself pregnant. Do you know what an abortion costs here? No? Well it's 2,500 Hong Kong dollars. Two hundred and fifty pounds. It was lucky that the station sergeant was deep into corruption. He could afford it. I couldn't.

'Anyway, the marriage staggered on for about ten years, and then she managed to snaffle a bloke who'd come out here for a short time. She went back to the UK with him, and what happened to her after that, Christ knows. That was five years ago now.'

The result had been to screw him up sexually, she discovered the first time they went to bed. He made love to her as though she were a Wanchai tart. And in order to satisfy him, she had to learn quickly just how the *yu daan* massage was performed. There was no other way. At first.

Because she found him physically exciting, and because she had felt angry for the way his life had gone, she had decided to turn him into a good lover and a contented one.

She had succeeded almost too well. Their physical life was now near perfect, but he had became deeply suspicious of her past and jealous of her future. He questioned her endlessly; probing as to who her previous lovers had been and what they had done to her. She only had to experiment and caress him in a different way for him to think that a new man had taught her.

Sometimes she was bewildered at her own perversity in carrying on what could only be a doomed affair with a man who could offer her nothing. Her family were shocked and dismayed that she had taken up with a *gweilo*. Her mother said, tight-lipped, it was just as well her father was not alive to see the day. But she knew that she must let the affair runs its course. The deities would decide the outcome, not her nor him.

He had his head between her thighs now, his hands stretched to clasp at her breasts. In a minute he would take her, and she would choose the position. She tried to vary their love-making so that he was never bored; often surprised. Now as he came up to lie alongside her, she rolled over on to her stomach, hunched herself on to her knees and presented her narrow backside to him. He was not a lot taller than her, and he knelt behind her, opening her legs then slid deep into her. He rode her fiercely as she crouched below him, her head in the pillows, his hands tugging at her nipples. She could hear her own little gasps of near-pain and pleasure and in the mounting crescendo it was suddenly all over for both of them.

He stayed kneeling behind her for a moment, his arms around her, and then they both rolled together to lie curled into each other on the bed.

'That was good,' she murmured, thinking of how much had changed in the six months they had been together.

'You are good,' he said. 'And I love you.'

'And I love you.' She told him, her head on his shoulder.

Normally he would fall instantly asleep after their lovemaking, but tonight he was restless beside her.

'What *is* the matter, Steve?' she finally asked him, gently stroking the thick hair on his chest.

79

He was still for a short while and then he said abruptly: 'The ICAC *are* investigating me.'

She sat up and stared down at him in the striped neon light that came through the shutters.

'What about?'

'I don't know exactly. It can't be anything too serious. I haven't done anything serious. In the past, before you, the odd massage I didn't pay for. Today the odd meal I don't pay for. Nothing else. But someone's informed on me.'

'How do you know?' Her voice was anxious.

'Kwan Ching told me. He has his own contacts. He said not to worry and if anything went wrong, he had a job for me.'

'What sort of job?'

'I don't know. I didn't ask. I was too shattered by what he had said.'

She thought for a minute.

'He probably informed,' she said. 'The little shit. It would be in character if he wants you for something. Can the ICAC prove anything?'

He sat up and lit a cigarette from the packet on the bedside table.

'I don't see how,' he said. 'There's so little to prove anyway. I've never taken cash, a cheque or a bribe, I've always figured it wasn't worth it. The free meals I've given them help for – just letting them know well in advance when the health inspector was coming and things like that. Nothing serious. But I suppose they could make a case out of it if they wanted to.'

'And what would that mean?'

'Investigation, interrogation, prosecution and then probably dismissal.'

She lay down again and stared at the ceiling.

'How many restaurants are involved?'

'Only two. The one I took you to that first night and that Peking House in Tsim Sha Tsui.'

'Will they rat on you?'

'I don't think so. I consider them friends.'

She thought about it. It was possible they considered him a friend, too. Stephen was one of the very few British police officers who spoke good Cantonese. He said he learned it from the tarts in Wanchai, but nevertheless the fact he could talk to the Chinese in their own language would give him an advantage. But not that much of a one.

'Suppose I went to those restaurants tomorrow and said I'd come to pay your account, and asked for a receipt and a series of bills?' she said. 'Would that help? Really pay them, I mean. Act as if you did actually have credit accounts with them?'

'It might be worth a try,' he said.

'I don't see it can do any harm,' she said. 'But I'm damned if I'm paying the massage girls.'

He gave a short, barking laugh.

'I doubt if that will be a consideration. The ICAC aren't into protecting whores.'

She tugged gently at his thick curly pubic hair.

'Well, now stop worrying,' she said. 'There's nothing we can do tonight. So sleep, darling. We'll sort it out somehow.'

Eventually his breathing slowed, and he began to snore gently while she lay, wide-awake.

The thought that was suppressing sleep was Kwan Ching and what it was exactly he had in mind for Stephen to do.

≈ 6 ≈

SATURDAY

Jade left it until nearly ten o'clock the next morning before she rang Poppy. She was fairly sure that her sister would have come back to the hotel very late, if at all. She herself had woken at eight thirty and plotted what to do with the day. The chilling coincidence of the late Dottie Adamson had caused her to regard the address book as if it might open up and bite her. She decided, instead, to find the orphanage where she and Poppy had been taken as babies.

She found the letter from Miss Tibbets in the document case she had brought with her and checked the address. It was at somewhere called Fanling, but there was no street name. Jade telephoned the concierge to find out where the place was and how to get there. And then she rang Poppy.

To her surprise Poppy answered the phone immediately.

'So maddening,' she grumbled, 'I couldn't sleep. I woke up terribly early. Jet lag, I suppose. I was just about to ring you. I'm bored stiff. Can we go shopping? Kwan says Hong Kong is a shopping paradise. He's given me all the names of the best places to go to. The Gucci here, he says, is almost half price.'

Jade sighed. 'I thought we might find the orphanage where Father and Mother found us.'

There was a pause.

'Why do you want to do that?' Poppy asked slowly.

'For heaven's sake,' Jade said. 'Do you ever think of anything except Gucci, Pucci and Fiorucci? Aren't you interested in your own origins?'

'Not really,' Poppy said, her voice cool.

'Well, you go shopping. I'm going to Fanling,' Jade said angrily.

'Fanling? Where is it?'

'In the New Territories. Beyond Kowloon.'

'You're very knowledgeable about the geography.'

'I've been talking to the concierge. They sent me up a map.'

Poppy was quiet again for a short moment.

'You're definitely going?' she finally asked.

'Definitely,' Jade said.

'All right. I'll come with you. When do we leave?'

'Almost immediately, if you're ready,' Jade said. 'There's a train from Kowloon Station at four minutes past eleven. We should be able to catch that.'

'Ok,' Poppy said. 'See you in the lobby in five minutes.'

They both arrived almost simultaneously to leave their keys; Jade just a beat ahead of Poppy.

'Now what?' Poppy asked as they went out into the street. It was a gusty morning, with weak sunshine and no sign of the rain that Jimmy Lee had predicted. But then he did not look like the kind of man who would be in tune with the elements, Jade thought. There was nothing peasant about *him*.

'We cross on the ferry to Kowloon and then we get a taxi to the station,' she said, deliberately switching her mind from Jimmy Lee.

82

'Can't we take Jimmy Lee's Rolls?'

'It's not worth it. Apparently it takes longer. And besides, I don't think we should be beholden to him.'

'I don't see why not,' Poppy said with a shrug, but didn't argue.

The Star Ferry was right across the road from the hotel and they used the underpass below the busy Connaught Road to get into the terminal. They joined what seemed a multitude of people pressing towards the pay turnstiles.

'Wall-to-wall people,' Poppy muttered.

A green-painted ferry boat, named *Morning Star*, was waiting. They pushed on board and settled themselves on the wooden bench seats looking towards Kowloon on the other shore. A Chinese sailor with white stars on his broad collar let out the ropes, and the ferry slid in a businesslike way out into the harbour. The boat was crowded with only the faintest sprinkling of Europeans. Chinese businessmen, mothers and babies, students and peasants sat or stood, ignoring the view in order to study the morning paper or engage each other in conversation, waiting for the brief journey to be over.

The view was spectacular. Jade turned to look behind when they were out into the wide channel and grabbed Poppy's arm.

'Look behind,' she said.

Poppy turned.

'Wow!' she said, impressed. 'It is amazing, isn't it?'

Behind were hundreds of pointing skyscrapers, a scene that reduced Manhattan, set in blue sea with green mountains behind rising even higher than the buildings.

'It's astonishing,' Jade said.

She twisted round to look behind while the ferry chugged on past harbour junks and sailing craft, all threading their way with confidence through the straits.

The passengers were all spilled out at Ocean Terminal in a pushing, hurrying mass up a broad walkway to the ferry terminal hall. There Jade said to the man who guarded the turnstile: 'Taxi?'

He answered in a clatter of Cantonese.

'We don't understand,' Poppy said cheerfully. 'Can you speak English?'

The man half-smiled at her pert little face.

'American?' he asked.

'No, English.' Poppy said.

'You want tour?'

'No – just a taxi, please,' Jade said firmly.

'Ok,' the man said on a falling note of resignation. 'You go round across road. Taxis and buses all there.'

It was just ten fifteen when they arrived at Kowloon station where they had a nasty coffee at the cafeteria that looked down over the station concourse. Then Jade said perhaps they should buy their tickets. Down below she could see a growing queue for the booking office. Whole families were bunched together between the two barriers that kept everyone in line. Bundles tied up in what appeared to be brightly coloured tablecloths were scattered over the tiled floors. Newcomers to the queue arrived with their bundles on bambooo sticks hung across their shoulders, which they kept in balance by an odd little shambling run.

Most of the women were in dark jackets and baggy trousers; the men in jeans and sweatshirts or short-sleeved shirts. The faces, seamed and prematurely old, were different from those around the hotel. This was, Jade realised, what she had expected Hong Kong to be.

'We should have gone in the Rolls,' Poppy said petulantly. 'It's going to be awful.'

Jade did not reply. She paid for the coffee and together they walked down the stairs into the booking hall.

'Why doesn't the queue move?' Poppy said, her voice impatient, after they had stood for a few minutes.

Jade peered ahead. 'The ticket office isn't open.'

The queue was lengthening behind them, spilling the length of the station, and the noise was growing. No one seemed to speak in normal tones. Jade had the impression that everyone in the station was only able to conduct a conversation at the top of their lungs.

It was a long wait. At well gone half-past ten the wooden window of the office flew up and two Chinese began selling tickets.

'Two returns to Fanling,' Jade said when they reached the head of the queue.

The train was waiting down an escalator, sitting alongside the platform in a tunnel. Here the noise, captured, was even louder. Transistors blared, and the shouting voices reverberated. The

84

carriages were already packed and it was a long walk before they found two empty wooden seats side by side. The train was old fashioned and not too clean, high ceilinged, with outdated metal fans hanging useless.

'Those people behind us will never find anywhere to sit,' Poppy said. 'Where do you think they're all going?'

'The train goes right to the Chinese border,' Jade said. 'Maybe they're going there for Chinese New Year. They look as if they are carrying food and presents.'

'They look as if they're carrying their homes!' Poppy said. 'What day is it?'

'Saturday.'

'Umm. Weekend.' Poppy looked at their neighbours. 'Bit different from last night,' she remarked. 'As I said, we should have taken the Rolls. Or hired a taxi.'

'I think it's interesting,' Jade said defensively.

'You wouldn't think it interesting to be on a football special to Manchester,' Poppy said. 'I reckon this is much the same. How long does the journey take?'

'Only an hour.'

Poppy groaned.

The hawkers arrived before the train had left the station, trading from plastic buckets full of chewing gum, toothpaste, cosmetics, umbrellas, strange orange-coloured food which could have been either fish or fowl or even red meat. An old woman in a tunic and trousers staggered under the weight of two buckets full of oranges.

'What are we going to do about lunch?' Poppy asked, thoughtfully regarding a bucket full of chicken's feet which appeared to have been dipped in orange breadcrumbs and deep-fried.

'We'll find something,' Jade said absently. 'Are you hungry?'

'Not at the moment. We ate again last night, at the Godown place.'

'What was it like?' Jade was conscious of making conversation.

'Tacky, but fun. Full of European blokes with Chinese girls.' Her voice sounded self-righteous.

'And what's wrong with that?'

'Apparently it's not done here.'

'Really,' Jade said, her tone sarcastic. 'What about Chinese blokes with European girls?'

'How should I know?' Poppy said.

The train had left the suburbs and came into green fields, speckled with what appeared to be small market gardens. Here and there were sudden azure flashes of blue as the sea appeared.

'What time did you get home?' Jade asked.

'Late,' Poppy said and shut her mouth into a trap. 'We talked about Grandfather rather a lot. Kwan's in shipping in a small way. He wants to be bigger. He's a great admirer of Grandfather. Of course, he's never met him – too young – but he says that McKenzie McKenzie is still the most influential of the shipping businesses here.'

'What sort of shipping is Kwan in, then?' Jade asked.

'I don't know. I didn't gather. But obviously he's very rich. His apartment . . .' She stopped dead, and Jade remembered how Grandfather had remarked that Poppy said whatever came into her head, without thinking. She had given the game away there.

Poppy, realising her mistake, changed the subject.

'Do you know where this orphanage is?' she asked.

Jade could not resist saying: 'Showing some interest at last?' Poppy did not reply and she went on: 'I only know it's in Fanling. But it must be a tiny little village – it's so near China. We won't have trouble finding it. The orphanage was run by a Miss Eleanor Tibbets when we were taken there.'

'How long were we there?'

'I don't know. I expect Miss Tibbets will tell us.'

'I suppose it's a good idea?' Poppy was frowning.

'What?'

'Poking about in our past. I mean we could have been like that . . .' She indicated a girl about their age wearing torn jeans and a striped tee-shirt who sat, her transistor to her ear, her expression vacant. She had a huge striped plastic bag on her lap, tatty clothing spilling out of the top.

Jade gave her a dismissive look.

'We could also have been dead,' she said crisply. 'We could have been living in China. Anything could have happened. I want to see where we started.'

'It would have been better to have gone shopping,' Poppy said, and they both fell silent, watching the countryside as the train trundled along.

They passed through Sha Tin, an extraordinary skyscraper city in the middle of a dusty yellow cloud. Then the the train stopped at

Tai Po Kau and Tai Po Market, two old Asiatic towns, suffering development scars. 'The next stop is Fanling,' Jade said.

As the train began to slow they saw to the right of the railway track what seemed to be hundreds of rough wooden huts, crammed with people, their furniture and cooking equipment spilling out into the narrow passageways between the rows. Old women sat on decrepit chairs in the sunshine; children flocked like starlings. A kneeling woman cooked in a wok over a kerosene stove; men in torn jeans and old-fashioned vests stood in groups gossiping.

'Is that Fanling?' Poppy said, horrified.

'I don't know.' Jade stared out of the window as the wooden slums went inexorably on, each gangway numbered in grim prison lettering.

'It's frightful,' Poppy said. 'Quite frightful.' And repeated, her voice fretful, 'We should have gone shopping.'

Suddenly the huts petered to an end and the train was pulling slowly into the station. The two girls climbed down the high steps from the train to the platform, and Jade noted that higher up the train, people were hanging from the windows and clinging from the footplates. Why didn't they walk through to where it was less crowded? she thought, irritated by the stupidity.

'Why are they so accepting?' she said crossly.

'Because they are Chinese, like you, dear sister. Look who's talking. You're one of life's accepters yourself,' Poppy said, half mocking.

'Oh, for God's sake . . .' Jade muttered.

In the street outside the station, the squalor of the huts was not visible, and they walked in warming sunshine into what appeared to be a pleasant and modern little town.

'Which way?' said Poppy sullenly when they reached a round-about. There were three roads from which to choose.

'We'll ask someone down there,' Jade said, pointing ahead.

'Who? Her?' Poppy said sarcastically, pointing at an old woman crouched on the grass verge, her head covered by a huge straw hat with what looked like a frilled pelmet hanging round the brim.

'We'll find someone,' Jade said, conscious of being conciliatory. It occurred to her that this whole rush trip to the East had perhaps not been sensible. They should have found out about the place. Read a little, bought maps; planned what they would do. She had done everything wrong. She should have asked someone about the orphanage before they set off this morning; found the correct address. Now they were in a small town, not far from China, where it was unlikely anyone would speak English. And Poppy was sulking, her pretty mouth compressed into a tight, angry line.

The road they walked along was bordered by a little stream with another unmade road behind. On a small patch of grass beside the stream two cows with their two calves lay idly chewing.

'Look at that,' Poppy suddenly said.

Across the road was a strange building. It was obviously a church and designed to be severe, but the Oriental temperament had taken over and on what was a basic no-nonsense chapel edifice were odd knobs and curlicues. There was a garden with a centrepiece of a Christian Christmas tree, still hung with presents. From inside the building came the soaring voices of a choir, singing what sounded like a faintly remembered hymn.

'Someone there will speak English,' Jade said, and set off across the road, her sister following behind.

Tentatively she went up the path to the church and climbed the few steps to the arched entrance. On the walls inside were pinned children's chalk and crayon drawings and as she stood hesitating, a young Chinese wearing a black suit appeared. He spoke to her in Cantonese.

She lifted her hands.

'I'm sorry,' she said. 'I don't understand. Do you speak English?'

'Indeed,' he said with a smile. 'Forgive me. I should have guessed you must be ABCs.'

'ABCs?' she said. 'No. I'm afraid I still don't understand.'

'Not American-born Chinese?' he asked.

'No. We were born here, but we were brought up in Britain,' she said. 'Would that make us BBCs?'

He laughed and turned to look at Poppy appreciatively.

'You are sisters?' he asked.

'Yes,' said Poppy.

'We're looking for the orphanage where we were when we were babies,' Jade said. 'We know it's in Fanling. It's called the Home of Those Who Care. It's run by a lady called Miss Tibbets.'

A group of healthy teenagers with an air of prosperity had appeared from inside the building to stand behind him, and he turned and spoke to them quickly in Chinese, obviously explaining.

'I'm so sorry,' he said eventually, 'but the orphanage does not exist any more. It closed sometime in the early 1970s. The flood of refugees from over the border became controlled at that time. Miss Tibbets' supply of children ended.'

Jade felt a searing disappointment.

'Oh,' she said. 'And Miss Tibbets?'

The man must have seen her dismay.

'She went away,' he said gently. 'To where, I don't know.'

'And the home?' Jade asked.

'It still exists. It is about two miles from here.' He hesitated. 'I could take you, but it may be a sadness for you. It is nearly derelict now. Perhaps it would be better not to see it.'

'I'd like to,' Poppy said suddenly. 'Would you really take us?'

The thin angry line had gone from her mouth and she was at her most winsome, smiling at the young minister.

He nodded. 'Our choir practice is finished,' he said. 'If you will excuse me for the moment I must get the chapel in order. Will you come in or would you prefer to sit in our garden?'

'We'll sit in the garden,' Poppy said. 'By your Christmas tree. You're Christian?'

'Baptist,' he said. 'And you?'

'Church of England, I suppose,' Jade said doubtfully. 'Or maybe Church of Scotland. Nothing really.'

'Perhaps your parents felt they would let you choose when you were ready,' he said, then with a murmured 'excuse me' he went back into the chapel.

'What an attractive young man,' Poppy said, watching him.

Jade looked at her despairingly. 'For God's sake, Poppy . . .' she began. 'You're not . . .'

'No, I'm not,' Poppy interrupted. 'I just think he's nice, that's all.

The young people were leaving the chapel and nodding 'goodbyes' as they left. And a minute or two later, the minister reappeared, dressed in jeans and a lightweight pale blue sweater.

'I should introduce myself,' he said. 'I'm Paul So.'

'I'm Jade, and that's Poppy—'

'McKenzie McKenzie Martin,' Poppy added.

'My goodness!' Paul So said. 'The shipping family?'

'That's right,' Jade said. 'Ian McKenzie McKenzie is our adoptive grandfather.'

'The daughter, Margaret, adopted you?' he asked. He was leading them back into the street.

'Yes.'

'From the Home of Those Who Care—' He shook his head. 'How extraordinary. You must have been children of refugees.'

'We don't know,' Jade said. 'That's what I wanted to find out.' Her voice trailed away.

'Well,' he said kindly, 'it's not impossible. Maybe I'll be able to find Miss Tibbets for you. The Baptists in Hong Kong gave her a lot of financial help with her work. Someone may know where she is.'

He had stopped in the street by an ancient brown Mini. 'Not very grand,' he said. 'But it will get us there.'

'I drive one at home,' Jade said quickly.

He looked faintly disbelieving, but smiled again. He smiled an awful lot, she thought. It was unexpected. One of the things she had noticed about the people they had met was how rarely anyone seemed to smile.

'It's quite a way down this road and into the country,' he said. 'In just a minute we'll go past the Luen Wo Market. You should stop there before you go back to Hong Kong. It's very – well – Chinese. Your Miss Tibbets was a familiar figure there in the 1950s and 60s. She used to come down and shop for her children. She carried a huge straw basket and she'd fight and bargain with the shopkeepers like any country woman. A difficult lady she was. Not too good tempered. Very fierce. Very strong. I remember her well.'

They had passed the market and a small area of houses where a temple with dragons guarding the roof dominated the road, and they were now into open country.

'Who were all those people living in huts at the side of the railway?' Jade asked suddenly.

His face clouded.

'Squatters,' he said. 'Waiting for rehousing. They may wait for years.'

'It's the most awful slum,' Poppy said from the back seat.

'But better than they could have expected in China,' he said. 'That's why so many still try to come. Mostly illegally.' Poppy was listening to him attentively and asked: 'Were you born here?'

'Yes, and my parents before me.'

'Were they Christians too?'

'Yes. Converted by missionaries.'

'Then what is the religion here?' Jade asked.

'Taoist. Or Buddhist – imported from India. A little bit of

everything. Most Chinese hedge their bets, as you call it. Most are pagans.' He said the word disapprovingly.

'Is *fungshui* part of the religion?' Jade asked, remembering the conversation of the previous night.

'Oh, no,' he said. 'That's a science.'

'I see,' she said and lapsed into a puzzled silence as the car bounced on down the road.

Gradually the buildings petered out and a lone structure appeared in a wooded area on the left. It stood deserted, a tall brick wall around it, with only the curving roof visible from the road. Tall trees, green and leafy, surrounded the building. It was set a few feet back, and Paul parked the car against the wall. There was no pavement here, and they walked to the big iron gates up a short pebbled path.

'That's it, the Home of Those Who Care, but I'm afraid it's not in very good shape,' he said apologetically.

They peered through the fretwork of the gates which were held together with a huge padlock. In front, there was a pebble path that ran for a few yards before curving to follow the contours of a large round fish-pond set in front of the house. Then the path met again at the other side where a flight of elegant steps led to a large verandah and two imposing but rotting wooden doors supported by stone columns. Above the front door was a balcony, large enough to take a salute, and the roof had the Chinese curls and dips, while dragons and tigers were carved in *bas-relief* around the stone of the balcony.

In front of the pool there was a thick privet hedge which divided the garden into two, crossways.

'Maybe someone's about,' Paul So said, and pulled the chain of a large bell that hung inside the gates.

'No, don't . . .' Poppy said, her voice strangled. She was clutching Jade's arm, and she was trembling, her face pale ivory and a thin line of perspiration over her top lip. 'No, don't. Don't go in. There are snakes, I remember. I know there are snakes.'

'Poppy, what is it?' Jade said, clutching her sister's shaking hands and holding them tight. 'What's the matter?'

'I'm afraid of this place. I remember it. I've seen it in the dreams. I don't want to go inside,' she said, her voice hysterical. 'Don't ring the bell. The snakes are black and gold and we were frightened. They killed them with sticks. They didn't bleed . . .' She tore her hands from Jade's and covered her face.

'Poppy – it was only a dream,' Jade said. 'You couldn't remember anything about this place. You were too little.'

Paul So moved forward and wrapped his arms around the girl. He held her very tight and close and just said: 'There, there. It was a dream. There are no snakes. I promise you.'

Poppy was calming a little when suddenly two dogs came running inside the gates. A variety of hound, they were liver-coloured with white spots and barking loudly. Behind them came a small Chinese woman in trousers and jacket.

'*Haih?*' she said.

'*Neih hou ma?*' Paul said, and continued talking rapidly, his arm still around Poppy.

The woman nodded, said something and looked sympathetically at the girls, then fished in the pocket of her jacket. She took out a huge bunch of keys and, carefully selecting the correct one, opened the padlock. Then solemnly she beckoned them in.

'She is a caretaker. I told her you were both at the orphanage here, and she says you are welcome to see the place.'

The woman was speaking again, quickly. Paul So listened, nodding.

'She says it is in bad shape because they have been making a kung-fu film in the house and not cleared up. Also some very dirty Thai's have lived here with their dogs. You must not be upset by the mess.'

'I don't think I want to go in,' Poppy was saying shakily.

'It will appease the spirits and the dreams will go away,' he said. 'Don't be afraid. There is nothing to be afraid of.'

Holding his hand very tightly, Poppy went through the gates. As they neared the pond, suddenly Jade recognised the view. There were the hedge and the flight of steps that were in the picture she had found of them both as children. The exterior of the house had hardly changed at all. She had never shown Poppy the picture, and now she opened her handbag and undid the zip at the back where she had put her father's letter to Miss Tibbets and Miss Tibbets' reply. With them was the photograph. Silently she took it out and handed it to Poppy, who took it and looked at it bewildered.

'Turn it over,' Jade said.

Poppy did so and read out loud: 'Jade aged seventeen months(?) and Poppy aged three months(?).'

Then she burst into tears.

Poppy wept quietly as they wandered through the house, but it had no message for Jade. It was large, with big high-ceilinged rooms that had been painted in powder-blue paint, now peeling off. The shutters hung loose; most of the windows were cracked or broken. Someone, probably the kung-fu film team, had put coloured cellophane over the windows which was peeling off in strips. The floors were filthy with animal ordure.

Inside, it was dark and cool. There were two fine staircases, but no kitchen or bathrooms. The only sign of running water seemed to be a tap on the narrow balcony that ran around the house and joined up with the large front balcony where stone-carved tigers snarlingly regarded the garden below.

The garden must have been beautiful. Now it had run wild.

'Those are lychee trees, and mangoes,' Paul So said, pointing. His other hand still held Poppy's, who was now crying in deep sobs.

With a wave of her hand she dismissed the trees. 'I can't bear to think we ever lived here,' she said.

'But it was not like this,' Paul So said gently. 'I was only a child myself, but I remember it as a happy place. Sometimes we village children would come here to play. It was different then.'

Jade was silent. She wished she could remember something of the place, but there was no sense of *déjà vu*, not one memory she could dredge up as they walked back to the gates. The house, the gardens meant nothing. She found it difficult to believe she had ever been here before. She could not understand why the effect had been so much more dramatic for Poppy. Maybe because Poppy had been frightened here, she decided.

The woman was waving them goodbye and speaking, smiling.

'What is she saying?' Jade asked.

'She wants you to come back when the lychees are in fruit. They are very good lychees, she says, and far too many for her.'

'Ask her if there are snakes in the garden,' Poppy said suddenly.

He spoke to the woman in Cantonese and she replied.

'She says sometimes,' he said.

'Are they black and gold?'

The woman answered a firm, quick *haih*.

'Yes,' said Paul.

Poppy sighed, long and deep.

'I knew it,' she said. 'I remembered right.'

She was sitting in the front seat of the car, her shoulders rigid, hands clasped in her lap, when suddenly she began to talk, her voice a rambling monotone as Paul put the key into the ignition.

'It's the place of the dreams, Jade,' she said. 'All those terrible dreams. All those nightmares when I was little. Do you remember? I used to cry and scream in the night and Kirsty or Mother used to come and try to quieten me. The dreams never went away, and when I was little I couldn't explain what they were. There was always noise and slant-eyed people. Bad people, I thought they were. It was years before I realised I had the same eyes myself. Then there was the snake dream. That came again and again in the night. This big black and gold snake, curled on the grass with water behind. It made a big circle, like a tyre, but its head was up waving, with little eyes and a spitting forked tongue. I knew it was danger-ous and someone must kill it. Then there was noise and sticks banging and people crying out and the snake was dead with its head lying separated from its body, but its tongue still flickered, and all the coils of its body writhed. It wouldn't die. It didn't want to die.

'I was always frightened when I was little, Jade. You were different. I was afraid they'd go away and I'd be alone. I had these dreams where everyone had vanished. There was no one at all. Only me, and I was cold and frightened. I knew everyone but me was dead. I couldn't bear it when mother went away in those days. Suppose she didn't come back? What would we do? I was never secure like you. I was always scared, so I was naughty. I made myself the centre of everything and I thought they'd love me more then, but they always loved you best, really. You were the good one. And I never felt you loved me. You were always disdainful when I was naughty, even when you were only a little girl. I wanted you to love me, because you were *me*. You looked like me. We were real sisters. We ought to have belonged to each other, because we didn't really belong to them, or to anybody else. We were the outsiders. But you never seemed to feel you were an outsider. You knew how to fit in. Nobody ever really loved me. Nobody ever has. And look at me in that picture, Jade – I was so ugly. How could anyone have loved me?'

Paul had not started the engine of the car. He sat quietly, his head bowed, and Jade began to cry, silently, fishing in her handbag for a Kleenex. She handed one across the seat to Poppy and leaned forward to wrap her arms around her sister. She laid her head on Poppy's shoulder and said: 'I didn't understand. I didn't realise you were unhappy. I'm sorry, Poppy. Please don't cry. Don't be upset.'

They were both quiet, and Jade felt she was closer to Poppy than she had ever been in her life. And the need to explain herself was very strong.

'You see, I thought they loved you best,' she said. 'You were prettier than me. How can you say you were ugly? And when you cried and screamed in the night, they all ran to you and no one took any notice of me. And I always had to look after you. It was always "watch Poppy, see she doesn't fall, see she doesn't hurt herself, see she's a good girl". I felt no one cared if I fell or hurt myself or wasn't a good girl, but I wasn't going to let them see. But it made me feel responsible and that I belonged. I knew you were the changeling, the little princess who had to be indulged. You were the stranger, but I thought you liked it that way because you never tried to be like me or even them. I was trying to make them love me in my way by being good and obedient. You were always yourself. I was jealous of you, Poppy.'

'But I was jealous of you—' her sister wailed on such a despairing note that Jade couldn't help but laugh. And the choked little sound made Poppy laugh too.

Jade took her arms from her sister's neck.

'Well,' she said, sniffing. 'I don't know. Why didn't we say all that years ago?'

Paul suddenly spoke. 'Because it wasn't the moment,' he said.

'Does it mean we'll like each other now?' Poppy asked him, sounding like a child.

He laughed.

'Probably not. That may take longer. But you've both made a start.'

Jade was blowing her nose.

'I'm sorry we involved you in all this,' she said to him. 'You just give us a lift and find yourself in the middle of a family drama.'

He didn't say anything, but made a gesture round his neck in the shape of a dog collar.

'Yes, but you are off duty,' Jade said, with a gulping laugh.

'I'm never off duty,' he said. 'Now come.' He started the car engine. 'You need food. I'll take you to the market for some lunch and then put you back on your train.'

He walked them through the narrow streets where toothless shopkeepers sold strange and pungent-smelling dried herbs and spices and where brilliantly coloured stalls of fresh vegetables tempted. The shops spilled into the street and many of the things on sale were totally unfamiliar to Jade. He took them into a scruffy small restaurant filled with noisy men where they ate food about whose origins Jade thought it best not to enquire too deeply. It was a restaurant they would never have dreamed of entering alone and in fact the food was delicious.

Then he left them at the railway station.

'I shall be in touch,' he said. 'I will find Miss Tibbets for you. It's time your ghosts were laid for ever, Poppy. Miss Tibbets is the one to do that.'

They shook hands, and with a backward wave he went back to the car, leaving them to wait for the train.

Jade was both surprised and delighted when she felt Poppy's hand slide into hers as they stood on the platform. But she realised that now after what had happened she simply could not explain that in truth they weren't related at all.

Standing on the platform at Fanling, Poppy felt the most extra-ordinary sense of peace. She understood her own nature well enough to know that it would not last, but for the time being she had a feeling of having been reborn. She felt a warmth of affection for Jade that she had not known for years. It was Jade who had brought her here and who had been responsible for beginning to lay her ghosts, as Paul So had called them. She had a sense, also, of having come home – which, indeed, she had. She felt comfortable, as if her skin fitted her properly. She belonged. Paul So had liked her, accepted her, been kind to her, as had Kwan Ching. She knew that Jade was convinced that she had been to bed with him, but she had not. He had taken her back to his flat and talked to her. It was as if he had been helping her to catch up on her education as an Oriental. He had given her little tips – telling her not to smile too much. It was rude to smile at strangers, he explained. They might think you were laughing at them. It was best, too, to hide your feelings and never say too much.

He had poured her two oversized and magnificent brandies and then he had driven her back to the hotel in a large black Mercedes and arranged to meet her again. He would show her Hong Kong, he said, the real Hong Kong that the tourist never saw.

She could see that Jade had been thrown by her transfer from the

Occident to the Orient. While her skin now fitted, Jade's had become uncomfortable; too tight and unfamiliar. She felt a surge of sympathy for her sister and slid her hand into hers.

Jade's expression of surprise and pleasure touched her. It *was* a pity they had not been closer.

They stood silent until the train trundled in and, once on board, Jade began to talk.

'Why do you think we were told so little about this place?' she said. 'What possible reason could Mother and Father have for keeping us so ignorant?'

'I suppose they wanted to pretend we were really theirs,' Poppy said. 'Don't all people who adopt children do that?'

'I don't know.' Jade sat frowning slightly and staring ahead as a transitor blared behind them. 'Aren't these people *noisy*,' she said with a sigh. 'No. I think there was another reason. Why was Grandfather so angry when I told him we were coming here? And then the papers—' her voice trailed away, and Poppy, who knew her sister better than her sister suspected, thought: She's hiding something.

'What papers?'

Jade looked uncomfortable.

'The picture I showed you of us, and the paper that said we weren't the children of the interpreter.'

'Ah, yes. Can I see that?'

'I haven't got it with me,' Jade said, too quickly. 'And other papers. About a ship disappearing, and a murder.'

Poppy felt her own curiosity prickle.

'A missing ship and a murder?'

'I'll show you.'

She watched as Jade carefully went into the zip compartment of her handbag and brought out two photocopies of newspaper cuttings which she handed over.

With the train joggling, she read both.

'And these were with the paper about us?' she said, certain that Jade had that paper too. She was going to have to get into Jade's handbag when she wasn't looking.

'Yes,' Jade said.

'Perhaps they don't mean anything. Perhaps they're just two cases that Father tried.'

'I think they are. But he must have tried hundreds of cases. Why keep them?'

Poppy shrugged.

'There was also an address book with all Hong Kong names and addresses,' Jade said. She paused, then went on: 'Something very odd happened last night. Do you remember they were talking about a murder, and that the house had bad *fungshui*?'

Poppy nodded.

'Well, the woman who was murdered, Dorothy Adamson, was the first name in Daddy's address book. And if that girl, Emma, had it right, she was killed on the same day as Daddy was run over. And, if you remember, she was murdered with broken scissors, just like in that other story about the Chinese all killing each other.'

Listening to her, Poppy thought how funny it was that Jade hadn't come to terms with being Chinese at all. She still kept herself separate, trying to belong to the world they had left behind. I ought to tell her, Poppy decided, but said instead: 'What do you think it all means?'

'I don't know,' Jade said hopelessly. 'Even Miss Tibbets isn't there any more. But I'm going to see all the other people in that address book and see if I can find out.'

'Find out what?' The mention of Miss Tibbets had taken Poppy back to those terrifying and yet cleansing minutes at the derelict home. 'It would be nice to find out where we came from and who we are. Do you think Miss Tibbets will know?'

Jade fidgeted uncomfortably.

'Maybe,' she said. 'Anyway, the whole thing is probably nonsense and a figment of my imagination.'

Poppy shut herself off from the din of the train around her and thought over what Jade had said. Finally she made her pronouncement.

'We'll just have to go and see all the other people in Daddy's book,' she said, 'and find out whether it's imagination or not.'

She sounded very positive, but her mind was really on her meeting with Kwan Ching.

He was waiting for her in the Captain's Bar when she came down from her room at seven thirty that evening. They had arrived back in Hong Kong at just after five, and she had made the time to go out and buy something special to wear. In a shop in the arcade that was part of the Mandarin Hotel, she had found a white shantung silk *cheong-sam*, delicately embroidered in white beads. And she had also bought a Chinese wedding coat. Embroidered with writhing dragons and snarling tigers on brilliant red silk, it weighed a ton and looked a million, she thought. The English salesgirl with the Roedean accent, recognising one of her own kind, had explained its history.

'All Chinese wedding clothes are red,' she had explained. 'The real Chinese think bad spirits are frightened of red. These coats are becoming rarer and rarer. So few women can do the embroidery any more.'

'That's why it costs £250, I suppose,' Poppy had said.

'Exactly,' the English girl laughed, 'but it's something that will last you all your life.'

Poppy wore the coat over the dress with the highest-heeled, strappiest white shoes she had, and she was conscious that every head in the hotel turned as she walked by. She had twisted her thick black hair high and held it in place with combs in a style that was nearly Japanese. She knew she looked special and she felt special, too.

His eyes had opened as she came to the table where he waited. The Captain's Bar was busy, but a little hush fell momentarily as she crossed the dance floor to join him where he sat at the back of the room. He already had an ice bucket on the table, and she was pleased to see that the distinctive Dom Perignon bottle nestled in it. The new, Oriental Poppy deserved only the best, she told herself.

'Good evening,' she said demurely as she reached him. He stood to greet her, and she thought he looked good in his dark dinner jacket. He was not quite smiling, but she could see he was impressed.

'You are getting married?' he asked.

'Not tonight,' she said. 'But it's beautiful, isn't it?'

'Very,' he said gravely. 'You must keep it safe for its real purpose.'

She wondered uneasily for a second if perhaps she looked to him as if she were wearing fancy dress. He could have seen the tinge of anxiety cross her face because he said: 'You look quite incredibly beautiful. Now sit, and have some champagne.'

'Thank you,' she said, taking the glass he offered and sipping it, her eyes, made up with black kohl, watching him over the rim.

'Tonight I think it has to be dinner at Gaddi's, the French restaurant at the Peninsular Hotel,' he said. 'I had planned to take you somewhere very Chinese, but such beauty must be shown off.'

And again she wondered if perhaps she was overdressed, too Oriental; but with a mental toss of her head she decided she did not care if she was.

She was astonished to find that the meal they shared in the big hotel, Kowloon side, as she was already beginning to think of it, was possibly one of the finest she had ever eaten. He explained to her that as Hong Kong was perhaps one of the richest places in the world, filled with the cleverest and most ambitious of both Chinese and Europeans, everything in the Colony that was there for the rich was of the best.

'In the old days the British used to send their black sheep, their misfits to "the colonies" – he made the word sound derisory. 'Today only the very best come here. It keeps us on our toes, too,' he added, 'but we can usually beat them.'

'Don't you mind all the Europeans and the fact that this is a British colony?' Poppy asked. She was eating a plateful of perfect *frais de bois*.

'Not really. We're very pragmatic people, you know. We look at Red China, we look at Taiwan and we look at the plight of the Chinese in Vietnam and we put up with the British.'

'Are they arrogant?'

He thought about it.

'Not so much these days. The older ones are. They're more stupid than anything. We say anything we like to them, and as long as we look as if we're kowtowing, they're happy. Most of them in the small jobs would only be clerks back home. Anyway, they all look the same to us.'

Poppy giggled. 'That's what Europeans say about Orientals. And blacks,' she added.

He just grunted and sipped at his brandy.

'What made you come here?' he asked suddenly, and the question sounded like an interrogation; more than mere conversation.

'Jade wanted to. I'd never even thought about it. She wanted to see where we came from.'

She told him about the day trip up to the orphanage.

'The place was filthy. Awful.' She put down her spoon and looked at the plate of fruit with a sort of gratitude. 'We were lucky to be taken away from there.' She shook her head and wondered:

100

'What do you think would have happened to us if Mother and Father hadn't adopted us?'

He shrugged.

'You'd have done better than most. You'd have been educated, kept clean and well fed. You were lucky even there at the orphanage. What were you? Daughters of refugees?'

'I don't know.'

'I expect you were,' he said casually. 'Two girls would be two too many mouths to feed. They would have just abandoned you.'

'Who?'

'Your real parents. Girl babies were expendable in those days.'

'Charming!' she said.

He shrugged.

'One way or another you've been very lucky,' he said. 'You must have been born under a good sign.'

She took up her glass, sipped the champagne and giggled. 'This is definitely better than an orphanage or those dreadful camps we saw today.'

They both laughed and then he said: 'What else did you find out about yourself in those papers?' He was still eating a strawberry flan, washed down with three-star brandy, and his attention seemed to be on breaking the pastry without shooting crumbs across the table.

'Not much about us,' she said. 'Jade got all excited because apparently our father knew that Dottie woman you were talking about last night who got murdered.'

'Why was Jade excited?' He was looking straight at her now, his eyes black and unfathomable.

'She seemed to think there was some connection. I don't know what she thinks really. She's a bit confused. It's strange. I never even wanted to come here; never even thought about it. It was her idea entirely and she's finding it difficult. She can't seem to think of herself as being Oriental at all. I'm not having the slightest problem.' She stroked the high neck of the *cheong-sam*. 'I feel more of a piece than I ever have in my life. I know it sounds very babyish, but I do feel as if I've come home.'

He nodded, still playing with the food on the plate in front of him.

'So what does Jade plan to do?'

'She wants to talk to all our father's friends here. She has an address book which she found with the other papers, so the idea is we'll go and find all of them.'

'For what purpose?'

'Search me!' Poppy said cheerfully. 'Can I have some coffee, please?'

He signalled the waiter and said:

'Tell me about Jade. Are you and she alike?'

She pulled a face.

'Not in the least,' she said. 'She's the goody-goody of the family. She was clever at school; always fussing over me because I was the little sister, trying to keep me out of mischief when I didn't want to be kept out of mischief. Then when we came home from Switzerland, Mother was going a bit funny in the head and Jade elected to look after her. She didn't have to – she just did it. She never moaned, I must say, but she's inclined to be a bit of a martyr. This is the first time she's ever broken out and done something for herself – like coming here. I didn't really want to come, and then I thought it might be fun and something different, so I came too.'

Poppy knew she was letting her tongue run away with her.

'It is fun, this place, isn't it? The shops are amazing, but Jade's all into solving the mystery of us and I don't really think it matters too much who our parents were. Might be better not to know. Jade really ought to be married with hordes of kids to look after,' she said, her voice confiding, 'but she's only had a couple of boyfriends that I know about. I suppose she hasn't had much chance, really. Would you believe, the only ambition she ever had was to run a nursery school. My God! And with Grandfather one of the richest men you can imagine.'

'I intend to be one of the richest men you can imagine,' he said casually. 'In fact, I have every intention of following, exactly, in your grandfather's footsteps.'

She giggled, knowing she was faintly high.

'Being rich is definitely better,' she said.

'Better than what?'

'Better than being poor, of course,' she told him.

He took her dancing somewhere she couldn't remember, and then they went back to his apartment. It was Hong Kong side, high on the Peak, which he explained was *the* place to live in Hong Kong.

'Once only Europeans could get up here to be in the cool at typhoon season,' he said. 'That, like so many other things here, has changed.'

The block of flats was luxurious in the extreme, but it was the view from his sitting-room window that fascinated Poppy. The windows looked across the bay to Kowloon and an amazing blaze of lights. The ships in the bay were lit – a cruiseliner at harbour was dressed overall, and above was a ripe moon and myriad stars.

'Jade would love this view,' she told him.

'You're really fond of Jade in spite of everything,' he suggested.

'Oh, yes,' she said. 'We don't really get on. We are very different, but this trip has helped. We ought to be close, don't you think, as sisters and with no one else in the world who really belongs to us?'

He smiled at her and slid his arm around her waist as they stood at the big picture window.

'Well, European-brought-up or not, you have a proper sense of family,' he said. 'Nothing is more important than family.'

There was an odd note in his voice and she looked at him questioningly.

'Do you have a big family?'

'No,' he said. 'Like you, I lost mine young.'

'Were you adopted?'

'Not exactly. No, I was luckier than that. Now, what do you want to drink? More champagne?'

'Why not?' she said.

It was after they had drunk nearly all the bottle that he started to ask questions about her grandfather. And when she thought about it later, she had drunk most of the Dom Perignon at the Captain's Bar, she had drunk most of the bottle over dinner, he had fed her a large brandy, then she had drunk a great deal more of the final bottle of champagne in his flat. And then he had suggested a snort of coke, which had seemed a good idea at the time. It wasn't the first time she had had coke, but this time the line made her very sick. She had to rush to his bathroom, but she felt good afterwards. Floating and free. She wondered if it had been something a lot stronger than coke, even though he had said as he had poured the line: 'It ought to be pure opium for Poppy, but this will have to do.'

And then he had started asking questions, and afterwards she could not remember exactly what he had asked or how she had answered. But he had been very, very inquisitive about her grandfather.

That much she did recall when she woke in his bed the next morning.

At first she could not think where she was. She felt very ill, as if her stomach was made of water. Her body hurt too. Her breasts and belly stung painfully as if they had been burned and her mouth felt swollen. The room was still in half-light with heavy shutters over the window, and there was someone lying next to her. Cautiously she turned her head and saw Kwan's head on a navy blue pillow. His long eyes were open and he was watching her, his face expressionless.

She tried to say something but her mouth was too dry. She tentatively felt her sore breasts and jumped under the touch of her own finger. She struggled to sit up and looked down at her body. Then she realised she had been burned. Her breasts and stomach were a mass of tiny red marks: cigarette burns. She recognised them instantly. She had once stubbed her cigarette out on the back of a man's hand when he was annoying her, and the burn had looked exactly the same.

She opened her mouth to scream, but Kwan's hand shot out like a snake and clamped over her mouth.

'You liked it last night,' he said. He pushed her back on the pillow and was leaning over her. 'And you liked this.' He was pushing her legs apart with his knee and then before she could find the strength to push him away he was grinding into her. She was sear and closed and she cried out, biting at his hand, but the pain between her legs was nothing to that of his body pressed on her, rubbing against the burns. She gave another choking cry and after that was not conscious of anything at all that was happening to her.

Jade, alone in her hotel room, had had room service bring her supper. Now she was busy with a map. With her father's address book at her side, she was carefully marking and noting the addresses and names of every person listed in the book.

There was no pattern, she discovered. Some lived on the far side of Hong Kong Island; others not far from where the Mandarin Hotel was situated. There was one address in Macao, and one in Kowloon.

She had decided to work from the map rather than the book. It would give a clearer idea of where she had to go. Meticulously, writing with a fine black pen in small, neat handwriting, she marked names and addresses and telephone numbers. When she had completed her task, she put the address book by the side of her bed and the map in the big zip pocket of her handbag.

Then she settled down to read one of the books on Hong Kong history that she had bought along with the map.

By ten o'clock that Saturday night, before Poppy had even left the Peninsular Hotel or finished her expensive French meal, Jade was sound asleep.

It was three o'clock in the morning when the phone rang in Michael Blake's apartment in the district of Hong Kong called Mid Levels, logically enough because it sits above Central and below the Peak on the north side of the island.

Michael had been sound asleep on the divan in the small dressing room that led off the flat's master bedroom. His wife slept there alone in what had once been their shared king-size bed. In the early days of their marriage, he had wanted a much smaller bed so that he could have slept closer to her, but she had never been very keen on contact. It was she who had insisted on the huge bed which dwarfed the bedroom, and she who with increasing frequency sent him to sleep alone next door.

Now she was shouting for him, her voice querulous.

'Do come and answer this thing. It's got to be for you.' Her crisp, nursing sister's voice had never lost its Midland vowels, nor he his, come to that. But doing a job in a world overrun by public-school types and their memsahib women, her voice always sounded like Nottingham and home, especially since she so rarely bothered to speak to him that he rarely heard it.

He swung himself out of the narrow bed and for a brief second sat still, staring at the floor. He knew he would start to cough when he rose to his feet. Carefully he tried it. And coughed. He padded across the floor in his pale blue pyjamas, tied clumsily at the waist; the jacket half-in, half-out, towards the insistently pealing phone.

'Who on earth can it be at this time of night?' Beryl was bleating into her pillow.

'How the hell should I know?' he said, suppressing another outburst of coughing.

Picking up the phone with one hand and reaching for a cigarette from the bedside table with the other, he said, 'Hallo,' aware that his voice was brusque.

'Mike?'

'Speaking.'

'It's Ian – Ian McKenzie McKenzie.'

Mike fumbled for the cigarette lighter and groaned softly into the phone.

'I might have guessed. Do you know what time it is here?'

'Three.' The old man's voice hadn't lost timbre, nuance, anything, Mike thought. It could have been the man of twenty years ago at the other end of the phone.

'So what do you want at three o'clock in the morning?' he asked.

'My granddaughters are there.'

'What! Here in Hong Kong?' Mike took a long drag of smoke to stop his coughing. 'Is that a good idea?' A yawn escaped in spite of himself.

'It is not a good idea,' Ian McKenzie McKenzie said in his precise Scots voice. 'It is a very bad idea.'

'Then why didn't you stop them?'

'Stop them!' The old man snorted down the phone. 'That Jade has a mind of her own. She's twenty-four years old. How could I stop her? She has her own money and her own spirit.' He stopped abruptly. 'Their father was knocked down by a car and killed in Los Angeles a week ago,' he said baldly.

Mike noted that even in death the old man couldn't bring himself to refer to Ralph as his son-in-law.

'I'm sorry. That's terrible. How's Margaret taking it?' he asked.

'She's not. She's not *compos mentis* any more. Her mind's gone away.'

Three flat little sentences, but Mike was silenced, remembering Margaret, her gaiety, her spirit and her total determination to get her own way and how much both Ian and Ralph, and, come to that, he had loved her.

'Yes. It's bad. But there it is,' Ian said.

There was silence until Mike said: 'What do you want me to do?'

'Keep an eye on them. Get to know them so that you can inform me of what they're doing. They're at the Mandarin. She found some papers about the adoption.'

'Who did?'

106

'Jade.'

Mike absently scratched the coarse grey hair on his chest through a gap in his pyjama jacket.

'So?'

'She's very bright. I'm afraid she might get curious. Just keep an eye on her. And Poppy.'

'And how am I supposed to get to know them?' Mike asked.

'Ring up with condolences about their father.'

'I hardly knew him.'

'You knew Margaret. That'll do.'

Mike felt his stomach churn at the mention of Margaret McKenzie McKenzie and the thought of her senility.

'Ok,' he said.

'Right. Now take down these telephone numbers and don't be worried to ring at any time.' The old man chuckled. 'It doesn't bother me.'

Writing down numbers meant turning on the bedside light, and caused an angry exclamation from Beryl as she heaved herself theatrically over to the other side of the mattress and pushed her face into the pillow.

'Sorry, dear,' he murmured, and then scribbled down three telephone numbers as Ian read them. He repeated them, promised to ring as soon as he had made contact, and hung up.

He sat on the edge of the bed for a moment. In the mirror opposite he could see a depressing reflection of himself: middle-aged, grey haired, running to overweight. A sad man in blue pyjamas who seemed to take off his authority along with his heavy glasses. He sighed and turned to look at his wife. One sun-tanned shoulder, gleaming brown, was above the white sheet. Her short, strong blonde hair was unfurled, stern against her soft brown neck. She had worn well, and as she shifted impatiently under the bedclothes, he started to sneeze. A long series of quiet, gentle sneezes, like a cat.

'No,' she said.

He put out his hand to stroke her shoulder.

There had been a time when his sneezing signalling sexual desire had made them both laugh. Now she only used it as an early warning system for when he was about to 'pounce' as she put it. It seemed years since he had pounced.

But he persevered, tentatively pulling back the sheets on the side of the bed where he sat.

'No,' she said. 'Go back to your own bed. You'll only fidget.'

He sat irresolute, and then shook his head, got up and briskly walked back towards the dressing room. A disappointed man with a large erection, a good career to go to in the morning, and a bad wife to come home to at night.

He sometimes wished it was the other way round.

$$\approx 7 \approx$$

SUNDAY

Gary Smith climbed off Cathay Pacific flight No. CX200 from London to Kai Tak, Hong Kong airport. He had what felt like pebbles in his eyes, feathers in his mouth and an injection of novocaine in his backside. A practically non-stop journey from the Highlands of Scotland through to South East Asia was not to be recommended, he thought, as he stood waiting for his luggage to appear. What had not helped was that the flight from Gatwick had been held up for two hours by a fall of snow which grounded the airport to a halt – a simple little fall of snow which any American pilot worthy of his salt would have regarded as fallen off a Christmas tree.

The plane was two hours late landing at Kai Tak airport. It was now nearly half-past eleven and he had until one thirty to make contact. The question now was whether to take his luggage to the Mandarin, leave it and set off for Wong Tai Sin or check his bags here at the airport. He did some quick mental arithmetic. Say three quarters of an hour to get to the Mandarin and leave his baggage. Half an hour on the MTR from Chater station to Wong Tai Sin. Another quarter of an hour to find his man. He could just about do it.

He was into a taxi immediately he was through Customs. 'Chop-chop,' he told the driver who had no hold-ups on the quieter Sunday morning roads. He checked into the Mandarin in five minutes flat, then out the back door to the entrance to the MTR. They had told him this was quite the quickest way to get himself deep into Kowloon. He fed his three dollars into the ticket machine and headed down the spacious underground hall to the escalator which led down to the platform. A train came in almost immediately – a pristine, shining train with comfortable seats and high carriages that very easily accommodated his six-foot height. 'Nice of the British to build the carriages high,' he thought, considering how most of the Chinese population were lucky if they topped five feet seven.

He had never been to the Wong Tai Sin Temple. All he knew about it was that it was in the most crowded part of Hong Kong. It was said that the people in the apartment blocks there lived in the highest density in the world.

'The place gets its share of tourists, and the people are so thick on the ground, you won't cause too much attention,' his control in Washington had told him. 'But get moving. We wouldn't want anything unpleasant to happen to those two nice girls, now would we?'

'I don't think they're involved,' he'd grunted.

'But we don't know. And neither do the others,' Control had pointed out.

The train moved at a remarkable pace, rocketing through tunnels, and Gary thought to himself that the Hong Kong MTR could teach the New York Metro a thing or two. The train was crowded entirely with Chinese, and a small child perched on its mother's lap fixed round black eyes on him unblinkingly. He could not tell if it were boy or girl, but either way it was fascinated, no doubt by both his height and his yellow hair.

'*Gweilo*,' the child whispered, and Gary grinned down from where he strap hung, causing it to hide its head on its mother's shoulder. The mother smiled apologetically, her mouth closed.

At Shek Kip Mei a man came on to the train with his wife and family. He was carrying a whole roast suckling pig on a tray. The wife had another smaller tray neatly piled with oranges which she attempted to hold in place with her left hand. At each successive station more people carrying food came aboard. A girl with a crisply roasted chicken; an old woman with a loin of pork, its rind glistening golden. The train smelt deliciously of food and Gary found his stomach turning in hunger waves. A day and a half of airport and train food had not been satisfying. He promised himself

109

a superb lunch at the Mandarin's Chinese restaurant.

Along with the carriers of food, he left the train at Wong Tai Sin. They streamed from every carriage and the smell of roast pork became almost unbearably tantalising to a hungry man.

There was no problem in finding the temple. He merely followed the food past the tall blocks of what appeared to be one-room apartments where washing decorated every balcony. The place was an ant heap, the tenements' inhabitants relentless; and yet there was no sense of hostility as there would have been in a New York ghetto. The Chinese, Gary had noted on previous visits to Hong Kong, had a trick of looking through the *gweilo* as if he did not exist on their streets. It gave Europeans an odd sense of depersonalisation for a while until they learnt to play the same trick back.

The guidebook that Gary had hastily bought at London Airport told him that Wong Tai Sin, the god to whom the temple was dedicated, was a Taoist who granted useful horse-racing tips and could also cure illness. He seemed to be a very popular god, Gary thought, seeing how the crowds grew in density as the long alleyway which led to the temple grounds grew closer.

It was this alleyway that interested Gary. It hit the eye in a blaze of red. Each of the dozens of stalls that lined both sides was selling Chinese lanterns, ready for the New Year, wind propellers on sticks which he remembered from his childhood, sheets of red paper and joss sticks. It looked more like a country fair than a place of worship. Lower down nearer the temple entrance were the fortunetellers' stalls, less colourful booths, the pitches for palmists, clairvoyants offering every type of prediction possible.

It would be one of these, the tenth pitch on the right, that he was looking for, and there should be a bird cage with two canaries and one linnet inside. There he had to stop.

He sauntered down the row of fortunetellers, their photographs displayed to inspire confidence, his camera over his shoulder, his guidebook just faintly sticking out of the pocket of his lightweight pale grey jacket, every inch the tourist. Mentally he was counting. He stopped and looked at the palmist's recommendations on the eighth stall to the left, hovered and then moved on. Around him the crowds pushed and shoved, elbows carving a way through the alley to the temple. The worshippers with food carried it head high for safety and those who had already prayed and made their offerings fought their way back to the streets and the MTR, carrying their offerings for their lunch. Gary grinned at the practicality of the Chinese who had decided the god could not be *that* hungry.

He reached the tenth stall on the right. The cage was there with three dispirited birds on their perches. A young man in patched jeans and a grubby blue short-sleeved shirt that flapped over his waist stood behind a table.

'Learn your fortune, sir,' he sing-songed as Gary hesitated by the stall. 'Good fortune. Lovely girls. Money. You win at horses. Try fortune, sir.'

Gary grinned.

'Ok, why not? How much?'

'Three dollar, sir. You throw *chum* at altar, bring back sticks that fall and I tell fortune.' The young man's face was broad, the expression begging, the eyes bright with intelligence.

'Ok,' Gary said again.

The man handed him a small bamboo canister which contained what looked like joss sticks, but the top of each stick was flattened.

'You get good fortune, sir, when you bring *chum* back. Ok, sir?'

'Ok.' The conversation was getting monotonous, Gary thought. He looked at the canister and grinned like a poor ignorant tourist who had been fooled again, then shoved it in his pocket where it made a bulge on the other side from the guidebook.

At the real entrance to the temple where the alleyway petered out, the air was full of floating black specks. People were burning red paper in a huge black heap, signifying the sending of money to their ancestors. An incense burner sent up choking smoke, and in the wide courtyards of the temple, people knelt on small mats before the altar, their food offerings on the ground, while they burned handfuls of joss sticks. The smoky air cut the eyes and the throat.

Happily the Chinese were giving him his usual cloak of anonymity. He walked through them like the Invisible Man into the courts until he found the main shrine. This was decorated with a drawing of the god's likeness and both sides of the altar were superbly carved. Sculptured animals perched on the ridges of the roof, and below, on the broad steps leading to the shrine, there must have been a hundred surprisingly young people kneeling and making their offerings while others shook the *chum* carefully letting a few sticks fall before the god.

Without kneeling, but squatting on his heels, Gary did the same. He had no need to separate those that fell from the canister from those which did not. All the sticks but one had writing on the broader surface of the top. The other had a white piece of sticky paper covering something.

He took the one with the paper and slipped it into his top pocket. Then he placed the ones which had fallen to the ground when he had shaken the *chum* in the pocket with the guidebook. The others and the *chum* itself went into the other pocket. He wandered on around the temple, taking a photograph of a smaller shrine where fewer people were gathered, and then ambled, head and shoulders above the crowd, back towards the alley of the fortunetellers.

He was aware of being glaringly conspicious in the small, dark throng and concerned that though it would be the easiest thing in the world for anyone to follow him, he would be hard put to tell if anyone were following him. He needed some cover, and he found it in the shape of a good-looking blonde and an older attractive brunette who were wandering around trying to look as if they were not staring at the worshippers. He moved to them with the kind of confidence that could denote to anyone watching that he knew them well.

'Hi,' he said. 'Are you gals feeling as outnumbered here as I am?'

In the space of seconds he had gained their confidence, passed on the *chum* and the fortune sticks, shown them how to throw them and led them, giggling, back to stall number ten and the three caged birds. He left them to have their fortune told in pidgin English. The young man had gone. In his place was a more convincing seer, a venerable gentleman with a wispy beard and a blue embroidered robe. The fortunes were satisfactory; the blonde was promised a tall, fair husband, a pronouncement made with a sideways look at Gary by Wispy Whiskers.

He walked them back to the MTR, bought their tickets – the least he could do, he reckoned – and waved them a goodbye at Tsim Sha Tsui station while he went on to Chater.

It wasn't until he was alone in his hotel bedroom that he took the fortune stick from his top pocket and peeled off the small patch of sticky paper.

Underneath it read: 'Six o'clock tonight Captain's Bar, Mandarin Hotel.'

He thought, not for the first time, how idiotic the work could be. All that way to get a message to meet someone in his own hotel bar. He shrugged and carefully put the small piece of paper down the

112

lavatory. Then he looked thoughtfully at the fortune stick and the message that was written on it in Chinese.

'I wonder if that was good luck or bad?' he said out loud.

It was the telephone ringing that woke Jade at nine thirty on the Sunday morning. Looking at her bedside clock she was astonished to see how long she had slept, and sleepily picked up the receiver.

'Jimmy here.' She sat up, trying to wake up. 'Are you still in bed?'

'As a matter of fact . . .'

'You are. Wasting the day,' he reprimanded, 'and when I have a beautiful junk and an exotic picnic waiting for you. I intend to take you round the islands. The sun is shining, there is a light breeze and it is a beautiful day.'

'I can't,' she heard herself saying. 'I have all sorts of things to do today.'

'It's Sunday,' he said, his voice patient. 'There is nothing you can do today except go to church, go to temple, sleep, eat, or go sailing around the islands in a beautiful junk.'

'I have people to call.'

'They will not be there. They will be at church, at temple, sleeping, eating or sailing round the islands in a beautiful junk.'

She felt herself weakening.

'And,' he said, 'it is time, as a girl born here, you saw the island of your birth. There will be no more discussion about the matter. I shall be at the hotel to pick you up in three quarters of an hour, not a minute later. And you will be in the lobby waiting for me so we do not waste another moment of this splendid day. Bring something to swim in. Preferably a bikini.'

She did not have time to reply. He had hung up.

Shaking her head and laughing to herself she got out of bed and padded towards the bathroom. What did one wear on a junk? she wondered, and settled on jeans and a sweater. She showered quickly, then rang through to Poppy's room to explain she was going out. There was no reply. She pulled a small face as she put down the receiver and wondered if Poppy had found Kwan Ching smelt the same as European men and indeed if there had been any difference at all to the heaven-knew-how-many European men that Poppy had had.

The thought made her wonder how Jimmy Lee would be. Was

there any difference? She could not quite control a faint urge to find out.

She had just come from the bathroom when the phone rang again. Expecting it to be Poppy, she picked it up and said 'Hello' reluctantly, wondering if her sister would be looking for company.

'Miss McKenzie McKenzie Martin?' a man's quiet and pleasant voice asked.

'Yes,' she said cautiously. This was not another educated Chinese. This voice brought back the sound of England.

'You don't know me. My name's Michael Blake. I knew your mother when we were both young. I was ringing to say how sorry I was to hear about your father and to ask if there is anything I can do for you. I'd like very much to meet you in any case.'

'You knew my father?' she said eagerly.

He seemed to hesitate.

'Not as well as I knew your mother, but we met a lot over the years. I'm afraid he rather pinched her from me,' he said apologetically.

She found herself unaccountably excited.

'Did you know me when I was little?'

'No. You were hardly in Hong Kong. Your mother was anxious to take you and your sister home as soon as she could.'

'Oh – I'd love to meet you,' she said. 'When can we?'

'Today if you like,' he said.

'Oh!' she gave a little tut of exasperation. 'I wish you'd called ten minutes ago. I can't now. I'm going out for the day.'

'You've made friends already?' he asked politely.

'It's a man—' she stopped. Explaining Jimmy Lee was going to sound very odd to one of her mother's friends. 'I'll tell you about it when we meet. Could it be tomorrow?'

'I have to work tomorrow,' he said, 'but if you would like to have dinner with me, we could go to the Pierrot Restaurant in your hotel. It's very beautiful and peaceful for Hong Kong.'

'That would be marvellous,' she said enthusiastically. 'I really look forward to that.'

'Me too,' he said. 'See you tomorrow, then. Bring your sister if she would like to come. We'll meet in the lobby at seven thirty. I'll ask the desk to call up for you.'

Once she had put the phone down, Jade realised she had already forgotten the man's name. Michael, definitely, but was it Brown or

114

Laker? Nor had she asked how he had known she was in Hong Kong. Undoubtedly to do with Grandfather, she thought, as she outlined her mouth in soft pink lipstick and gathered up a large navy leather shoulder bag. She took one last look at herself in the mirror, small and slim in jeans and a navy and white striped tee-shirt and as an afterthought she picked out a navy cashmere cardigan – in case it turned cold. Then she left the room, hurrying to meet Jimmy Lee in the hall downstairs.

He had his Rolls and his chauffeur waiting outside the hotel and he explained that he kept his junk moored on the other side of the Island at Aberdeen.

'I have a reason for choosing to keep it there,' he said, 'but I will explain when we are sailing. You don't object to going across the Island?'

'Of course not,' she said.

He was dressed in designer jeans and a casual navy blue sweater – an outfit similar to her own, and in the morning sunlight his hair seemed less black and greasy. He looked casual and relaxed.

The drive took about quarter of an hour and she would not have been able to explain why but she found herself relieved that there was a crew of two on the junk. Both seemed professional sailors. Neither of them seemed to know Jimmy well, and he gave his orders briskly and in Cantonese as they swung out from the Aberdeen yacht club harbour, a light wind catching the beige sails and the motor *putt-putting*.

The boat was made of polished scented teak, pleasing to the touch, and the small cabin was comfortably furnished. As they stood watching the skyscraper blocks of Aberdeen, she said: 'It's a beautiful boat. Is it yours?'

'Yes,' he said. 'A company boat like most of the better junks. I don't keep a permanent crew – I just hire seamen as and when I need them. Junks are quite complicated to sail.' He was opening a bottle of champagne as he spoke and the cork came out with a satisfying pop.

'Shouldn't you be working today?' she asked.

'You've forgotten that it's Sunday. And besides, you are a potential customer, aren't you?' he asked, handing her a glass.

'Well, maybe,' she said, 'as long as you give good discounts.'

'Your Scottish upbringing is showing,' he told her. 'But if the Miss McKenzie McKenzie Martin is a little short of money, my

115

main business is the exportation of fun fur coats. Can I interest you in a patchwork coney jacket?'

'A *rabbit*?' she said with Lady Bracknell intonation, and they both laughed, leaving her a little more at ease.

The junk was sailing past the back of a group of large floating restaurants and moving into an open channel between rows and rows of battered old hulks, near derelict dredgers and unloved junks, laid in rows like rotting teeth in an old mouth.

'Raise your glass,' Jimmy Lee said as they entered the channel. 'To my old home.'

'Your home?' she said. 'Where?'

'I told you I was of the boat people. There are the boat people and their homes.'

She looked, bewildered, at the masses of boats strung together in insanitary squalor, washing hanging from bulkheads and cabin windows, dogs lazing on the decks, fish drying in strings hanging like primitive necklaces in the sun.

'You were brought up here?' she asked.

'Yes,' he said. 'My family were boat people. We lived here in picturesque poverty. Tourists used to come and gape at us and take our pictures from a dollar ride in a Sampan. This is a typhoon shelter, you see, so all the boats cluster for safety, but they never go to sea. Tourists would watch us, wonder at the way we lived and take our pictures. When I was about four I can remember my mother's fury as a *gweilo* photographed me. I was sliding down a rope to swim in the harbour. They thought I was cute. The visitors still treat the boat people like a zoo, but the sampan ride costs six dollars now, and there are a great many more tourists than when I was a child.'

He gave some rapid orders in Cantonese to the crew, who began to carefully navigate the junk up narrow channels which formed a kind of watery street between the rows of boats.

'Interesting, isn't it?' he said. 'Primitive, of course, but I sometimes wonder if life here on the water is not more pleasant than there.' He stabbed a finger at the tenement blocks that dominated the waterfront. 'The authorities would like us all in those blocks. But the boat people are reluctant to move.'

'How did you escape?' Jade asked, genuinely curious.

'My father was killed at sea in a typhoon and an uncle took me in. He was a furrier in a small way. He had me educated at a Catholic

116

school here and for a short time in London where I worked in the fur department of Harrods, and that was more or less that.'

'It's a bit like Poppy and me, isn't it?' she said slowly, still fascinated by the life on the boats they passed by. 'You might have still been a boat person and I might have been a peasant in China. Life is very strange.'

'In terms of good joss you did very well,' he said. 'In Hong Kong you cannot get a great deal higher than being a McKenzie McKenzie – unless, of course, you have the incredible good fortune to be a Jardine or a Matheson.'

'What's a Jardine or a Matheson?' she asked.

He shook his head in mock despair.

'Don't you know anything about Hong Kong at all?'

'Not really,' she admitted.

'Jardine and Matheson are the biggest Hongs – merchants, if you like. They have fingers in every pie. They say that the power in Hong Kong is held by the Jockey Club, Jardine Matheson, the Hong Kong and Shanghai Bank, and the British Governor – in that order. McKenzie McKenzie could well come next.' He laughed. 'You must be giving the *gweilo* here a very puzzling time. Should they invite you because you're McKenzie McKenzie's adopted granddaughters, or should they not invite you because you're Chinese?'

Again she had that sense of not knowing what he was talking about and wanting to protest why shouldn't Europeans invite them.

'I don't think anyone knows we're here,' she said instead. 'Oh – except some man who rang me this morning who used to know my mother.'

'Who was it?' Jimmy asked. He seemed to be concentrating on a sampan moving gently towards them.

'Can't remember his name. Laker, Brown – something like that.'

'They don't sound very alike,' he said, giving her a sharp look.

'Well, he was called Michael anyway.'

'And what does he do?'

'I don't know. He didn't say.' She looked at him curiously. 'Does it matter?'

'Of course not,' he said quickly, and changed the subject. 'So, you know nothing about your grandfather?'

'Only that he owns a big shipping company, that my father worked for the British end, and that he's my granddad and an

117

amazing man. He's nearly eighty and you'd think he was in his mid-sixties.'

As she spoke of him, she felt a pang of guilt. She must telephone him.

'He's a legend in South East Asia too,' Jimmy said. 'There's a story, and it's very probably true, that he was a pirate at one time.'

'Grandfather a pirate!'

'He's been a pirate all his life, really,' Jimmy said drily. 'But apparently, aged about fourteen, he was a real pirate. At that time the South China Sea was full of them. They say it's how he got the money together for his first ship.'

'I can't believe it,' Jade said positively. 'What would he have been doing here at fourteen years old? He'd have been in school, surely?'

'I don't know. But I do know your grandfather was born here. His father was in one of the services. But I don't remember any more of the story. You'd have to ask your mother.'

'My mother wouldn't remember either,' Jade said. 'She's ill. She's lost her memory. Completely.'

'Has she?' said Jimmy. 'Completely?'

'Yes. Completely.'

'What a terrible thing to happen,' he said, but the statement lacked conviction, and again Jade felt a *frisson* of uneasiness.

He might perhaps have sensed her discomfort, because he immediately changed the subject yet again and began pointing out the surrounding islands. They had already sailed quite some distance from Hong Kong and he explained that he had planned to take her to Lantau Island where they could swim ashore.

'The island is larger than Hong Kong and still very countrified,' he told her, 'but it's rapidly becoming developed. There'll be an airport there by 1990 and it will all be modernised.'

'Won't that be a shame?' Jade asked.

He looked genuinely surprised.

'Of course not,' he said. 'All that land going to waste? It'll take some of the overflow from Hong Kong and Kowloon. They say officially there are five and a half million people in the Colony. Everyone knows it's nearer seven million. They have to be housed somewhere.'

'So will the beach be crowded?' she murmured, hoping that it would be. She did not want to be alone with him.

'No. Not at all. We'll go south of Cheung Sha where the beach is inaccessible from land and you can have the South China Sea all to yourself.'

He broke off to give some instructions again to the crew, and then asked if she would like to eat before or after they swam.

'Will it be hot enough to swim?' she asked. There was a stiff breeze billowing the beige sails of the junk; they hardly needed the motor.

'The bay is very sheltered,' he said. 'We'll eat now while we're sailing and then swim afterwards – agreed?'

'Fine,' she murmured.

He served the meal himself – a delicious concoction of different cold seafoods, served with unusual and delicate sauces. They sat in comfort in the cabin; the table covered with a white cloth, the food served in good china and with only chop-sticks as eating implements. She was clumsy with them, and he laughed at her, arranging her fingers around the ivory and coming closer than he needed to. She found herself very aware of him, but her uneasiness persisted. His hands were so small; the bones so fragile looking and his waist in the denim trousers seemed as narrow as her own. His face was broad and his feet in espadrilles seemed almost feminine, but his shoulders were surprisingly strong and the arms below tough and muscular. He was built quite differently from any man she had ever known.

He made her laugh while they ate, telling stories of the small and subtle ways that the Chinese scored over the *gweilo* who lived in their midst, yet while she laughed she felt disloyal and uncomfortable.

'You don't really like those stories, do you?' he finally said as a bowl of *kumquats* was put on the table.

'Of course,' she said, 'they're very funny.'

'You'll have to come to terms with who you are one day.' he said without elaborating. 'Let me tell you just one more story. The property developers have just finished knocking down the Hong Kong Club. It was a fortress for the Europeans. They felt safe there and there has been much agitation and pressure to leave the building standing. The *South China Morning Post*'s columns were filled with retired and irrascible British colonels protesting against its demise. Now here in Hong Kong we have an honoured and powerful Chinese citizen who won a first-class honours degree at one of your Oxbridge universities many years ago. He was back here when the time came for him to receive his degree and he was told that it would be presented to him by the Governor at the Hong Kong Club. He arrived on the appointed day – only to be sent around to the servants' entrance. Why? Because he was just a Chinese. His letter concerning the Hong Kong Club to the *South China Morning Post* told this story and requested that he might wield the first pick to begin demolishing the building. This letter ended the correspondence.'

Jade was silent then murmured: 'That was terrible.'

'Indeed,' he said. 'But now, more tea. We are nearly there.'

While they drank a final cup of tea he kept the conversation non-controversial, pointing out comic little bumps of islands rising like the Loch Ness monster from the sea and the big island they were nearing, where a small town was set deep in a bay.

'That's Lantau,' he explained, and once the small houses were well past, he instructed: 'Go and put your bikini on.'

She had put the yellow and black striped bikini pants under her jeans and the top was in her handbag. She changed in the cabin and, when she returned, he was wearing a blue bathing slip, sitting, his legs dangling over the side of the junk. As she came on to the deck, he slid into the sea and struck out for the shore.

'Not too far for you?' he shouted up at her.

'No, it's Ok,' she said, diving neatly over the side and into the water.

It struck cold – almost as cold as the sea off the coast of Ayrshire where childhood holidays had been spent, but she warmed quickly as she swam strongly to the beach ahead. It was quite a distance, further than it had looked from the junk.

The sand was fine and yellow; there was no one to be seen, and they flung themselves breathlessly down and lay panting quietly. Behind the beach was a curtain of rich green verdure and, beyond, bare brown mountains. It was still; slow white rollers broke on the shore, a sea hawk, wings trembling, above. After a while he said: 'Let's find some shelter out of the wind.'

He took her hand and they ran along the shoreline until he pointed out a small cove.

'We'll go in there,' he said.

Out of the wind the sand was warm under her feet, the sun warm on her back, her bikini cold on her body, and his hand holding hers cool and firm. She gave a little shiver, and he looked at her quickly.

'You're cold?'

'A little.'

'Is it that wet bikini?'

'I suppose so.'

There was quiet like a silent bar in music, then he said: 'Turn around.'

Obediently she did so and, standing with her back to him, she felt his fingers dealing with the narrow strap which held the small bra in place. She felt the wetness of it fall away from her and then his hands slid around under her arms to cover her small breasts.

'They are cold,' he murmured into her hair, and she stood still and silent as his hands made gentle circular rubbing motions that she could feel were making her nipples stand proud. She was aware she ought to move away, but what he was doing was pleasurable, the attraction was there and, most of all, curiosity.

He was pressing against her back, his body still damp, and she could feel the hard ridge of him pushed against her buttocks. She thought suddenly that he was the shortest man she had ever known, the only one who came remotely near to her own height, and she wondered what difference it would make to lovemaking. It might be better, she thought. They could kiss while he was in her.

He was turning her face to him, but he did not kiss her. He bent his head to bite and lick at her breasts, and she stood looking down at the glossy black wet hair against her skin, wondering whether she should stop him but not sure how. It was already too late. His mouth on her breast was sending urgent messages to the rest of her body. She felt a warmth and excitement and could hear herself begin to pant a little.

He lifted his head, and pushed her hair back with his hand, then whispered in her ear: 'Lie down now.' The heat of his breath made her shiver and, still without speaking, she dropped, first on her knees and then twisting to lie full length on her back in the softly gritty sand.

He lay beside her, leaning up on one elbow and looking down at her. Then he began to roll the bottom of the bikini down over her thighs, touching them with fluttering movements as he did so. She helped him to get the wet mass over her feet, and then his head went back to her breast while his left hand insistently pushed her legs apart. She felt his fingers teasing at her, front, middle and back, all at once, and wondered how his small hand could stretch so, but heard herself cry out: 'What is it? What are you doing? Oh, that's good . . .'

She could not bring herself to touch him, but he did not seem to mind. It seemed to please him to excite her until she was no longer aware of the surroundings, the harshness of the sand on her skin or the light breeze that teased along with his fingers and tongue. Then she said: 'Please, now . . . now . . .'

He rolled over to cover her with his length and she clasped him to her, aware of his slight weight, the narrowness of his waist and small hips and buttocks. She had been right. As he rode her, he was able to kiss her, his mouth duplicating the movements below until she had to push his head on to her shoulder. The two pleasures were too much to bear at once. She found she could easily wrap her legs around his narrow waist and pull him even closer to her and she clung to him, aware of no love or affection, but of extreme sexual excitement, conscious only of deep, deep enjoyment until quite suddenly it was over for both of them.

They fell apart almost immediately, and she lay on her back staring at the scudding clouds high in the sky. Then she fell asleep.

Gary, having slept most of the afternoon, was in the Captain's Bar at five minutes to seven. He carefully selected a seat in the corner, along from the few steps that led down from the foyer, a glass panel decorated with a chess motif behind his head. He ordered a Scotch on the rocks, and waited.

At seven o'clock precisely, a Chinese man came down the steps and looked around. He spotted Gary in the dimly lit corner, waved, came across to the table.

He was taller than usual, and dressed in a finely tailored lightweight dark suit with a shirt that gleamed white in the near-dark. His tie was conservative, deep blue with small white dots; his shoes were Gucci; he wore heavy horn-rimmed spectacles with slightly darkened lenses and his black hair was combed neatly across his forehead. He carried a soft expensive-looking bag with webbing handles.

Gary, seeing him in a crowd, would never have recognised him as the fortuneteller from the temple of that morning.

'Hi, fella,' he was saying, holding out his hand. Climbing to his feet, Gary automatically took it, and they shook hands with a show of considerable enthusiasm. 'Great to see you,' the man was saying loudly. 'How you been?'

'Fine, fine,' Gary said, noting that the American accent was authentic. 'And you?'

'Busy. You know how it is.'

'Sure, sure,' Gary said. 'What'll you have?'

'Bourbon and America dry. Plenty of ice.' He was pushing the bag under the seat and settling himself down as Gary beckoned the waiter and gave the order.

'Now tell me, how are things back in LA?' he asked, continuing the fatuous conversation for the waiter's benefit as he reappeared with the drinks on a tray. 'Boy, what could I do for a night on the town with a willing American chick again. Same meat all the time gets to be a drag.'

The waiter had gone, and the man grinned.

'I'm Sam Tu,' he said.

'Hi, Sam. Gary Smith.'

'Hi, Gary.' They both resisted the impulse to shake hands again. 'Any trouble getting here?'

'Nope. There's a cruddy pair of jeans and cheap blue shirt and some worn-out kickers in there,' he kicked the bag with his foot. 'Turn that bag inside out and it looks like it's been carrying shit. I changed in the john at the ferry. Too much going on there for anyone to notice.' He had seated himself so that only Gary could see his mouth movements. 'But I don't think there was a problem. I'm sure they didn't follow me. I think they trust me. Jesus! It's taken long enough. I been stuck here six months, but it's beginning to happen. They were keen to recruit me when they found I could speak some English. If I burst into pidgin, take no notice. It's just that it's been a long time.'

He stopped for breath and Gary asked: 'Where in the States did you learn?'

''Frisco. We got there in '64. My folks got into Hong Kong from Canton by the '62 exodus from China. We were lucky. They didn't send us back. We did nearly two years in a camp here, cursing the Brits and wondering if we'd been better off staying home, and then we got to the Gold Mountain.' He grinned. 'I was eight and disappointed as hell there wasn't any gold. Christ, I never thought I'd have to go through the whole thing again. This time I got back in via Vietnam. And there I was, in one of those damn camps again. I got out of it, though. I'm shacked up with a chick in Wong Tai Sin, earning a crust as the fortuneteller's apprentice while she adds to the family fortunes by lying on her back.' He took a long swig of his drink and then asked: 'Have you been here before?'

'Couple of times,' Gary said, thinking he'd found himself a character here. 'God knows what I'm doing this time, though. I'm watching a couple of dames – the McKenzie McKenzie daughters, but I'm not convinced at all they've anything to do with it. We ought to be watching Granddad – not the girls.'

'The McKenzie McKenzies, eh!' Sammy Tu whistled through his teeth. 'How come we Orientals are supposed to be so wily when you get the Mandarin Hotel and the McKenzie McKenzies while I finish up in Wong Tai Sin with a Hong Kong whore?'

'Serves you right for speaking Cantonese,' Gary said.

'No chance not to,' Sammy said. 'My old lady can still only say half a dozen words in American. If I didn't speak Chinese she wouldn't be able to bawl me out. Anyway, let's have another one and get down to business.'

This time Sammy ordered, speaking Cantonese. 'Just showing off,' he grinned, and when the drinks were served he lowered his voice and said: 'Right then, the initiation's on Wednesday. and to tell you the truth I'm shit scared.' He shook his head and sucked briefly at his teeth. '*Heung chu* – Incense Master to you, Gary – is a guy called Kwan Ching. A very superior brand of Chinese he is. A businessman into shipping importing and exporting. He runs the whore I'm shacked up with as well as doing a lot of other funny things that'll interest you and me. Who 489, the head guy, is I don't know yet. It may take time.' He paused. 'How do you want to keep in touch? You can't keep temple-visiting – they'll think you're converting. I can't keep coming over here and I don't like using the telephone. The kind I'm supposed to be doesn't go in much for telephones, and once I'm initiated they'll be watching me even more closely.'

'Post?' Gary suggested.

'Slow.'

'Then how?'

Sammy had obviously thought it out. 'There's a particularly god-awful all-night club Kowloon side called Big Fat Hot Lips.' he said slowly. 'The broad who owns and runs it is an ex-whore who had the sense to save. An American. Quite a gal. She lets my broad hustle there. She doesn't know I'm American. I keep up the pidgin with her, too. But she knows me and I get in there quite a bit. She's generous with the Scotch when she's had a few herself. Go there, make like a customer, and I'll make sure my broad seeks you out. If you need me, go there and ask for her. She'll find me. And if I need you, she'll tell you.'

He grinned. 'You'll have to pay. It'll add to the family income.'

'Ok,' Gary said. 'What's her name?'

'Mi,' Sammy said. 'She's cute. But the surroundings aren't like this.' He pointed at the room with his chin in the Chinese manner. 'Anyway, Mi's clean,' he said, suddenly awkward. 'I see to that. Self-defence,' he added, brazen.

'And the name of the American girl?'

'Suzie. Suzie Shaw. You'll like her if you can catch her sober.'

'Right.' Gary mentally filed the information away and groaned at the idea of night after night at the Big Fat Hot Lips. 'Let's have one for the road and call it a day. I've got to try and meet up with *my* pigeon.'

As it happened, the contact was made with no difficulty at all. Sammy Tu had taken himself off, presumably to the gentleman's lavatory on the pier head to change, while Gary finished his drink. He signed the bill and walked out of the bar and into the foyer. Coming through the swing doors, with a casually but smartly dressed young Chinese behind her, was Jade. Her sudden appearance hit him somewhere midway between his solar-plexus and his sexual equipment. He was remembering her loud and clear and recalling the small swell of her breasts, hidden now under the loose tee-shirt she wore, and how tender she was when he had been with her.

Her eyes widened appreciably and her mouth fell open as she saw him.

'Gary Smith!' she said, her voice astonished. 'I don't believe it.'

He grinned at her, hoping the heat her presence had generated didn't show.

'You owe me money.' he said.

'So I do. How awful. I'm so sorry—'

'Shh.' He was laughing. 'It was a great excuse to follow you. How are you, baby?'

'Fine.' He could see she was suddenly confused and embarrassed. She turned to the man behind her and said: 'Jimmy, I'm

125

sorry. This is an old friend of mine. Gary Smith. Gary, this is Jimmy Lee.'

Jimmy Lee was looking positively wary for a Chinese, Gary thought, but he stuck out his hand, forcing the other man into offering his. Then he shook it just a little too tightly for the smaller, more fragile bones. Jimmy Lee, he noticed, did not wince.

'Did you get everything sorted out in LA?' he asked Jade, claiming her attention.

'Yes.' She was nodding her head. 'It wasn't difficult. My grandfather arranged everything. But I never thanked you for your help.'

'You had other things on your mind,' he said easily. 'Hey – won't you both join me for a drink?'

He was wondering who the hell Jimmy Lee was, and feeling slightly aggrieved at his presence. Particularly as Jade had the look of a lady who'd been up to mischief; but her smile, once over the shock of recognising him, had been remarkably sweet. He found himself thinking again about how she had been in bed.

'I'm afraid I can't,' Jimmy Lee said, his voice apologetic. 'I just explained to Jade that I have an appointment that I must keep this evening. Perhaps another time.'

'Sure,' Gary said. 'But how about you?' He took her hand and squeezed it.

She looked flustered.

'That would be nice. But could I just go up and change? Could you wait? I've been out all day.'

'Go ahead,' he said. 'No problem.'

Tactfully he slipped back into the bar leaving Jimmy Lee to walk the girl to the desk. He saw him leave and decided there was no point speculating on his identity. Jade would have the answer. He had just settled down again and called for another drink when the waiter came back to his table.

'Phone call, sir,' he said.

'Who is it?' Gary asked.

'Lady,' the waiter said. 'Lady in hotel.'

He wandered to the phone at the end of the room by the bar, thinking she wanted time to take a bath or something, but when he picked up the receiver and said: 'Hallo,' her frightened voice, near to hysterics, cut him short.

126

'Gary, please can you come up here to room 714 – quickly. Something awful's happened.'

He was lucky that the lift came swiftly and the bellboy let him out on the right floor and pointed the correct direction to walk for room 714. His stride made no sound on the thick carpets, and the silent corridors were deserted. He found the room and knocked gently. Jade immediately opened the door, her face very pale.

'I'm so pleased to see you,' she said. 'Come in.'

He pushed past her along the strip of passageway lined with wardrobes, noting that the bathroom was on the right.

'What is it?' he asked. 'What's happened?'

'Something frightening,' she said from behind him.

He was into the bedroom, and saw nothing. The room was neat and orderly.

'What is it?' he asked.

'On the bed,' she said.

On the large double bed were a pair of broken scissors, placed neatly in the centre of the heavy bedspread. The steel glinted evilly, and they lay with the points of the two blades pointing towards each other.

'Broken scissors?' he said, turning to look at her where she stood hesitant in the doorway into the room, as if she were terrified to go near the bed. 'Are they what frightened you?'

She nodded. He walked over to the bed, and using his handkerchief, picked them up.

'How did they get there? Do you know?'

She shook her head. 'It's rather a long story,' she said apologetically. 'But I do have reason to be scared,' she added defensively as if she didn't want him to think she was making a fuss over nothing.

'Why?' he asked. 'Tell me. There's plenty of time.'

It did indeed take some time while she showed him the newspaper cuttings she had found and the papers regarding the adoption. He listened intently, trying to place her scenario in his own while she told him the background of what had happened after she had said goodbye to him at Aspen. None of it made a lot of sense to him.

'So it was broken scissors that killed the Chinese family in the newspaper cutting,' she finally said. She was sitting on the bed, her hands clasped in her lap, her face anxious. 'And then, the other night at dinner with Jimmy Lee, the man you just met, and some other people, they were talking about a murder on the peak. A woman called Dorothy Adamson had been killed – with a pair of broken scissors.'

'It's a fairly common weapon here,' he said, his mind working overtime.

'Yes, that's what everyone says, except that when I looked at my father's address book that night when I got back here, Dorothy Adamson was the first name written in it. And it seems she had died on the same day as Daddy.'

She was looking at him, her eyes fixed steadily on his face, still wearing the day's jeans and tee-shirt. Her expression begged for reassurance, but he was trying to put these new developments into his own jigsaw, without success. He was not interested in disappearing ships. At least he didn't think he was interested in disappearing ships. What sounded like ritual Triad murders were more promising, but where did they belong in his puzzle? On the face of it, there had to be some connection.

'Where is your father's address book?' he asked slowly.

'Here.' She turned to the bedside table. 'Oh—' She was moving the heavy lamp, opening the drawer underneath the beside table. 'It's not where I left it,' she said, her voice puzzled. 'I think it's gone.'

He moved to look at the bedside table's twin.

'Maybe this side?' he said, but there was nothing there.

'It's gone,' she said, and if Chinese eyes could be wide, those she turned on him were.

'Maybe the maid has put it away,' he said reassuringly. 'We'll look. What size and colour is it?'

'Only small – just an ordinary address book. Red leather.'

Without speaking they searched the room, looking in drawers, in her empty suitcases, even in her toilet bag. The address book was nowhere.

'I think we need a drink,' he said eventually. 'What do you want? A brandy?'

'Yes, please.' She was calm and very thoughtful as he selected the drink, poured it, took it to her, and then put his arms around her.

'Is there anything you haven't told me?' he asked, looking down.

'Nothing. Except that Grandfather didn't want us to come here.

He said it would be culture shock. Do you think perhaps there was something else he was concerned about?'

'Maybe,' he said.

She was sitting on the edge of the bed, swirling the liquid in her glass.

'Jimmy Lee said Grandfather had been a pirate when he was young,' she said slowly.

'It's meant to be true.'

'You know about him?' She was looking at him almost suspiciously.

'Everybody knows a little bit about your grandfather,' he said.

She was staring at him, her eyes narrowed.

'Why are you here?' she asked abruptly, and he could see she was beginning to think.

'Looking for you.'

'Why?'

'I told you. You owe me money.'

'It's an expensive way of debt-collecting.'

'I wanted to see you again,' he said, his voice patient. 'I went to Scotland. They said you'd left for Hong Kong. So I came to Hong Kong. I can afford it, Jade.'

He could see she was not convinced.

'Hey,' he said softly. 'You don't have to be suspicious of everyone, you know.'

'I'm sorry,' she said, but he realised she still wasn't trusting him. He decided not to push it – let it go for the moment – as she said: 'Do you think Poppy's room is all right? Will they have done anything there?' She stopped, clapped her hand to her forehead and said: 'They gave me a message from her at the desk. I haven't read it. I'd forgotten all about it.'

'Well, read it,' he suggested.

She went to her handbag and took out the small sheet of paper.

'It's only to say she won't be back tonight,' she said, handing it to him. 'She's going out again with Kwan Ching.'

'With who?' he said urgently.

'Kwan Ching. Someone in shipping we met the first night we were here.' She looked at him sharply. 'Why, is something wrong?' Her voice was suspicious.

'No,' he said. 'It was just a name I thought I recognised.'

Poppy and the Incense Master together, he thought, his mind

racing, looking at the name written on the message sheet. Now there was a turn-up for the book! Were the McKenzie McKenzie girls involved after all? It still didn't make sense, but he was going to need time to think it out. For the moment Jade was standing very close to him, small and brave, and he remembered the night in Aspen and most urgently wanted to enjoy her softness and sweetness again.

'You need distracting,' he said, and lifted her bodily as he had lifted her in the Limelight Hotel – was it only nine days ago? It seemed much longer, and also as if he had known her much longer.

He laid her on the bed and she looked up at him unprotesting. Then she suddenly giggled and said: 'I still have the information that was in the address book.'

'You do? Where?'

'Never you mind,' she said, sounding triumphant; her expression was so self-satisfied that he had to laugh down at her in spite of his awareness of her lack of total trust.

'I'm not going to be beaten,' she told him, as if the message was for him.

'But who are you fighting?'

She was silent for a moment. 'That's it. I don't know. But I feel I'm fighting something.' The look she gave him held a question.

'If I were to make love to you, would you fight me?'

Her expression lightened.

'No.'

'Are you sure?'

'Yes.'

'In that case, why don't we get ourselves undressed?'

'Yes, why don't we?' she said, sounding slightly breathless.

When Jade woke, the bedside light was on, casting a gentle glow over the bed where she lay naked next to Gary Smith. He was sleeping deeply, a small whistling noise coming with each breath he took. She smiled indulgently at the sound and lifted her arm cautiously to look at her watch which was still on her wrist. It was gone ten o'clock. They had been in bed for three hours, most of the time making love, and even just thinking about what he had done to her with such finesse made her inner muscles contract and lifted her hips involuntarily from the bed. His closeness had driven away all her anxieties.

For a brief moment she felt a strong sense of guilt at having made love to two men in one day. That was Poppy behaviour, and she found herself wishing that Gary Smith had reappeared in her life a few hours earlier so that the Jimmy Lee incident had not taken place. But there was something exciting about what she had done. And besides, she told herself in a flash of virtue, she had only let Jimmy Lee make love to her because it would have been embarrassing to have refused him. But an inner honesty told her it had been more than that. Curiosity had been an attraction too. She had wanted to see what it was like to be taken by a Chinese – by someone who looked as she did. She had found him attractive, but when it came to it, he had felt the same inside her as any man and she wished she had looked at him more, touched him more. But in the end he had just been a man fucking her. His skin colour and the slant of his eyes changed nothing.

The difference between the two men was that Gary Smith she could love. She wondered what he would think if he knew that only an hour or two earlier another man had entered her. Would he care? Or was she just an exotic lay? Had she been that, would he have followed her all the way to Hong Kong? There had to be something more. Her common sense defeated sexual euphoria and told her that the something was certainly something quite different.

The same pang of uneasiness that had hit her when she saw him standing in the lobby struck again. She wanted to think he had followed her for emotional reasons, but she doubted it. She now felt she had told him far too much in the fright of finding the broken scissors. These he had now flung into the wastepaper basket. She'd tell him no more, she decided.

She thought of him and how he had knelt before her while she sat spread on the bed and kissed her while she held his head until she climaxed. Then she thought of Jimmy Lee and his thrumming fingers. Two men, both exciting, and the remembrance of her acceptance of them was rousing her again.

She wouldn't let Jimmy Lee touch her again. That was over and done with. But Gary was different. She lay on her back staring upwards. He was the type she went for; big, dependable, not particularly exciting on the surface, but reassuring. But she was sure there was more to Gary and she intended to find out what it was. He seemed too good to be true, boringly good. She liked big, blond men. The only two other men had been big and fair and, come to think of it, boringly good as well. The one in Switzerland, her ski instructor, whom even at eighteen she had been grown-up enough to realise was no more than a small fling and a way of losing her virginity: for a ski instructor he had been very dull and solemn, but she felt herself to be ordinary and felt more comfortable with men who were ordinary too.

The big red-headed boy in Scotland whom she had met secretly – knowing her father would have a fit if he realised she was involved with a crofter's son – had been kind and loving too. Not at all suitable, of course, though that arrangement had gone on for nearly three years.

Poppy had always had the fun and the freedom. Perhaps it wasn't such a bad idea to take a leaf out of Poppy's book and do a little throwing of caps over windmills herself.

And, with the thought, she leaned to nibble gently at Gary's earlobe to wake him. She felt like being made love to again.

≈ 8 ≈

MONDAY

Jade woke at six thirty in the morning, alone in her bed, and for a few seconds uncertain where she was. There was a heavy smell of wine. Then she remembered. She and Gary had eaten in the room, drunk a bottle of Côte de Rhone and then gone back to bed. Cautiously she reached out for him, but he was not there. Sometime in the night while she slept he must have returned to his own room in the hotel.

The remains of their meal were still in the room, unattractive on the large trolley, and she remembered he had put the 'do not disturb' notice on the door when they had gone back to bed. She lay there thinking that she would push the trolley into the corridor when she got up. The scent of the heavy wine was faintly unpleasant so early in the morning.

If it were half-past six it must be ten thirty at night at home in

Scotland. Her grandfather would not have gone to bed. She decided to call him and picked up the telephone, giving the number to the operator. Then she lay back on her pillows, still drowsy, the receiver at her ear. The call went through remarkably quickly and as usual Mary, the housekeeper, answered. Mary would never go to bed until Ian McKenzie McKenzie had settled down for the night and she said immediately that no, he had not gone to bed, he was in the library.

Jade waited, and in seconds she heard her grandfather's voice wavering over the miles. There was a faint echo on the line.

'Jade?' he said. 'And are you well?'

'I'm fine, Grandfather.'

'And Poppy?'

'She's fine too. How's Mother?'

She heard her grandfather's sigh. 'No better. No change.'

There was a silence while Jade accepted the fact.

'And you, Grandfather?' she asked.

'I'm well.' His voice was brusque. 'But what's happening there?'

'Well . . . She hesitated, not sure how much to tell him. 'It's very beautiful –' he grunted '– a friend of Mother's called me yesterday but I can't remember his name. He said Father pinched Mother from him—'

'Must be Michael Blake.'

'That's it. Do you know him? I'm having dinner with him tonight.'

The old man chuckled.

'Be sure he gives you a good one. It'll be on his expenses.'

'Who is he?'

'A protégé of mine. He works for McKenzie McKenzie. He'll explain. He's all right. Now, what have you been doing?'

'We went to the orphanage in Fanling.' She waited for a reaction but none came. 'It was derelict. Poppy remembered it and was upset. Miss Tibbets has gone. I want to find her.'

'What for?'

'Well, maybe she knows something about us.'

'She won't,' he said positively.

'And, Grandfather – do you know someone called Dorothy Adamson?'

'Indeed.'

'She's dead. She was murdered. About the same time as Father was killed. Isn't that extraordinary?'

The silence was so long that for a minute Jade thought they had been cut off.

'Hello,' she said tentatively.

'I'm still here. Poor wee Dottie. Who killed her then?' He sounded sad and tired.

'Someone with broken scissors.'

This time she was waiting for a reaction but none came.

'A very common weapon in Hong Kong,' he said, his voice totally expressionless. 'And what else have you done?'

She could hardly have explained the most positive things that she and Poppy had been doing, so she said: 'Sightseeing. We've met some interesting people, but you were right, Grandfather. It is a culture shock for me. Poppy's taking it much better.'

He snorted. 'Well, you would go. Now listen, mind what Michael Blake tells you. And if you need anything go to him. I'm glad that he's got in touch with you.'

'Did you tell him to, Grandfather?'

'I did not. But it's no bad thing that he found you. How did he?'

'I don't know. I think there must have been something in the newspapers. Other people have found us.'

'Who?' His voice was sharp, almost anxious.

'Only tradespeople. No one else.'

He grunted. 'Will you ring me again in a few days?'

'Yes, if you want.' She paused. 'We are all right, Grandfather. I'm glad I came.'

He grunted again and she could see him in her mind's eye; standing, holding the telephone. his back straight. He never sat to speak on the phone.

'We'll hope the end of it doesn't bring tears,' he said. 'Watch yourselves, now, and mind Poppy. Don't let her get into mischief.'

Too late, she thought, remembering she had not seen Poppy for longer than a day now, but she said dutifully: 'Of course, Grandfather.'

'Well, I'm away to my bed,' he told her. 'And mind yourself too,' he added gruffly.

Gently she put down the phone and lay back staring at the ceiling, wishing she had asked him if it was true he had been a pirate and who Dottie Anderson had been in their lives. But she was fairly sure she would have received no answers. The sense of being immersed in a mystery struck her again. She felt as if she were performing a ritual dance that someone she did not know had choreographed for her – a dance she had been persuaded into performing and that would go on willy-nilly until the finale. Briefly she felt afraid and wondered if it would be a good idea to ring Poppy for company. But then she remembered that Poppy was off with Kwan Ching, and that even had she been back at the hotel she, Jade, would have been given no thanks for calling at a quarter to seven in the morning.

It was also too early to ring Gary Smith. In any case, she would be shy and a little embarrassed to do so and she was still uneasy about his role in events. Best to bury the sudden attack of loneliness in sleep. She would sleep until nine, and then, using the map which was still in her handbag, ring the seven or so people who had been in her father's address book, the missing address book.

Who had it, she wondered, and why?

She only slept fitfully and at eight thirty hauled herself out of bed. She pushed the trolley which was irking her into the corridor and rang for her breakfast. She bathed, washed and blow-dried her hair, and, still in her Paisley patterned silk dressing gown settled down by the telephone, the map she had so meticulously – and fortuitously – marked on the bed beside her.

The number that intrigued her the most was that of a Peter Leigh who lived at somewhere on the other side of the island, called Stanley. She dialled the number and heard the phone ringing out. After a few moments a crisply English voice said: 'Hallo.'

'Could I speak to Mr Peter Leigh?' she asked.

There was a silence and then the voice said: 'Who wants him?'

'Mr Leigh doesn't know me,' Jade said. 'My name is Jade McKenzie McKenzie Martin.'

'One of the daughters?' the woman said almost rudely.

'That's right. May I ask who is speaking?'

'I'm Fiona Leigh. I was married to Peter.'

Was? Jade thought, but said: 'I'm sorry . . . is he not there?'

'My husband is dead.'

'Oh!' Jade felt a sense of shock. 'I'm so sorry . . .'

'What did you want him for?' The woman's voice was hostile.

'Well, you see my father was killed by a hit-and-run driver just a week or two ago and I found his Hong Kong address book,' Jade said. 'Your husband's name was in it. I thought I should inform

135

him, and I wondered if perhaps he would have been able to tell me something of my . . .'

'When exactly did you say your father was killed?' Fiona Leigh interrupted.

'Well, actually it was on 7 January.'

Jade heard the woman's intake of breath.

'I think we'd better meet,' she said, her voice reluctant.

Stephen Norris was having a bad morning. He was at his desk at the Wanchai Police Station, dealing with the usual mass of paperwork that cluttered his job and fretting as to whether or not the other European officers were less friendly than usual. If the ICAC were investigating him, he would be ostracised in case it was catching. Yet everyone seemed to be much the same as usual for a Monday morning just before Chinese New Year – somewhat hung-over and irritable at the pressure of work. Perhaps any off-handedness he sensed was merely in his mind.

His confidence in the day was not improved when Emma rang.

'I'm at the flat. I've been to those two restaurants of yours,' she said abruptly.

He looked at his watch. It was nine forty-five. 'So early?' he said.

'I wanted to catch them before they got too busy.'

'And?'

'I went through the whole bit about paying your accounts up to date, but they wouldn't take any money. They said you didn't owe anything. But they were – well, odd. I think someone has got at them.'

He felt his stomach plummet.

'What did you say?'

'I decided to leave it. If I'd tried to explain, it might just have made things worse. So I let it go.'

He could feel himself sweating gently; the light short-sleeved cotton shirt he was wearing was clinging to the back of his neck and his armpits.

'Were they friendly?'

'Not very.'

'Fuck!' he said. 'Now what?'

'I don't know. But I'll think of something. Don't worry.'

'Don't worry!' he said. 'That's a bloody stupid thing to say!'

'Not really,' she said, her voice cool. 'There's no point in

136

worrying and, besides, it's probably all a false alarm. Kwan Ching could be winding you up. And nothing's the end of the world.'

'Sometimes your common-sense assessments of every situation get me down,' he told her, almost shouting down the phone.

He was staring gloomily out of the fly-specked window into the scruffy street outside when the telephone rang again. He turned back to his desk and picked it up.

'Inspector Stephen Norris,' he said.

'Steve? It's Kwan. Can you come over to my place?'

More trouble, he thought, and said cautiously: 'Yes, Kwan. Where is your place and why?' He was conscious that his voice was sour.

'I can't tell you why until you get here, but it's up on the Peak.'

'Kwan, I can't just leave here and come swanning up to the Peak. I'm at work on duty.'

There was a stretched silence.

'Call it insurance,' Kwan said finally.

Stephen groaned.

'Fuck it, Kwan, I'll *need* insurance if I'm missing from here for too long.'

'Take down the address.' The Chinese man's voice was suddenly cold and authoritative and Stephen found himself reaching for a pen and paper. 'I'll expect you here in twenty minutes.'

What the fuck does he want, Steve was asking himself as the taxi he found bucketed through to Central and then began to climb. His instincts told him that it was not going to be good news, and the conviction grew that it was Kwan who had shopped him to the ICAC – if indeed they were investigating him. As he paid the fare and went into the building he had a very positive sense of being manipulated and he didn't like it.

A houseboy let him into a flat so opulent it bordered on the vulgar and led him through to a large, white-carpeted sitting room with red lacquered walls and black lacquer furniture.

There was no one there, and the houseboy left, muttering that someone would be with him in a moment. Almost instantly he heard the door open again and Kwan came into the room. He was wearing a black silk dressing gown with a red dragon embroidered on the back and Stephen noticed how broad the man's shoulders were for his height. The thought went through his head that Kwan

Ching was a tough little bugger and no doubt a handy man to have around in a fight.

'Ah,' Kwan said. 'Good morning. I'm glad you could make it.'

Stephen gave him a resentful glare and asked: 'What's it all about?'

Kwan sat himself in a red satin-covered chair and crossed one leg over the other so that a short but powerful leg showed through the kimono.

'Nothing very much. I want you to take Poppy McKenzie McKenzie back to her hotel for me.'

'Can't she get herself back to the hotel?'

Kwan stroked his own knee.

'It's unfortunate,' he said, 'but she has the heroin habit and I'm afraid I over-indulged her. It might be a problem for me, a Chinese, to take her back. And she is not well enough to go alone.'

Stephen stared at him.

'She's a junkie?'

Kwan nodded.

'And you indulged her?' His voice was sarcastic.

Kwan nodded again and Stephen was silent. It didn't make sense. Wealthy Chinese did not use heroin. Hong Kong might have the worst addiction problem of anywhere in the world, but it was a coolie or a *foki*'s habit; strictly for the peasants. He bet his bottom dollar that if Kwan Ching had been indulging the girl, he'd got the stuff specially, hadn't taken any himself, and had some other purpose in mind. Not seduction, he decided; the McKenzie McKenzie kid would have been anybody's, that was obvious.

'How ill is she?' he asked.

'Pretty bad.'

'How much has she had?'

Kwan shrugged his shoulders. 'God knows. But I want her out of here.'

'Why pick on me?'

'You're the only European I can ask. And besides, with a policeman, she'll be quite safe.' His voice was grave, but Stephen could hear the mockery beneath. He was used to the nuances of the Chinese when dealing with the *gweilo*. There was nearly always mockery underneath. Kwan had walked across to a lacquer cabinet, engraved with gold tigers. He opened a drawer and took out a small packet.

138

'I think you had better give her this,' he said, 'otherwise she may be in a bad way in a few hours time. It's Chinese white. Good grade. She mainlines the stuff. The syringe is in her handbag.'

Stephen was working out what to do. He had no desire to get involved and he was pretty sure that the frozen-faced little bastard standing in front of him had some good reason for getting him involved, but on the other hand he felt he couldn't leave the girl here. He wasn't one for chivalrous gestures in the normal, way, but Kwan Ching gave him the creeps.

'Where is she?' he asked abruptly. He had deliberately not taken the packet.

'In the bedroom. I'll take you to her.'

They walked in silence out of the big living room and down a passageway lined with paintings of the immortals. Kwan opened a panelled door and behind was a bedroom that repeated the red, black and white theme of the living room. Lying on her side on the bed was the girl. She was wearing a *cheong-sam* under a red Chinese wedding coat, and her long black hair hung tangled down her back and partly over her face. Her eyes were shut; there was a basin on the floor by the bed and the room smelt sourly of vomit.

'Time to go,' Kwan said loudly. 'Stephen is going to take you home.'

'Dressed like that? At this hour!' Stephen said.

'I think she looks very beautiful,' Kwan said.

'Arrange a taxi,' Stephen said, looking at the girl who had not moved.

'I was going to send you in my car with the chauffeur,' Kwan said.

'Thanks, but no,' Stephen was suddenly authoritative, aware that in a taxi he was his own master. 'I'd rather take a cab.'

'As you wish.' Kwan shrugged and left the room.

'Come on, Poppy,' he said gently, pushing the basin away with his feet and trying to shut his nostrils against the smell. He gently lifted her to a sitting position and tried to pull her to her feet. 'Like the man said, it's time to go.'

She opened her dilated eyes and looked at him vacantly. With his help, she got off the bed and he moved her slowly towards the door. It was like pulling an automated doll along. 'Gently does it,' he told her.

There was no sign of Kwan Ching. It was the houseboy who

accompanied them down in the lift and into a waiting taxi. And before the door closed, the boy leaned into the cab and put the white packet on Poppy's lap.

'Plesent for you,' he said straightfaced, and Stephen swiftly picked it up and put it in his pocket as the boy gave instructions to the driver.

As they pulled away from the big block of flats, and when he was sure that the houseboy was back inside, he spoke quickly to the driver in Cantonese. They did not want the Mandarin after all, he said. He gave the man his home address in Causeway Bay, quietly sweating as he did so that Emma would still be there.

He had decided that he could not walk into the Mandarin with Poppy in her present state, that it would be unforgivable to let the other one, Jade, see her sister like this; also he wanted time to think. He stole a look at Poppy where she sat next to him. She was deathly white under the ivory skin, catatonic. He guessed she'd injected fairly recently, and she looked on the verge of an overdose to him.

He found himself shocked by her condition. In Hong Kong the sight of a junkie was not unusual. From the safety of a police car he had seen hundreds of emaciated men in ragged clothes collapsed in doorways in the Walled City, all of them caught in the same desperate trap as the girl sitting next to him. He had seen Hong Kong's rehabilitation camps for men so far gone on heroin that they looked like survivors of the German concentration camps. But he had never seen a beautiful and rich girl who had the habit, not in Hong Kong, though he knew addiction was common among the rich in the West. The sight troubled him. He thought back to the night at the Furama. He would never have guessed, never in a million years.

To his relief Emma had not left when he rang the bell of their apartment. 'I've got a problem,' he said over the intercom. 'Are you alone?'

'Yes,' her distorted voice came back. 'What is it?'

'Just hang on,' he said. 'You'll see.'

He had no trouble getting Poppy into the lift and up to the flat. She moved where she was led, a beautiful doll robot in expensive clothes. As the lift gates slid back, Emma was coming down the corridor towards them. She saw Poppy, took in the evening clothes and then, as she came nearer, the girl's face and eyes.

'Oh, my God!' Her hand went to cover her mouth.

'Let's get her inside,' he said.

Poppy was a deathly pale green, her pupils were enormous and she was moving very slowly. Emma had taken her other arm, and together they led her into the comfortable sitting room of the flat.

'Lay her on the sofa,' Emma said, and between them they sat the girl down, Stephen lifting her legs once her head was on a cushion.

'Is it an overdose?' Emma asked.

'I don't know. She doesn't look as far gone as the OD's they bring into the station. Kwan said she has the habit, mainlines and he over-indulged her.'

'Kwan!'

Stephen looked at her uneasily.

'Yes, he rang me to come and get her from his flat.'

She made an angry little exclamation.

'Sometimes for a policeman you're not very bright,' she said. 'What do you do with an OD in the station?' she was looking at Poppy who seemed to be breathing very shallowly.

'We lie them down, on their sides so they can't swallow their tongues and choke themselves, and then we send for a doctor.'

'Then we'd better send . . .' Emma was already turning Poppy on to her side and rearranging the pillow under her head.

'I don't know that that's a good idea,' Stephen said. He could not think how he would explain the situation to any reputable doctor.

'Why not?'

'Well, I'm going to have to implicate Kwan or how else can I explain how she got into that sort of state? And there's this . . .'

He took the white packet from his pocket.

'What is it?' Emma asked, her voice deeply suspicious.

'Heroin. For when she needs it again. He said she'd be in a bad way.'

'You are a *fool*!' Emma said, snatching the packet from him. 'Has any of it spilt in your pocket? Shake your jacket out of the window. Get rid of it.'

While he was taking his jacket off and opening the window he heard her determined footsteps march to the bathroom and then the sound of the lavatory cistern running. She'd got rid of the stuff, perhaps wisely, he thought, though what they'd do if the girl freaked out without it . . . He was standing staring at Poppy when she came back.

'Kwan's really cornered you, hasn't he?' she said tartly. 'I wonder what for? Is this girl going to die on us?'

'I don't think so,' he said. 'I told you, she isn't as bad as they often are.'

'And we can't call a doctor.' She bit her lip. 'What do we do? Get her back to her sister?'

'She might die if we moved her too much,' he said doubtfully.

'Will she sleep it off?'

'Sometimes they do. But I expect she'll be pretty rough when she wakes up.'

Emma gave a sigh that expelled every bit of air from her lungs.

'We'd better let her sleep then. I'll stay here with her. You go back to the station and see if you can find out discreetly if there's something positive we ought to be doing. Then as soon as I can I'll get her back to the Mandarin. From now on you stay out of it.'

The relief of unloading the problem on to Emma was so great he knew he was leaving the flat with unseemly haste. Emma was right, he was a fool, he thought gloomily as he waited for the lift. But he never would have acted so stupidly if Kwan hadn't given him the tip about the ICAC. That had unnerved him. And if the girl did die on Emma's blue shantung silk sofa, then they'd be investigating him all right. His own mates would be investigating him. He was sweating again as he hurried into the crowded street working out which of the station sergeants would be the safest to ask exactly what the doctors did for a heroin addict.

And his mind full of the pale and pretty girl who had lain so still once they stretched her out, he began to feel enormous guilt that he had not called a doctor.

Emma went to the kitchen to make herself a cup of coffee once the door had closed behind Stephen. Poppy McKenzie McKenzie Martin was sleeping, her pulse alarmingly slow, the pallor still pronounced, but she was at least resting and breathing, if precariously.

The coffee in her hand, Emma sat herself in the chair opposite the sofa to keep watch and to wait until Stephen phoned, hopefully with some instructions. It would all take about twenty minutes to half an hour before she heard, she thought, hoping that the girl would survive that long.

While Emma sat, her mind rearranged the things she had intended to do today. Mentally she worked out the phone calls she must make later and the appointments that would have to be changed. The business would survive without her for one day, and today it was going to have to, she decided, wondering how she was going to get Stephen out of the mess he seemed to have landed himself in. One thing was certain. She had to get Poppy back to the hotel in one piece, behaving reasonably normally and with neither Stephen nor her involved. It might not be easy.

He still hadn't phoned twenty-five minutes later, but Poppy seemed to be improving. Her chest was making some small movement and she seemed to be breathing more normally. Emma went over to the sofa and took the girl's hand. It was clammy, but not so deathly cold as it had been.

'How do you feel, Poppy?' she asked very distinctly, her voice deliberately hard.

The girl's smooth eyelids fluttered.

'Away . . . away . . .' she said. 'It's all gone away.'

'Would you like some coffee?'

'Umm . . .'

Coffee couldn't hurt. She hoped it couldn't hurt. She went to get her cup and half lifted Poppy's head so that the girl could take a sip or two. She drank and then slid back down with her head on the pillow.

'I feel sick,' she said plaintively but distinctly.

'Do you want to be sick?' Did being sick help if the stuff was in the blood stream?

'Yes—'

Emma tore to the kitchen for a bowl, and was back only just in time. The girl was retching violently but it seemed she must have been sick before. Her stomach appeared to be empty. She instantly fell back asleep. Looking at her, Emma decided things were improving a little. It would be better if Stephen did not have to go around the station asking how to deal with a heroin case. She went to the phone and quickly dialled the Wanchai number, asking to be put through to him. He sounded like a man in need of a good stiff drink when he answered.

'Thank God,' he said. 'I thought it was going to be Kwan Ching.'

'Well, it's not. It's me. You can relax. I think she's a bit better. She's just been sick and she's sleeping more normally. I think we should just leave things as they are and I'll get it sorted out. Ok?'

'Are you sure?'

'Certain. Stop worrying about it. I'll cope from now.'

She didn't think he would argue, but without giving him time to do so, she hung up. She might as well wash her hair, as she had a strong feeling it was going to take a while before she would be able to get Poppy back to the Mandarin.

Fiona Leigh had said to come to lunch, so when Gary Smith called, Jade had to explain that she would be unable to see him.

'I have a dinner date too,' she said. 'It's a friend of my mother's – a man called Michael Blake.'

'Who's he?' Gary asked, sounding disgruntled.

'I don't know. He works for McKenzie McKenzie.'

'Doing what?'

'I don't know. I'll tell you tomorrow – if we can meet tomorrow.'

'Can I book you for lunch *and* dinner?'

She laughed. 'Unless something better turns up.'

'Like who? Jimmy Lee?'

'Jimmy Lee's not better than you,' she said, meaning it.

'Right,' he said. 'But I'll talk to you again today sometime.'

She put down the phone feeling unaccountably happy. It still troubled her that he had followed her so far, for no believable reason, but her suspicions were at war with attraction. It wouldn't be difficult to fall in love with Gary Smith and perhaps he was halfway to being in love with her. If, of course, there was not an ulterior motive for his wooing of her. But would a man be able to make love with such tender finesse, she wondered, if he meant a woman harm? And she tried to convince herself that he could not.

It pleased her that he seemed so genuinely uninterested in her race. Even Jimmy Lee, the one Chinese she had encountered, seemed more concerned to prove that she was Asiatic than accepting her as the person she was. She had always chosen lovers in the past who seemed indifferent to the fact that she was unusual. Thinking about it on the taxi ride to Stanley it suddenly occurred to her that maybe neither of them had had the imagination even to notice.

She arrived at Mrs Leigh's just before one o'clock. The house was a terracotta refugee from the Côte D'Azure, where two alsatians barked madly from behind big wrought-iron gates. A Chinese woman in black trousers and tunic hurried out, shushing them away before unbolting the gate and letting Jade through.

Jade followed her to where her hostess was waiting, standing on a mirrored verandah that reflected Jade, the garden and the view as she walked up the gravelled path.

Mrs Leigh was not a young woman; maybe early sixties. She had hazel eyes with signs of grief around them. Her bony face, beaky nose and short springy grey hair all sat on the body of a much younger woman.

'Do come in,' she said, turning into the house while Jade followed her into an open hallway and into a drawing room on the right. 'Drink?'

'Vodka tonic, if you have it please.'

Mrs Leigh nodded, clapped her hands and the Chinese woman glided back. There was a clattering exchange of Cantonese and when the maid nodded and left the room Mrs Leigh settled herself on the big Chesterfield opposite the chair that Jade had selected.

'I am so sorry to hear about your father,' she said formally.

'And I your husband,' Jade said and paused before asking, her voice hushed: 'What happened?'

'He was sailing and the yacht exploded. They said it was the gas bottle in the kitchen. The craft went down immediately and we never saw him or any of the crew again.'

'How dreadful,' Jade said.

'But the extraordinary thing is,' Fiona Leigh went on, her voice hesitant. 'that it happened on 7 January.' She paused to allow Jade to take in the significance of what she had said.

'The same day as my father,' Jade said quietly.

'Yes. And there was another. A woman—'

'You mean Dorothy Adamson,' Jade interrupted.

'Yes.'

'Was that on the seventh as well?'

'Yes.'

The two women stared at each other in silence. Neither spoke while their drinks appeared and were served. Then when they were alone again Jade said: 'I'm very confused. Tell me, how did your husband know my father?'

'They had business dealings. My husband was a ship designer. He designed several ships for McKenzie McKenzie and for other ship owners as well.'

Jade nodded. 'Was one of them the *Brian Leigh*?' she asked, convinced the answer would be yes.

'It was. Named after our son,' Mrs Leigh said and added sharply: 'Why do you ask about the *Brian Leigh*? That wasn't designed for your grandfather.'

'Because,' Jade said slowly, 'I think the ship must have something to do with whatever is happening. You see, when my father died I was given a packet of his papers.' She was opening the zip compartment of her large handbag. 'Including these,' she said, holding out the photocopies of the clippings concerning the *Brian Leigh*. Quite deliberately Mrs Leigh let the papers hang spare in Jade's hand, making no move to take them. It was as if she knew very well what they said, and her face showed momentary displeasure and perturbation.

'It's all such a long time ago,' she said. 'I don't remember it very well. Peter was anxious, of course, when the *Brian Leigh* enquiry was going on, but that was just professional concern that one of his ships could disappear like that. They did think it might be a design fault. Of course, it wasn't. Peter was brilliant. And disappearances are not uncommon in the South China Seas. There are so many reefs and in a small boat like a schooner it's hard to take a reading when the seas are high . . .' She seemed to be talking to herself. Then interrupting her own monologue, she said abruptly: 'I've had lunch served in the garden. Is that all right?'

'Lovely,' Jade said. She knew there were more questions she should be asking but the atmosphere was not right and she sat sipping her drink thoughtfully.

'Why are you here?' Mrs Leigh asked, almost as an accusation.

'Originally I just wanted to find out about my background,' Jade said slowly. 'I'd hardly thought about being Chinese until my father died and then I decided I ought to see where my real roots were. That was the only reason for coming here, but since then all these odd and frightening things have happened. I had just thought my father's death was an accident. But now I'm not sure. Three people to die on the same day who all knew each other? It can't be a coincidence, can it?'

'I wouldn't have thought so,' Mrs Leigh said quietly. 'I wouldn't have thought so at all.' She rose to her feet, tall and stately. 'Please come through now.'

Following the squared shoulders and straight back down the length of the drawing room to where French windows opened on to a pretty patio, Jade had the sense of having lost Mrs Leigh. She was convinced that the woman was regretting having made the invitation. She made slightly too much fuss about settling Jade at the round table covered with a white damask tablecloth. A lychee tree's bright green leaves gave shade, and once they were seated, Mrs Leigh made elaborate explanations about who did the cooking and where the meal – a simple one of cold meats and salad – had come from. There was a bottle of good white wine and Mrs Leigh talked on inconsequentially about life in Hong Kong and asked politely after the health of Jade's grandfather and her mother, though it appeared Mrs Leigh had never met Margaret McKenzie McKenzie.

Jade tried some tentative questions about life in the 1950s but Mrs Leigh was vague about her early days in Hong Kong, though she admitted she had lived in the colony since then. With no encouragement to real conversation, Jade found herself making equally superficial remarks and suffering considerable frustration. They talked about the sunny sheltered garden where old-fashioned English flowers bloomed in spite of the lateness of the year. 'So difficult in this climate,' Mrs Leigh sighed, and the meal dragged on.

They were eating a dessert of ice-cream when Mrs Leigh said: 'You mentioned other papers. What were they?'

'About a group of Chinese being murdered, but with no explanation as to why.'

'How extraordinary,' Mrs Leigh murmured, and this time she did seem surprised.

When coffee was served, Jade's patience was wearing thin.

'Mrs Leigh,' she said as she very deliberately stirred cream into her cup, 'I intend to find out what has been going on here and to learn if there was some reason for my father's death. To put it bluntly, I think he was murdered, and if he was, I want to know why and by whom.'

Mrs Leigh sat motionless, the white parting in her hair distinct as she looked down at the table. A bird that Jade could not identify chattered in the tree that shaded their meal. When the bird quietened, the garden was very still.

'Mrs Leigh,' Jade persisted. 'Don't you feel the same way?'

The woman sighed and lifted her head, and the narrow hazel eyes were glistening moist.

'The answer is no,' she said.

'You don't care?'

There was the faint breath of another sigh and Mrs Leigh said: 'My dear, you are very young. How can I explain to you? My husband had a long and distinguished career in this place. If he, your father and poor Dottie Adamson were all murdered . . .'

'Dottie Adamson *was* murdered. That is a fact.'

'Indeed, but if they were murdered it must be for some reason, and I am not sure that I want to know what that reason was. I loved my husband very much. We were married for nearly forty years and we had three children who grew up to give us great pleasure and happiness. I have always considered that we were an ordinary family who had had great good fortune. If there was something in his life which he did not wish me to know at the time, he would not wish me to know it now. So the answer to your question, Miss McKenzie McKenzie, is that I do care. Of course I care. I miss him more than I can say and every day without him seems to become longer rather than shorter. But I want him left in peace and I want to be left to mourn my dead. I should not have asked you to come here. It was a mistake. And when you have finished your coffee I am going to ask you to leave.'

'Oh!' Jade found that tears were beginning in her own eyes and she was not sure if it was the woman's dignity as she stated her case or whether the rejection had wounded her.

'I'm sorry to be unkind,' Fiona Leigh said gently. 'And you must do what you wish, but maybe you will come to the same conclusion that it is better if they are *all* left in peace.'

'You know something,' Jade said accusingly.

'No. I promise you. I know nothing. But if I did, I would not tell you. And now I am going to ask my chauffeur to take you back to your hotel. Our meeting was a mistake.'

Her voice held a note of finality which Jade could do nothing but accept. She put her napkin on the table and rose to her feet. Her coffee cup was not empty but Mrs Leigh was standing, totally in control, and there seemed nothing else to do. She was deeply embarrassed at the direction the conversation had taken, but a conviction lingered that Fiona Leigh had been the one to garner information while she, Jade, had learned nothing more than that the *Brian Leigh* had been designed by Peter Leigh and that Peter Leigh had died on the same day as her father.

Fiona Leigh said carefully correct goodbyes at the door, and stood on the verandah until the big Mercedes, driven by a young

Chinese, went down the drive to the gates which were open and ready for Jade's departure. As the car swept through, the Chinese woman almost ran from where she had been standing out of view to lock them again. And then the front door of the big white house shut. It seemed to Jade that it closed on secrets.

Suddenly it dawned on her that under the iron control Fiona Leigh had been afraid.

It was half-past one. Emma had made herself a small snack, her hair had dried, and she sat in a big chair in her living room watching Poppy while she slept.

The ashtray was full of cigarette stubs, and now she needed a drink. She got up to pour herself a vodka tonic and sat again, looking thoughtfully at her charge.

It was time she unloaded the problem. Poppy had tried again to be sick and was now resting more normally. If people who took drug overdoses in suicide attempts had to be kept moving, maybe it would be no bad thing to get the girl on her feet, but she would have to dress her in something more in keeping with the time of the day before they left the flat for the Mandarin.

She lifted the lightweight travelling rug that had been covering the girl and smiled at the *cheong-sam* and the wedding coat. She had seen it happen before with Western-born Chinese who came to the Colony – a desperate plunge into the Oriental. Sometimes it lasted; sometimes the confusion between the Western way of life and that of the East sent them scuttling back home in their jeans and tee-shirts.

'Poppy,' she said loudly.

The girl's dark eyes flickered open.

'Time to get up, Poppy.'

This time the eyes opened and Poppy stared up bewildered and licked her dry lips.

'It's Emma, isn't it?' she said, her voice faint.

'That's right.'

'What am I doing here?'

'We brought you here from Kwan Ching's. You were –' Emma hesitated '– very sick.'

Poppy shut her eyes again and then opened them.

'I don't remember anything,' she said. 'Not since . . .' She turned her head abruptly to the side. 'Oh, God!' she said. 'He hurt me.'

'Who did? Kwan Ching?'

149

'Yes. I felt sick. He burnt me.'

'*Burnt* you!'

'Yes. With cigarettes. But I didn't remember him doing it. He gave me some stuff. I thought it was coke. I don't think it was.' Her voice trailed away, tired.

Emma sat on the edge of the sofa and gently began to pull the other girl into a sitting position.

'Where did he burn you?'

'My body—'

Emma carefully began to remove the wedding coat; the white silk *cheong-sam* beneath was crumpled, and she saw that the front of it was covered with small yellowish marks.

'Can you sit up properly?' she asked.

'I'll try,' Poppy said. 'I feel so sick . . .'

'I want to get this dress off,' Emma said. 'But I can't do it unless you cooperate.'

Poppy did not speak, but struggled to sit upright, halfheartedly wretching, and then to half stand, swaying on her feet as Emma tried to pull the *cheong-sam* over her head. When she started to move the fabric over the girl's belly, Poppy cried out, a little sound; more a whimper.

'Oh, please . . .' she said.

She had indeed been burned, and the blisters, raw and red, had wept and stuck to the silk. Taking off the dress would be very painful.

'Wait a minute,' Emma said. 'Try to keep sitting up if you can.'

She hurried to the kitchen for a china bowl which she filled with warm water. From the bathroom she took some antiseptic which she poured into the water and found a sponge. Then she returned to the living room where Poppy was still sitting upright, dazed, on the sofa.

'This may hurt a little bit,' Emma warned and slowly she damped the silk of the dress in little dabs of warm water until it loosened away from Poppy's hurt flesh. Slowly she rolled the dress back, wincing at the sight of the burns in the sparse pubic hair, and on the smooth flat stomach. The breasts were the worst. They were a mass of bleeding blisters, and Emma gritted her teeth with anger as gradually she was able to free them from the silk, gently bathing all the while.

'Did Kwan Ching do this to you?'

'I suppose so,' Poppy said dully. 'I don't remember. He did all sorts of things . . .'

The dress was off, and Emma flung it on to the floor. Poppy had fallen back and lay quite naked on the couch, her slight, delicate body horrifically scarred. Now Emma could see the marks of the needle – eight distinct injections with a small bruise surrounding each one. They had not been done gently. But, she noted, there were no old scars.

'Poppy,' she said abruptly. 'Do you use heroin?'

'No,' Poppy said. 'Is that what he gave me?' She sounded as if it didn't matter. 'I've sometimes snorted coke, but nothing more.' Her eyes were closed and her voice so weary that Emma decided the girl hadn't the energy to tell a lie.

'Umm!' She decided to say no more for the moment, and contemplated what to do about the burns. There were far too many to cover with any kind of plaster. They ought to be bandaged, but there was no bandage in the flat. The only thing to do was to dress her in something clean and loose, preferably cotton, Emma decided, mentally going through her wardrobe for a garment that would be suitable.

In the end, she found a long tee-shirt dress which she normally wore to the beach. It had a high round neck, short sleeves and hung loose. It shouldn't cause any pain.

'I'm going to take you back to the hotel., Poppy,' she finally said gently, 'so that Jade can look after you.'

Poppy made a stronger attempt to sit up.

'No, please don't,' she said. 'I don't want her to see me like this. She'll only say it was my own fault. And I don't think I can make it. I feel terrible.' She looked terrible. Her teeth were beginning to chatter, and she was groaning quietly, clutching at her stomach.

Emma chewed at a fingernail. It seemed inhuman to make her move, but she had to go. Stephen couldn't take the responsibility and that was what might happen if they kept her in the flat. What the hell was Kwan Ching up to? she wondered. The girl should really go to the police and make a complaint but in a sense she had been to the police and Stephen had done nothing about it. And if the story got out of an assault on a McKenzie McKenzie girl, the Colony would be agog. All in all, for everyone's sake, it would be better if Poppy McKenzie McKenzie Martin put

151

what had happened down to experience and was more careful who she went out with in future, Emma decided.

She rang down for a taxi and firmly made a grumbling Poppy get to her feet and move towards the door. Eventually the girl, still groaning quietly, came uncomplainingly. She seemed to have lost all will. Emma had no idea how long it would take to hook someone on heroin but those eight injection marks meant that Poppy had had a lot, and recently. If she *was* hooked, she was in for a bad time, particularly as her fix had gone down the lavatory.

'Just don't let Jade see me,' Poppy said.

Both the hall porter and the taxi driver gave them curious looks, but she ignored them as she half-pushed Poppy into the back seat of the cab and told the driver to take them to the Mandarin.

'What's your room number?' she asked.

'Seven eighteen,' Poppy said. She had small beads of sweat on her upper lip, and her head was back on the seat, her eyes closed. 'I've got the most terrible pains,' she whined. 'I think I want to be sick.'

'Try not to be. We'll get a doctor soon,' Emma said soothingly, her mind racing as to how she could explain why she was with Poppy if she did call one.

In the event there were no explanations needed. Jade was not in the hotel and nothing ruffled the hotel staff, who calmly handed over the room key. Once in the bedroom, Emma helped Poppy back into bed and sat beside her. She was a strange green colour, and she seemed to twitch as she lay. 'Please don't leave me,' she said. With a sort of despair, Emma realised that she could not possibly go. It would be too cruel. She took Poppy's small hand in hers and held it tightly.

'Try to sleep if you can,' she said. She was still petrified that Poppy might die.

She herself dozed a little, and she had been in the room about twenty minutes when the telephone rang. She answered it cautiously and a Chinese voice announced that the Reverend Paul So was in the lobby to see Miss McKenzie McKenzie Martin. Emma was instantly alert. A priest? Perhaps someone to pass the problem to. She desperately needed to involve someone else and made an instant decision to take a chance on Paul So. It might be disastrous, but there weren't that many choices.

'Send him up,' she said.

It took exactly three minutes from putting down the phone before there was a quiet knock on the room door. Unconsciously she had timed the arrival, while worrying if she had done the right thing or not. It was not in her nature to be unkind or to abandon someone who needed help. Her normal reaction would have been to take Poppy to a hospital, make sure that Kwan Ching received his just deserts for what he had done to the girl, and generally organise what looked like chaos into order. But she had Stephen to think about, and whether he had acted foolishly or not she loved him and he was important to her. She knew he was not as strong as she, but his weaknesses made him all the more appealing to her. She needed someone to use her strength for.

She opened the room door. The man standing outside, his hat in his hand, a smile on his face, was attractive, she thought in the split second before his face dropped and quickly recovered.

'I'm sorry,' he said in Cantonese, hiding his disappointment. 'I was looking for Poppy McKenzie McKenzie Martin.'

He cares about her, Emma thought, but said: 'She's here.' Then abruptly: 'Are you a friend of hers?'

'Well, I would like to think so,' the man said quietly.

'She badly needs a friend,' Emma said. 'Come in.'

He hesitated.

'Is there a problem?' he asked.

'You might say that,' Emma said, knowing she sounded panicky.

Paul So followed her down to the small lobby and into the bedroom. Poppy had fallen back asleep and was faintly snoring.

'My God. What happened? Is she sick?' he asked, staring at the bed and then to look back at Emma, his whole face a question-mark.

Emma hesitated and then made what might be a dangerous decision. She liked the look of Paul So. His face was gentle, and there was something about even the way he stood that made him appear protective. His expression looking at Poppy showed deep concern and real dismay.

'She's been very badly treated,' Emma said rapidly. 'A man called – well, it doesn't matter – took her out. He's filled her with heroin and he's burnt her all over. She's in a bad way. She ought to be in hospital, or with a doctor, but how do you explain that Miss

McKenzie McKenzie Martin has got herself into that kind of mess?' She stopped and asked abruptly: 'Do you know how quickly it takes to get hooked? She's acting like someone with withdrawal symptoms.'

'No,' he said. He was still looking at Poppy's face on the pillow. 'A Western man?'

'No. I'm afraid not. We can't blame the *gweilo*.' She moved towards the bed. 'Look—' she pulled back the sheet so that just the top of Poppy's scarred breasts showed. 'She's like that all over. And look—' she pointed at the arm with the eight puncture marks which lay above the bedclothes. 'You see. She said she doesn't take it. And I believe her.'

'Does her sister know?'

He was involving himself, she thought thankfully.

'Her sister isn't in. She's more anxious than anything that her sister shouldn't see her like this.'

He nodded slowly.

'I can imagine that. I think I understand why.' He too moved towards the bed and tenderly stroked Poppy's forehead. Her eyes flickered open and she looked straight up at him.

'I thought you'd turn up sometime,' she said quite distinctly and smiled.

He sat on the bed and took her hand.

'So what are we going to do?' he asked, and turned to look at Emma, his dark eyes questioning. 'And who are you and where do you come into all this?'

Paul So was not a man to lie to.

'I met her at a dinner party. The man who did all this to her has some sort of hold over my man. We were landed with the problem. And I didn't know what to do. Going to the police and asking for help would have been bad for us and bad for her. It can only be a scandal, Reverend. You know who she is.'

He nodded, thought for a moment and then said: 'I think I will take her back to my home in Fanling. My mother will look after her, and there we can call a doctor so that she is properly treated. There will be no difficulty with the doctor. He will accept the situation on its face value.'

'You don't think she'll die?' Emma asked anxiously.

'No. I don't think so. I would imagine that the man you tell me about would stop short of killing her. Now she just needs care and love.'

Emma let her breath escape and realised she had been holding it.

'If I were a *gweilo* I'd say you were a miracle,' she said.

He laughed.

'The Lord works in mysterious ways,' he said. 'Miracles can come in all shapes and sizes. But they are not miracles, they are the work of the Lord. Perhaps I was sent.'

'Yes, well maybe,' she said, faintly embarrassed. 'What shall we do about the sister?'

He pursed his lips.

'Maybe a lie is in order,' he suggested. 'I shall tell her that Poppy has come back to Fanling at my invitation to visit my family, leave my telephone number and ask her to ring me. Or is she in the hotel?'

'She wasn't when we came in.'

'Good. Now if you will just get Poppy dressed then perhaps we could put some of her things together and be off without delay. I have my car outside.'

'Of course,' Emma said, grateful he asked no more questions about her own involvement. Grave-faced but with a harsh indrawing of breath when he saw Poppy's burned body, he helped to lift the girl while Emma dressed her in a loose cotton frock she found hanging in the cupboard, and then he packed toothbrush and toilet things from the bathroom while Emma sorted out underwear and clothing.

Eventually he wrote a note to leave with the desk for Jade and then they left, each holding one of Poppy's arms.

Once she was in the car he turned to Emma and said: 'Perhaps it would be better if you forgot where Poppy has gone. Would it help? Would it be better if you just said you took her back to the Mandarin and left? That would end your involvement.'

'I think it would help,' Emma said quietly.

'Then why don't you do that?' he said. 'And stop worrying. She'll be perfectly safe now.'

'I know,' Emma said, gratefully. 'And thank you.'

The note from Paul So did not surprise Jade; she read it with a sense of resignation and disappointment. She had hoped that perhaps Poppy would be a companion in Hong Kong, but nothing changed. When they had been small, Poppy had always left her to play with some other more interesting and lively child; once grown up, she would be off if a man crooked his little finger. She had seen that

155

Poppy was attracted to Paul So, and what Poppy wanted, Poppy got.

So she pushed the message to the bottom of her handbag and forgot about it.

She was cheered to find her bedroom full of flowers from Gary Smith and a note that said: 'Tomorrow is far too far off. Be good.' She held the card tightly in her hand and smiled around the room at the roses, the orchids and the small pot of *kumquats*. She couldn't help feeling elated in spite of all the anxieties.

She showered leisurely, thinking about Fiona Leigh, and then wearing her white towelling robe, settled on the bed with the map which she now kept with her all the time. Which one should she ring next? Stanley had been far away. Perhaps this time someone nearer. One of her red crosses on the spread-out street map was against a street to the west of the Mandarin called Bonham Strand, the name in her neat handwriting, Kim Ting, and beside it the telephone number, which she gave to the hotel operator.

Mr Ting answered sounding young and surprised, but agreed she could come and see him when she explained that what she had to say was too complicated for the telephone.

She hastily pulled on jeans, a sweater and some sandals and hurried down. She was in a taxi in five minutes and on her way. The part of Hong Kong they quickly arrived at was completely different from anywhere else she had been. The streets were steep and narrow with lanes going off in all directions, and each tiny shop seemed to house an artisan of some kind. The area was busy with people making ropes in the open air, cutting keys and cobbling shoes. Old men walked, ignoring the heavy traffic, carrying birds in cages, and the taxi eased its way past open-fronted grain shops, snake restaurants and tea houses where the caged birds sang.

Bonham Strand was a street of old four-storey tumbledown buildings with ornate balconies and carved balustrades, more Chinese than anything Jade had seen before. The address was in an old block of white-painted flats which were in better condition than most of the property.

Kim Ting had said the fourth floor, and she walked up the stone steps to his front door. It opened before she could push the bell.

'I'm Jade McKenzie McKenzie Martin,' she said, catching his quickly hidden look of surprise that she was Chinese.

'Come in,' the young man said. 'I heard the footsteps on the stairs and guessed it was you.'

He had a fat baby perched on his hip and a two-year-old peered round the jamb of the door. Jade couldn't decide if it were a boy or a girl.

'My sons,' the young man said proudly. 'Tu here is the baby. That's brother Joey on the stairs. Come in. I'm sorry it was such a long climb.'

She muttered that it didn't matter and followed him into the flat.

'I'm sorry my wife isn't here, but she speaks no English so perhaps it's as well,' he said. 'I work at the court and I'd just got home when you called. She's gone out to do some shopping.'

The room that he led her into looked down over the teeming streets of Western. It was large and comfortable with heavy, dark pieces of furniture and several deep sofas. It smelt spicy, as if joss sticks had been burned there.

'Do sit down,' he said. 'Would you like tea? Or would you prefer a coffee?'

'I really don't want anything,' she said.

'A brandy?' he suggested.

'No thank you. I'm fine.'

There was an awkward silence. Joey was clinging to his father's leg and staring at Jade with unabashed curiosity. Kim Ting kept his hand on the child's hand.

'Well?' he prompted. 'What can I do for you?'

She explained about his name being in the address book and her father's death.

'Sir Ralph was your father?' Kim Ting said. 'In that case I'm afraid you don't want me. You want my father, and he is no longer with us.'

'You mean he's dead?' she said stupidly.

'Yes.' The voice was patient.

'When?'

'*When*?'

'Yes. Exactly when.' She put emphasis on the word exactly.

'Just over a year ago now. On 7th January.'

Jade was silent until he said: 'Is anything wrong?'

'Well, yes, there is really,' Jade said. 'Can you tell me how your father and mine knew each other?'

'My father was his court translator.'

157

Jade began to laugh with a touch of hysteria.

'Then you should be my brother,' she said.

'I don't understand.' His voice was cold and cautious.

Jade hesitated. It was difficult to know what to say. 'You see, as you must realise my sister and I were adopted,' she said slowly. 'My parents told us that we were the children of father's translator, and that he and his wife had been killed in a car crash.'

Kim Ting nodded without speaking.

'But obviously we weren't your father's children. And it was only when my father was killed this month that I found out we were both refugee children taken from an orphanage.'

'And that worries you?'

'No, not that. Not at all.' As economically as possible, she explained the series of 7th January deaths, ending: 'It's too much of a coincidence, isn't it?'

His round face was very grave, and he rubbed his rather broad nose with his finger thoughtfully.

'It is indeed a coincidence,' he agreed.

Trying to keep the story as uncomplicated as possible, she told him about the papers she had been left and the story of the *Brian Leigh*.

Kim was shaking his head.

'I have never heard of the *Brian Leigh*,' he said. 'And I don't see how my father could have been involved at all.'

'If he was the translator on the enquiry?'

'They wouldn't have had a translator. With no jury the proceedings would have taken place in English. You have to understand it's a ridiculous system here. Though ninety-nine per cent of the population are Chinese-speaking, all court cases are conducted in English. If you were to find yourself in court, even speaking the perfect English that you do, because you are Chinese, the judge and the counsels would have their own interpreter who would solemnly tell you everything that had been said, translating it into Cantonese or Mandarin.'

'A fat lot of good that would be,' Jade said. 'I wouldn't understand a word.'

He grinned.

'Well, maybe they'd make an exception in your case. But even if counsel, the judge and the accused are all Chinese-speaking, proceedings are still in English, with the translator telling the

158

accused what's going on, and translating his replies.'

'So,' Jade said slowly, 'in cases where people didn't speak English, that would give the translator a great deal of power.'

'Well, I suppose so, if he wanted to use it,' Kim said defensively. 'I'm a translator myself. Followed in my father's footsteps as the *gweilo* say, but we don't do that. We have a very close relationship with the judge we work for. Attitudes are a little different than in Britain, and a good British judge knows how to bend the rules to allow for differences in Oriental thinking. My judge, if he just wants to frighten the hell out of an offender, will tell me to give him "homily number three" which I solemnly deliver in Cantonese. They rely on us a lot.'

The small boy was whispering urgently in his father's ear.

'Back in a minute,' Kim Ting said. 'Hold the baby, will you?'

He was gone for a minute or two, and Jade sat looking down at the face of the sleeping child on her lap. I must have looked like that, she thought, and she decided that it wasn't a bad way to look at all.

'So,' he said when he came back into the room. 'What do you want to do about it all?'

'I don't know,' she said. 'I think I ought to warn the other people in the book.'

'Well,' he said, straight-faced, 'if your 7th January theory is correct they're safe for another year. Perhaps you should find out if something originally happened on a 7th January.'

She stared at him.

'Of course,' she said. 'That's it. I'm an idiot.' She was fumbling in her handbag for the photocopies of the newspaper cuttings. 'Just look at this,' she said when she had found the right one.

He took it from her and started to read out loud. '*Today in the High Court Yu Tai Cheung, twenty-nine, and Kwan Ming Shing, thirty, both unemployed seamen, were committed to trial for the murder of Wan Yu, a stevedore, on 7 January 1959* . . . 'He stopped. 'I see,' he said.

'Read on,' she told him.

He read the rest silently and then said: 'They killed the whole family. It'll be something to do with the Triads.'

This was a new thought and one which she seized upon.

'The Triads? They're gangsters aren't they?'

'Like the Mafia, only Oriental. Sometimes they're very small criminal groups. Sometimes they're rich and powerful. These sound like very small fry, but revenge is a great part of their code.'

'Maybe your father and mine were at their trial. Maybe they sentenced them to death.'

'Maybe,' he said doubtfully, 'but where does the *Brian Leigh* come in?'

'Heaven knows,' Jade said.

He got up from his chair and walked across the room and picked up the baby from Jade's lap.

'You know,' he said reflectively, 'I think your Mrs Leigh is right. Best to leave it. Has it never occurred to you you could be in danger yourself? And your sister.'

His words alarmed Jade. Was Poppy really with Paul So or had she disappeared?

'Whatever you do,' he said solemnly, 'I think you should be very careful.'

'If something bad did happen to your father, don't you want to do something about it?' she asked.

'We Chinese do not like to disturb our ancestors,' he said gravely.

She sighed and shook her head.

'I'd better go,' she said, helpless in the face of their differences.

'Are you sure you won't take some tea before you leave?' It was a polite formality, and she almost smiled thinking that this was the second time in one day she had been sent off with a flea in her ear.

'No, thank you,' she said, equally polite, 'but it's kind of you to offer.'

He was edging her towards the door.

'Even small-fry Triads are dangerous,' he said. 'Please be careful.'

'Of course,' Jade murmured.

'You may have trouble getting a taxi, but the streets are quite safe. Indeed this is a most interesting area of Hong Kong to explore. There are many things to buy.'

He was suddenly speaking to her as if she were a Westerner. He had retreated and she felt a keen sense of disappointment. She shook his hand quickly.

'Goodbye,' she said. 'Please don't come down.' She bent and

said: 'Goodbye, Joey,' to the child, and gently stroked the baby's cheek. Then she turned and ran down the stairs.

Michael Blake knotted his striped silk tie with care and swore. It had still turned itself around the wrong way underneath.

'I reckon,' he said to his wife, 'that I could tie a tie better when I was fifteen than I can at fifty.'

'You could do a lot of things better then,' she said spitefully.

He sighed. There didn't seem any point in answering her.

'What time will you be back?' she said. 'If you're late I'll have gone to bed. Don't disturb me. You'd better sleep in the other room.'

'Yes, I'd better, hadn't I?' he said absently. He had managed to make the tie behave and he slipped on the dark jacket of his suit over his white shirt, shot his cuffs a little and regarded himself critically in the mirror. He didn't look at all bad. The suit, made by Mr Ahmin Cheung, one of Hong Kong's better tailors, fitted him perfectly. His heavy-rimmed glasses suited him, and his thick, prematurely grey hair, no doubt caused by the miseries of twenty-five years of marriage to Beryl, was neatly combed. He looked what he was: successful, but with the small anxious face of a man who had spent a lifetime trying to keep the peace.

'You'd better go,' Beryl said. She had been changing into a long black dressing gown, dragon embroidered. Michael sometimes thought that if he ever saw another dragon he'd go on a rampage. Since she had been in Hong Kong his wife had become obsessed with them. She had dragon-based lamps, dragon upholstery, dragon dressing gowns and brooches. It was a pity a real-life dragon didn't come along and make a bonfire of the lot with one puff of his fiery breath, he thought fancifully. But Beryl interrupted his musings on the ubiquitous dragon as she always interrupted his musings.

'I must say you never take me to the Mandarin,' she said.

He looked at her surprised.

'Would you like to go?'

'Not particularly. But you never even offer.'

'I'll offer in future, dear,' he said cheerfully.

He felt better. The prospect of a night away from the television and Beryl swathed in dragons was one to savour, particularly as there was every chance that the McKenzie McKenzie Martin girls might be attractive. The thought of two pretty girls over dinner lifted his spirits, had him whistling and slapping on extra after-shave on his high forehead. He liked women. He lusted after women, though he had to admit that all those he had known had caused him pain. It was his bad luck he had married such a cold and unkind one. But he had never even contemplated divorce – other people got divorced. Not Michael Blake. Beryl, awful as she had become, was his responsibility.

He was escaping out of the front door while she headed, predictably, towards the living room and the 24-inch television set. He'd had the forethought to bring her home a box of chocolates, and he didn't doubt that she'd spend part of the evening on the phone nattering to her equally unlovable girl-friends. But for tonight he was free.

He drove his old Bentley to the Mandarin, chucked the keys at the doorman, and walked rapidly across the lobby, his heels making purposeful noises on the marble floors.

He asked the desk to ring Miss McKenzie McKenzie Martin and tell her of his arrival, and said that he would wait in the bar. He had a taste for a gin and tonic and a mental picture of himself presented itself: debonair, suave, lounging, watching the girls, sipping his gin, clinking the ice and revelling in a bit of night life and the change from the interminable home routine.

Jade MMM, as he thought of her, arrived commendably quickly, but alone. He had forgotten that she would be Asiatic, and when the small girl at his elbow touched him gently and said: 'Mr Blake?' he looked down at her, startled.

She was very small, her face smooth; the skin like gossamer, ivory gossamer, he thought romantically. Her mouth was like a red butterfly, and her little pointed chin turned enquiringly while she waited for his answer. He could have kissed it. Her eyes with their flat lids might have been painted on, so perfect did they appear to him, and when she realised that he was indeed Mr Blake, the butterfly opened into a smile that made him think of a quite different part of her body.

And he began to sneeze – a long series of small, sharp sneezes, like a cat.

'Are you all right, Mr Blake?' She sounded genuinely concerned.

'Hayfever,' he managed.

162

'Poor you,' she said, as he listened in wonder to the soft, immaculate English voice.

He was groping desperately for his handkerchief, afraid he'd forgotten to bring one, but it was there in his pocket, and he blew his nose firmly.

'Sorry about that,' he said briskly. 'What will you have?'

'A vodka tonic, I think.'

'Of course,' he said, and ordered with what he hoped was a nonchalant wave, but one that nearly sent his own gin and tonic flying.

'Where's your sister?' he asked, guiding her to a table by taking her elbow, a courtesy that sent shivers through him and nearly started the sneezing again.

'At Fanling,' she told him as she sat, smoothing the pleated skirt of her white dress over her knees.

'What's she doing there?' he asked.

Jade seemed to hesitate and said uncertainly: 'She's with the family of a man called Paul So. He's a Baptist minister.'

'A Chinese?' Michael said, conscious he was sounding disapproving.

'Yes, but a very nice man.'

Her voice was defensive, and he could have kicked himself. After all, she was Chinese.

'I see,' he said, and then added, 'No, I don't see. What's it all about?' He was remembering Ian McKenzie McKenzie's strictures to keep an eye on the two girls. He offered her a cigarette, which she refused and he lit one for himself.

'I really don't know.' She started to tell him the story of her visit to Fanling and finding the orphanage, but his mind was more on the movements of her beautiful mouth than what she was saying. 'I could tell he liked her and she liked him, so I suppose they've just got together,' she said lamely.

'You don't sound too sure about it.'

'To tell you the truth, I've never been too sure about anything when it comes to my sister,' she said, laughed and then looked surprised at herself for having told him. But he was used to people surprising themselves by telling him things that they hadn't meant to.

They made the usual sort of conversation that clears the minefield when two strangers meet with a long evening ahead of them and, their drinks finished, he led her to the Pierrot restaurant on the twenty-fifth floor. The night-time view was spectacular, but he cursed himself quietly for picking the place as they walked into the elegant room. The windows were long, nearly to the ground, and he had no head at all for heights.

'Which would you prefer?' he asked, praying she'd give the right answer. 'To look at the view or the people?'

'Oh, the view, please,' she said without hesitation, and he felt the sweat that had started under his armpits at the thought of staring out into nothing for the next two hours vanish. He wasn't too happy knowing the void was behind him, but of the two alternatives . . .

Once they had ordered from the French menu, she leaned her elbows on the table, looked at him with what he would have described as a beguiling expression and said:

'Did you know my father?'

'Not well,' he said cautiously. 'I knew your mother better. Just as a friend, of course,' he said hastily, 'though I was crazy about her.'

'But she's a lot older than you.'

He felt absurdly pleased she had noticed.

'Well, I suppose so. Not a lot. And in those days she was such a –' he searched for the word ' – such a girl. So gay, in the old-fashioned sense before they ruined the meaning. Merry, I suppose one would say today. She was ageless and I adored her.'

'Did she love you?' Jade's voice was sympathetic.

'Not a bit,' he said truthfully. 'She just thought I was a boy, which I suppose I was. But she had an extraordinary quality of creating devotion. Your father would have done anything in the world for her. So would your grandfather. Come to that, so would I. But she never asked me,' he said with a rueful grin. 'Anyway, it's all far too long ago.' He didn't add that Ian McKenzie McKenzie had been furious when they didn't marry and that the old man had had him, Mike, earmarked as a son-in-law.

'She's very different now,' Jade said.

He wanted to say he didn't care to hear about it, but he wasn't supposed to know, so he said casually: 'In what way?'

'She's senile. Really senile.'

It wasn't hard to look shocked. He still could not comprehend it.

'Can nothing be done?'

'Nothing. We were in Los Angeles trying a new cure – which wasn't working – when father was killed. He was knocked down by a hit-and-run driver and died instantly.'

'That's terrible.'

'Yes,' she said. 'It was on 7th January.' She was looking at him as if she had said something very significant.

'7th January,' he repeated. It seemed somehow to be expected of him.

She looked him straight in the eye.

'Did you know Dorothy Adamson?'

'Indeed.'

'Well, she too died on 7th January.'

'It was the seventh, was it?'

'Yes. And someone you might have known called Peter Leigh died on 7th January too. And so did my father's translator, Kim Ting, only it was last year.'

'Good heavens!' Mike found himself feeling genuine alarm.

'They were all in my father's address book. There aren't that many names. Only seven. Do you think I ought to warn the others?'

'What about?' He was stalling for time, needing to think.

'That they might die, too.' Her voice had dropped and she suddenly sounded very young and a little melodramatic. He wanted to tell her he wasn't concerned about the other names in the address book, only about her.

Her voice lowered so he had the pleasure of leaning nearer to her. She told him the story of her two encounters of the day, and he listened gravely, his anxieties growing.

'Do you think it might be something to do with the Triads?' she asked when the narrative had finished. 'That's what Kim thought.'

'Perhaps,' he said cautiously. 'I hadn't realised that Peter and Dottie went on the same day. And anyway, the Peter thing seemed to be an accident. I suppose they didn't try to cover it up with Dottie.'

'You see,' she said triumphantly. 'You think there's something, too. Who was the Dottie woman?'

'Well, she was brought up with your grandfather for a while. He was very fond of her.'

'Why was that?'

'Well—' he hesitated, wondering how much he should tell her.

'Your great-grandfather was a lieutenant in the army out here at the turn of the century. Apparently his wife was very beautiful, very silly and very extravagant. In the end he couldn't pay his mess bills and he shot himself. His wife went into shock, apparently went off her head as well and was sent home to England. Dottie Adamson was the daughter of a sort of missionary lady who had married a Chinese – quite unheard of in those days – and she was hired to look after your grandfather until the mother came back. He was only a little boy, of course. Anyway, the mother never came back and your grandfather never went back to Scotland to join her.'

She was listening agog, her fork poised to her mouth, the piece of lamb on it cooling.

'Go on,' she said.

'There's not much more to tell. Dottie and your grandfather were brought up as brother and sister. She was a year or two younger than him, and adored him.'

'Umm,' she put her food in her mouth and chewed thoughtfully.

'Do you know anything about the *Brian Leigh*?'

'Not a lot. Though I should. I'm a Lloyd's agent.'

'What's that?' she asked. 'I thought you worked for Grandad.'

'I do. I place his insurance for him with different underwriters. Lloyd's agents never do the work as a full-time job.'

'Do what exactly?' she asked.

'Well, when a ship is lost, or thrown away . . .'

'Thrown away?'

'Scuttled. Do you know what that means?'

'Of course.'

'Well, when a ship is scuttled or there is some mystery about its disappearance, or where the cargo has been stolen, the Lloyd's agent has to nose around, acting a bit like a detective and trying to find out if the sinking, the accident or the loss is genuine or if it is a shipping or an insurance fraud. You have to know a lot of shady characters.'

'Like the ones who did the murders?'

'Yes, like those.'

'Did you know them?'

'No. I wasn't an agent in 1959.'

'But you know about the *Brian Leigh*?'

'I've heard a little about it in shipping circles because it was such an odd story what with the Shackleton going missing as well.'

'If you'd been a Lloyd's agent then, what would you have thought had happened to it?'

He considered.

'At a guess, I'd say it was something to do with the ballast. At that time they often used gravel for ballast, particularly in small craft like the *Brian Leigh*. How big was she? Do you remember?'

'Five hundred tons,' Jade said.

'Big for a schooner, but still a small ship. The trouble with using gravel is that if the hold or the ballast tanks aren't absolutely full, it shifts. It also gets wet, with what we call a slurry of water on top which makes it even heavier. If the *Brian Leigh* had gravel on board and there wasn't enough of it and she hit some heavy seas, the ballast could have slid, pulling her under. It's only a theory. If you're using anything that shifts as cargo or ballast it has to be supported. For example, the holds of grain ships are divided with steel walls so that the grain can't shift and make the ship nose heavy – to put it in landlubber terms,' he said, smiling.

'So if that was the case, there was nothing particularly mysterious about her disappearance?'

'No. About ten ships a year disappear on average around the world. Usually only about three of them have been thrown away. The rest are fortuities.'

'Fortuities?'

'Natural causes, acts of God, something straightforward.'

She was nodding, interested in what he was saying, and he was enjoying imparting information. He'd have to watch he didn't get carried away.

'Supposing she had been thrown away, though. What would be the reason?'

'Only for the insurance on the hull. She carried no cargo as I recall.'

'No.' Jade was shaking her head and the thick hair swung like a curtain. 'It was her maiden voyage.'

'Then there wouldn't have been any point in sinking her. I seem to remember your father decided it was an act of God at the time – or what we'd call a fortuity.'

'How could I find out more about it?'

He puffed and shook his head.

'It was a long time ago. I could ask if you could look at the bound volumes of the period at the *South China Morning Post*. The editor's a mate of mine.'

Her face brightened.

'That would be interesting. Do you think he'd let me?'

'I expect so. If I came along with you.'

'Would you?'

'Pleasure,' he said, picking up his wine glass and sipping to avoid showing just how much of a pleasure it would be.

She was biting her perfect lip.

'When could we go?'

'Tomorrow morning?'

'Super! Can you get off work?'

'No problem,' he told her.

She gave a little sigh of pleasure and then said: 'Where do you work? Will it be a nuisance?'

He laughed. 'I work in the McKenzie McKenzie building,' he said. 'It's in Central. You can see it from the ferry. It's that green marble-looking one, but it's only eighteen storeys so it's due to come down soon. Much too small and old for Hong Kong.'

'Is that Grandfather's?' she asked, her voice astonished.

'Of course.'

'My goodness!' she said. 'He never even mentioned it. But then, he didn't want us to come.'

She wanted to talk more about her mother and her grandfather as they had been in the early days, and he answered her questions, but all the while his mind was nagging over the information she had given him. Something was seriously wrong. Ian had been his mentor, almost his father, since he'd arrived as a green little insurance clerk from Nottingham all those years before. He had caught the old man's eye and promotion had come rapidly. He knew Ian had been up to mischief in the distant past, but he didn't want to know the details. Never had. He himself had been a director of McKenzie McKenzie for twenty years and the place was straight, he'd swear it. But there were sometimes rumblings and grumblings of a more buccaneering past.

And he was finding conversation difficult. On the one hand, this faultless girl, intelligent, listening, wide-eyed and stunningly beautiful, was engaging his mind in erotic fantasies. At the same time he was trying to assess a potentially difficult and dangerous situation which might mean peril for her. There had to be peril for someone with all those people getting themselves knocked off all over the place, he thought.

His overactive imagination saw her stretched, broken, naked, her long hair tangled, her mouth open in pain and death, victim of a Triad assassination. He visualised another more pleasing scene, when he arrived just in time to save her from the broken scissors, from rape, disfigurement, death. And the gratitude that made her fall into his arms.

His mind seemed to be dashing about on three levels, because his voice was saying: 'I wish I could tell you something about yourself as a baby, but I rarely saw your mother after she married Ralph Martin. I couldn't bear to, and I got married rather quickly myself.'

'And has it been happy?' she asked, her eyes shining across the table.

'Oh, not too bad,' he said. 'Just like any other marriage, I suppose. Do you have a young man?'

Her eyelids dropped and she said shyly: 'Well, there is an American. Can you imagine? He followed me here.'

Oh, my dear, he was thinking, of course he followed you here. Any man with any balls would follow you to the ends of the earth. But he said jocularly: 'Well, I don't blame him.'

'I met him in Aspen.' She was confiding, he realised, and felt older. 'Then he went to Scotland and we'd left, so he followed on here.'

Bells were ringing in his head.

'He must be rich as well as in love?' he suggested.

'His father is a solicitor in Tennessee,' she said.

'And what does he do?'

'Well, he sells private jets.'

'And how old is he?'

'Thirtyish.'

'What a lucky young man.' He was conscious of his voice being sour, but quite apart from the disappointment of learning there was someone younger, richer and much more suitable, it didn't sound right.

'Did you know him for long in Aspen?' he asked, busy with buttering a piece of bread.

'Just a day. But he'd been following me from the time we left Los Angeles.' Her voice held a defensive note, as if she too knew it didn't wholly ring true.

Mike was beginning to feel distinctly alarmed. Beautiful she was, but in all the circumstances his intelligence, no longer dwelling on fantasies, was informing him that something was wrong.

'I'd like to meet this young man,' he said. 'Just to make sure he's good enough for you.' He was doing his best to sound like an uncle.

She laughed.

'I don't see why not,' she said. 'I'll be having lunch with him tomorrow. You can have a drink before with us or something when we get back from the newspaper.'

'I might do that. Where are you meeting him?'

'In the Captain's Bar, I expect. He's staying here.'

'And what's his name?'

'Gary Smith.' She spoke his boring name in a way that made it special, and he felt regret for lost youth, lost loves, so many things. But practicalities came before pangs.

'Would you excuse me for just a minute?' he asked.

'Of course.'

He put his napkin on the table and got to his feet, trying not to think of the long window and the big drop behind him. He muttered 'excuse me' again, and hoping that she would assume that he was going to the gents, he headed for the nearest telephone, where he dialled on Hong Kong's freephone system while he lit a cigarette.

Sounding like home, it *burred*, just three times, and was answered.

'*Wai!*' a voice said.

'Is Mr Watson-King at home?' he asked.

'Waitee minute,' a strangled Chinese voice said, and the receiver went down.

'Hello, who is speaking?' The old Etonian tones of Arthur Watson-King came over loud and clear.

'Arthur,' he said. 'Mike Blake. How are you?'

'Fine. And you?'

'Fine. How's the security business?'

'Booming. We bought two new armoured trucks this week, but it's bloody near impossible to get honest staff. That armed robbery the other day was one of ours. Did you read about it?'

'No, I missed that. Rotten luck. How much went?'

'Not too bad. Only 100,000 Hong Kong dollars. Could have been worse. Anyway, what can I do for you?'

'Bit of guidance, old boy,' Mike said; he always found himself playing the old-school-tie role with Arthur. 'I've got to meet a chap tomorrow who wants to borrow money. Seems to be in some sort of security business himself. Could you check him out?'

'Who is he?'

'Gary Smith. American. Comes from Tennessee. Thirtyish. Been here a couple of days. Staying at the Mandarin.'

Arthur Watson-King grunted.

'Roger!' he said. 'I've got to get the old bod moving Hong Kong side tomorrow. Where do you want to meet?'

'Bull and Bear?'

'Done. What time?'

'About one thirty would suit me.'

'Good God! You want service, don't you? All right. See you then.'

The phone call had taken just a little longer than he meant it to, and leaving the telephone booth full of smoke he hurried back to the table. Jade had put fresh lipstick on while he had been away, he noted. As he sat down he was careful not to push his chair too far back towards the window.

'Sorry about that,' he said.

'Doesn't matter,' she said cheerfully, and then: 'Was Grandfather a pirate?'

'Good heavens!' She certainly knew how to bowl them. 'Where did you hear that?'

'Two people have mentioned it. Someone called Jimmy Lee, and Gary had heard it too.'

'It's one of those legends that grow up around the kind of character that your grandfather is. I've heard it myself, but I think it's a figment of people's imagination. Remember, I'm nearly thirty years younger than him so I wasn't around at the time, and I'm only a fairly humble employee. I don't know that much about the family history. Anyway, who is Jimmy Lee?'

'A Chinese man I know. He owns a fur company. Green Butterfly Furs. He's rather nice.'

There was a crease between her brow that he would have liked to have reached out and smoothed, as if the idea of Jimmy Lee, whom he filed away with Green Butterflies, troubled her. Instead he lit a cigarette and called for the bill. She had declined a pudding and was finishing her coffee.

'Would you like to do anything else? Go to a nightclub or something?' he asked.

'No thank you,' she said politely. 'To be truthful, I'm not mad about nightclubs.' Then, not letting up: 'Who would know if Grandfather had been a pirate?'

'Why, is it important?'

'I don't know,' she said, still frowning. 'I suppose it might be.'

He was busy with his credit cards; not looking at her, he said: 'Not many left who were around then, I'm afraid, my dear. Why don't you ask your grandfather?'

'I think I might,' she said. 'Do you think he'd mind?'

'Not if you asked,' he said. 'I might get a dusty answer if I did.' Let the old boy sort that one out for himself, he thought.

She declined a brandy, pleaded ready for bed, and he dropped her off at her floor, promising to collect her in the morning; then he hurried home. He wanted to get to a telephone. The old bugger had said to call any time. He'd take him at his word.

This time he used the telephone in the room he had made into an office in his apartment. Beryl had gone to bed, not even bothering to leave the hall light on, but he wasn't too displeased. His head was still full of pictures of Jade. Beryl would only mar them.

He dialled one of the numbers that Ian McKenzie McKenzie had given him, working out that it was three in the afternoon and the old man would probably be at his desk. Someone, possibly a secretary, gave the news that Mr McKenzie McKenzie was not in.

'Is he at his home?' Mike asked.

There was an almost imperceptible hesitation and then the voice said cautiously that he might be.

Mike hung up and rung the other number. It seemed to ring for a very long time, and then, surprisingly, Ian McKenzie McKenzie answered it himself.

'Ian? It's Mike.'

'Hallo, Mike.' The voice sounded very tired. 'You don't bring more bad news I trust?'

'Not good, but not terrible. Why, What's happened?'

'Mary's dead. You remember Mary. My housekeeper.'

'I remember her well.' Mary, as he recalled, would only be in her late sixties. 'What happened?'

'A letter bomb, addressed to me. She opened it. She always

opened the mail. It arrived this Saturday, postmarked Los Angeles; sent parcel mail.'

Mike whistled.

'Are you all right?'

'Shaken, but Ok.' He was silent and Mike asked:

'It wasn't posted on 7th January by any chance, was it?'

'As a matter of fact it was. How did you know?'

Mike groaned.

'I had dinner with your Jade tonight. Pretty girl.' He couldn't resist saying it even in the middle of all this carnage. 'She's very bright. Dottie's dead.'

'I know.' Ian's voice was heavy. 'She told me that when she told me she was meeting you.'

'So is Peter Leigh.' He heard a distinct moan. 'And so is Kim Ting. They all died on 7th January.'

'But Kim's been dead over a year.'

'Yes, but it was the seventh.'

'Jesus Christ!'

'Jade has an address book. It was Ralph's. All their names and addresses were in it, and there are more. Can't you get her back home, Ian. She's nosing around. She's curious about the *Brian Leigh*, I don't know what's happening but I suspect she'll get herself killed – or worse,' he added gloomily.

There was a long silence as the phone gently crackled.

'I'm coming out there.'

'Don't be bloody silly,' Mike said, his voice alarmed. 'There's no point in putting yourself in the firing line of whatever's going on. What *is* going on, Ian?'

'Revenge, of course.'

'Revenge for what?'

'Too complicated.' The old man's voice was decisive again. 'But who? That's the question. It's a hell of a long time ago. I want to get there; sort it out.'

'For Christ's sake, Ian. I don't want to be brutal, but you've got to be nearly eighty. Leave it alone.'

The snort that came clear over the line from Scotland made Mike quickly take the phone away from his ear.

'What's that got to do with it. It's going to take a day or two, that's the only thing. I'll have to stay here for Mary's funeral. See her decently put to rest and sort things out a bit. Then I'll be there. The place is swarming with police and reporters at the moment. Now listen, just keep an eye on those girls. Can't you get Poppy shacked up with someone? If she's kept off the streets, she at least might be safe, though with Mary dead here, and Ralph in Los Angeles, where is safe?'

'She seems to be staying with some Chinese Baptist minister out in Fanling at the moment—' Or was she? he suddenly wondered.

'A Baptist minister!' Ian's voice rang with total disbelief. 'Well, if you say so. She ought to be all right. And Jade?' His voice was gruff again.

Mike hesitated, wondering whether to mention the American.

'I'm keeping an eye on her, sir,' he said, deciding not to worry the old man any further.

'You do that, laddie,' Ian said. 'And make a good job of it. Keep in touch and I'll be there as soon as I can.'

He hung up, and Mike sat staring at the phone. The old man still played the cards close to his chest. In the room only the small desk-lamp was lit. Around him there were pools of darkness and the room itself seemed watchful. Suddenly he shivered, his imagination doing overtime again. His name wasn't in the book, and he hadn't had anything to do with the old business, but there were too many people dying.

Before he went to bed he didn't bother to put out the lights he had turned on.

$$\approx 9 \approx$$

TUESDAY

Poppy opened her eyes to a grey light that seemed to have a core of red cold on her face, and the sense that her limbs were being pulled apart one by one. She heard herself groan loudly; as she did so there was a small movement in the room and soon afterwards the feel of a cool hand on her forehead.

'There, there,' a voice said.

She groaned again, louder.

'I feel terrible,' she complained into the grey. Cautiously, as if she were made of glass, she tried to move, but she hurt everywhere, and she felt sick and queasy.

'You will feel terrible,' the man's voice said calmly. 'But you'll be better soon.'

She lay and thought about where she was, and realised that perhaps the comforting voice and cool hands belonged to Paul So.

'Paul?' she ventured.

'Yes. Could you bear a little light?'

She struggled to sit up, and he put his arms behind her shoulders and helped lift her. Once she was nearer to being upright, she could see that the red glow came from a small shrine at the end of the bed against the wall facing her. It seemed to be a figure, in a red surrounding, lit with red candles and with a pile of small oranges placed in front.

'I thought you were a Christian,' she said petulantly.

He laughed. 'You must be a little better,' he said. 'The shrine is my mother's. It can do no harm and, who knows, it might help.'

She could see his dark shape moving across the room to the window where the greyish light came in. He seemed to be opening shutters, and then more light came. still grey, but stronger.

'I'm thirsty,' she said. 'I feel ghastly.'

'I know,' he said. 'Here, drink this.'

He poured something from a pitcher that was set on a table beside the narrow bed where she lay. She could see now that he was wearing a dressing gown, not dissimilar from the one that Kwan Ching had worn, and thinking of Kwan Ching she whimpered like a sick puppy.

'What is it?' he asked, as he held a bowl to her lips to drink. She sucked at the slightly bitter liquid greedily.

'Nothing,' she said and sank back on the small hard pillow. 'What was that?'

'Something good for you,' he said. 'Something from the doctor.'

She nodded and then, staring up at the ceiling, said: 'What happened, Paul?'

'I was hoping that you would tell me that.'

She considered for a moment.

'When I feel better,' she said. Whatever he had given her to drink had been comforting and sleepy-making. 'I'll try to remember it then.'

There was sunlight in the room the next time she woke, and Paul was still there. He was sitting in a deep rattan armchair and he seemed to be reading the Bible. It looked like a Bible, small, black and leather-clad. He was wearing gold spectacles that made him look a little prissy and older. But he took them off as soon as he saw she was awake.

'How do you feel?' he asked.

'Not good. What's the matter with me?' she asked.

She did not feel good. Her body seemed to be wracked with stabbing pains and she was weak and still sick. She felt she could not remember how it was not to feel sick, and yet there had been the times when she had felt so free, floating; a bird released from the heavy earth. Remembering how marvellous that had been, thick tears pushed themselves from under her eyelids.

'Your friend gave you a great deal of heroin,' he said gravely. He was standing and looking down at her. 'Eight separate injections of it. How long were you with him?'

Her head seemed to belong to someone else, and she tried hard to concentrate on what he was asking her.

'What do you mean, how long?'

'How many hours?'

'I don't know.'

'Then when did you meet him?'

'It was – oh, God, it was—' She couldn't think. The plane journey, Fanling, everything was muddled in her mind, and the sharp cramp-like pains were making her jerk.

'Was it the same day you met me?'

She thought.

'Yes, it was. It was that night. We went to dinner and then I went back to his flat . . .'

She stopped, remembering the snort of cocaine that hadn't been cocaine and then vaguely what had happened afterwards and she began to cry.

'He did awful things to me,' she said. 'Awful sexual things. He hurt me. And I wasn't all right. I couldn't have stopped him. He'd

176

said it was cocaine, but I was sick, and after I was sick he did all the things. With bottles, and he burnt me. He kept hurting me, but I couldn't really feel it and I didn't seem to mind. It wasn't me. I was just floating and watching and then when I woke up, he did it all over again, and I don't remember anything more after that.'

Paul had gone white and tight-lipped, but he went on calculating out aloud. 'So you went out with him on Saturday night, and you left him sometime on Monday morning. Your girl friend didn't tell me when. It sounds as if you were with him for about thirty-six hours.

'What day is it today?' she asked, aghast.

'It's very early Tuesday morning,' he told her. 'It seems he was trying to turn you into an addict. But why?'

She thought about what he had said and considered her pains and aches.

'Would I feel better if I had heroin again?'

'Yes.'

'Then I want some.'

'No.'

'Why not? You're cruel, too. You don't know how it feels.'

'Listen, Poppy,' he said, and took her hand. 'It only takes twenty-four hours for someone to have a psychological dependence on heroin. It takes forty-eight hours to make them physically dependent. He could have killed you, he gave you so much, and he might have thought that the eight injections were enough as you're such a little tiny thing. But he's not going to win. You're not going to be an addict. We'll get over this bad time, and everything will be normal again, and then you must forget it.'

'Can't I have just a little bit? I want to feel good again. Float. Have the pain go away.' She made her weak voice wheedle.

'No.'

'Please.'

'No.'

'You're cruel!' she hissed, and burst into noisy sobs. 'Cruel! Cruel! Cruel!' and her fists pounded feebly on the bedclothes.

'Only to be kind,' he said sadly. 'Now, come, try to sleep. And drink this.'

'That nasty bitter stuff? I won't.'

He gave a despairing little laugh.

'Then I shall ring up Jade and tell her to come and get you.'

She brooded on that for a moment.

'Oh, all right,' she said and obediently took the cup from him.

Emma woke to find that Stephen was lying with his arm round her, pressed into her, his mouth at the nape of her neck, an urgent erection pushing between her legs. She was barely conscious when he whispered: 'Turn over.' Grunting gently, she did as she was told, aware she had not cleaned her teeth and trying to keep her breath away from him. Almost frantically, without any preliminaries he pushed her legs apart and, dropping his weight full on her, he pushed into her.

She cried out in pain.

'Steve – I'm not ready,' she protested.

'Just let me,' he said, his face buried on her shoulder. 'I need you, Emma. I need you.'

She made herself relax, and he was in, deeply, riding her violently. She was still uncomfortable; her face pressed into his shoulder, barely able to breathe while he seemed unaware of her as person or even as a body. It was one of those occasions when his lovemaking was no more than fucking. It had little to do with love, and everything to do with relief from whatever troubled him.

He was panting, his buttocks rising and falling in strong, sure movements. She wrapped her arms around him tightly so she was lifted with him, biting at the shoulder that impeded her breath.

Neither spoke, though she too was panting as he probed deeper and harder and faster. Then he was crying out as he always did at the conclusion and he collapsed on top of her, breathing hard and suddenly completely relaxed.

'Oh, it helps the tensions, Em. It helps the tensions,' he said.

'And what are the tensions?' she asked, thinking she might have a few herself today. He had left her high and dry.

But something was troubling him. He had been silent before they had gone to bed the night before, refusing to discuss his day or what she had done about Poppy. Used to his moods, she had taken little notice and sat with him while he slumped in front of the television before suggesting that they went to bed early. He had taken one of his rare sleeping pills and had been snoring ten minutes after they were under the covers. Now he rolled away from her and lay flat on his back staring at the ceiling.

'What did you do with Poppy?' he asked abruptly.

He sounded like a man asking for information that he did not want.

'Why?' she asked. 'You didn't want to know last night.'

'I'm not sure I want to know now,' he said. Then he added, still not looking at her, 'Kwan Ching says she's not at the hotel.'

'That's right,' she said calmly.

'Then where is she?'

She considered.

'I really don't know,' she said finally. 'Does Kwan Ching care where she is?'

'He seems to want her for something.'

'To pump more heroin into?'

'How the hell should I know?' His voice was not angry – more resigned.

'Well, we're not her keepers,' she said lightly. She sat up and swung her legs over the side of the bed. 'I'm going to have my bath.'

He put out a hand and gripped her arm.

'He wants to know where she is, Em,' he said.

'I told you. I don't know.' She was surprised at the strength of her determination to tell Kwan Ching nothing. A mental picture of Poppy's burnt and abused body flashed through her mind. She could still smell in her nostrils the aftermath of the girl's vomiting. She made a sudden and positive decision that she would tell Kwan Ching nothing. And if that meant telling Stephen nothing, he'd have no information from her either.

Gently she pulled her arm free. 'Tell Kwan Ching I took her back to the Mandarin, I undressed her and I put her to bed. And after that, I left. Suggest that maybe she died. Perhaps he ought to look in whichever mortuary the Mandarin use for their clients who are inconsiderate enough to die on them.'

He was sitting up, naked and hairy, his penis still not quite relaxed, but he would be no good until the evening. She would have to wait.

'I've already told him I dropped her there by taxi,' he said. 'And why did you say "that's right" when I told you Kwan Ching said she wasn't at the hotel?'

'I didn't say "that's right",' she said pertly. 'I said "is that right?" Quite different, darling. Quite different.'

She moved quickly away from him, heading for her bathroom, and slammed and locked the door behind her, deciding to make it a very leisurely bath. With luck he'd have left for work before she emerged. He could make his own coffee this morning.

Lying in the bath, moving the warm scented water with her hands to splash her body gently, she thought over the problem. The problem was what was Kwan Ching up to? What did he want with Stephen? And what did he want with Poppy? And just how dangerous would he be to cross? He was quite obviously something to do with a Triad society – but then so were most Hong Kong Chinese businessmen, and the Chinese police force, and every other ruffian on the street. She'd had her suspicions about her own father while he was alive. But there were Triads and Triads. There were those who joined for the connections – not unlike a little bit of Western Freemasonry turned bent – and those who joined with criminal intent. It seemed fairly certain that Kwan Ching was there for criminal reasons, and not doing too badly either. As she soaped herself thoughtfully and delicately, her ancestry told her to keep out of it; shop Poppy and the Reverend if necessary and not get herself into any potentially dangerous situation. Her schooling and the standards of behaviour dinned into her at the terribly British Heathfield girls school were nudging her to go to the authorities, regardless.

A compromise was the answer. She'd keep her mouth shut and shop no one. But there was one thing she would have to do.

And that was to tell Jade.

She could hear Stephen slamming about the apartment, and still she lay in her bath, enjoying the tranquillity, until eventually he banged on the door and shouted: 'Are you coming out?'

'Not yet,' she said lazily.

A baffled silence.

'I've got to go in a minute.'

'I know.'

He tried the doorhandle and found it locked.

'Emma,' he said. 'I want to talk to you. What am I to do?'

'Absolutely nothing,' she suggested.

'It's not that easy.' She only just caught the words. He had lowered his voice, and it occurred to her that maybe there were things he had not told her. And maybe, she decided, they were things she would rather not hear.

'Go to work, Stephen,' she said as if he were a schoolboy. 'We'll talk tonight.'

She could still hear him moving about while she carefully rubbed hair conditioner into her pubic hair to make it softer. She dried herself and stroked in body cream, her eyes shut to enjoy her own caressing fingers, wishing she had not let him come so quickly. She thought how ridiculous to feel merely randy when the pair of them were sliding, willy-nilly, into a plot in which they did not belong – or *she* did not belong. Maybe Stephen had elected himself a member of the cast.

After he had slammed the front door, she left a decent interval to be sure he was not coming back and then wrapped herself in a blue towelling robe and padded out of the bathroom to the phone.

Jade was not in, the hotel informed her. She gave a quick little 'tut' of annoyance. 'Then I'll leave a message, please,' she said, and tapped her fingers impatiently as she was put through to the message clerk. It was best not to say anything specific, she decided, just in case. Everything would be better left vague.

The message said: 'See you at four in the lobby this afternoon, Tuesday. Emma.'

The only problem now was whether or not Jade would turn up.

'I'm a little bit early,' Mike Blake said apologetically when Jade arrived downstairs to meet him. 'I just wondered if you'd like—' The man was sneezing again and groping desperately for a handkerchief and Jade quickly fished a Kleenex from her handbag and handed it to him.

'Gosh!' she said. 'Fancy getting hayfever so badly at this time of year.'

He blew his nose and looked around for somewhere to put the Kleenex, then, giving up, shoved it in his pocket.

'Sorry about that. It's ridiculous,' he said, taking off his glasses to wipe his eyes with his own handkerchief. He had nice brown eyes, Jade noted, and very long lashes. 'What I was about to say is that you'll be very welcome at the *South China Morning Post* – they're all excited to have a McKenzie McKenzie visit. I wondered if you'd like to go by tram. Just for fun. The newspaper is at Quarry Bay – not the prettiest part of the Island, but the tram goes all the way, clanging merrily over every inch. And you get a good look around from the top deck.'

'Sounds fun,' Jade said.

'It is rather,' he said.

She enjoyed the tram and she enjoyed his company. He had a quick sense of humour and he laughed a lot – a rather deep and chuckling kind of laugh that she found attractive. On the ride on the swaying tram, covered with brass and brassy advertisements, he pointed out some of the more bizarre names on the shingles which almost made an archway over the pavements.

'How about the Magnificent Trading Company there?' he said, making her look at a brilliantly lit sign over a tatty old building. 'And the Incredible Shoe Company. Do you fancy a pair of shoes from the Incredible Shoe Makers? One for me there – Billion Gents Tailor. Hong Kong's full of marvellous signs. The *gweilo*'s favourite though is the Thumbs Up Toilet Paper.'

'You're making it up,' she said accusingly.

'No, really. It's true.'

'Thumbs Up Toilet Paper!' she said. 'That's hilarious.'

He was still making her laugh when they went into the scruffy building near the waterfront, the home of the *South China Morning Post*. They had to pick their way over rubble, and he explained that there was more land reclamation going on at this end of the Island. Inside the unprepossessing entrance, they crowded into a small lift and he walked her through a corridor down to the newsroom.

'My mate's not in this morning,' he explained. 'But he's rung through and someone's been given instructions to help you.'

It was a surly-faced girl with a strong Australian accent who got up from a desk in the corner of the big room and came towards them.

'You must be Miss McKenzie McKenzie Martin,' she said, without waiting for a reply. 'I'm Marlene McConnell. We've got the volumes you wanted to see ready, but since you're here, I wonder if I can ask you about your grandfather. We've just received the news.'

'What about Grandfather?' Jade asked, conscious of sounding panicky and feeling Michael Blake's hand take and tighten on her arm.

'Jade—' he started to say.

'After all, he was very fortunate, wasn't he?' the girl ploughed on relentlessly. 'Why do you think they did it?'

'Did what?' Jade said, staring into the girl's pruriently eager face.

'Why don't you shut up?' Michael Blake said loudly. 'She doesn't know.'

He turned Jade so that her back was to the girl, and he looked down into her face. His hands were on her shoulders as if he were holding her together.

'Your grandfather is all right,' he said rapidly. 'He was sent a letter bomb . . .'

He stopped.

She felt as if nothing could ever surprise her again.

'And?' she asked, aware of her own dangerous calm.

'It killed his housekeeper.'

'Mary?'

He nodded.

At first she felt relief that it wasn't her grandfather, and then she felt guilt that it was Mary. Her face seemed to have stiffened and she could not think of anything to say.

'I should have told you,' Mike was saying through the fog. 'But you seemed so happy, I thought I'd break it later.' He turned to Marlene McConnell. 'She has nothing to say,' he said. 'She knows nothing about it. Can you get someone from your library to photocopy everything on the *Brian Leigh* and we'll take the cuttings away?'

'But—' the girl started to say.

'Just get the photocopying done,' he said authoritatively.

Even in her misery, Jade was aware of the emotions chasing across the girl's face: indignation at being bossed about by someone who was not her boss, determination to continue questioning, and finally in the face of Michael's cold stare, shrugging and going back to her desk to pick up the phone.

They had the photocopies in twenty minutes. They sat together in the small library waiting, and he held her hand. She clung to it gratefully and then said: 'Michael – was it anything to do with 7th January?'

He hesitated and sighed.

'The letter was posted from Los Angeles on 7th January.'

'I thought it might have been,' she said quietly. 'The same day as Daddy.'

His hand was something to hold on to, and she squeezed it hard.

'Do you think they'll try to kill Poppy and me?'

'Your names are not in the book.'

'No,' she said. 'But neither was Grandfather's, or poor Mary's. Grandfather will miss her so badly.' She was determined not to cry where the unpleasant young Australian girl might see her and make capital from her tears. She took a deep breath and said: 'I hate to admit it, Mike, but I'm getting a little frightened.'

'Nonsense,' he said. 'Nothing's going to happen while I'm around.'

She looked at him and managed a smile.

'But you look so anxious,' she said.

'That's my natural expression,' he told her.

She shook her head.

'I've been thinking,' she said. 'It's getting obvious that Grandfather must have had something to do with all those people being killed all those years ago. But what? Is it something to do with being a pirate?'

She knew he wouldn't answer her, and he didn't. He just held her hand very hard and looked more anxious than ever.

Then the thought suddenly struck her that he had *known* about the letter bomb to her grandfather. How? She took her hand from his and said coldly: 'Who told you about the bomb?'

She was aware that her voice was unfriendly, but she was beginning to feel surrounded, almost suffocated, by people whom she could not quite trust.

'Why, he did, my dear,' he said promptly. 'Remember, I work for him. Apparently you had told him we were meeting, and he telephoned me to ask me to break the news gently.'

It sounded too glib.

'And why didn't you tell me right away?'

'Because you were happy. Because you were enjoying the tram ride. I was waiting for the right moment. Had I known that that predatory little bitch would—' He broke off and took her hand again. 'You can trust me, you know,' he said quietly, and looking at his brown eyes, magnified by the heavy glasses, she realised she could.

'I'm sorry,' she said. 'Come on. Let's go from here back to the hotel. We'll look at the cuttings there.'

They found a taxi without much difficulty, but it was a more sober ride back into the central district of the Island, except that once when the driver bounced his cab around a corner and Jade lurched against Michael, he began to sneeze again.

'Are you sure that's not a cold?' Jade said when she had counted ten sneezes and tired of saying 'bless you'.

'No. No. Just hayfever,' he managed, tucking himself in the corner of the seat against the window. 'It happens all the time.'

But he seemed quiet as if he were not feeling too good for the rest of the journey.

At the hotel there were three messages waiting for her: one from Gary to say he would meet her in the Captain's Bar at a quarter to one, one from Jimmy Lee asking if she would like to go to the races with him tomorrow, and one from Emma, which announced baldly that they would meet in the lobby at four o'clock.

'Funny,' Jade said, 'I don't remember arranging to meet her. I wonder if she means Poppy?'

'Who is she?' Mike asked.

'A Chinese girl I met the first night we were here. She's nice. Educated in England and runs a wine and spirit business.'

'What's her second name?' he asked. 'I might know her.'

'Isn't it silly?' Jade said, 'I don't know. I must have been properly introduced, but I don't remember.'

'And Jimmy Lee's your Blue Butterfly fur man?'

'Green,' she corrected.

He nodded briefly and called a waiter, ordering coffee. They had settled themselves in the Clipper Lounge, and he had spread out the cuttings on the table in front of them.

'Well, there you are,' he said. 'They're going to be boring reading. Shall I go through half of them for you?'

'Ok,' she said. 'Lucky dip.'

She scrabbled about in the papers, and handed him a small sheaf, taking the rest for herself. 'Just tell me anything that you think might have any bearing on it all,' she instructed him.

'Right, ma'am,' he said and then they were both quiet. He was reading, she noted, amused, with his glasses off.

'Interesting,' he muttered after a few minutes. 'The ship wasn't properly registered. She was only sailing on a temporary pass.'

'What does that mean?' she asked.

'Not a lot. The owner wanted the ship registered in Australia, but if the temporary pass from here was issued, she'd have been deemed registered in Hong Kong anyway.' He was still skimming the words. 'She had temporary oil tanks,' he said. 'Three of them. They could have upset the stability. And it *was* gravel ballast.' He read aloud. *'There was a quantity of gravel ballast in the forward end of the hold. The witness did not see any on the deck.'*

'Who was the witness?' Jade asked.

Michael skated back through the cutting.

'A Mr Kevin Parker of the Orient Islands Shipbuilding Company,' he said.

Jade felt the spurt of the pure satisfaction the seeker feels when he finds the hidden.

'And,' she said, deliberately dramatic. 'He's another of the names in father's address book.'

'Is he now?' said Mike. 'Well, we'd better see what else he said.'

He ran his finger down the columns looking for mentions of Parker. 'Listen to this: *Mr Parker said that a small rectangular water-tight door was fitted in the fore engine bulkhead for access to the hold from the engine room. It was also through this door that one had access to the voyage fuel tanks . . .* hmm,' he said. 'I wonder what they wanted that for. There were two hydraulic deck cranes fitted as well, with a capacity of three tons . . . Hang on – there's more about the door.' He read out loud again. '*The door had instructions on it that it was not to be opened without the master's permission and without a suitable entry being made in the log. The door was fitted with a lock and only the master had a key.*

'And there's more about the ballast.' He quoted: '*To the best of his knowledge, Mr Parker said that the gravel ballast was not secured. It had been ordered from another company and he could only guess its amount at about 200 tons.*'

Jade, ignoring her own papers, was listening intently, and finding herself irritated by her lack of understanding.

'And,' Michael said, 'here we get the Lloyd's man putting his oar in.'

'Your predecessor?' she asked.

'Two before me,' he said. 'A John Marchmont. He said that the ship could only be classified after arrival in Australia and the door found to be satisfactory. The door had to be replaced by one of the approved type or the bulkhead had to be permanently closed.' He clucked quietly. 'Well, well, well. No proper registration and no proper classification.'

'You'd better explain what that means,' she said, her voice resigned.

'Every ship has a classification,' he said. 'It's marked on the vessel, just on the Plimsoll line. And the "class", as we call it, proves the ship has been built to a safety specification approved by a classification society. Then every four years a ship has to go into dry dock and be tested for safety and seaworthiness to renew its classification. Before anyone will insure the vessel, they want to know what "class" it has. If it has a British classification, the insurer feels pretty content. He's happy about a Norwegian classification, too. He's not so keen on an American one, and a Russian one positively gives him the shivers. There are a lot of classification societies, but insurance underwriters are very cautious about most of them. Lloyd's underwriters, for example, approve only eight.'

She had been listening and reading at the same time and the word 'ballast' had caught her eyes in the reports of the enquiry.

'You might be right about the ballast,' she said. 'A surveyor of ships from the marine department testified that when he visited the ship to check the loadline markings – whatever they might be – he noticed she was over to an angle of ten degrees. He spoke to the first officer who said that on the previous day the vessel was slightly over to port and that on moving the ballast she keeled to starboard.'

'She was lolling,' Mike said.

'That's right. That's what the man said. And on the next day when he visited the ship before she sailed, he found there was surface water in the hold. A lot by the sound of it. It extended sixty feet forward of the afterhold. He made them clear it out, and when he came back before she sailed, the water had gone and it was completely dry in the hold. But he also says the ballast moving wouldn't be serious.'

'Curiouser and curiouser,' Mike said.

'But twelve men died,' she said sombrely. 'All the crew and a representative of the company.'

'Which is why there would have had to be an enquiry,' Mike said. 'Listen to this: *Asked whether it had been his desire or recommendation that the owner's representative, Mr William Nutley, should travel on board the schooner, Mr Owen Brent, the owner, replied in the negative . . .*

'Owen Brent?' Jade asked.

'Owen Brent. He's not another, is he?'

'He is.' She felt herself shiver. 'I wonder if he's still with us. What else did he say?'

'He said: *Very repeatedly and over a long period of time, I had advised and requested Mr Nutley to proceed to Australia by air. His presence here was rendered unneccessary. More particularly I requested*

187

him to execute work in Australia for me at a date as early as possible. Apparently he chose to override that advice and request and board the vessel.'

'And was never seen again?' Jade said.

'And was never seen again.'

She sighed: 'And then there is this mysterious other vessel stranded on Swallow Reef. It looked like the *Brian Leigh* from the air, it had the same number of crew, but the wrong markings.' She quoted again from the papers in front of her: '*A Shackleton aircraft which was subsequently lost while searching for the* Brian Leigh *had reported sighting a vessel which was later found not to be the missing vessel.*

'*This other schooner had the marking YF. At that time it was established it had been registered in Formosa.*'

She sat mulling over everything they had read and the implications of the not unsurprising discovery that two more of the seven people in the address book were also connected with the enquiry and the *Brian Leigh*.

'What do you make of it all?' she asked him.

He put his glasses back on and lit a cigarette, then tutted gently through his teeth.

'Well, if I'd been sitting on that board, I'd have given an open verdict. The enquiry declared it an act of God, therefore the insurers would have had to pay up, though it's unlikely she was properly insured with neither a proper registration or classification.'

'Do you think that schooner on the reef and the *Brian Leigh* might have been the same boat?' Jade asked slowly. 'Could they have changed the markings or something because the ship hadn't proper classification and wasn't registered properly?'

'Yes, that would have been possible,' he said. 'But why did they want the door and the cranes on a maiden voyage when she wasn't carrying any cargo? It could have waited until she'd reached her home port and she could have got her classification here in Hong Kong. It's all very odd.'

'This afternoon I'll ring Mr Owen Brent and Mr Kevin Parker.' she said. 'With some trepidation, I might say.'

'Must you?'

'Yes.' She wanted to explain that what had happened to the *Brian Leigh* and to her father and the other people who had died all seemed to be inextricably confused with her need to discover her origins. She was convinced it was no coincidence that the papers about the *Brian Leigh* had been in with those concerning her and Poppy's beginnings. She felt that solving one mystery might lead to solving the other. But realising the need to know was becoming obsessive she found it simpler just to answer him with the one word: 'Yes.'

He shook his head and stubbed out his cigarette half-smoked.

'All right. I can't stop you doing anything, but will you please do nothing without telling me first.'

She laughed.

'All right,' she mocked. 'Now in –' she looked at her watch '– five minutes' time I'm going to meet Gary Smith in the Captain's Bar. You'll come with me. At three thirty I am going to telephone the numbers that I have for Owen Brent and Kevin Parker. And at four o'clock I will be meeting my new friend Emma. After that my movements are vague.'

'I shall call you at six,' he said, his voice decisive, 'and you'll be a good girl and be in your room to take the call.'

'Very well, sir,' she said demurely.

'Come on,' he said, in a resigned way. 'Pick up those papers and I'll walk you around to the Captain's Bar.'

'Very well,' she said again, adding: 'You are bossy.'

'You need bossing,' he grumbled. 'How many more names are there?'

'Two,' she said.

'Who?'

'One English name – someone called Michael Broadbent – and a Chinese name I can't remember.'

'Michael Broadbent used to be an underwriter,' he said thoughtfully. 'He retired some years ago. I haven't heard of him since. I suppose we'll find he insured the *Brian Leigh*.'

'Maybe,' she said, her mind now on meeting Gary.

But Mike was a very 'safe' sort of person, she decided as they walked down the flight of stairs from the Clipper Lounge, across the hall and down again into the bar. Perhaps it was his connection with her grandfather, but he did seem to be an oasis of sanity. Gary excited her, but she wasn't sure of him or his motives, which was spoiling everything. Yet even so her stomach contracted when she saw him sitting at the bar, tall, blond, head and shoulders above everyone else. And he spotted her almost as soon as she was through

189

the entrance and started to walk towards her, his expression wary when he saw she was with another man.

'Good morning, Gary,' she said, as he neared. 'Am I late? Can I introduce a friend of my grandfather's, Michael Blake. Mike, this is my friend Gary Smith.'

'Hi,' Gary said, and Michael Blake said a formal: 'How do you do?' The men shook hands, and then taking the lead, Gary took them to a table near the bar where it was a little lighter.

'What have you been doing this morning?' he asked Jade.

'Mike took me out to the *South China Morning Post* offices and we did some research on the *Brian Leigh*.'

'And what did you find out?'

'Curious things,' she said. aware that Michael Blake had become very quiet and watchful. 'Didn't we, Mike?'

'Very curious things,' he said. 'Let me get some drinks. What will you have, Mr Smith?'

'It's Gary,' he said. 'Scotch on the rocks, please.'

'Jade?'

'Oh, a screwdriver,' she said.

The ever-present waiter was hovering, and Mike ordered the drinks, then he turned so he could see straight into Gary's face and said with a smile: 'And what brings you to Hong Kong?'

'Jade,' Gary said promptly. 'I've been chasing this girl all the way from Aspen, Colorado. And I've just caught up with her.'

'I can understand why,' Mike murmured and began sneezing again which put a temporary stop to the conversation.

'You travel a lot?' he asked when his handkerchief was back in his pocket.

'Quite a bit,' Gary said. 'I sell private jets.'

'And how many have you sold here?'

The question was almost rude, Jade thought, but Gary didn't seem to notice.

'Just one so far,' he said decisively.

'You're planning to do better?' Mike suggested.

'Hopefully.'

The drinks were served and there was a thorny silence which Jade felt she had to end.

'And what have you been doing this morning, Gary?' she asked.

His eyes, unfocused, looked across the bar.

'Not a darn thing,' he said. 'Didn't get up until ten thirty. Fixed

190

for us to have dinner tonight on a floating restaurant and went across on the Star Ferry and back for fun. And here I am.' He turned back to the table. 'What's your racket, Mike?'

'Shipping. I place insurance for McKenzie McKenzie.'

'I thought the old guy had his own underwriting business.'

'Not for his ships,' Mike said.

'Mike's also a Lloyd's agent, Gary,' Jade put in, and Mike looked as if he wished she hadn't mentioned it.

'Yeah?' Gary's look sharpened. 'That must be interesting.'

'Some of the time,' Mike said and looked at his watch. 'Listen, Jade – I'm sorry. I have to go. Got an appointment round the corner in five minutes. I'll call you later. eh?'

He left without a fuss. A brief nod to Gary, a fifty-dollar note on the table to pay for the drinks, and he was hurrying out of the bar; a small man with a purposeful stride who always looked as if he were going somewhere important.

'Who is he?' Gary said, his voice suspicious. 'And how did you meet him?'

The questions did not seem to be casual.

'Why?' Jade asked, quite deliberately letting her tone become belligerent.

He drew back in dismay.

'Hey, cool it,' he said. 'I come in here and you arrive with another guy and I'm not supposed to be curious?'

'He's someone who works for my grandfather,' Jade said. 'He knew my mother when she was young. He's nice.'

'He seems Ok,' Gary said. 'Now what did you find out this morning?'

Again she felt the question was loaded. She wasn't sure whether or not she was becoming paranoid, but paranoid or not, she decided to be cautious.

'Much too complicated to explain now,' she said gaily. 'Where are you taking me to lunch? I'm starving.'

And as he explained about the Peking Restaurant across the road in the basement of the Alexandra Building, she was pleased to sense that under his surface easy acceptance of her brush-off there lurked a thwarted air.

Michael Blake walked briskly along Connaught Road, settling his jacket on his shoulders, checking his cuffs were showing just the

191

right amount and smoothing back his white hair which was being snatched by a brisk wind from China which gusted across the wide street. The Bull and Bear was only a few minutes walk away, and he was going to be early for his appointment with Arthur, but that didn't matter.

The Bull and Bear, as British as the *News of the World*, was always full of Hong Kong British policemen, mingling in an uneasy half-truce with ex-British police officers who now sat, as employees of the ICAC, in judgement on their one-time colleagues. He liked listening and observing. He often picked up a useful titbit.

It was a funny old world, he thought, when you had to have ex-coppers investigating current coppers, and of all the phrases that had been made from the initials of the Independent Commission Against Corruption, the best was Interference in Chinese Ancient Customs. The Chinese weren't corrupt by their own standards. They just believed in bribery as a way of life. And why not if it worked? The colonial British could never accept it was horses for courses. And had never grasped the 'when in Rome' principle.

However, there was the I Can't Accept Cheques – which many of the Hong Kong police force could and frequently did, providing they were drawn on an overseas bank, preferably Swiss. Cash was better, of course. The phrase the public used was I Can't Abide Cops – which most of them couldn't. A good cop could fuck up the system rotten, just when someone had got a good racket going.

He was looking forward to a chat with Arthur Watson-King. With his own working-class roots, not quite dug out from the North, he was fascinated by Arthur. Arthur was class all the way through. And it wasn't class that just came from the drawled public-school accent or the conventional tweedy clothes. The idea of Arthur Watson-King in slip-on shoes, jeans or a pale blue suit was unimaginable. He was old school. He lived in Hong Kong so he had had the courtesy to learn the language, he drank gin at lunchtime and whisky at night, he had an air of natural authority that would have had the bolshiest of trade union officials cleaning his shoes. He was built like a brick shit-house, he must have been nudging seventy and he was a China-watcher and a member of MI6. As Mike helped out in that direction occasionally himself, he knew it.

And if there were anything wrong with Gary Smith, Arthur would know.

The 'olde-worlde' door of the Bull and Bear, copied from somewhere in Suffolk, was before him. He pushed it and entered. It was twenty-three minutes past one, and the vast figure of Arthur was already there, his huge frame perched on a too small stool, a large drink on the bar in front of him. He was talking to Phyllis, the equally large, elegantly dressed landlady who had been known, legend had it, to remove two drunken and obstreperous matelots from her pub in one throw: two sailor-heads, minus sailor hats, firmly under each arm, four navy-blue-clad legs dragging over the red patterned Turkey carpet and out through the door; riffraff dispatched, she returned to the bar, greeting her sober customers. A duchess greeting her weekend party guests.

Without being asked, Phyllis motioned the pretty barmaid to put up a gin and tonic.

'Good morning, Mr Blake,' she said, and vanished as discreetly as her size would allow. Phyllis knew more than she let on, Mike thought.

'Morning, Mike,' Arthur grunted. 'It's a bit crowded. Bar do?'

'Have to. Nowhere to sit,' Mike said, falling into Arthur's clipped pattern.

'Din's enough to drown a pneumatic drill,' Arthur said. 'Not much important to tell you anyway.'

'CIA?' Mike asked. His summing up of Gary's clean-cut looks, the honest wide-open blue gaze, the all-American boy aura, plus the ambiguity of answers, had suggested to him the American secret service.

'No.' Arthur took an appreciative swallow of his gin.

'A goodie or a baddie?' Mike asked, not sure which he wanted the answer to be, bearing Jade in mind and the way she made him sneeze.

'Goodie. DEA. One of their drug enforcement agency blokes. Working here with our cops and an American Chinese who's undercover. In some safe house, I believe.'

'Drugs?' Mike was shaking his head and putting out a half-lit cigarette. 'Tell me then, why's he latched on to the McKenzie McKenzie girls?'

'What McKenzie McKenzie girls . . .?' Arthur started to say, and then nodded ponderously. 'The two Ian's daughter adopted?'

Arthur had been China-watching for so long in his life in the

New Territories that nothing that had happened in Hong Kong since the beginning of time had escaped him.

'That's right.'

'Must be in their twenties now.'

'That's right.'

'And this DEA bloke's tied up with them. They here? The girls, I mean.'

'They're here.'

Arthur took a slower sip of his gin, tasted it and took another.

'Wonder if the old man was ever involved in drugs?' he said and it was a question.

'He hasn't been involved in anything for years,' Mike pointed out.

'There was a period about twenty-five years ago when we thought he might be,' Arthur went on, not having his train of thought spoilt. 'But he wasn't. He was up to something else. Maybe the DEA don't know it was something else.'

'What?'

'Can't remember now,' the old man said vaguely and mentally Mike cursed him for a lying bastard. Arthur never forgot a thing.

He signalled for a replenishment of drinks and now that the serious business had been attended to, the old boy took out his pipe and carefully filled it. All of this took time – thinking time.

'So something's up,' he finally observed.

'You might say that,' Mike said. 'A lot of odd goings on. Ian received a letter bomb.'

'Heard it on the overseas news.'

'Sir Ralph Martin was killed by a hit-and-run driver in Los Angeles on 7th January.'

'You don't say.'

'So were Dottie Anderson and Peter Leigh.'

'Noticed that. Odd. Same day.'

'Well, that day was 7th January too.'

'Realised that. So, what are you thinking?'

Speaking rapidly, Mike went through the story – Jade's story, just as she had told it to him. Arthur listened, his Mount Rushmore face impassive, his pipe between his teeth.

'Interesting,' he said when Mike had finished. 'Triads, obviously. Bit of revenge. What for, I wonder?'

'Something to do with the *Brian Leigh*, of course.'

The huge face and head, still above him even though their owner was seated, remained impassive.

'No idea, old boy. But I've always wondered how the court of enquiry came to that fortuity decision when hanky-panky it had to be. And then it was just a month or two after Ralph Martin led that enquiry and gave that questionable decision that he packed up bags and went home with Margaret and those two children, never to be seen in South East Asia again. Chickens coming home to roost, maybe, all these years later.'

Mike sighed, exasperated.

'Look,' he said. 'I'm worried about the girls. Maybe this Gary will be some protection. Maybe not. He's involved with the older one, Jade, but not just for her Oriental eyes, I'm certain. We have a whole string of deaths and a bunch of mysterious and vengeful Triads. I know about old Ian's piracy. What I don't know is where this fucking ship comes into it, and why is a drug enforcement officer from the USA getting himself involved?'

'Umm.' Unmoved by Mike's hissing anger – shouting would have been impossible in the crowded mock-Tudor bar – Arthur said: 'Well, Triads and drugs go together like Adam and Eve, wouldn't you say? Maybe your vengeful Triads are into drug-running. No reason why they couldn't be up to all sorts of things now, is there, knowing how they do carry on?'

'Is the girl going to be safe with this Gary Smith?' Mike persisted.

'Long as she's not up to something.'

'She's not.'

'Probably not a bad thing having him around then. Mind you, sounds as if they'd have done her in by now if they wanted to. The DEA man's probably suspicious. Still, the more suspicious he is, the closer he'll stay with the girl. Bit of protection, don't you think?'

'I suppose so,' Mike said, wishing he was doing the protecting himself and getting the benefits that went with it – a thought that made him let out one short, sharp sneeze.

'You ought to watch that cold,' the old man said. 'Shouldn't delve too deep into things if I were you. Old McKenzie McKenzie wouldn't like it. That's all over now. Hang on to your job. You're getting on for retiring age, and it's not easy. As for the rest – well, thanks for the gen. Don't worry too much about the girl. She's not on the list and you're not on it either.' He gave a short, barking laugh. 'Got to get back to the office now. Have a look at those two new armoured cars I told you we took on. Not bad having a growing business when you're my age. It's having a Chinese wife does it. They keep you young.'

The thought of a Chinese wife led inexorably to thoughts of Jade which in turn led to a fit of sneezing. He was still sneezing when Arthur, ducking his head, vanished into the street beyond the low pub door, leaving Mike to wonder about the veiled threat that had gone with the old man's suggestion to stop delving into the affair of the *Brian Leigh*.

Gary had not been in the best of tempers when he arrived at the Captain's Bar to meet Jade. He had just spent an uncomfortable half-hour with a toffee-nosed British chief superintendent at the Hennessy Road police headquarters. The man had been reasonably helpful, but played his cards close to his chest and obviously resented Gary's presence on what he kept referring to as 'his manor' or 'his patch'.

'What you chaps don't realise,' he said, 'is that the Triad operation is very small here. They're no more than fragmented groups of thugs. Street gangs, if you like. A damn nuisance, but under control. The days of the big powerful operators are gone. We've seen to that.'

Tactfully, Gary had tried to point out that in the view of the DEA the big operators were quietly creeping back in.

'We've seen no sign of it happening here, old boy,' the chief superintendent had said. 'But any help we can give . . . Try not to get into any trouble, won't you?'

'Condescending bastard,' Gary had muttered to himself as he left the building for the windy, noisy street outside.

Finding Jade with another man had not improved his temper, particularly as Gary's sensitive nose had detected that the diffident Mike Blake, blinking behind his glasses, was not as harmless as he looked. He himself was sick of playing the good-time Charlie all-American graduate. He felt like smashing someone's face in. And he felt like taking Jade to bed.

She was behaving in a decidedly paranoid fashion and continued to do so throughout lunch in the red and gold, crystal and mirror restaurant. All through the Peking duck she asked him damn-fool questions about his childhood in Tennessee, his years at Harvard and his family. He decided to play her game and described a home that sounded like something out of *Gone With the Wind*, schooldays from a bad 1940s B-movie, and went on being engaging, charming and cheerful.

She didn't trust him, that was the problem. And he could hardly blame her, but neither could he explain. That wasn't in the rules. And while they were fighting with a chewy dessert of bananas dipped in toffee that had set like a rock, he asked if she still planned on having dinner with him that evening.

'I thought we might eat on a floating restaurant at Aberdeen on the other side of the Island,' he said. 'It's touristy, but fun. Great fish. Do you like fish?'

'I do, and it sounds lovely,' she said.

He gave a relieved sigh and then grinned at her.

'I thought you'd gone off me,' he said.

She looked embarrassed, flushed under the delicate ivory of her skin and then said: 'I'm sorry, Gary. I have a lot on my mind. I just don't want to talk about it right now.'

'Right,' he said, 'but when you do—' And the quick questioning look she gave him made it clear that whatever suspicions she was entertaining had flooded back; he cursed himself for being an idiot.

He paid the bill and they left the restaurant and rode the escalator to street level in silence. He wanted to take her arm. He wanted to tell her she was safe with him. He wanted to take her to bed. But he said: 'Feel like a walk?'

She hesitated as he looked down at her while the crowds parted around them. Then she looked at her watch.

'I'm sorry, Garry, I can't,' she said. 'I've got one or two things to do and someone to meet at four.'

It was obvious she had made up her mind she wasn't going to tell him a damn thing.

'Ok then,' he said. 'Seven all right for tonight? Meet in the lobby?'

'Fine,' she said, not looking happy.

'Until then,' he told her and bent his head to kiss her. 'Be good.' He hesitated. 'And more important, be careful.'

'I will,' she promised before precipitously leaving him as the traffic lights changed and she ran across the road. He stared after her tiny hurrying figure and then set off himself at a sharp pace, walking towards Wanchai. He needed to use up surplus energy, and as he walked he wondered who she had to call; and, more worrying, who she was going to meet.

Jade's attack of paranoia was still with her as she hurried in through the back door of the Mandarin and up to her room. Gary was altogether too pat, too glib, and she had definitely decided that right back as far as Los Angeles airport where she had first spotted him that he had been following her. It would have been nice to have believed it was because of her fatal attraction, and indeed, she might have been able to kid herself that this was the case if so many other mysterious and frightening things hadn't been happening. Regretfully she had to tell herself that either he was involved in all that was going on, or maybe he was just a fortune hunter. It occurred to her that she was really rather rich; something she had rarely thought about before.

The unfortunate thing was that the acceptance of both these possibilities did not stop her fancying him like mad.

With her room door shut, she resolutely put Gary Smith out of her mind and set her map, now getting raggedy round the edges, in front of the telephone. She was going to call two numbers: the one for Owen Brent and the other for Kevin Parker. As the phone rang out the first of the two numbers, she carefully put a line through both names. Now there were only two people she had not contacted – a Chinese, Chan Koh Leung, whose address and telephone number were in Macao, and one other, a Michael Broadbent, whose address was in Tsim Sha Tsui, Kowloon side.

She found herself nervous as she waited for the phone to be answered. Eventually a plummy Sloane Ranger voice, incongruous at the end of a Hong Kong telephone, announced: 'Brent Cargoes.'

Jade asked for Mr Owen Brent. but the affected voice said: 'Mr Brent retired four years ago. He no longer lives in Hong Kong.'

'Could I speak to someone who might know where to find him?'

'The managing director's secretary might help,' the girl said. 'She used to work for Mr Brent.'

The managing director's secretary could not help. Mr Brent lived somewhere in New Zealand. As far as she knew he was in perfectly good health, and if it was really important she could forward a letter through his lawyers. But Mr Brent had given strict instructions that his whereabouts were to be kept private.

Kevin Parker's number led to a discontinued line.

At least there was no bad news – so far – she decided as she went back downstairs to meet Emma.

There was no sign of the Chinese girl as she came into the lobby. She hovered, and then felt a slight tap on her shoulder. At first she did not recognise the girl behind her, wearing huge dark glasses and with her hair hidden under a black scarf tied turban fashion.

'I'm so pleased you're here,' Emma's voice said urgently. 'Can we leave quickly? I want to talk to you away from here. Don't take too much notice of me, please.'

She headed out of the hotel door, brown-booted legs striding below a brown leather coat, and swung right and then right again to the tunnel under Connaught Road. Jade hurried a pace behind, wondering what the hell was going on now.

Once down the stairs and in the wide tunnel, Emma let her catch up.

'What is it?' Jade said, conscious of sounding irritable.

'I'll explain,' Emma said. 'I'm sorry about the abrupt message. You weren't in and I had to see you. I couldn't explain. I'm so glad I caught you. I must talk to you. Let's get on a bus. There's hardly ever anyone on them at this time.'

She had been striding purposefully while she talked in disjointed, nervous fragments and they were up the other stairs and on to the harbour side of the road. Heels clacking authoritatively, she hurried Jade along the waterfront and down to a large bus station. 'Any bus will do,' she said. 'Just let's get the first that's leaving.'

It turned out to be a number six, marked to Repulse Bay and Stanley. Emma paid the fare downstairs, led the way to the empty top deck and the front two seats. Then she sat down and sighed.

'I'm sorry to act in such a dramatic fashion,' she said, 'but I don't want anyone to see us together. I was afraid someone in the hotel might have recognised me from yesterday and reported back.'

'Why shouldn't the hotel see you with me?' Jade asked, her irritation growing. 'And who might report back?'

'Please, let me explain. It's about Poppy.'

'What about her?' Jade grabbed the bar in front of the seat as the bus lurched forward. 'Has something happened to her? She's supposed to be with a man called Paul So. I knew I shouldn't have let her go off alone . . .'

'Easy!' Emma said. 'She is with Paul So, but she's very sick. She didn't want you to see her in the state she was in. Paul just turned up

199

at the right moment. Oh, shit. I'd better start from the beginning, hadn't I?'

'Please,' Jade said, still gripping the bar too tightly for the lumbering progress of the bus through the Central traffic.

Emma did not spare her any of the details – the burns, the heroin, the possibility of addiction.

'And now Kwan's searching for her,' Emma said. 'I think he wants to turn her on. To heroin, you know. So he mustn't find her. I don't think they know I took her to the hotel, but if they bribe one of the employees and one of the employees saw me, they might just remember I was there when Paul drove off with her, and guess I know where she has gone. That's the reason for the dark glasses and the scarf,' she explained, starting to take both off. 'And why I didn't want to talk to you in the hotel. To tell you the truth, I'm alarmed.'

'That makes two of us,' Jade said. She had listened in mounting dismay to the story, her first reaction total horror, then anger with Poppy. Only Poppy could have got herself into such a terrible situation, but along with the anger was a heart-wrenching concern. How could anyone do such frightful things to anyone as small and as beautiful as Poppy?

'I'd better get back to Fanling right away,' she said.

'Why?' Emma said. 'She doesn't want to see you. That was her biggest worry.'

'But it's my responsibility,' Jade protested. 'Someone has to look after her.'

Emma shrugged.

'Let her sort herself out,' she said. 'She's a big girl now. She got herself in – let her get herself out. Anyway, you could lead Kwan Ching right to her if he's watching you.'

Jade was silent, old habits dying hard, but Emma was right, she realised. Poppy would be safe with Paul So. More important at this moment were the reasons for what had happened.

'Why would Kwan be doing this?' she asked.

'He's some kind of Triad, I'd imagine. And he's involved Stephen because Stephen is a policeman, but not a very convinced one, and therefore easy meat. Businessmen here, Triads or not, like to have a tame British inspector in their pockets if only for an emergency. But why he should want to turn your sister on, I don't know. Maybe he's just wicked.' She turned her head to look very hard at Jade. 'Do you know?' she asked.

Jade's tired mind registered that the road was high and down below she could see a race course with, incongruously, race horses being exercised on the roof of a building.

'I've no idea,' she said distractedly. 'It is something to do with the Triads. All of it.' She felt a pressing urgency to go away somewhere, by herself, in a room with the door shut against everyone and think. Her head needed sorting our; the confused welter of possibly significant, and maybe useless, information she had garnered needed coordinating into some kind of mental filing system. She felt if she could get it all neat and tidy in her head, then maybe she would find out what she and Poppy were all about.

The bus was lurching up a steep road, its roof tearing at the branches of trees as it tore around bends over the mountain she had seen from the Star Ferry. She needed to hold the rail in front in earnest now and she was feeling slightly sick from the movement, the dizzy drops to the side, and the news of Poppy.

'What shall I do?' she asked, aware of sounding feeble.

'You didn't telephone Paul?'

'No. I just thought Poppy was up to mischief again. She usually is.'

'Well, phone him. From a call box would be best. But I wouldn't go near Fanling. If someone were following you, they'd find Poppy, wouldn't they?' She crashed briefly into Jade as the bus hurled itself around a bend. 'I wish you'd tell me if you have any idea of why Kwan's done this to your sister. It might be easier to work out what to do. We should tell the police, you know. Except . . .'

Jade forced her mind to work.

'Except that it would be bad for Stephen and a great scandal for the McKenzie McKenzies.'

'That's right.'

'Maybe he wants to blackmail Grandfather,' Jade said.

'Maybe. It feels more like revenge, though. The Triads are hot on revenge.'

'Then why haven't they done anything to me?'

And Emma said brutally: 'Maybe they haven't got around to it yet. Listen, why don't you go home and take Poppy with you. Like it or not, you're caught up in something pretty unpleasant. Your sister . . .' Her voice trailed away. 'It would be better to go.'

Emma's head was turned to look at Jade, her hand over Jade's on the barrier. 'He nearly killed her. It was so close,' she warned.

Go home. It was probably the best and the most sensible advice.

'I can't,' Jade said. 'Not yet.'

'Why not? It's stupid to stay here.'

'It's more complicated than you know.' It seemed to Jade that Emma was in a similar situation to her – caught up in something that she didn't understand and that was not of her doing. Her anxiety for her policeman boyfriend had come through loud and clear while she had been telling the events that led to Paul So taking Poppy to Fanling, but there was also a genuine concern for Poppy. It occurred to Jade that maybe Emma would be able to see the path through the quagmire of disconnected pieces of information. 'Could you bear to listen to a long story?' she asked. 'And will you promise not to repeat it to Stephen?'

'The less Stephen knows about anything the better,' Emma said positively. 'I love him, but for a policeman he's a bit of a fool at times. He'd never have made inspector if he hadn't been white. Maybe it's because he's a *gweilo*. He's the first *gweilo* man I've ever been involved with. He doesn't understand how to watch his own interests. Are they all so foolish?'

'Maybe. I don't know,' Jade said, her mind skittering back over the few men she had known. Would Gary Smith know how to watch his own interests? He would, she decided. His own interests would probably come first.

Jade was only halfway through her long story when the bus pulled into Stanley Village. Emma had chain-smoked while she listened, her face intent. 'We won't get off,' she said as the bus huffed to a halt. 'We'll sit here until it turns round and goes back again. Now – we'd got to the translator. What did he think?'

'Triads,' Jade said. 'But he didn't want to get involved either. He said the Chinese don't like disturbing their ancestors.'

'Quite true,' said Emma briskly, 'and then . . .?'

Jade went on, telling the events in a wealth of detail which she found was helping her to order her own thoughts. The bus started up again and they were past Repulse Bay and dragging over the steep hills to the north of the Island before she had finished.

'Umm.' Emma lit another cigarette with a heavy gold lighter. The floor of the bus beneath her feet was littered with butts. 'So, you have a situation where most of those who have been killed so far were involved with the *Brian Leigh*. But not all. Miss Tibbets has just disappeared. She and the Dottie woman don't appear to have been concerned with the ship. And you've no evidence that your grandfather was. Poppy, who *nearly* died, couldn't possibly have a connection. So there's another aspect apart from the ship, and it must be that massacre on 7th January. Right? Somehow you have to link those two, the ship and the massacre. But if I were you, I'd go home, and quickly. Not,' she added, 'as though it sounds as if Scotland's particularly safe.'

'And what do you think about Gary?' Jade ignored going home for the moment. Emma's reaction regarding Gary was important.

'Oh, he's following you. He's probably some sort of undercover policeman. Hong Kong's thick with them. He picked you up in Los Angeles, you say? The letter bomb came from Los Angeles. Another connection to sort out.' She paused. 'Why does it matter? Are you lovers?'

Jade nodded, mute.

'I'll rephrase the question. Do you love him?'

'I could.'

'But you're suspicious?'

'Exactly.'

'What's he like in bed?'

Jade hesitated, slightly embarrassed, then said: 'Very good.'

'Well, enjoy him, but don't indulge in pillow talk.'

'That's what I decided to do.'

'And make another decision – go home.'

There was no hesitation this time. 'I can't.'

'Why not?'

'I want to know who I am.'

Emma turned to look at her and gave a short laugh.

'A very lucky girl. When you were born, the refugees slung their baby girls in the harbour. And look at you.' The movement of her hand took in Jade's Gucci shoes, her Yves St Laurent silk suit and the heavy gold bracelets and one heavy gold chain which she always wore.

'That was a very flip answer,' Jade said reproachfully. 'I'm not really a McKenzie McKenzie now, am I? I'm a Chinese girl from God-knows-where and all right, I was lucky. Grandfather didn't want us to come here. He said it would be culture shock and he was absolutely right. Emma, I'm so confused. I've been brought up a European—'

'So was I. I went to school at Heathfield.'

'But you came home to your own culture. Look, you speak your own language, you talk about the *gweilo*. For Christ's sake – I even have to fight with a pair of chopsticks, and it's no good saying that's a bit of trivia, which I know it is, but since I've been here I feel that the East is tripping me up at every turn. I feel totally disorientated. I need to know who I really am, and then I can perhaps go back to who I was. If you can't understand that, you're less sensitive than I thought. I want to be like you – straddling both worlds very comfortably.'

'Most successful people in Hong Kong do,' Emma said.

'But I'm not managing it. I can't make my foot land properly in the Oriental world. Every time someone makes a joke about *gweilos*, I feel they're getting at me, and then I have to realise that they're making the joke because I'm not a *gweilo* and they think it's not offensive. And there I am all indignant and wanting to leap to what's virtually my own defence. It's very confusing. And if you can't see it . . .'

'I can,' Emma said authoritatively. 'But don't worry about the word *gweilo*. They use it themselves. It's no longer offensive. I can also see that you're going to stick it out here and probably get yourself killed in some Triad vendetta that goes back to before you were born. Wastefully, because you'll never find out who you were because you never properly existed in Chinese terms. You know Poppy's mother flung herself into the harbour – and they still do that today. How on earth do you think you can ever discover who you *were*? I don't doubt you were just dumped somewhere; a baby girl, another mouth to be fed and one that wasn't going to grow up productive. How could *anyone* trace your background? There are millions like you. I exaggerate, but there are a hell of a lot. Why don't you just concentrate on who you've become and start from the principle that you began when your parents adopted you.'

Jade sighed.

'You are pragmatic people, aren't you?'

'*We* are pragmatic people,' Emma said, nudging her. 'Take the best of both worlds.'

She made such a brave attempt at a broad and Western wink that Jade could only laugh. Afterwards they sat in thoughtful but companionable silence.

'By the way,' Emma said as the bus came in sight of the Star Ferry terminal. 'What's the last name on your list?'

'It's Chinese. Can't remember,' Jade said. 'Wait a minute.'

She fished in the zipped compartment of her bag and took out the tattered map. She had written the Chinese name in the blue space for ocean as the map did not cover Macao.

'He's in Macao,' she said. 'He's called Chan Koh Leung.'

'Say that again!'

'Chan Koh Leung,' Jade repeated obediently.

'I don't believe it,' Emma said softly. 'Chan Koh Leung!' She spoke the name with singsong inflections that Jade had not managed. 'It can't be!'

'Why not?' Jade asked. 'Who is he?'

'Another pirate of sorts,' Emma said. 'And if he's still alive, a very old one. Your Chang Koh Leung is one of the richest men in South East Asia. We call him the Gold King because for years he controlled all the gold in this part of the world. Outwardly he was always respectable, but Jade, I most certainly wouldn't want to tangle with him.'

Paul So had been holding Poppy very tight. Holding her like a cracked china doll that threatened to shatter if the pieces weren't clasped together. Though she was more alert, her pains had grown in intensity so that she twitched and moaned, her body jerking as if it were being pulled apart.

He had found it very disturbing to hold her so close. He had been forced to lie along the length of the bed with her and he was ashamed and angry with himself that he could feel desire when she was so pathetically sick. Eventually she had dozed, her body still jumping, but he had felt she no longer needed him to be so close, and half relieved, half disappointed, he went to sit back in the chair where he could watch over her.

His mother had been keeping them supplied with food, which Poppy had been unable to face, and making up the draughts which the doctor had suggested and which he had coaxed her to drink. There was little to be done but let the girl sweat it out, the doctor had said. The withdrawal symptoms would pass in a couple of days as the drug had been administered to her for such a short period. Again he had warned not to give her any opportunity of touching heroin again.

'If she takes it,' the doctor had said, 'she will be chasing the dragon for the rest of her life, and her life will be a short one.'

He was dozing himself when he heard the telephone ring in the hall of the house and the *foki*'s shambling footsteps as the man went to answer it.

'Wai?' he heard him shout, and then a babble of Cantonese, and then silence.

Moving quietly, he went to the door and out of the darkened room into the bright sunlit hall outside.

'What is it, Pao?' he asked.

'A woman who does not speak Cantonese,' Pao told him, shouting up the stairs, 'Asking for you, sir.'

It would be Jade. Girding himself to tell lies, he went to the phone.

'Hello,' she said. 'Paul? It's Jade.'

'I guessed it would be you,' he said, making his voice hearty. 'How are you?'

'I'm fine,' she said impatiently. 'How's Poppy?'

'Fine,' he said cautiously.

'She really is?'

'Of course, why shouldn't she be?' he asked, fishing. Perhaps Jade had some inkling all was not well.

'Paul – I've seen Emma. The girl who was with Poppy when you turned up at the hotel. She's told me everything.'

'I see,' he said slowly.

'She says it's a bad idea for me to come there in case I'm followed. I'm in a phone box now. What do you think?'

'Why is she afraid you would be followed?' he asked, puzzled.

'Because Kwan Ching – the man who did all those things to Poppy – is looking for her. He wants to know where she has gone.'

'He has asked you this?'

'No. Not me. Oh, it's too complicated to explain. But what do you think?'

'I think that if your coming would in any way endanger Poppy, you should stay away,' he said. 'It's most unlikely that anyone will look for her here – unless, of course, your friends tell him. Or you tell him.'

'That won't happen,' she said decisively. 'But how is she?'

'Not good. But she will be better in a day or two. Then I think you should take her home to safety.'

There was a long silence, and then Jade said: 'Is it no great trouble to you to keep her there?'

'None at all,' he said.

'It's just that there are things I have to do here. It may take longer than two days. Could she stay on if necessary at your home?'

He had to be careful to keep his voice from showing the pleasure her request brought him.

'Yes. She will be safe with me.'

'And I'll keep ringing you whenever I can. I'm sorry I didn't ring before. I thought it was just Poppy being irresponsible again.' Her voice sounded resigned and he was angry that she should always think the worst of her sister.

'None of this is her fault,' he said firmly.

She sighed. 'I suppose not. Could I just ask if you had any luck tracing Miss Tibbets?'

'No. I did not. In fact, that was the reason for my call at the hotel – to tell you both that no one seems to know where she has gone.' He did not add that he had wanted to see Poppy again, and that he had done nothing but think about her since he had left them both at Fanling station. 'But I have not stopped making enquiries.'

'Are you sure it's no trouble?'

'None at all. But it may take a little while as I have to look after Poppy for the moment. She cannot be left alone, and my mother's English is very poor. They would not be able to understand each other, so I cannot leave them for too long.'

'You are kind. I feel terrible. I should be doing more.'

There was guilt in her voice, but he knew that she was glad to be free of the problem of her sister. The moment of rapport between them outside the derelict orphanage had not lasted very long, he thought sadly.

'I don't know how I'll ever thank you,' she was saying.

'There is no need,' he said. 'In a sense, I'm doing my job.'

'I suppose so,' she said doubtfully. 'Look, I'll call tomorrow.'

'I shall look forward to that,' he said, trying to make his voice warm.

He put down the telephone and padded back to Poppy's room. He opened the door quietly to see she was asleep. He closed it with great care and ran downstairs to the sitting room where his mother was sitting sewing in an old-fashioned hard-backed chair.

'Mother, could you listen for her?' he said. 'I must go to the chapel for half an hour to tidy some odds and ends.'

His mother looked up, and her shrewd eyes, set in a mass of deep wrinkles, looked at him steadily.

'Yes, I'll watch her for you,' she said. 'But Paul, is this wise to keep the girl here? You are not making trouble for yourself, are you?'

'Mother – it is the Christian thing to do.'

She did not speak, but the look she gave him said that she could see more than Christianity was involved.

'And, Mother, she may have to stay for a while. Do you mind?'

'No. As you say, it is the Christian thing to do.' A smile hovered around her lips. His mother had never been a wholehearted Christian. 'But is she worth your anxieties?' she asked, the smile gone. 'I cannot help but ask myself how a young girl could have found herself in such a situation. She cannot have been prudent, my son.'

'None of this is her fault,' he protested for the second time in minutes.

She sighed. 'If you say not. If she wakes while you are out, I will dress her burns again.'

'If you would,' he said. 'Be gentle with her, Mother. She has had a sad life.'

'As a McKenzie McKenzie?' she said slyly, her lips pursed.

He laughed. 'Well, she has not been happy.'

'Few of us are happy,' his mother said. 'Go. Get youself to the chapel.'

He drove to the chapel a little too fast, and hurriedly dealt with the post and made arrangements for his assistant pastor to run the youth club that evening. Then he drove to Luen Wo Market to buy some country-fresh fruits and green vegetables. Pao's wife could make her a soup. That would be nourishing, and the fruits would perhaps cool the thirst she felt constantly. She was so thin, almost transparent, so that her skin glowed as if a light behind was flaring before going out. He thought about what Jade had said and what his mother had reiterated. He felt pain, and wondered perhaps if he could save Poppy from herself. For even besotted as he was by her and her fragility, he had to accept that she had not indeed been prudent. Yet at the thought of what the man Kwan Ching had done to her; the indignities and hurts he had inflicted, he felt he wanted to kill the man, slowly and painfully, and preferably with bare hands. Quickly he asked God to forgive him.

It was nearer three quarters of an hour before he was back, and his mother was leaving the bedroom with a small tray holding medical things.

'She is resting,' she said. 'And I think she is quieter.'

He nodded and went into the room. Poppy was sitting up in bed, her arms over the bedclothes, quite still and staring ahead. The last of the evening light came through a gap in the shutters and the room was brighter than she had been able to bear it before.

'I've been thinking, Paul,' she said without preamble as he came and sat on the edge of her bed. 'I've been punished. That's what all this has been – punishment.' Her voice was weak, but while he had been out, it was obvious that some turn for the better had taken place. He did not know quite what to say; it seemed best just to listen, so he took her hand and she curled her fingers around his. 'Kwan was punishing me for all the others. That's what it was.' She turned her head away from him. 'You see, Paul, I've always been bad, but since I grew up I've been bad in a different way. There were men. So many men you can't imagine—' Now she turned to look at him so that her confession would be more abject. For that's what she was doing, he realised. She was confessing. 'It began when I was fourteen and I had this boy when we were skiing in St Moritz. He was very rich, older than me and well, *très snob*. He –' she hesitated '– made love to me, if you can call it that, and afterwards he made a crude joke about my being a Chink as he called it. I hadn't really even thought about it until then, and anyway I didn't mind being a Chink. I knew I was pretty. I knew I could get anything I wanted and I'd always had lots of girlfriends because I was fun. They didn't mind that I was Chinese. I heard that joke and lots of others in the next few years from white boys and I decided I didn't like Western men very much, but I needed them. I really need you to love me now,' she said matter-of-factly. 'If you did, I know I would feel better. Sex is necessary to me.' She paused, and again he felt the power of desire, but he knew she was not asking him to make love to her. She was just confessing. 'So I started deliberately using them. I did awful things. I'd lead them on, let them make love to me and then manoeuvre things so they knew I didn't care tuppence about them. If they were at my place, I'd kick them out of bed and my house the minute they came. It was as if I had an ejector seat from my bed. I couldn't bear them near me after they'd done it. I burnt one once, with a cigarette, like Kwan Ching did to me, but I

209

only did it on his hand, and only one burn. There was a man I met once who liked to be tied up, so I tied him up and I just went off and left him there. I had these fantasies that he might die like that and the thought pleased me, though I really knew that he'd be rescued by his cleaning woman the next day. But I loved the thought of his embarrassment. I played with that, enjoying it, imagining the scene, and serve him right, I thought. They were nearly always pick-ups. I never gave myself the chance to like anyone. I suppose it wasn't satisfactory and I wasn't happy, and I could hardly tell anyone what I was doing or explain. You see, I really liked that boy when I was fourteen. But he hurt me. He made me see I wasn't at home. I didn't belong. Oh – it's so confusing because as much as I despised them all, at the moments when they were inside me and close to me physically, I felt I belonged. I wasn't lonely while they were fucking me – because that's all they were doing, Paul. They weren't loving me. But you know how men are, how they gasp and how important and urgent it is, and how desperately they need a woman for those few minutes before it's all over. It *felt* like they loved me. But when it was over, I wasn't going to give them the chance to hurt me. Not ever. I got rid of them.'

He felt as if he were choking and he was terrified she might see how much he wanted her.

'Have you never felt really loved?' he managed to say.

She considered the question, sliding down into the bed, tired by talking.

'My mother loved me and Kirsty loved me when I was little and I was very sick. It was always best when I was ill. Maybe because I was good when I was ill.' She managed a small stifled giggle. 'I suppose when I was sick I hadn't the energy to be bad. But my mother started to change. She began to go senile after we left school, and now I can't bear her. Isn't that dreadful? But I can't. That mindless, mad female isn't my mother. I don't know her and she doesn't know me any more. You can't imagine what it's like not to recognise your own mother. Not, of course, that she really is my mother, but I never felt she wasn't before. She's gone away and left me behind, and she cared about me once. My father always like Jade best and Grandfather never approved of us in the first place, and then when he did get around to accepting us, it was Jade he liked – goody-goody smart-aleck Jade. And she's no better than I am, Paul. She'd like to be just as promiscuous, except she hasn't the courage.

So she goes on about picking men who like her for herself and who don't care she's different. None of us is different. She's not different and neither am I. Everyone's the same really.' She shook her head violently. 'I thought maybe men who *looked* the same as me would be different and that I might find one to love. And look what happened. The most terrible things that have ever happened to me were done by a man of my own race. So I'm not going to find peace here, am I? I suppose I'm just unlovable.'

She had been clinging to his hand so tightly that the bones hurt, and though he was appalled by everything she had said, he heard himself speaking as if without reference to himself.

'I could love you.'

She struggled to sit up again and sat staring at him.

'Then love me. Make love to me now,' she said. 'Oh, please, Paul.'

He released his hand and then drew her into his arms so that her head was on his shoulder.

'No,' he said.

'Why not?'

He gave the simple answer.

'Because that is not love and this is my mother's house. We are both her guests.'

'Is that the only reason?' She was testing him in some way, he realised.

'No. I would need to know you better, to be sure I really loved you and you loved me in return before I took your body. You forget,' he said gently. 'I am a pastor. For me, the act of sex is a sacrament. If I loved you and you loved me, I would want to marry you, and for ever afterwards I would require that I was the only man in your life because you most certainly would be the only woman in mine.'

She had pulled her head back so that she could see his face, and when he finished speaking she was silent. and then she burst into a huge sob, followed by more and more. He held her tight, soothing and rocking her, her tears wet on his shoulder, and he let her cry until she stopped.

When her sobs had subsided into small, dismal sniffs, he wiped her face with his handkerchief and she looked at him, her lower lip still quivering.

'What do you want me to do?' she asked.

'Nothing,' he told her. 'Just get well again and we shall see. You need time, Poppy. You've been rushing through life without love, without God and both are there if you seek them. You will find out.'

'Can I stay here?'

He nodded. 'Jade and I have decided it is wiser.'

'Jade?' Her voice was alarmed. 'She doesn't know, does she?'

'Yes. Emma told her. She says Kwan Ching –' the girl shivered at the mention of the name ' – she says he is looking for you. But you are safe here.'

'Why does he want me?' she asked pathetically.

'Jade thinks to give you more heroin.'

'But why? I've never done anything to him.'

'We don't know. I ought to go to the police, but taking into account who you are . . .'

'Please don't do that. It would be too awful. I'd have to say what happened. Please don't.' Her small hands were clawing at him in panic and he held them in his.

'I'm not going to. Now relax.'

'I'll try,' she said and leaned back on the pillows again. 'I just wish I understood why he'd done it,' she said. 'It was so cruel. Perhaps he always does it to girls, do you think?'

'Maybe,' he said, unable to help her. He was totally puzzled himself as to Kwan Ching's motives. 'But now you must try to forget all about it.'

'Don't tell me to put it down to experience,' she said with a flash of her old spirit.

'That's exactly what you must do,' he said calmly. 'Now, could you eat something?'

She contemplated and then gave him a radiant smile that seemed to erase the tearmarks as if her face had been polished.

'I could,' she said. 'Do you know, I'm starving.'

Jade had got herself back to the hotel in time for Mike's call at six o'clock after having found a phone box and made her call to Paul So. She had decided, hurrying back to the Mandarin, that Poppy was in the safest place. Obviously her sister was part of the mysterious vendetta, and it looked as if Kwan Ching was not yet satisfied with the degree of revenge he had inflicted. She felt a sharp brief lance of anxiety for herself and looked back over her shoulder as she walked briskly through the tunnel under Connaught Road

Mike's phone call had come on the dot and, remembering Emma's strictures not to use the switchboard, she asked him if he could come quickly to talk to her. He arrived, still suffering with his hayfever, and sat quietly in her room on her bed, while she told him what had happened to Poppy and Kwan Ching's involvement in the near tragedy. He carefully wrote down the name without comment.

The mention of Chan Koh Leung shook him out of his silence. He looked thoroughly alarmed and said: 'And what do you propose to do about him?'

'Go and see him if he's still alive,' she said.

'He is alive, but a Triad society blew up one of his hotels on Macao. He's feeling decidedly sick.'

'How do you know?'

'These things get reported in newspapers, my dear,' he said patiently.

She accepted that and said : 'So now we have gold cropping up. Do you know anything about this Chan Thingummy?'

'Everyone in South East Asia knows about Chan Thingummy,' he said and went on to explain to her how in the late 1950s and early '60s the price of gold had been pegged by an international agreement.

'It was called the Bretton Woods Monetary Agreement,' he said. 'I can't remember the exact price, but it was somewhere around thirty dollars an ounce then; in China, people would pay nearly double to get hold of gold. Portugal had been excluded from this agreement and Macao belongs to Portugal. Your Chan Koh Leung bought gold perfectly legitimately from the Bank of England or the USA at the right price, and then sold it at a premium to anyone who cared to buy. How it left Macao to be smuggled into the outside world was none of his business. He had a ready-made market – people in South East Asia put their money in gold. The gold smuggling that went on out of Macao and into other territories at that time was just unstoppable. It doesn't happen any more since Hong Kong made importing gold legal.'

'Then how does he fit in with it all?' she said. 'I'll have to go and see him.'

He became very agitated then, trying to dissuade her from doing anything so foolhardy. Finally he said: 'If you do go, take your boyfriend or take me. Don't go alone.'

'My boyfriend?' she said. 'Did you like him?'

213

'Not much, but more important—' He hesitated and then said. 'He's all right. You'll be safe with him.'

She felt a sense of relief that was almost physical and opened her mouth to ask questions. Before she could speak, he was looking at his watch. 'I must go,' he said. 'I've urgent phone calls to make.' He picked up the message paper that was on her bedside table and without any apology said: 'This chap who's asked you to the races – are you going?'

The question surprised her.

'I think so,' she said.

He grunted. 'I'll ring you in the morning. For God's sake be careful.'

He had only been gone five minutes when her phone rang. It was Jimmy Lee asking if she would accept his invitation. The races were in the evening, tomorrow, he said. Floodlit, of course.

Though she had told Mike that she would probably go, she had not really made up her mind. She considered while Jimmy Lee waited, and made a decision to accept. It was possibly dangerous – Jimmy Lee and Kwan Ching were associates, but she wasn't going to find out anything sitting on her bottom in the hotel room. She made arrangements to meet him at six thirty in the evening at the hotel and he would drive her to the new race track at Sha Tin.

'Don't dress up too much,' he said. 'Sha Tin is not like your Royal Ascot. But we'll have dinner somewhere pleasant after. The last race is at ten fifteen. And we might leave before then.'

She put Jimmy Lee out of her mind, having decided to have a headache when he suggested dinner, and began to prepare for her evening with Gary, her heart ten degrees lighter from having heard Mike say, 'You'll be safe with him.' She had her suspicions that Mike himself was not quite the simple character he appeared, and therefore his grudging approval was a green light to open up to Gary. They were both probably in the same line of business, whatever that might be, she thought as she ran her bath, though Gary was a much more likely candidate for the role of secret agent. Mike's sneezes would give him away if he were trying to be unobtrusive.

If only Gary would stop playing games with her it would help. She might then get to know him properly. Their lovemaking had been the best, but otherwise there was an impression of dealing with the husk of the man; finding no substance. If Emma was right and he was some kind of agent, and if Mike was right and he was 'Ok', the situation could only improve.

All things considered, she felt positively light-hearted as she poured herself a glass of champagne from the fridge and put on a brilliant red silk dress, bare-backed and plunging in front. Feeling liberated, she left off her bra, contemplated panties and settled for nothing more than a pair of the finest ten-denier tights beneath the dress. She used lipstick with a heavier hand than usual and let her hair flow free down her back. Experimentation with a soft, black crayon made her eyes look larger and yet even more Oriental, and the girl in the mirror who looked back at her was ready for a good evening, ripe for mischief and ripened for love.

His face when he saw her walking towards him in the lobby was naked pleasure. She realised, triumphant, that however convoluted his reasons for following her around the world he cared about her now, and she was smiling as she swirled to meet him.

'You are incredibly beautiful,' he said, standing as though he was afraid to touch her.

She stood on tiptoe to kiss him on the cheek and said demurely: 'Thank you.'

He was looking at her as if he had never seen her before.

'What's happened to you?' he asked.

'I'll tell you all about it over dinner,' she promised him, while her eyes promised much more.

It was a clear moonlit night and he had hired a Mercedes to drive to the other side of the Island. The interior of the car smelt of leather, a small expensive glow illuminated the dashboard and the heater gently purred. The atmosphere between them had changed. The small space of the front seat felt more intimate than bed had ever been. As he drove she let her hand creep on to his thigh and left it there. He looked at her quickly, smiled, and then turned back to the winding road.

They had to take a small ferry boat out to the huge floating restaurant which lay in astonishing brilliance out in the harbour.

'There must be more than a million lights on that boat,' she marvelled as they waited for the ferry.

'We'll count 'em,' he promised her.

The first glass of champagne went to her head; by the third she felt deliriously happy. She flirted with him and he responded most satisfactorily, and by the end of the meal she had given him chapter and verse of everything that had happened over the past few days. She held nothing back.

He held her hand very tightly across the table as she told him about Poppy and he looked both angry and concerned.

'Thank God it wasn't you,' he said.

'No.' She shook her head. 'It wouldn't have happened to me. I'm too sensible.'

'It could happen to anyone,' he said firmly, and she had a sudden mental picture of herself on a deserted beach with Jimmy Lee. Gary was right. It could have happened to her.

When she had finished, he said: 'My darling, this must stop. You've gotten yourself caught up in some Triad vendetta. Jade, Triads are not jokes. They are dangerous. Let it go. Drop it. Go home before anything else happens.'

With some very good wine topping the champagne, she felt confident enough to take on Triads and the Mafia at the same time.

'Everyone wants me to go home,' she said, light-headed and light-hearted, convinced of her own immortality. 'For you, I'll think about it. But the answer will be no. I'm too involved. I want to know the answers.'

'In that case,' he said, 'wherever you go and whatever you do, I go with you. Right? No more sneaking off to meet strange men, no more wandering around South East Asia alone. Promise?'

'Promise,' she said. 'With pleasure. But what about selling your jets?'

'Fuck the jets. I have the rest of my life to sell them. I'd kind of like to think you were around, too.'

'What does that mean?' She widened her eyes at him over the rim of her glass.

'Exactly what it says. I don't want you dying or getting hurt or even being frightened.'

'I thought you were proposing,' she said cheerfully, enjoying her own presumption.

'Not yet,' he grinned. 'But I'd like us to last long enough to think about it.'

She looked down at her plate and the put down her fork.

'Gary – why are you really here?' she asked abruptly.

'To be with you and to sell private jets,' he said promptly.

'Gary – I'm not a fool.'

He looked around the huge, brightly lit room, full of chattering

216

Chinese and clattering chopsticks and she could see his mind working. Then he said: 'If I were to tell you, I'd only add to your problems. Give me a few days and I'll come clean if I can. Ok?'

'Ok,' she said, nodding her head rapidly. 'Now I want to go dancing.'

'So we'll go dancing. Anywhere in particular?'

'Poppy went somewhere called the Godown, full,' she said, of Chinese girls with *gweilo*, which is apparently against somebody's rules. Imagine Poppy worrying about rules! Let's go and break rules.'

'Ok,' he said, laughing at her. 'It's not very swish.'

'Who cares?' she said with a gesture that sent her wine flying.

The remainder of the evening was a haze. On the ferry ride back from the boat a group of tipsy French tourists sang children's roundelays she had learned at her finishing school in Switzerland. She joined in and, for the few minutes that the ferry took to cross the water, she was part of their group while Gary held her hand.

The Godown, where they drank more champagne, was a blur and a blare of loud music and noisy Australians. And then they went back to the hotel to her bed.

He started to undress her, smiling at the small, slightly glassy-eyed figure as she stood in front of him, her dress a splash of red silk on the floor, her breasts bare and wearing nothing but high-heeled shoes and sheer tights.

'You'd better remove those,' he said. 'I'll only make them run.'

Trying to be careful, she slid the tights slowly down her legs while he waited. Then, completely naked, she stood up and said triumphantly: 'There!'

'They've made a funny mark all down your tummy,' he said, tracing the line of a seam from her waist to below with a questing finger. She laughed. 'They always do,' she told him. 'Haven't you noticed before?'

'You,' he said, 'are drunk,' rolling the 'r'.

'I know it,' she said mournfully.

There was no urgency about their lovemaking; it was sweet and slow and they savoured each other in a way that was different from other times. She wanted to hold him very close to her. She felt truly safe for the first time in days, and suddenly she was asleep in his arms.

The lights were on when she awoke, and he was still in bed with her. As she moved cautiously, his eyes opened.

'All right?' he asked.

'I have the most dreadful thirst.'

'Deserved,' he told her, and getting out of bed, he padded naked across the room to the fridge where he took out and poured her a bottle of Perrier water.

'Was I awful?' she asked him as she sipped it, aware that sleep had not entirely dissipated the alcohol.

'No,' he said, surprised. 'You were just having a great time.'

She lay back on the pillow and stared at the ceiling.

'You know, that's right. I was having a great time.'

'Well, don't sound so astonished,' he said. 'Great times can't have been thin on the ground for a girl like you.'

She sat up and hugged her knees.

'Oh yes they have been,' she said. 'My own fault, of course. Thinking about it – and I've been thinking more in the past few days than I've ever thought in my life – I reckon someone must have programmed me at an early age as to how lucky I was, and how I must be a good girl for the rest of my days to make up for it.' She shook her head. 'Do you know, Grandfather said something to me after Father's funeral. He said I'd played Martha to Poppy's Mary for far too long. And it's true. I've always been the dutiful one, looking after her when she was little, and then, just as things might have changed, looking after Mother when her mind went. I didn't object actually. It just seemed what I had to do.

'But you know when you think about it, poor old Martha was an idiot wasn't she? There she was, rushing around, serving, working her socks off for everyone, and what thanks did she get? Jesus just said that Mary, who sat at his feet having a good time listening to him and, frankly, doing sod-all, had chosen the better part. There's no justice.'

He had lit a cigarette and was sitting on the bedside, listening.

'What brought all this on?' he asked tenderly.

'Champagne in copious quantities and you. I had a great time with you. I got smashed. I knocked my wine glass over and I sang with a lot of strange people. I don't remember much about the Godown place, except – ' and her voice dropped to a conspiratorial whisper ' – I was a Chinese girl with a *gweilo*! How about that!'

'You were a girl with a guy,' he said firmly.

'Of course I was. I don't care if you care, but I'm going to tell you

I've had two proper lovers before you.' She considered. 'God – they were dull. There was a ski instructor, Franz, or was he Fritz? Can't remember just at this moment. Doesn't matter anyway. Do you know, he always washed his hands before we made love. Funny that, but they do say the Swiss are antiseptic. He lasted a winter, passed the time. Don't ask me what he was like in bed. I don't remember. I only remember this obsession with washing his hands. He washed them after, too,' she said thoughtfully, adding: 'I'd have thought there were more important bits to wash.

'And then, of course, there was dear old faithful Alistair back home on the croft. Now he and I have been lovers, if you can call it that, for the past three years whenever I was able to get away from Mother and his dad was out doing whatever crofters do. It was fortunate for us that he had no mother to get in the way.

'Alistair is nice. He is kind. He is gentle and he is as dull as dull can be, but I figured I was pretty dull too, and so we matched quite nicely. Nothing would ever have come of it, of course. Father would have had a fit at the idea of me marrying a crofter's son, though believe me, I could have done a deal worse.' She paused and considered. 'The truth of the matter was I didn't love poor Alistair, but it was nice to have someone of my own. A sort of secret to hug while Poppy was carousing around with all and sundry. I used to think 'I've got someone, too, but mine loves me.' And he does. He's big and rawboned with red hair and he'll never be the brain of Scotland, but he does love me and I wish I could love him back. It's not fair that I don't.' She stopped suddenly. 'Do you mind me telling you all this?'

'No.'

'You're sure?'

'I'm positive.'

'So there we are. And as it's confession time, I let that Jimmy Lee make love to me – though I think you'd guessed, hadn't you?'

He nodded.

'Now why did I do that? Answer, because I felt like doing that. I fancied him. And I was curious about him being Chinese and me being Chinese. I don't know what I expected. Poppy shocked me by telling me that European men think that Chinese girls' cunts go sideways. Can you believe it! Did you think that?'

'I never did think that,' he said gravely.

'Well, apparently some do. Maybe it's a British fallacy, if you'll pardon the pun. So maybe I thought Jimmy's penis would go sideways or do something different. Well, it didn't and now my curiosity is all satisfied. I don't like him much, though I am going to the races with him tomorrow. I have my suspicions that he's the key to the whole thing, or why did he pick us up at the airport? Come to that, why did you pick me up at the airport? Why are people always picking me up at airports? Don't answer – I know, you'll tell me in a day or two if things work out.' She sat silent for a moment and then said: 'Is there any more champagne in that fridge?'

'Indubitably,' he said.

'Then let's drink it.'

'Why not?' he said. 'I'll get it.'

'So there I am in Scotland with Alistair tucked in the wings, Father dead and Grandfather insisting that I do not take care of Mother for another moment. And it has only just dawned on me what a relief that decision of his was. My God, looking back, I was out of there so fast at the first chance, wasn't I? I mean I'd gone before you got there. Looking for my roots, I told myself. I don't think I meant it then. I was escaping. And, oh boy, was the escape a culture shock. Grandad was right. Now I *do* want to find my roots. At this moment I feel I'm suspended, swinging between the Western and Eastern hemisphere. Most uncomfortable. And what with that and the mystery. And you—' She took a glass of champagne from him. 'You who aren't remotely dull though you've been doing your best to appear so.' She took a very long swallow of her drink. 'Do you know what I feel? Don't answer – I'm going to tell you. I feel free, liberated, released. I feel I can do exactly what I like. I could stay here. I could go back to England and the flat in Eaton Square and whoop it up for a while. I could return to being Martha and a good girl. I could become much, much naughtier than Poppy. I can do what I like. Isn't that the most amazing situation to be in? How many people in the world are that free? And once I have sorted out this bizarre mystery that seems to be going on, I shall then consider with the greatest gravity, exactly what I am going to do with my life.'

She emptied her glass and slid gently back down on to the pillows. 'Now what do you think about that?' she said, but before Gary could answer, she was asleep.

He leaned and kissed her forehead, pulled the blankets over her, turned out the lights and slid away.

Back in his own room Gary settled down to think out logically everything Jade had told him. He could still not quite see where her jigsaw fitted into his jigsaw, but there had to be a missing piece that once found would make the picture clear.

He was pretty certain that his original reasons for trailing Jade all over the USA were spurious, unless the DEA were clairvoyant or a damn sight cleverer than he had thought. But some curious quirk had proved them right. Kwan Ching was part of Sammy Tu's plot, which meant he was part of Gary's. He was also very much part of Jade's plot, which meant that willy-nilly she was involved and so were her family. Kwan Ching was important, which might just mean that Jimmy Lee was as well, since the two seemed to be confederates. And from the little Gary had seen of him, Kwan Ching was a natural for the role the DEA had cast for him.

The complication for Gary came with the very positive affection he was beginning to feel for Jade. It made the hair rise on the back of his neck to think that she was involved, unwittingly, with a bunch of Triads and he didn't care how blasé the British chief inspector might be about 'street gangs' and 'young thugs', he was gold-plated certain that Kwan Ching did not fall into that cosy category.

He debated whether to wander over to the Big Fat Hot Lips and discuss the situation with Sammy, then decided against it. It was getting on for Wednesday morning, and Wednesday morning Sammy was getting initiated. Best not to cause any confusion.

His reading of the situation was that the DEA had been right in their thinking that Ian McKenzie McKenzie had been trafficking in heroin a long time ago. But not any more. And for some reason the deaths were revenge, Triad revenge, for something that had happened in the past. Which put Jade, soft, delicate, vulnerable Jade, in no small danger.

Where the ship and the gold man in Macao came into it, beat him.

He thought for a long time, then, wishing he were on home territory, he decided there was no way around it. He was going to have to ring that pompous prick of a police superintendent and put him more deeply in the picture.

The other thing he was going to do was to get himself a ticket to the races.

It had been just about the time that Jade was climbing on to the ferry to go across to the Jumbo restaurant when Mike Blake managed to track down Arthur Watson-King at the Foreign Correspondents Club. He swore softly when whoever answered the phone said he was there. The Foreign Correspondents Club was not a place he relished, crumbling as it was, ready to be pulled down for more of Hong Kong's never-ending redevelopment. The only thing that the place had to offer was the best view of the harbour from the gentlemen's lavatory window. The journalists were crumpled, like the place itself, drinking themselves stupid and dreaming of Fleet Street, Wall Street and their little grey homes in the West.

'What the hell are you doing there?' he asked when Arthur had lumbered his way to the phone.

'Sticking my nose in where it isn't wanted,' Arthur said. 'What's up?'

'Just one or two things to tell you.'

'Urgent?'

'You might say so.'

'Want to toddle round here?'

'Not a lot, but I will. Listen, Arthur – one thing. You a member of the Jockey Club?'

'Almost a founder, old boy.'

'Right,' Mike said crisply. 'You're taking me to the races tomorrow.'

'If you say so,' the old man said on a lugubrious note. 'But try to get a few good tips, will you, old chap. Make it worth my while.'

≈ 10 ≈

WEDNESDAY

The persistent buzz of the alarm woke Sammy Tu with quartz efficiency right on the button of five o'clock. He groaned loudly into the dark room and tasted his mouth experimentally to check just how much too much he had drunk the night before. Mi, crammed against the wall in the narrow bed they shared, had stirred sleepily at the sound of the alarm and whimpered quietly to herself. She had come in an hour or so ago and Sammy had not been properly asleep when she crept into bed. The anxieties of the ordeal ahead had kept him tossing and restless.

Now he slid quietly out of the bed himself and padded naked across the small room and out the door to where the washing facilities were in the 'H' bar of the building. No one was going to see him at this hour. He went into the stinking lavatory and then, shivering, made his way to the small sink. He thrust his head under the freezing water and made some effort to clean up. This was the worst of living in the huge old primitive housing-estate of Wong Tai Sin – no shower. When and if he got back to the States, he was going to spend two weeks in a hot shower without coming out.

He dressed quickly in his torn jeans and white vest and he put on a shabby matted-wool cardigan. He was going to have to walk to Cray Street into Shek Kip where the initiation ceremony was to take place; it would take at least an hour and it would be cold out there.

The part of Kowloon where he walked was silent, though he saw the occasional Triad protectors, light-footed in their white sneakers, patrolling their territory. By full daylight he would be one of them.

He walked quickly in his own sneakers, shivering a little from the cold morning air and from anticipation of what was to come. Infiltrating a Triad society was not to be undertaken lightly, and if you were rumbled, you were dead. But he wasn't going to be rumbled, he told himself.

He was outside the right number at Cray Street in good time to find three other uneasy-looking men of about his age lurking.

They did not acknowledge each other, and with his arrival a car drove up and an older, chunkily built man put his head out of the window and beckoned to them.

'I am the Vanguard,' he said to Sammy who was standing the nearest to him. 'Get in the car.'

'He's the Vanguard,' Sammy said cheerfully to the others to keep his spirits up. They did not reply but squashed into the back. Sammy had taken the seat next to the driver.

Once they were all in, the car quickly took on the smell of unwashed bodies, and the Vanguard drove as if he wanted to get the stench from out of his car. He swerved around corners, took back streets and appeared to be trying to confuse them as to the direction in which they were going. Sammy tried to watch for street names without it appearing too obvious.

The journey took five minutes, perhaps a little less, and then the car drove into a wide street of grim factories. It was Castle Peak Road, Sammy saw. He caught a glimpse of a factory sign on a corner building that read Green Butterfly Furs, and then the car turned left at the corner, then sharp left again. There it stopped at the back of the building.

The dusty, drab street of factories was deserted, and the four men followed their guide to where there was a small door, signposted Staff Entrance. The Vanguard pushed at the door and it swung silently open, unlocked. The man grunted and nodded them through. A flight of stairs faced them running up from a small hall with a clocking-in machine. At the top of the flight of stairs they came to a big open hallway, concrete floored and with large wooden doors that were padlocked. But the gates of the big industrial lift were open. The Vanguard pointed, still not speaking, and the men filed uneasily past the metal grille gates. Their guide followed them and pressed the button for the basement; the gates closed automatically and ponderously the lift began to drop.

No one was speaking and Sammy stole quick looks at the other recruits. They were as ragged and as badly dressed as he was; young, with hard, seamed faces. One, whose hands shook uncontrollably, he decided must be on heroin. But all three were whip-muscled under their not-too-clean clothes and Sammy thought they would be pole fighters – of the breed who practised martial arts in parks every day at break of dawn.

As the lift came to a shaky stop, the inner gates flew back, but the outer door was locked. They stood in the glare of the uncovered electric light-bulb hearing the sound of keys fumbling outside, and then the lift gate slowly opened.

They were in a huge basement store room where fur pelts were hung or flung in undisciplined piles, spilling out of packing cases. It was bitterly cold – so cold the area must have been refrigerated. To Sammy's surprise, there were a good number of people already in the room, and he spotted the young fortuneteller from the temple who had introduced him to the society. Since that day, it had been said that 'the blue lantern was hanging' at his home. He was on trial for membership of the Triad society.

A heavy wood table which could have been used for spreading the pelts for inspection was in the centre of the basement. That would be the altar, he thought. A red piece of paper with some writing on it was pasted to the table. Sammy's grasp of Chinese characters had been lost over the years in the States, and he could not understand what they said. He had had to tell the fortuneteller that he was illiterate when the matter of his joining had come up. The fortuneteller had said that did not matter. It was his proficiency in speaking English that mattered.

Before the altar he could see a container holding rice. Pushed into it were three red paper flags, again decorated with characters that he could not read.

A good-looking young Chinese of a different class to the initiates was standing in the background with Kwan Ching, the Incense Master. The other one had to be the head man, K489, the Hill Chief, but Sammy did not recognise him. Both the Hill Chief and Kwan Ching were in traditional mandarin robes that, sold, would have kept a Wong Tai Sin family in food for a month. They were separate from the rest of the people in the room. Plainly they considered themselves superior and both moved with the dignity of mandarins. Sammy could imagine them both wearing the pigtail, now so long outlawed in China.

The Hill Chief made a sign to the Vanguard, who had been watching him intently, and then the Vanguard bowed low in the old manner before signalling the four recruits to come forwards towards the altar.

'Kneel. On your left legs,' he instructed.

All four men did so and Sammy could smell the nervous sweat, like rotting fruit, on his neighbour.

The Vanguard turned to the altar, where he was lighting joss sticks. Sammy counted more than two dozen, and then these were handed ceremoniously to the Incense Master, Kwan Ching, who had moved majestically forward. The room was very still now and the lights seemed too bright – so bright they'd spotlight him for a fraud; they'd smell he was a fraud. He was sweating like a pig even in the cold of the room. But then the men with him were sweating too.

Kwan Ching was reciting poems in a slow monotone and then he knelt to put the joss sticks into the container with the flags and the rice. He turned to face the recruits.

'Is it true that you are all here voluntarily?' he asked loudly.

Sammy added his mumble of 'yes' to the others, wishing himself back in his own bed in San Francisco.

'Take these,' said Kwan Ching, holding out a joss stick for each man. 'Hold them with four fingers of your left hand, five of the right and with the lighted end to the floor.'

There was a certain amount of fumbling as the men arranged the sticks in their freezing hands. 'No,' the Vanguard hissed at one. 'Four fingers left hand, five fingers right hand.' The man muttered an apology.

'Now,' Kwan Ching said, 'dash the joss to the ground as you shall be dashed to the ground and extinguished if you break your sacred Triad oaths.'

The men threw down the sticks almost simultaneously and the pungent scent of their burning flared up briefly and died.

'Now, swear these oaths,' Kwan Ching said, and it seemed to Sammy that the man addressed him only. 'Repeat after me: *After having entered the brotherhood of this society, I must treat the parents, brothers, sisters and wives of my brethren as my own people. I shall be killed by five thunderbolts if I do not keep this oath.*'

Kwan Ching spoke the oath in two parts so that the men would remember the words. That didn't seem like too bad an oath, Sammy thought, but there were more to come and his left knee was giving him hell long before he and the other initiates had sworn them all.

He swore to help his brethren to bury their parents and brothers by offering physical or financial assistance, and agreed he would be killed by five thunderbolts if he pretended to have no knowledge of their troubles.

He agreed to be killed by myriads of swords should he not

provide his brethren with board and lodging or if he did not recognise their signals. Still mild enough.

Myriads of swords were the penalty for betraying Triad secrets even to his own family. He almost grinned at the one which said that if he happened to have arrested one of his brethren owing to a misunderstanding, he must release him at once. It tidily wrapped up a large proportion of the Chinese members of the Hong Kong police, he thought. And to his knowledge none of them had been knocked off by five thunderbolts. It seemed the oaths worked!

He swore to do no harm to the Incense Master or any of his brethren; he swore not to commit indecent assaults on his brethren's womenfolk, nor to embezzle from them. The oaths went on and on, brilliantly covering every family and criminal eventuality. They swore never to inform, but to warn other Triads if the authorities wanted them. It was fortunate for the owner of the Green Butterfly Fur Company that one oath demanded that he would not disclose any address where his brethren stored their wealth or have any malicious ideas about the wealth. Myriads of swords would keep the gleaming furs safe.

Sammy had become fascinated by the inventiveness of the oaths. They linked all Triads into a protective group which allowed back-up for any illegal acts. But at the same time, he was finding the ceremony intimidating. He was not far off being frightened. After the last oath was sworn, the Incense Master handed them each another joss stick which was flung again to the ground and extinguished. At this, a soft ripple of a sigh ran through the silently watching people beyond the altar.

And then Kwan Ching drew a ceremonial sword from beneath his robe and walked behind the kneeling recruits. Sammy felt the flat of the sword come down on his back in a sharp pat, and then Kwan Ching moved on. The fortuneteller had explained this part of the ceremony so he would know how to respond.

'Which is harder?' Kwan demanded of them. 'The sword or your neck?'

'My neck,' the recruits mumbled.

'And the threat of death will therefore never cause you to reveal the society's secrets,' Kwan Ching said, and advanced upon them with a thin-bladed kitchen knife. Using the point, he pricked each man's finger until blood ran.

Sammy was first to lick off the blood.

'It is sweet,' he said loudly and clearly.

They were then allowed to stand, and each rose, creaking to their feet; knees temporarily set. They had to walk over three pieces of red paper, pretending they were stepping stones, and after this they moved, left leg first, over burning paper. They were given a piece of apple to eat and a bowl of water to drink and then one of the watchers moved silently down the length of the basement and returned with a live chicken, its legs tied together. As he laid it on the altar, it made vain attempts to escape, its little eyes bright in the light. The Incense Master gathered them round, and each man placed his right hand on top of Kwan Ching's, holding the sword. Then, with one sharp blow, he cut the chicken first in half and then in quarters.

Sammy had never realised a chicken held so much blood and his own ran cold as Kwan Ching brought down the sword, his eyes gleaming, his expression satisfied. Sammy wiped a hand over his brow, pretending he was looking for blood splashes, but he was hiding a sudden spurt of fear. In spite of the mumbo-jumbo, Kwan Ching was for real; a tough, sadistic little bastard, and Sammy's quarry.

He was given his Triad number and paid for it – $20 to the Incense Master, $5 for the pot containing the rice and the flags, and $50 to the fortuneteller who had introduced him to the society. From now on, this man would be his protector.

And then, with great ceremony all the paper used in the ritual was burnt, the joss sticks were extinguished, and it was over.

Only then did Sammy realise he had been scared all the way through.

He was hovering, wondering what happened next, when the Hill Chief with Kwan Ching at his side came towards him.

'Is it true that you speak some English?' the man said in English.

'That is so,' Sammy told him.

'We may wish you to become the Straw Sandal – the 432,' the Hill Chief said.

The Straw Sandal was the group's messenger; the liaison with other branches. Sammy felt his heart lift and start to beat a little too fast. What they had hoped was beginning to happen.

'It's a great honour, so soon,' he said hesitantly.

'It is,' the Hill Chief said, his voice stern. 'You work at the temple, I am told.'

228

'When there is work.'

'You will start work here. As a warehouseman in this basement. I have heard good reports of you. It will be better if you are at hand. You will begin at eight thirty tomorrow.'

Sammy hesitated.

'Sir,' he said humbly. 'Forgive me, but have you the right to give me work here?'

'I do. The Green Butterfly Fur Company is mine.' Sammy saw the man was boasting. 'I am the Hill Chief and my name is Jimmy Lee.'

Sammy bowed, suppressing the urge to ask how much he would be paid.

'My Lord,' he said. 'I am grateful.'

There was an uneasy silence and then Kwan Ching said:

'You may go now.'

With the other initiates, who still seemed stunned by the ceremony, he went up in the lift and, led again by the Vanguard, was let out of the factory's staff entrance. Still no one spoke, and out in the street in the thin light of dawn each one melted away like a grey cat into the night.

When Poppy opened her eyes she was conscious of something being different. The small shrine still glowed red at the foot of the bed, the shutters let in grey morning light, the bed was the hard pallet that she had become used to over – how long was it? She realised she had no idea.

And then it dawned. What was different was that the cramp pains had gone; the sick feeling was no longer with her. She felt better.

Cautiously she sat up, afraid movement might change this pleasing situation, but it did not. She saw that Paul was in his usual place, seated in a hard chair near the window, writing in a large book.

'Don't you ever go to bed?' she asked him, her voice drowsy.

'Ah!' He put down the pen and the book and came towards her. 'Are you better? The doctor declares that this morning you should be well again.'

'I am better,' she told him. 'I feel right.'

'Nevertheless you must rest and let us look after you a little longer,' he said. 'Would you mind if I opened the shutters?'

'No. I don't think the light will trouble me now.'

'Good. I'll call Mother to bring you some food.'

He moved away from her to return to the window. As light flooded in mixed with thin sunshine, she saw he was wearing a dark sweater and slacks. He was very attractive, she thought as she settled herself back on the pillow and lay quiet. He went out for a moment and then returned to his hard chair. It was peaceful just resting and listening to the rustle of his papers and the faint scratching of the pen.

'What are you doing?' she asked after a while.

'Writing Sunday's sermon.'

'What's it about?'

'The new life in Christ. This Sunday we have a dedication to a baby and three baptisms. Then the congregation will partake of the Lord's supper.'

She lay thinking about it.

'What will you say?'

'I shall explain the relationship of the new believers to Christ. Before we were all sinners, separated from God. Those we baptise will have a relationship with God because of Christ filling their lives as he fills all our lives. I shall quote from the book of John which tells us our history as Christians.'

'Read some of it to me.'

'If you wish.'

She lay with her eyes closed, hearing him turning the thin pages, and then his quiet voice saying: *'Jesus said: Let not your heart be troubled; ye believe in God, believe also in me. I am the way, the truth and the life; no man cometh unto the Father, but by me.*

'If ye had known me, ye should have known my Father also, and from henceforth ye know Him and have seen Him.' He paused and then: *'If ye love me, keep my commandments and I will pray the Father, and He shall give you another comforter that He may abide with you for ever.'*

'I don't know if I could believe it,' she said slowly, 'but the words are nice. *Another comforter that He may abide with you for ever.* I like that. What happens when you baptise people?'

'They are immersed in water. Just as John the Baptist did to those he baptised.'

'What, really immersed? Made wet?'

He laughed.

'You must come to the chapel on Sunday and see for yourself.'

'I haven't been to church for years.'

'That's not important. You will be welcome. But I'm afraid the service will all be in Cantonese.'

'Then perhaps it would be better if you just showed me the chapel. Can we go there? I'd like to see where you work.'

'It's not exactly work,' he said as Pao came in through the door with Poppy's breakfast on a tray. She sat up, muttered a thank-you, and thoughtfully sipped the cup of tea.

'Paul,' she finally said and waited.

He looked up from his work.

'It's going to be a problem, isn't it? Me, I mean. Not being able to believe like you. I don't think I ever could. You see, I think getting wet like that is – well, just silly. I have to be honest with you. I have to say.'

He sighed.

'Believing in anything – even just believing in yourself – is an act of faith,' he said. 'Yes, and your feelings could be a problem. But why don't we just wait and see. Patience is needed, Poppy. We have found ourselves in a strange situation.'

She was still again, resting back on her pillow and watching him while he worked. She felt an enormous sense of peace; it seemed that she could communicate with him without words and that made for quietness and calm. But it *was* a strange situation. She knew that he loved her, but the reality of love was so remote to her that she was unable to describe to herself exactly what it was she felt for him. Was it love? What was love? The word that sprung to mind was that he was precious, and like anything precious she wanted to hold on to him.

She dozed again, and after a while when she woke the room was empty, but someone had laid a kimono and a large bath towel by her bed. She took these to be an invitation to get up. She knew where the bathroom was from the times Paul or his mother had led her there. This time she set off alone and found that, almost as if they had anticipated the time she would wake, the bath was full of hot water.

No one came near her until she had returned to her room and dressed herself in a shirt, skirt and shoes that Emma had packed when they left the Mandarin. She had no idea what time it was and was debating what to do when there was a gentle tap on the door.

'Come in,' she said, and Paul's head appeared.

'Ah,' he said, without coming into the room. 'You *are* better.'

'I *am* better,' she told him. 'But my watch has stopped. What time is it?'

'Nearly midday,' he said. 'Are you well enough to walk to the chapel with me?'

She thought about it.

'A bit tottery,' she said, 'but to go out will do me good.'

She held his hand as they walked along the country road back towards Fanling. The pavement was narrow and there seemed to be a lot of traffic on the road, so he kept close to her, protectively. The words he had read – *Another comforter that he may abide with you for ever* – were going through her mind, but she couldn't relate the comforter either to Jesus Christ or to God. It seemed to her that the comforter was Paul So.

'Is it as good to believe in another person as it is to believe in God?' she asked suddenly.

'Perhaps not as good, but it is important to believe in something or someone.'

'It may take me a while to believe in God,' she said. 'For the moment, I shall believe in you.'

'Don't forget I am fallible,' he told her.

She thought about it and said: 'So is God.'

He did not argue with her.

It took about twenty minutes to reach the little chapel and inside she stood staring around the simple room, a wooden cross on the wall beyond a table which she decided must serve as an altar. The bench seats were plain, the walls undecorated, but large blue crosses were set into the windows. The place had none of the atmosphere of the churches she had trudged around in Rome and Paris as part of her education, nor even of the Anglican chapels in which she had sat, bored, every Sunday at school.

She wondered why her parents had never made religion of any importance at all, and thought that perhaps as she and Jade had come from a different culture it was right to let them make up their own minds when they were ready. Then she remembered that Paul had said that the first time they had met.

Tired, she settled herself in a pew in the middle rows and looked around while he went into a small room at the right of what to her looked more like a stage than an altar. She was completely relaxed and unusually happy when she heard a diffident voice – a voice she recognised – say 'Excuse me' – from the back of the chapel.

Bracing herself, she turned slowly. 'Hallo, Jade,' she said.

Her sister was just inside the door, hot and dishevelled, clutching her large handbag and dressed in jeans and a green sweater.

'Poppy!' she said. 'Thank God! You're all right.'

At the same time Paul had come back into the body of the chapel.

'Ah,' he said when he recognised Jade standing in the doorway. 'You've come.' He paused. 'Was that wise?'

She was hurrying down the centre aisle towards them.

'I had to,' she said. 'I was worried. I came here to the church because I thought someone would tell me where you lived. I didn't expect to find you here.'

She sat down on the seat beside Poppy, placing her handbag between them and, taking a tissue from it, dabbed at her upper lip where a bead or two of sweat showed.

'Are you certain you weren't followed?' Paul asked. His voice was cool and he did not look at all pleased.

'I'm certain,' Jade said. 'Positive. I was very careful. I took the ferry to Kowloon and then I went into that Chinese arts and crafts shop at the Ocean Terminal. I wandered about there and came out by a different entrance. Then I walked for a bit, window shopping, and caught the MTR to Sha Tin. From there I stood in a bus queue and took one of those funny little buses that only hold fourteen people. It brought me here. I planned it exactly before I left the hotel. No one followed me. If anyone had, I could just have looked at the orphanage again and gone straight back. But I wanted to see Poppy.'

She turned, took Poppy's hand and held it tight.

'Are you all right now?' she asked.

Poppy was no more pleased to see her sister than Paul appeared to be. She had been enjoying the peace of being with him, the opportunity to rethink her life, and here was Jade, clucking, and who any minute now would be organising. She did not wish to talk to her sister about what had happened. She had no desire to share her humiliation with Jade, whose concern was genuine enough, but unwelcome.

'I'm fine,' she said, conscious of sounding sulky. 'It took you long enough to get here,' she added, working on the well-tried principle of attack being the best defence.

'Well, I thought—' Jade began, then stopped and said: 'It doesn't matter what I thought. But it seemed wiser to stay away.'

'Then why didn't you?' Poppy said.

'Poppy!' Paul's voice was reproving her, and that was Jade's fault too, Poppy decided. 'Jade is here now,' he said.

'Well, I don't want to talk about anything that has happened,' Poppy said. 'I just want to forget it.'

'Is she better?' Jade asked, speaking directly to Paul.

'Yes. Everything will be all right now if she stays here a little longer.'

'Is there anything I can do?'

'Just don't start organising,' Poppy said.

She could see Jade's eyes fill with tears, but she could not bring herself to be warmer. Aware she was behaving badly, she folded her arms tight across her chest and sat staring at the wooden cross on the wall.

'You look tired,' Paul was saying to Jade.

'It was a long journey,' she said. 'I came on impulse. I seem to keep doing the wrong thing on impulse lately.'

He nodded sympathetically, which considerably irritated Poppy.

'Can I get you anything?' he asked.

'I'd love a glass of water.'

'Of course,' he said. 'Come with me.' He beckoned to the side door of the chapel.

Jade got to her feet and threw Poppy an appealing glance, but she ignored it and kept silent. She watched as Jade followed Paul down the side aisle of the chapel and out to where there was a little garden and maybe a kitchen or a church hall of some kind.

Jade had left her handbag on the pew. Looking at it, Poppy had a sudden vision of them both on the train back from Fanling to Kowloon. She remembered Jade's discomfort when they talked of the papers that told they were not the children of their father's translator. She also remembered how she had been convinced that the papers were in the handbag. It had been her intention to read them at some time to find out exactly what was embarrassing Jade. Now seemed like the perfect opportunity.

The zip of the black Gucci handbag was open and Poppy went straight to the big inside pocket. A map was there and some smaller papers. She took them out quickly, not sure how long she had before Jade and Paul returned.

She was lucky. The first paper was an envelope with an old Hong Kong stamp addressed to Sir Ralph Martin. Inside was a letter and another piece of paper – a newspaper cutting. It was about a woman throwing herself into the harbour and abandoning her baby. Then she turned to the letter and read it swiftly. It said:

Dear Sir Ralph

You may have seen the enclosed in the *South China Morning Post*. I have the child. She is a perfect age to be sister to the other child you saw. This new one is sickly and will need much care. I would imagine she is no more than three months old, though she is so small and frail it is hard to tell.

The other child, whom I have called Jade, has taken to the baby and is careful of her. It grieves me, but I will let these two leave my home. You can do more for them than I.

I am sending a photograph under separate cover for you to show your wife so that she can make her decision.

It was signed Eleanor Tibbets.

Poppy had been so engrossed in the letter and the implications of what she was learning that she was not aware that Jade and Paul were back in the chapel, walking down the side aisle.

She saw Jade's face in a flash, as if caught by a camera, registering naked dismay at what Poppy held in her hand. And Poppy, staring at her, heard herself saying, with a note of delight that she could not conceal:

'You're not my sister at all!'

Gary Smith was a thoughtful man as he hurried back to the Mandarin after his second interview with Chief Superintendent Morrison. The man was still a pompous prick, but he wasn't the fool he had seemed. He'd listened to Gary tell the story as Jade had told it the night before, and had made decisions without any hesitation. The licensing officer, whose name Gary had not been able to provide – Jade could not remember it – would be found and used.

'Will you be able to trust this guy?' Gary had asked. 'He seems to have behaved well in the Poppy situation, but Kwan Ching's scared the shit out of him.'

'We'll check him out – and thoroughly. Don't worry,' Morrison had said. Then he grinned, a thin, cold, razor-slash grin. 'We've had other information in this morning, too. Your story tallies with someone else's. These McKenzie McKenzie girls must be quite something.'

'I've never met the sister,' Gary had said, 'but if she's as good-looking as Jade . . .'

'No one seems to have met the sister, except Kwan Ching and our nervous licensing staff officer. Would you think she's safe with this pastor? Will Ching find her?'

'I should think she's safe enough,' Gary had said drily. 'I gather the company of men of God is not her usual scene.'

'And it looks as if poor old Dottie Adamson's murder is tied in with it all. More revenge, I don't doubt.' Morrison had ponderously shaken his head, and then asked abruptly: 'Do you happen to know what the Triad gang call themselves?'

Then Gary had shaken his head. 'I haven't been in touch with my contact. I'm seeing him tonight. He'll know.'

'Well, our other informative fellow who's a nosy sort of chap tells me they call themselves the Broken Scissors Gang. In the light of Dottie Adamson and that twenty-year-old broken-scissor massacre that seems to have been worrying your friend Jade so much, I'd say that was interesting, wouldn't you?'

'Very,' Gary had said, remembering with a shiver the gleaming broken scissors on Jade's bed the night he arrived in Hong Kong; and he had started to worry about her again.

He worried more when she was not at the hotel. She had left him a message which read: *'Don't be cross, but I've gone out. It is important to me. You weren't around to tell. See you later.'*

He recognised her reluctance to tell him what she was doing as nervousness to commit any action to paper and wondered where the hell she could have gone. Macao? Unlikely. She had promised not to go there alone. Kowloon, looking for the last name on her list, Michael Broadbent? Fanling, to see Poppy?

He decided that would be most likely. She'd have gone to see Poppy – he hoped, without being followed.

His other problem as he sat in his hotel bedroom was how Sammy had got on. Was Sammy Tu, who had become as American as Boston Beans, now a fully-fledged Triad? Safely? Gary chain-smoked as he sat deciding what to do. He couldn't see Sammy Tu until late that night at the Big Fat Hot Lips and that meant that he was going to have to leave Jade unguarded. And Jade was going out with Jimmy Lee who he was pretty sure was no companion for a nicely brought up young lady. He felt a stabbing sword of jealousy as he thought that Jade had let Jimmy Lee make love to her. He hadn't wanted to hear the background to her sexual encounters the night before, but she had been too wound up to stop talking and telling, and so he'd sat there and listened patiently, wishing she wasn't spilling her secrets. But then the thought struck him that these days to have only three encounters to confess wasn't at all bad. He had had a hell of a lot more himself.

It was half-past twelve and Stephen Norris had just been about to slip out of the Wanchai Police Station and get himself a sandwich and a beer when the summons came that a Chief Superintendent Morrison wanted to see him over at headquarters, and now.

All desire to eat disappeared; his stomach felt liquid. This was it. Kwan Ching had not been lying. The ICAC were after him.

It took too long getting through the traffic to Hennessy Road, and the chief superintendent was visibly impatient when Stephen was ushered into his office.

'You took your time,' the man said. He was burly with cold blue eyes and a superior expression, and Stephen felt there would be no quarter from that direction.

'I'm sorry, sir,' he said, 'it was the traffic. It gets worse . . .'

The chief superintendent grunted.

'Well, Norris,' he said, 'you seem to have got yourself mixed up in a right old caper.'

'Sir?'

'Know a man called Kwan Ching?'

Stephen took a deep breath and held his hands so that their faint trembling would not show.

'Yes, sir.'

'What do you know about him?'

'He's into import and export, has his own ships and owns a few clubs and massage parlours.'

'And has he been telling you that the ICAC are after you?'

The question puzzled Stephen. He decided to answer honestly.

'Yes, sir.'

'And what did you do to cause this?'

'Took some free meals at restaurants. Only two restaurants. I gave one of them prior notice when the health inspector was coming.'

'In that case it seems you're the officer we're looking for.'

There was something not quite right with the conversation, and Stephen said: 'Are the ICAC investigating me, sir?'

'Not that I know of,' Morrison said casually. 'They seem to have rather bigger fish to fry these days. They're leaving the Force alone and upsetting local government. It's possible that Kwan Ching did inform on you. Some sort of partiality complaint, but a few free meals and one tip-off to the health inspector don't constitute too much of an offence.'

'Then why are you looking for me, sir?' he asked.

'We've had a couple of tip-offs of our own that a chief inspector, a licensing officer, has got himself involved with Kwan Ching and been acting as Sir Galahad to one of the McKenzie McKenzie girls – but without reporting what was going on. You should have reported it, Norris.'

'I know, sir,' Stephen said miserably.

'The informants didn't know your name. That was our only problem. I've been all through the staff licensing officers this morning. As you're the only one shacked up with a Chinese girl, it made it easier.'

Stephen decided to keep quiet. He was still uncertain which direction the conversation was taking. Who were the informants? Emma? Jade?

'Did Kwan Ching promise you a job?' Morrison asked.

'Yes, sir.'

'That was our information. And what sort of job was it?'

'He never said, sir. He just said that if I had real problems with the ICAC and was suspended, he'd have something for me to do.'

'Well, consider yourself suspended.'

'Yes, sir,' Stephen said woodenly.

'From your current duty, that is. You're going undercover. Find out what he wants you to do – and do it.'

'Sir?'

Morrison sighed and fiddled ostentatiously with a gold Parker pen between long, fingers.

'Your friend Kwan Ching is the Incense Master of the Triad group. The American Drug Enforcement Agency are after him. They believe he's responsible for smuggling a flood of heroin into Los Angeles and they want him. What they don't know yet is how the operation works. They have a man, undercover in the group – poor bastard – and someone else working on the outside. You don't need to know the whys and wherefores, but the McKenzie McKenzie girls are caught up in it too.'

Stephen's mind was beginning to work normally again. It had

238

dawned loud and clear that he wasn't really being suspended and that it looked like he was about to be working on something a good deal more interesting than handing out licences. 'I'm not surprised Ching's a Triad, sir,' he said. 'He asked me to help get a couple of men lion-dancers' licences recently. You know they're always Triad members.'

'Another bit of impartiality, Norris?' the chief superintendent said mockingly.

'Not really, sir. There was no reason why they shouldn't have the licences. They'd no record. Tough little couple of buggers they were.'

'And well into martial arts, I suppose?'

'Well, the lion-dancers always are, sir. And the station is keeping an eye on them. But the business with the McKenzie McKenzie girl was strange. He'd nearly killed her, sir, and I'd swear she wasn't a junkie.'

'And where is she now?'

'I don't know. My girlfriend, Emma, put her somewhere and wouldn't say where. I suppose she thought Kwan Ching would get it out of me and it was better if I didn't know. He still wants to get her, sir. He's not yet finished whatever he's up to. I think it's revenge of some kind.'

'Well, as long as she's safe and stays that way, she's not our problem.'

Stephen's mind was ticking like a clock now.

'Do you know where she is, sir?'

'I do.'

It was bloody Emma, sticking her nose in, Stephen decided. No, it couldn't be. Not if they hadn't been told his name.

'So,' Morrison was saying, 'now you go to Kwan Ching and say that you don't care whether or not you're being investigated, you're up to here –'' he made a slicing movement at his throat '– with the police force and ask him how about that job he was offering. Take it, and keep me informed.'

'How do I do that, sir? Any particular method?'

'Public telephone when you're sure you're not being watched. We'll inform you what to do when you make contact.'

'Shouldn't I know the names of the DEA men?' Stephen asked.

The superintendent gave him a sharp look.

'Not yet,' he said deliberately. 'Not until we're absolutely sure

239

that Kwan Ching can't bend you around his little finger too easily. Personally, I've got my doubts about the whole thing. We've had heroin under control here in Hong Kong for a long time now. The Americans always overreact.'

Stephen felt a flash of irritation at the man's superior attitude but, feeling no comment was needed from him, he just nodded.

'From now on you're "Needle",' Morrison said. 'That's your cover name. Goes well with Kwan Ching's little group. They call themselves the Broken Scissors.'

It seemed to Stephen that Morrison was watching him for some response; that he should have known about the Broken Scissors.

'Never heard of them, sir,' he said.

'You'll learn,' Morrison said. 'You'll learn.'

The expression on Poppy's face and the note of joy in her voice as she said: 'You're not my sister at all,' left Jade feeling that she had been slapped around the face. The feeling was so strong that she wanted to hit back. She wanted to retaliate more than she had ever wanted anything in her life. She took four long paces, and finding herself in striking distance of Poppy, hit her around the face with all the strength she could muster.

'How dare you touch my handbag,' she said.

Poppy's head sprung sideways on her delicate neck and a red hand imprint was clear on her cheek. For a moment she looked astounded. Then she leapt towards Jade, her hands claws, red nails bared.

'You bitch!' she spat.

'Poppy! Jade!' Paul So was between them instantly. 'This is God's house.'

'In that case,' Jade gritted, 'we'll go in His garden. I think I'm going to kill her.'

Free of Paul, she marched down the chapel to the garden door. She turned to see that Poppy was struggling to go after her, but Paul held her tightly. Suddenly she bit his restraining hand, and his grip loosened for the moment. Like a cat, she was running after Jade, claws out again, her face furious.

By the time Paul had disentangled himself from the pews, the two girls were rolling and fighting in the small patch of grass outside. Jade was only aware of a red mist of rage. Her fists were pummelling at Poppy and she was not feeling the blows that Poppy returned.

She could hear panting, breathing and Poppy hissing imprecations while she herself swore with fishwife force.

She must have been on top in the mêlée, because suddenly she felt herself being picked up bodily, a dizzying vision of green grass and trees and blue sky unfocusing before her eyes as the world went up and down. And she was over Paul So's shoulder pounding his back, while Poppy still lay panting and coughing on the ground.

'Now stop it,' he said. 'Stop it. Both of you.'

He set Jade on her feet, but carefully positioned himself between the two of them. Jade took a deep breath and stared down at Poppy.

'Ok,' she said. 'We won't fight any more. But I just want to tell you something, Poppy McKenzie McKenzie Martin. If it gives you pleasure to find that we're not sisters, it's nothing, nothing, nothing to the pleasure it gives me. You've been my albatross for twenty-one years. Well, I'm finished with albatrosses. Fresh out of them from this moment. And how dare you reproach me for not coming sooner? I thought, and I thought rightly, you were just having one of your sordid little fucks. Well, this time it went wrong, didn't it? You got what you've been asking for for years. But lucky as ever to fall on your feet with a man like this to look after you.' She turned to look at Paul who stood silent. 'Just don't you let her wreck your life, Paul So. Because she will if she gets half a chance. And I'll tell you for free: nobody – not her, *nobody* is wrecking mine from now on.'

She turned to go, and then spun around again to where Poppy still sat, half dazed.

'I didn't tell you we weren't sisters, Poppy darling, because I actually thought it might make you unhappy. Can you believe I was silly enough to think it might distress you that neither of us had anybody in the world? Well, now we haven't and I hope it's as much of a relief to you as it is to me. You can go to hell your own way from now on.'

Trembling, she marched back into the chapel and collected her handbag, amazed at herself for remembering to do so. Then she walked out of the street door into the thin sunshine of the day and headed for Fanling station.

She had to wait for a train, and stood on the concrete platform surprisingly calmly. She contemplated as to whether she was saddened that Poppy had not run after her when she left the chapel and decided that she was not. The sense of freedom that had begun the night before was growing. Her life was changing direction, entering a new phase, and that could only be exciting.

On the train her eye began to feel stiff and painful, and she noticed that her hands were scratched. The Chinese sitting near her were looking at her from under their eyelids, trying to observe without being seen.

She took out a mirror from her handbag and looked at her face. She had the beginnings of a fine shiner, and a bad scratch down one cheek was beginning to sting. Her hair was dishevelled and she looked exactly what she was: a girl who had been in a fight. She laughed out loud. What would Jimmy Lee think!

It was nearly four o'clock by the time she was back at the hotel, and she found a message was propped by her phone to ring Gary Smith.

He answered before the second ring.

'Thank God!' he said. 'Are you in your room?'

'Yes,' she told him.

'I'll be right there.'

He took her in his arms immediately the door was closed behind them, held her tight and said: 'Will you please not disappear like that. Where have you been?'

Her head was comfortable on his chest and she muttered: 'Fanling.'

He drew back to look at her and said: 'I thought—' then stopped. 'For Christ's sake,' he said, looking at her face. 'What happened?'

'Poppy and I had a fight.'

He looked disbelieving.

'Poppy did that to you?'

'Hopefully she's in worse shape,' she said cheerfully.

'What happened?' he asked again.

'She went through my handbag. She found the letter that explains we aren't really sisters and she was so pleased with the news I lost my cool and hit her. In a church.' She started to laugh. 'It was funny really. The poor pastor man was so upset. Shocked to the core, he said: "This is God's house." So I went out into the garden and hit her some more until he separated us. Then I sort of told her to get lost and came back to Hong Kong again. If you're interested, she seems fit as a flea. Or she was until I walloped her.'

He was smiling too. 'You're getting very militant,' he said.

'I feel militant.' She added cryptically, 'I'm through with albatrosses.'

'Around your neck?' he suggested.

'Around my neck.'

'I'll buy you a rope of freshwater pearls instead,' he promised. 'Now let's go out.'

He took her to the top of the Peak where they ate rich cream cakes and drank good coffee, the panorama of Hong Kong and Kowloon spread below. They came back down by the funicular, laughing like lovers as they clung to each other at the steepness of the descent.

'It is said,' he told her solemnly, 'that when this was first built in the days of your Queen Victoria, the British used to send their Chinese servants up and down first to make sure it was in good working order.'

'That's British!' she said.

For the last short distance back to the hotel they took a taxi. She was running late for her meeting with Jimmy Lee. He took her to her room door and kissed her.

'For God's sake, be careful. Don't go anywhere with him alone. And remember I won't be far away.'

'You'll be at the race course?'

He nodded. 'I'll hang around the paddock.'

'I'm glad,' she said.

It was six o'clock and Michael Blake was tidying his desk, making sure his in-tray was empty and the out-tray had been taken to the post when the telephone call came through.

He listened to the authoritative voice at the other end of the line, sighed, and said: 'I'll be there.'

He put down the phone slowly, then picked it up and dialled.

'Arthur,' he said, 'the races are off. Duty calls. Can't make it. But put a fiver on Top Fortune if you get the chance. I'm told it's a cert.'

Quiet in his office, he sat thoughtfully, worried. It occurred to him that the overhandsome young man from the DEA wouldn't let Jade out of his sight. He'd be there. It would be all right.

Gary had been shopping for a rope of freshwater pearls at a jewellery shop Kowloon side off Nathan Road. He took his time and had a beer on the way back and it was half-past eight when he returned to his room at the Mandarin. It was his plan to be at Sha Tin well before the fifth race at nine forty-five. He had plenty of time.

The message button was winking on his telephone. Impatiently he picked up the receiver and asked for the message clerk, who told him to ring Mi, gave the number and said it was urgent.

Swearing softly, he punched out the digits and a woozy female American voice answered.

'Big Fat Hot Lips.'

'Is Mi there?' he asked.

'Honey,' the voice said, 'Mi's always here. Hang on. Don't go away.'

He waited and after a few seconds another voice, this one having trouble with English, came on the phone.

'Gary? Is Mi. Where are you? I lonely. You must come. Now. Right away. I very wait.'

'I'm on my way,' he said curtly, and putting down the phone, added: 'Shit!'

He decided that the ferry and then a taxi would be quickest, and sweated all the way until the driver put him down in a blazing lit Kowloon street where a neon-red sign of horrendously fat lips hung six feet across the pavement from a first-floor window. He'd arrived.

He paid off the cab and ran up a dingy flight of wooden stairs into a big barely lit room. Two drunken British sailors were drinking and shouting at the bar and a few tired looking Chinese tarts sat in rows on bench seats against the wall.

As he came in, ducking his head to miss the door jamb, a woman came towards him, white-skinned, henna-headed, a rose behind her ear and wearing a black dress with a plunging neckline that had seen a lot of better nights.

'Who sent you, honey?' she attempted to purr. 'Welcome.'

'Hi.' Gary thrust out his hand and smiled. 'You've got to be Suzie. I've heard about you from Mi.'

'Mi? You lookin' for Mi?'

'That's right.'

'She's right there.' The woman sighed like someone to whom nothing good ever happened and moved back to the bar. 'Have one on the house, honey,' she said back over her shoulder. 'We don't see too many like you.'

A very small Chinese girl had scuttled up with the awkward little half-run of the Chinese who had been agricultural people.

'Gary. I miss you. Now you come,' she said. 'I waited very enough for you.'

She had the broad moon face of the Cantonese, but her mouth was full and deeply outlined in pink. She had used a curtain of mascara on her eyelashes so that her eyes appeared bigger, and though her nose was broad, it was neat. Dressed in a cheap Western-style too-short, too-low-cut, sexy white dress, there was still something innocent in her expression.

'Mi, I tried, but I've been busy,' he said.

She pouted.

'Too busy for poor Mi. Poor lonely Mi! You come back my place now?'

'I come back your place now,' he agreed. If Sammy wanted him that fast, there had to be a reason. But he realised his chances of getting to Sha Tin in time to guard Jade were very slim indeed.

Jimmy Lee was meticulously on time and his first words when he found her in the lobby were: 'My dear girl, what have you done to your face?'

She had tried to hide the rapidly developing swelling with make-up, but the shining red persisted in coming through. By morning it would be black.

'A silly fall,' she said.

'A bad fall,' he corrected her.

She was conscious that it was their first meeting since the afternoon on the beach, but he was acting as if nothing had happened between them. He was casually dressed in an English blazer with brass buttons, a gleaming white shirt and striped tie over dark trousers. She had worn a brilliant green Yves St Laurent suit – a colour that would stand out in a crowd. She wanted Gary to be able to spot her without difficulty.

'It's good to see you again – even with a black eye,' he said. 'I have the Rolls outside.'

It occurred to her as they were ushered out through the revolving door by two porters that going with him alone in the car was not a good idea. But the white Rolls itself was so reassuring, the chauffeur so correct and Jimmy himself so courteous that her confidence grew. She had no plan in mind of how to handle the evening, but maybe she would learn a little more about the rich and mysterious Jimmy Lee.

They drove straight to the race course through the tunnel across the harbour, through another tunnel and then in a growing mass of traffic to Sha Tin where she had already been once that day.

'How is your sister?' Jimmy asked suddenly.

'Fine – I think,' Jade said casually, but instantly alert. 'Enjoying herself, I imagine.'

'She never seems to be around.'

'That's true. We've always done our own thing. She and I don't get on all that well.'

'Where is she tonight?' he persisted.

'God knows. The last time I heard from her she was off with your friend Kwan. I assume she's either still with him and it's a big romance or, if not, I ought to be calling the police.'

'I'm sure that's not necessary,' he murmured.

His face in the half-dark of the car was unreadable, but Jade had a happy feeling that he was both puzzled and annoyed.

'Have you seen Kwan?' she asked.

He was silent.

'Not for a day or two,' he said finally. 'I had not realised that he was spending time with your sister.'

'Quite a lot by the look of it,' Jade said, thinking, Your move.

It was a surprise move he made.

'I was sorry to read about your grandfather,' he said. 'Has he recovered from what must have been a terrible shock?'

'He's bound to have done,' Jade said cheerily. 'My grandfather is quite indestructible.' Then she became solemn. 'But it was a terrible thing to happen. I can't understand people who do things like that. Monsters! Why would anyone want to harm an old man and kill an old woman? I don't understand violence or violent people. Do you understand that kind of mentality, Jimmy? I simply don't.'

'Nor I.' His voice was grave.

'I am so pleased,' she said fervently and he gave her a quick sharp look as she stared at the press of traffic, telling herself she really shouldn't play dangerous games.

The huge floodlit stand of the Sha Tin race course was ahead now, and they crept in line with other cars into the members' car park. Elevated walkways leading from the railway station were black with scurrying people, and a light rain had begun to fall. It did not seem to have a discouraging effect on the incredible throng.

'My God! It's crowded,' Jade said.

'We like to gamble,' he said, sounding as if he meant more than he was actually saying, while she wondered what his gamble was. 'And,' he added, his voice lighter, 'we like horse racing.'

'So I see,' she said, amazed by the sheer number of people and hoping that Gary would be able to find her among them all.

She was not impressed with the entrance where they fought through a press of people, but once they were up on the seventh floor in a cheerfully furnished restaurant and bar that looked out over the track, she saw that the place had a certain magic.

There were two tracks, one grass and one sand, and straight across at the winning post opposite where they sat was a vast television screen which, he explained, followed the racing and also what was happening in the paddock.

'I'll take you down there and you can inspect the horses before you bet. Would you like to look at the race card?'

He handed her the white race card with the yellow and blue emblem of the Royal Hong Kong Jockey Club on the front. 'We are in time for the first race,' he told her. 'It's a pity I do not have a horse of my own running tonight.'

The first race was at seven forty-five. Jade's eye ran over the list of nine runners and, telling herself again that she shouldn't play games, she said: 'I fancy number four.'

'Ah, which one is that?' he asked.

'It's called I Win,' she said, and smiled like honey.

His face never changed expression, but he said: 'In life, I personally always win. But of course, not everyone can, and if you will take my advice, you should put your money on number five – Top Fortune. It stands a better chance.'

'No,' she said, 'I'll stick with my hunch.'

But to her chagrin Top Fortune did indeed win, romping home by two lengths.

'But I shall not have won a fortune,' he said. 'Now let us go down to the paddock.'

There were six races, the last to be run at ten fifteen. Dutifully between each one she followed him down to the paddock, a wide open space floodlit and elegant with potted plants, looking all the time for Gary. She placed herself in the most conspicious places, but there was no sign of him at all, and at nine thirty, back in the upstairs bar and restaurant, Jimmy said casually: 'We shall leave before the last race and avoid the crowds. I have a little surprise for you. I think you will like it.'

'What sort of surprise?' she said.

'You will see. It is waiting for you at my factory, which is Kowloon side – on our way back. I thought we would stop there briefly and then we shall go on to dinner.'

'I don't know—' she began to say.

'It is all arranged,' he said. 'No arguments.'

Her mind began to race. He could be going to give her a fur coat which she did not want, or it could be something much nastier.

'Let's go back down to the paddock,' she said brightly. 'There's just time before the race.'

'If you wish,' he said. 'And what will you back this time?'

She was looking at the list.

'Message, I think,' she said praying for one from somewhere. 'The jockey is in dark blue and pink. My favourite colours.'

'Message?' he said. 'In that case I shall bet on Very Best Wishes. The horse is a little old at nine, but he could do very well.'

They took the lift yet again down to the paddock, and again she stood near the brightest lights, in the emptiest spaces, but Gary did not appear.

The race was run, and Message came fifth, but Jade took superstitious comfort in the fact that Jimmy lost too.

'And now what?' she asked herself. Short of vanishing to the ladies room and not coming out again, or trying to disappear into the throng in her brilliant green – literally running away from him – she wasn't at all sure what to do except that every jangling nerve told her that going to his factory was not a good idea at all.

'Shall we have just one more drink before we go?' she suggested. 'We can toast your winnings and console ourselves for my losses.'

'If you wish,' he said, but without enthusiasm.

Her mind was racing as he walked towards the bar, but she couldn't seem to come up with a solution. Once she was in the Rolls with him, pleading a headache – anything – would hardly stop him if he was determined to take her to his factory.

She decided to go to the ladies room to give herself breathing space and she had just turned away from the view over the race course when a voice boomed:

'Ah, there you are! Been looking for you everywhere.'

It was a miracle. It had to be a miracle. She rushed across the room and flung herself at the tall, safe figure of Ian McKenzie McKenzie with Michael Blake hovering behind. 'Oh, Grandfather!' she gasped. 'Am I pleased to see you!'

'I have a room I use for business,' Mi was telling him as they clattered down the dingy wooden staircase from the Big Fat Hot Lips Club and into the street. 'Is not very nice, Gary, but Sammy wait there for you.'

'Ok, Mi,' he said. 'No problem.'

Of course there was a problem, he told himself as they walked down the brightly lit street, Mi just a pace ahead of him and moving surprisingly quickly on her absurdly high heels. It was now creeping on for nine o'clock and time was running out.

The walk was a short one, and Mi suddenly plunged into a gloomy doorway and up a flight of steps, the twin of those at the Big Fat Hot Lips. This time there were two floors to navigate, and then she opened a green-painted door on a landing on which were three other identical doors.

'We here,' she said.

She beckoned him in and swiftly shut the door behind them. It was true the room was not very nice. There was a washbasin and a pile of towels on the floor beside it; and a bed and a rattan chair on the bare wooden floor. The overhead light swung gently in the draught, and the walls were covered with posters of Chinese opera singers and Western pop stars.

The bed was occupied. Sammy Tu was stretched along it, his feet up, shoes on the floor, his head against a pile of pillows, smoking.

'Hi,' he said.

'Hi.' Gary looked around and then settled himself in the rattan chair, turning it to face Sammy. 'How'd it go?'

'Would you believe, I have a full-time, paid-up salaried job.'

'Yeah?'

'Warehouseman at the business of K489 – the Hill Chief.'

'And who is K489?' Gary asked, helping himself to a cigarette from Sammy's pack.

'A guy called Jimmy Lee. Owns a company called Green Butterfly Furs.'

'Jesus Christ,' Gary said softly, dropping the lit match that was in his hand. 'You're sure?'

'Certain. After the initiation –' Sammy gave an involuntary little shudder '– he and Kwan Ching spoke to me. Jimmy Lee hired me as warehouseman. I started there today.'

Gary had struck another match and lit his cigarette. His mind was on Jade, at the races with Jimmy Lee and unguarded.

'Sammy—' Mi was speaking in Cantonese, and Sammy shook his head at her.

'Stay here,' he said. 'When you go, go with Gary. Ok?'

'Ok,' she said and seated herself on the end of the bed, hands folded in her lap.

'She wanted to go back to work,' Sammy said. 'I haven't told her about the job yet. Maybe she won't have to go back to work. Anyway, quite apart from warehouseman, I have another even more responsible job.' His voice was mocking. 'Would you believe, this DEA agent is to be Straw Sandal – the gang's messenger.'

'That means they'll want you to travel with the stuff,' Gary said. 'Jesus! What a break.'

'If I live to enjoy it,' Sammy said. 'But I guess that's what they have in mind for little 'ole English-speaking me.'

'Any clues to how the operation works?'

'Give me time,' Sammy said plaintively. 'But there are shipments of furs, packed and ready to go in the warehouse. They look respectable enough. There's a consignment for Neiman Marcus, another for Bonwit Tellers, one for Saks – all to the Los Angeles branches.'

'Do they go direct?'

'No, through a central warehouse in Echo Park in LA.'

'So the stuff must be in with the furs?'

'Must be. But I can't believe that the customs don't have the furs out to check. There'd be duty on a consignment of that value.'

'So how?' Gary said softly.

'I'll find out tomorrow. I'll get into one of those cases and have a good look.'

'Is that safe?'

'As warehouseman I'm in charge,' Sammy said. 'I'll manage it.'

'No.' Gary's voice was firm. 'Leave it. You'll be travelling with the stuff more than likely. We'll tip off the Customs. Let them find it. It's too dangerous. You'll blow your cover if you're not careful.'

'Hey, listen,' Sammy said. 'I've been here six months, living in pig's shit. I want to finish the job.'

'We have nearly finished the job,' Gary said. 'Don't take chances. And that's an order.'

For a moment Sammy looked mutinous and then he sighed.

'Ok,' he said.

'I'll check back anyway,' Gary said. 'Washington may want us to hand over to the Brits.'

'Oh, come on!' Sammy protested.

Gary laughed shortly.

'I must say I don't fancy that myself: "What you chaps don't realise is that the Triad operation is very small here." ' He mimicked Chief Superintendent Morrison. 'They've got it all under control, old chap, old boy, old fruit.'

'They sure as hell ain't got the Broken Scissors gang under control,' Sammy said. 'I suspect that heroin smuggling is not all they're into.'

'Well, we'll have to hand over to the Brits unless we can establish how they get the stuff in, and where it's processed,' Gary said. 'Where do the furs come from?'

'China mostly, I guess. The Chinese mink, anyway. But China's not part of the Golden Triangle. I don't know anything about furs, but I've never heard of anything in that line coming from Laos, Burma or Thailand.'

'How about Yunnan Province?' Gary suggested.

'What about Yunnan?'

'It is said they produce more opium than anywhere in the world,' Gary said. 'The Chinese have never managed to control it.'

'No real proof of it,' Sammy said. 'But if it's true, the opium goes through the usual Golden Triangle routes. And Yunnan's pretty far south for nasty little creatures like mink.'

'Are you sure the furs *are* mink?'

'Until I look, I don't know. There's an awful lot of rabbit skins about the place, and other stuff I don't recognise except that it sure as hell ain't mink.'

'Rabbit? No reason why Yunnan Province couldn't produce rabbits,' Gary said.

Sammy snorted.

'Rabbits and opium! Some combination.'

Gary was thoughtful.

'I guess you're going to have to get a look at what goes in those cases. Or we wait until they pack up a new consignment.'

'That could be weeks for all I know,' Sammy said. 'I don't think I can stand Wong Tai Sin much longer.'

Mi made a little sound of distress and spoke rapidly in Cantonese to Sammy.

'Ok! Ok!' he said. 'She's telling me to be careful,' he said to Gary.

'And she's right.' Gary's voice was decisive. 'We wait until they start packing up a new consignment. Take no chances. We do it gently. We've all the time in the world.'

'And supposing I get sent off with this lot before they start packing up another?' Sammy asked.

'Then we think again.' Gary told him.

'If you say so,' Sammy said, his voice resigned. 'So what's been happening your end?'

'I'm going to tell you quickly,' Gary said. 'No wealth of detail, because I don't think the detail is going to help you. I want to get away to the races.'

'Oh yeah?' Sammy's look was sarcastic. 'Got a sure-fire tip?'

'Jade McKenzie McKenzie is at the races with your Jimmy Lee. I'm meant to be keeping an eye on her because his friend and yours, Kwan Ching, has already nearly killed her sister.'

He launched quickly into a précis of the events of the past days; the murders and the tenuous apparent involvement of Jade and Poppy.

'It hasn't slotted together yet, but it will. Get your wily Chinese mind working on it, will you?'

'I'll try,' Sammy said. 'You'd better get on your way. You'll just about make it.'

'I'm off,' Gary said. 'Listen – I'll stagger into the Big Fat Hot Lips late tomorrow. You can be spending some of your new-found wealth at the bar. Ok?'

'Ok,' Sammy said, and grinned. 'Now pay Mi for her time. I don't get any bread until Friday.'

'Get lost!' Gary said, stuck up two fingers and hurried from the room.

It was gone half-past nine. But he'd make it.

Or he would have done if the Lion Rock Tunnel had not been completely blocked by a bus that had broken down and paralysed the traffic for a mile back. His taxi inched its way along, the minutes ticking by. It was five past ten and the two lanes were creeping past each other when he suddenly spotted the white Rolls. As it nudged past his taxi, he saw Jimmy Lee in the back. Alone.

'Oh, God!' he said. 'Oh, fuck!'

And he leaned forward to tell the driver to turn back – if he possibly could.

Ian McKenzie McKenzie had dealt with the situation brilliantly.

Introduced to Jimmy Lee, he had pumped the man's hand, thanked him for entertaining his granddaughter and finished by saying: 'You'll not be minding if we take her off now? I'm wanting to hear her news. We'll be having a wee bite of supper at the hotel. Will you join us? You'll be welcome.'

Jimmy Lee had declined. His face had tightened into a mask, and when Ian McKenzie McKenzie had let go of his hand, Jade noticed that he surreptitiously wiped it with his handkerchief, before pretending to blow his nose. Yet he seemed not to be able to take his eyes off the big Scotsman. He'd lost his cool, Jade decided, without being sure why.

Within seconds he had gone, leaving her with her grandfather and Mike Blake, who was grinning broadly.

'Are you all right?' Ian asked.

'Fine,' Jade replied. 'How's Mother? Is she any better?'

'The same,' her grandfather said, 'no worse, which is a blessing.' He seemed not to want to talk about it and stabbed his finger at the door through which Jimmy Lee had vanished.

'And how did you find *him*?'

'It's sort of a funny story,' Jade said defensively.

'I imagine it might be,' her grandfather said.

He and Mike had arrived in Mike's old Bentley and they set off for the drive back to Hong Kong with Jade attempting to parry her grandfather's questions.

Finally Mike turned from the wheel and said: 'Why don't you come clean, Jade? I've told him most of it anyway.'

'All right, if Grandfather comes clean with me,' Jade said, and asked: 'Were you ever a pirate?'

He chuckled softly.

'Aye. Aged fourteen. I never had so much fun in my life. I was a wee cabin boy on a big old junk. It wasn't piracy like you'd imagine. We'd moor alongside the big liners in harbour or at anchor at night, find a rope or a way to shin up on board and just clean out the cabins, while the passengers were dining or dancing. It was more like burglary, really, but on the high seas they call it piracy. Very profitable it was, for a poor orphan boy.'

Jade opened her mouth to ask another question, but he cut her short.

'Anyway, enough of that. What's all this about Poppy? And where did you get that black eye?'

'Poppy's fine and I had a silly fall.'

'Humph!' It was obvious he did not believe a word. 'Well, we'll be talking about it all tomorrow. I'm an old man and I've been on an airplane fourteen hours. I'm in no mood to concentrate. I'm having myself a nap.'

A traffic jam in the Lion Rock Tunnel made the journey a slow one. With her grandfather's gentle snores coming from the back seat, Jade whispered her fears of the evening to Michael Blake.

'Gary Smith promised to be there,' she said, 'but I never saw him.'

'He probably couldn't find you in the crowds,' Mike suggested.

'Maybe.' She was doubtful. 'Do you think he's all right? Nothing could have happened? He's some sort of agent, isn't he?'

Mike sneezed, but she disregarded it. Her mind was on what had happened to Gary.

'I really don't know,' Mike said, after he had given his nose a good blow, one hand on the wheel, eyes looking ahead. 'Maybe. But he's Ok.'

'You said so.' She was silent for a moment. 'It's just as well you turned up.'

'I'd have been there earlier, but I got a call to meet your grandfather at the airport and I talked him into coming out to Sha Tin. Just in case.'

'Thank heavens,' she said fervently.

They were quiet for the rest of the journey back to the hotel, Mike concentrating on driving once the crush had cleared. He muttered that there must have been an accident, then relapsed into silence. Jade found herself surprisingly tired. Tension, she decided, and wondered what Jimmy Lee had had in mind. Maybe she had missed a mink coat. Or a patchwork coney jacket. Or a fate worse than death.

Her grandfather woke with a snort and a smacking of lips when they drew up outside the hotel and a boy opened the car door. Wearily Jade climbed out and waited for the old man as he heaved his bulk from the back seat. Together they walked into the hotel foyer while Mike made arrangements for the car to be parked.

They were nearing the reception desk when Jade heard her name called. It was Gary, striding across the foyer, his face alight, and she found her feet running to meet him.

'Thank God, sweetheart,' he said. 'You're safe. What happened? I've been so worried.'

He was hugging her, picking her bodily from the ground, and holding her tight to him, kissing her on the lips

'Humph!' Ian McKenzie sounded like a bullfrog. 'And who is this?' he asked loudly.

Gary carefully placed Jade back on the marble floor of the foyer. Flustered, she said: 'Gary, this is my grandfather, Ian McKenzie McKenzie. Grandfather, this is Gary Smith.'

'Gary Smith?' her grandfather repeated.

'That's right, sir, Gary Smith.'

There was an awkward silence as Mike joined them, an overnight bag swinging from his hand.

'Ah,' he said. 'Evening, Gary, you've found each other. That's good. Now let's get you booked in, Ian, and then we can all have a calming, peaceful drink.'

'Good thinking,' Gary said, a little too heartily.

As they reached the reception desk, the clerk looked up.

'Mr McKenzie McKenzie?' he said.

The old man nodded.

'Something was left to be given to you when you arrived.' He called a boy and spoke to him rapidly. The boy nodded and went to the message desk. He was back in seconds.

'Here, sir,' he said, and handed Ian McKenzie McKenzie a white paper fan – the twin of the one that Jade had received on her first day in Hong Kong.

There was only one difference. Hanging from the delicate ivory frame was a label. And on the label was written. '*In memoriam*'.

$$\approx 11 \approx$$

THURSDAY

Out of some unspoken deference to Ian McKenzie McKenzie's presence, Gary had gone to his own room the night before. Jade found at first she could not sleep and then she woke far too early.

She lay staring into the darkness recalling her grandfather's face as he had looked at the white paper fan.

'Well, well, well,' he had said softly. 'An interesting wee gift.'

'It's the same as we had,' she had said, staring at the delicate ivory and ugly paper. 'Jimmy Lee gave both Poppy and me one exactly like that the night we came to Hong Kong.'

'Jimmy Lee is that young Chinese you were with tonight?' her grandfather asked, tapping the fan lightly on his hand, his face still unreadable.

'Yes.'

'Sir,' Gary had interrupted, 'you know—'

'I know very well,' her grandfather had said. 'Is this Jimmy Lee a Triad to your knowledge?'

'He is,' Gary had said. 'He is the Hill Chief of a gang who call themselves the Broken Scissors.'

'Is he indeed?' her grandfather said. 'And who is the White Paper Fan?'

'I don't know. The Incense Master is a man called Kwan Ching . . .'

'The man Poppy was involved with,' Michael Blake put in.

'I know –' Gary had given a twisted grin '– who Straw Sandal is.'

'But not White Paper Fan,' Ian McKenzie McKenzie had said softly. 'Well, maybe the position is open. I shall have to meet these young men, I think.'

'Will someone *explain*,' Jade had said. 'The Broken Scissors? Are they the same people . . .?'

'This is no time and no place to discuss it,' her grandfather had said very firmly. 'I'm away to my bed. I've been up far too long this day. And if you've any sense, you'll be away to yours, Jade. Maybe this young man will see you safely to your room.' He turned and said: 'Michael, come with me a moment.'

He had bent to kiss Jade on the forehead.

'I hear you want to meet Chan Koh Leung,' he had said. 'Well, we'll be off to Macao together in the morning – if Michael can get us tickets on the hydrofoil, that is. He tells me you have to book in advance these days.'

'You could go on the company launch,' Mike had suggested.

'No, we'll take the hydrofoil. It's quicker. I've always believed time is money. I'll expect you down here at ten o'clock sharp, young Jade. Goodnight.'

He had strode off towards the lift with Michael Blake, who gave a little half-wave, following him.

'What was that all about?' Jade had asked, exasperated.

'I expect he'll explain to you himself, tomorrow,' Gary had said. 'He's right. This is no place to discuss anything. Let's get you to your room.'

'Well at least tell me what the White Paper Fan is,' Jade said as they walked towards the lift. 'Remember, I do have one myself.'

'And you never told me about it.'

'It didn't seem particularly important.'

'I'd have been worrying earlier if I'd known,' Gary had said. 'The White Paper Fan is a senior Triad who gives the gang advice on administration and finance. Each Triad group usually has two or three of them. But it seems that Jimmy Lee's group don't have anyone fulfilling the role. Not that I know of, anyway.'

'How long have you known that Jimmy was a Triad?' she had asked him.

'Only since this evening for certain, or believe me, I'd never have let you go to the races with him. Now, no more questions.' He had taken her hand, given it a squeeze, and left her with a promise that he would see her on her return from Macao and another warning to be careful . . .

When she arrived in the lobby in the morning, Michael Blake was already waiting, explaining he had the tickets and was coming with them.

'Oh, good,' she said, giving him an impulsive kiss on the cheek which seemed to start him off sneezing again.

He was still sneezing when Ian McKenzie McKenzie appeared, tall and upright in tweeds, looking more as if he were off to the grouse moors than a hydrofoil trip.

'Don't you be giving me that cold, Michael,' he warned.

'Not a cold, sir,' Michael said, blowing his nose. 'Hayfever.'

Ian gave him a doubtful look.

Jade wanted to ask questions, but she felt this was perhaps not the moment. Her grandfather looked tired, and Mike had already ordered them a taxi to the Macao ferry terminal. She sat quietly while they talked about shipping.

'If you really want to join the business out here, you'll be needing to learn all this,' her grandfather suddenly said to her. 'Do you still think it would be better to work here than in London?'

The question caught her by surprise.

'I don't know.' Her voice was hesitant. 'I'd have to think about it when I'm less confused.'

He grunted.

There was a small wait at the terminal and then they piled on to the hydrofoil, fighting through a mass of jostling Chinese.

'They're away gambling,' her grandfather said. 'Gambling mad, they are. It's illegal here in Hong Kong, so there's an exodus come every weekend. Macao has casinos. But don't expect Monte Carlo. It's not the same.'

She decided to start her questions when they were settled in their seats, beginning with an innocuous one.

'Grandfather, do you know Michael Broadbent?'

He looked at her from under his bushy brows.

'The underwriter? Mike tells me his name was in your father's address book.'

'Has Mike told you everything?' she said crossly.

'Just about. Yes, I did know Michael Broadbent, but he's no longer with us. He died in his bed at the Radcliffe Hospital in Oxford of cirrhosis of the liver about three years ago. Nothing to do with Triads. It was what you'd call self-inflicted wounds. Broadbent liked a drink.'

'And Owen Brent?'

'Safe and well somewhere in New Zealand, as far as I know. We've not been in touch for years. I've no reason to think anything has happened to him.'

She nodded.

'And you've no idea where Miss Tibbets is?'

'Of course I know where Miss Tibbets is,' he said. 'Living in Venice.'

'Venice!'

258

'Venice. Now be a good girl and let me sleep. That's all these hydrofoils are good for. You can't see a thing.'

She herself dozed from the throbbing movement and puzzled about Miss Tibbets and Venice, deciding she'd have to pump her grandfather more when his was in a more communicative mood.

The journey took just over an hour. She was not impressed with Macao when they landed, nor indeed with the Hotel Lisboa, an edifice with a huge circular tower overlooking the sea and a sea wall which seemed to run right round the peninsula all the way to China. Inside the vast entrance hall of the hotel, again circular, a giant glass chandelier hung over the marble floor. It should have been imposing, but somehow it was not – just tacky, she thought.

Her grandfather, ignoring the surroundings, strode across the lobby and into the hotel's casino where crowded tables were set up for games that Jade did not recognise. There were a couple of roulette wheels and a baccarat table, but mostly the sport seemed to be Chinese, involving a lot of clicking tiles.

While she and Mike trailed behind, her grandfather plunged down a flight of stairs to the lower level casino and turned into a smaller saloon where, in one section, a room was signalled. '*Sala de Bacarat para VIP*'. There were screens in front of the door, and as they neared, a red-coated Chinese attendant stepped forward, barring the way. Ian McKenzie McKenzie spoke to him in rapid Cantonese, the young man nodded, went into the saloon, then came back and motioned them through.

The red-carpeted room was empty, lit by a large chandelier, and sitting at one of the green baize tables was a solitary man, waiting. His head lifted, like a bloodhound snuffling, as Ian McKenzie McKenzie came into the room. And then his expression changed from one of anticipation to real pleasure.

'Ian!' he said. 'I do not believe it!'

He rose from his seat and came towards them, a short, very fat man whose body quivered forward rather than moved. The head was bald, the yellow skin deeply wrinkled. Narrow, bright eyes peered from turtle folds.

'Well, how are you, old man?' Ian said gruffly. 'Waiting for a game?'

'Always I am waiting for a game,' Chan Koh Leung said, 'but no one wants to play my stakes any more. To play for less would be boring. Do you want to play?'

'You know I never gamble on cards.'

The Chinese laughed, chins shaking, and then stopped to gasp for air.

'Then what brings you back?'

'My granddaughter here.'

Chan Koh Leung stepped forward and looked at Jade, nodding his Buddha head.

'She has turned out well.'

'She has been interfering in things that don't concern her.'

'So I see,' he said, straight-faced.

'Things in the past.'

'And—'

'She wanted to warn you.'

'I see.' He stroked his nose with a fat forefinger. 'Shall we go to my suite then. If you are sure you don't want to play . . .'

'I'm certain.' Ian clapped him on the shoulder. 'It's early. Later there will be punters.'

'I always come too early,' the old man said. 'How is it with you, Ian? Do you find that sleep is not so necessary? And do you find there is no one left to talk to?'

Ian McKenzie McKenzie nodded. 'Great age can be a burden,' he said.

As they moved towards the door, two men in dark suits appeared, discreetly flanking Chan on both sides. The red-coated guard who had let them in walked in front, and Jade had the impression that behind someone else followed.

They took a lift to the tenth floor, the bodyguard crammed in awkwardly with them, and walked along a carpeted corridor into a large room with a view over the sea and of a long, slender, imposing bridge which curved to an outer island. Once inside, Chan sank breathless into a large chair.

'And what do they call you?' he asked Jade who had not yet spoken.

'Jade,' she said.

He nodded ponderously.

'A good name. It suits you. Sit down – and you?' He pointed to Michael Blake. 'Who is he?'

'My agent here. He is to be trusted. His name is Michael Blake,' Ian said.

'Good morning, Michael Blake,' Chan nodded. 'Why do you

not sit down now? We shall have some brandy.'

He pressed a button and a white-coated young boy appeared quickly with a tray with four balloon glasses and a bottle of Hennessy. He poured generous measures, handed them around, then left the tray and the bottle and went from the room.

'Now, Jade, what was it you wished to warn me about?' Chan asked, his head sunk on his chin and watching her with sharp black eyes.

She hesitated, afraid of sounding melodramatic.

'I believe someone wants to kill you,' she said. 'You see, my father is dead. He was killed on 7 January, and I have his address book. Most of the people in the book have been killed. They tried to kill Grandfather as well. I think it is a Triad gang called the Broken Scissors who are doing these things.'

He nodded.

'They have tried to kill me,' he said. 'But I am not easy to get near. They blew up one of my old casinos, Ian,' he said, turning to where Jade's grandfather was half leaning, half sitting on the window-sill, staring out at the view. 'Unfortunately for Wan who owned it, and fortunately for me, they had not learned I had sold it.'

'Wan is dead?' Ian asked.

'Wan is alive, but Wan is not well and he is angry.' He turned back to Jade. 'And you wanted to come to warn me. That was a good and kind thing to do.'

'Well,' she said slowly. 'I thought you might tell me what it was all about in return. No one seems to know.'

'What is it you want to know?' He was sitting very still.

She put it as succinctly as possible.

'Why all the people were killed and about the *Brian Leigh* and, if I can find out, where my sister and I came from.'

She noticed how he and her grandfather exchanged a look, and then Chan chuckled deeply.

'We do not have all the answers, young lady, but shall we tell her about the *Brian Leigh*, Ian? That was one of our best.'

'*My* best,' Ian said firmly, coming to sit down on a hard-backed chair. He swirled the brandy around in his glass. 'Your most legitimate.'

Chan chuckled again.

'There is little profit in honesty,' he remarked.

'I am rich enough,' Ian said.

'But without those midnight ventures when we were boys, you would not have been. Remember. How agile we were then.' He sighed. 'I could always get on board before you. I was quicker every time. The times they nearly caught us . . . Without those days of piracy you would never have been rich. How would you have bought your first ship, eh? Tell me that. You talked me into the *Brian Leigh*. There was no profit in it for me. But,' he shrugged, 'we had been brothers in crime. I had sworn to help you.'

'And I never asked again,' Ian said.

'And I would not have done it again,' the old man said spiritedly. 'But perhaps it was fire insurance in a way, eh?'

Michael Blake was refilling Chan's glass, and the old man drank, smacked his lips, sighed and said:

'It's all a long time ago now. You see, Jade, in the late 1950s and 60s the price of gold had been pegged by an international agreement.'

Jade nodded. 'I know about that. Mike told me,' she said.

'Gold was hard to obtain, and we Chinese like our money in gold. The peasant does not trust banks, or stocks and shares. He likes to feel his wealth, heavy and shining, in his hand; know it is under his pillow. It was at this time that I decided to leave Hong Kong and make Macao my home for what we shall call personal reasons. Portugal was exempt from this Bretton Woods Agreement. Macao belonged to Portugal and this meant that I could buy gold, perfectly legitimately, without quota, and bring it here. And then I could sell it here at any price it would fetch. How it left here after that was, I decided, no business of mine. I was not smuggling. But my customers were when they took the gold into territories where the Bretton Woods Agreement held. There was a lot of gold smuggling in those days,' he said thoughtfully, adding: 'Disgraceful.'

'You old villain,' Ian said affectionately. 'Still full of humbug.'

'Humbug?' Chan's head turned slowly to look across the room reprovingly. 'What is that?'

'Same as it's always been,' Ian said cheerfully.

'One day Ian came to see me here,' Chan went on. 'He had a problem—'

'Not exactly my problem. The respective Banks of England and Australia's problem,' Ian interrupted. 'A three-ton consignment of gold, worth one million pounds sterling in those days, had been sent from Perth in Western Australia for the Bank of England to sell.

Except it never arrived. The cargo turned out to be lead specially pressed in the shape of ingots and gilt-painted. Crude, but sufficient to pass muster for the weight of the cargo. Gold is very heavy.'

'They were very clever criminals who planned the job,' Chan said, and sighed. 'Regretfully I never had the opportunity to ask them exactly how they did the switch. But I liked their style. The lead was an expensive touch – but it did not cost them the million the gold was worth.'

'The Australians were a wee bit upset at their gold vanishing,' Ian said. 'They swore it had been on board when it left them. They wanted to know what had we British done with it. We, of course, insisted it had never arrived – but how to prove it?

'It was fortunate for everyone that London managed to keep the loss quiet. It was never reported in the newspapers, and an army of insurance investigators and Lloyd's agents got moving. Someone got a tip that the gold was on its way to Macao. Which was when I paid my visit to Chan.'

'Ian guessed I'd be involved in the deal, and wanted to know where the gold was. I did not wish to tell him, but for old times' sake I agreed to help.' The old Chinese pursed his mouth, remembering a difficult decision. 'I was able to tell him from certain information I had acquired that the gold was on its way across the Timor Sea in a schooner bound for Macao. The British were right. The gold had been switched in Australia. Now it was on its way, addressed to me. I had contracted to pay the men who had it somewhat less than the Bretton Woods price. I had made myself a very good deal.' He nodded wisely and said: 'Well, they were in no position to argue. They had to unload their treasure trove, and I was going to do the noble thing and take it off their hands.'

He chuckled again and sipped at his brandy.

'My only problem,' he continued, 'was that I had a certain reputation among gentlemen of the kind who were bringing the gold and I did not wish to spoil this mutual trust we all shared. I could not be seen to be aiding authority. But it was Ian who was asking me for help.' He paused. 'Do you realise how much richer I would have been had I not helped you on that occasion?' he said reproachfully.

'You'd have only gambled it away,' Ian said, moving from the window to sit down in a large armchair.

'So what happened?' Jade asked, fascinated.

'Yes, what next?' Michael was looking thoughtful, almost disapproving; as if he were hearing something unacceptable.

'I conceived a plot,' Ian McKenzie McKenzie said, thumbs tucked into his armpits, fingers fanned tapping his chest, palpably pleased with himself. 'First we had to trace the schooner carrying the gold. An RAF Shackleton went searching, and there she was, about 500 tons, with Formosa markings. She could have been any small cargo vessel going up into the South China Sea. We needed another vessel that looked just like her.

'We had a wee bit of luck. We found the *Brian Leigh* at Cheoy Lee Shipyards. She was being built for an Australian company and was nearly ready. I did a deal with an Aussie called Owen Brent who owned her. He was pleased to oblige. He said, I remember, that seeing as Australia only produced about three per cent of the world's gold, it was not on if someone was going to steal that much of it.

'So there it was. I was going back to piracy for expediency's sake.' His eyes took a faraway look. 'It was the biggest haul I ever made, and I've never been able to talk about it.

'The *Brian Leigh* looked much the same as the other schooner. The only difference was that she was much, much faster, so we needed extra fuel tanks and also deck cranes to lift the gold, but without those, from the air, you'd have been hard put to tell one from the other. We also had to make sure that our ship neither had proper classification nor was properly registered. She was going to have to vanish and become another ship entirely. That's why the spare bulkhead door was put in, carefully not up to specifications. We also needed to give some good reason why she might not have been seaworthy. We made her loll from her ballast before she even left harbour. We built up a lot of circumstantial evidence and a mystery.'

'It went very well,' Chan said, sounding satisfied.

'What about the owner's representative, though?' Michael Blake asked. 'Was he in it, too?'

'You mean the unfortunate Mr William Nutley.' Chan shook his head sadly. 'Owen Brent, his boss, did everything possible to stop him sailing with the *Brian Leigh*, but he wouldn't listen. He would go. In the end, to have persuaded him further would have made him suspicious.'

'So what happened to him?' Jade asked.

There was a long silence and the two old men looked at each other, both hard-eyed. The schoolboys recalling a prank were suddenly tough professionals.

'He vanished, too,' Ian said, shutting his mouth like a trap, and Chan swept the narrative on, leaving no space for questions.

'When the *Brian Leigh* set off on her maiden voyage, Ian was on board – though only the crew knew it. He had a hand-picked crew of Chinese we knew from the old days. They intercepted the schooner off the Philippines – she was called the *Soul of the South*, I remember. They boarded her, they took the gold—'

'Those cranes on deck came in very useful,' Ian said. 'Heavy stuff, gold.'

'And once they had it on board, they sent the *Soul of the South* to the bottom. A pity, but necessary.'

'And what about her crew?' Jade asked.

Her grandfather ignored the question.

'We had to beach ourselves on a reef after that to change our markings. We became another ship. We repainted her, took off the cranes, replaced the bulkhead, got rid of the extra fuel tanks and we sailed her back to Hong Kong where no one recognised her as the *Brian Leigh*. In Hong Kong the authorities quietly took the gold off and it was freighted back to Britain by the supposedly missing Shackleton. The plane had been deliberately declared missing. We wanted to build up a really complicated mystery – to protect Chan's credibility with his customers.'

'A brilliant touch, the missing Shackleton,' Chan said. 'Your idea, I recall.'

'I don't remember. I think we dreamed it up together,' Ian said.

'What about the insurance?' Michael asked.

'Just the question I'd have expected from you,' Ian said approvingly. 'No difficulties. Whoever had owned the *Soul of the South* was not about to report her disappearance, it seemed. No insurance claim was made. Maybe they suspected they'd been twigged, eh? The *Brian Leigh* was more of a problem as she had officially sailed from Hong Kong and officially never arrived in Australia. It would have suited us all not to have had the court of enquiry, but the law says when there is loss of life, there has to be one. With the crew gone missing and Mr Nutley no longer with us, it had to be done.

'We might have kept it out of court but for that obstinate fool Nutley,' he added. 'The Chinese crew might have been considered expendable in those days, but not an Australian businessman.' He gave a short, sharp laugh. 'The insurers had to pay up when Ralph pronounced it a fortuity. It was a bit hard on Broadbent who'd been the underwriter, but the Aussies eventually saw him right.'

'And hard on William Nutley?' Jade suggested. She was hardly able to believe what her grandfather was saying.

'And on Nutley,' he agreed, suddenly sanctimonious. But then his tone sharpened. 'But you can't make omelettes without breaking eggs, my girl.'

There was silence, and then Chan chuckled.

'We set a fine puzzle. I don't know when I have enjoyed myself so much since.'

'And did Father know what was going on?' Jade asked warily.

'Of course he didn't,' her grandfather said, his voice hearty. 'He just led the enquiry and made his decision in the normal way.'

'But it was a surprise verdict,' Michael Blake said.

'It was a fortunate one,' Chan corrected him. 'The Australians got their gold back and Owen Brent eventually got his Schooner back under a different name.'

'And did you really get nothing out of it?' Jade asked Chan.

'A little amnesty for things past. That was all,' he said.

'And were there other eggs broken for this omelette?' Michael asked.

'Not a one,' Chan said, his face suddenly inscrutably Oriental.

'What about the *Brian Leigh*'s crew?' Mike asked.

'They just dispersed,' Ian said casually. Too casually, Jade felt.

'So none of that explains these 7th January deaths,' she said. 'Nor the Broken Scissors gang.'

'All of that must have been something to do with your father,' Ian said, his voice positive. 'After all, the names were all in his address book. I hardly knew Kim Ting.' He turned back to Chan. 'Enough of that. How's your health, man? How's life treating you? By God, it's good to see someone who remembers the old days.'

Her brandy glass still full in her hand, Jade sat listening as they reminisced, and she was certain that she was still a very long way from the complete truth.

Michael Blake had the same impression. He was torn between his admiration for and loyalty to Ian McKenzie McKenzie, but a feeling persisted that a great deal that was important had been left out. He ought to ring Arthur Watson King and give him a tip-off, but he suspected he wouldn't be telling Arthur anything he didn't already know. This was probably what Arthur had meant when he said in the Bull and Bear that McKenzie McKenzie had been involved in something – not heroin – long ago. But Ian McKenzie McKenzie had been in British government employ, in a casual way, for many years. Perhaps the *Brian Leigh* had been his first legal caper. Still, there were definitely too many gaps in the story.

Ian had suggested Michael take Jade downstairs and show her the gambling while he and Chan talked.

'We don't want to bore you young ones,' he said. 'It's a goodly while since Chan and I met.'

Downstairs they had wandered around the crowded, dingy gambling room with no desire to play themselves. He bought her a drink at a scruffy bar and they half-heartedly put a few coins into a one-armed bandit. The Chinese women playing them stood with shopping bags full of coins, automatically putting money in, one coin after the other, in catatonic fashion, expecting nothing to happen.

'Did you believe it all?' she asked as they sat perched on stools at the neon-lit bar.

'I did,' he said, puffing out a stream of smoke. 'But I just thought there was more to tell.'

'Me, too,' she said. 'But he won't tell us anything he doesn't want to, will he? Mike, I don't like to think he was dishonest.'

'In my experience most very rich self-made men are always teetering on the brink of dishonesty in some way or another,' he said. 'I shouldn't worry too much about that. Besides, he has been straight for years and helpful to his country.'

'An agent?'

'Not entirely. Part-time.'

'But he knows. I'm sure he knows about the murders.'

He pursed his lips.

'I'm afraid he probably does.'

'And why does he want to see Jimmy Lee and Kwan Ching? That can only be dangerous.'

'Your grandfather's style has always been confrontation,' he told her, thinking how beautiful she was and wanting to talk about something quite different. 'But there's a lot more protection about than you'd think. There are two plants in the Broken Scissors now. It won't be long before the gang is broken up.'

'But for what?' she asked. 'Murder?'

'No, heroin smuggling.'

'How do you know?'

He shrugged. 'I have a contact. I tell him things and he tells me things. It can be of mutual benefit in my job.'

'Then why do you think Gary Smith is following me?'

'It seems the DEA have always thought your grandfather was into heroin at one time. It may be he was in the early days. It's easy for a ship owner. When your father suddenly went to Los Angeles where this latest heavy importation is going on, they just thought it politic to keep an eye on what the McKenzie McKenzie family were doing there. You going to Aspen, which is another drug centre, must have made them curious. But I suspect it was only a routine check. Until, of course, you suddenly leapt on to a plane and came to Hong Kong, where they believe the stuff is coming from. Circumstantially it looked interesting, and all undercover work of that kind is done by patient following up of any small possibility.'

'What's the DEA?'

'The American Drug Enforcement Agency,' he told her. 'Your admirer works for them.' He was conscious again that his voice was sour as it always was when he spoke of Gary.

'He doesn't sell private jets?'

'He might. He'd need a cover.'

'Why didn't he tell me?' she said sadly.

He would like to have agreed with her, and say what a shit the man was, but it would hardly be just.

'He couldn't. I expect he'll explain when this is all over.'

'Do you work for something?' she asked suddenly.

He hesitated and then thought, What the hell!

'Only sort of freelance,' he said. 'I'm meant to be a China watcher, but other things happen sometimes. I took over from your grandfather when he went back to Scotland.'

'What about those white paper fans? Why did Jimmy send us them? And Grandfather, too?'

'That intrigues me,' he said. 'I don't know the answer. But I have a theory, and if I can check it out, I promise to let you know. But it's probably only my overactive imagination.'

The only trouble with working as warehouseman at the Green

Butterfly Fur Company, Sammy felt, was that it was so fucking cold. A man could freeze his balls off in the chill down there. He had a small office with an inadequate heater near where the big elevator came into the warehouse. He had the keys that padlocked the outer gates of this so no one could come into the basement from above without his knowledge or permission. He also had the key to the staff entrance at the back of the building. Other than those two exits, there was a hinged heavy wooden flap in the wall at the far end of the warehouse which lowered so that the consignment could be winched in and out when it arrived in heavy reinforced cardboard boxes.

The fact they had given him the keys had cheered him. He must be trusted. But at night after he had locked up, he had to hand the keys personally to Jimmy Lee in his opulent office on the third floor and let himself out through the main entrance which closed on an automatic lock. Then the basement was secure until the morning when the nightwatchman opened the staff entrance and Sammy had to get the keys again from the third floor.

On this second morning he had brought in a piece of wax to take an impression of all three keys. One never knew when they might come in handy.

The place was still puzzling him. That morning there had been a delivery of skins tied in a huge bundle. They were marked 'Chinese mink' followed by the word '(weasel)' in brackets. They had arrived via the lift rather than the goods entrance.

'Mr Lee's checked them out. They can go out for working when they're needed,' said the man who brought them down.

'Does Mr Lee inspect all the skins before they come down here?' Sammy asked.

'Every single one. He's as shrewd as a weasel himself,' the man said.

Part of Sammy's job was to check out skins when the foremen from different departments came down to get the fur for cutting. Then, throughout the day, boxes of made-up coats came down for storage, but these were then taken away again via the goods hatch and returned later in the same plain van. The packing cases went out casually sealed, then came back securely sealed.

Something obviously happened to the coats between the time of a box going out of the warehouse and its return.

What he would have to do was to check out one of the returned boxes and that would not be easy. They were as impregnable as Alcatraz.

About midmorning a man from the packing department arrived, pushing a large box on a trolley. Sammy unlocked the lift gates to let him into the warehouse and said cheerfully: 'What have we here then?'

'A load of rubbish,' the man grumbled. 'Fun furs for export. Just bloody rabbit.'

'I'm new here,' Sammy said. 'What's a fun fur?'

'Have a look.' The man wrenched the lid back, ignoring the stapling.

Sammy leaned into the box and took out a black and white checkered fur coat.

'Rubbish or not,' he said, 'it'd help down here. It's like fucking Siberia.' Larking, he started to put the coat on. 'It's not even lined,' he said.

'They go out for that,' the man said. 'Some other factory somewhere else finishes them. Someone will come for them later.'

'Right,' Sammy said.

After the man had gone, as the box was open, Sammy had a quick scrabble through. He could find nothing. Just a dozen or so roughly made fur jackets, squares of skins machined together with little finesse. They would sell very cheaply, he guessed.

Someone did indeed come for them later, and delivered another box back through the goods entrance. Like the other heavily sealed boxes, it was marked with the name of an American store and the address in Echo Park. There were no shipping instructions.

There were fifteen sealed boxes ready for freighting and Sammy was fretting to pass on information and to get his skeleton keys made, but the Green Butterfly Company did not allow its employees out of the building throughout the day. A generous meal of noodles and chicken was served on the premises; everyone was given half an hour to eat and then sent back to their jobs.

It was mid-afternoon when the telephone in his chilly cubicle rang. Jimmy Lee wanted to see him.

He locked all the doors behind him so that the basement was safe and made his way to the third floor. He knocked on the door of the office and entered. Lee was sitting at his desk, surrounded by open cupboards filled with furs of a far superior quality to those in the warehouse. At his side was Kwan Ching.

Obviously Jimmy Lee did not believe in preliminaries.

'Have you ever been to the United States?' he asked abruptly.

'Never, sir,' Sammy said.

'Would you like to go?'

'To the Gold Mountain? More than anything.'

'Good.' Jimmy Lee nodded abruptly and turned to Kwan Ching. 'That seems right then?'

Kwan Ching nodded.

'We want you to accompany the fur shipment to Los Angeles. Make sure it arrives safely. But you will also be carrying something else.'

Sammy did not speak, but made his face a question-mark.

'Heroin. It is to supply our brethren with finance in Los Angeles. You will deliver it to the Broken Scissors Triad group there.'

Sammy drew a deep breath.

'How shall I carry it?' he asked. 'Will it be safe?'

'You will follow orders. The heroin will be in condoms and you will keep them in your anus leaving Hong Kong and when you enter USA. There will be no danger.'

'I trust you, sir,' said Sammy, careful to keep his voice humble.

'Good.'

'And when is this to be?'

'You will leave on Sunday. We shall give you more instructions before then. There are things to do and to tell to our brethren in Los Angeles. I trust your English is as good as you have told us.'

'If you wish proof, you can tell me all these things again in English,' Sammy suggested. 'I would understand.'

'Let's take his word for it,' Kwan Ching said; then turning to Sammy, 'You may go back now. We will see you again tomorrow.'

'Thank you, sir,' Sammy said, still humble, and scuttled from the room.

Not enough time, he was thinking as he went down in the service lift to the basement, unlocked the gates and let himself back into the warehouse. Nowhere near enough time. It was blindingly obvious that he, Sammy, was to be fall guy in the operation. The Customs would be tipped that he was carrying heroin, and while he was being searched and arrested the furs would slide through. That was the plan, except that Kwan and Jimmy Lee did not know that he was DEA. But whatever happened his cover would be blown.

He needed to see Gary quickly. He needed his keys cut. And he needed to find out exactly how the heroin was to be shipped and where it came from. And he had only one day in which to do it.

Emma was already at home when Stephen let himself into the flat at just after six in the evening. The hi-fi was on playing something he recognised as highbrow and modern. He couldn't stand Emma's taste in music and also it was too loud for a man who had the kind of headache he was suffering.

She turned the music off immediately he came into the room, leaning from the sofa where she was stretched, her slim arm inviting within the loose sleeve of a red satin kimono.

'How did it go?' she asked.

'Too easy,' he said, taking off his jacket and dropping it on to an armchair. 'I don't know what to think.'

She had raised herself from the sofa in one fluid movement and gone to the drinks tray where she was pouring him a gin. Ice clinked soothingly in the glass as she added tonic.

'Well, tell me what happened,' she said. She handed him the heavy glass and turned to pour herself a brandy and soda.

'I start officially Monday. But Kwan Ching wants me to go in on Saturday for what he calls a briefing.' He took too heavy a swallow of the gin and collapsed into the armchair, heedless of his jacket lying there.

'How did you get around explaining why the police had let you go so quickly?'

'I told him I'd resigned two weeks ago and they'd told me to go away and think about it. I said I'd thought and wanted the resignation to stand.'

'And he accepted that?'

'Completely as far as I could tell.'

She was back on the sofa, one well-shaped leg bare and free of the red satin.

'And what is this wonderful job he's offering you?'

'Chief security man. But not for him. It's for Jimmy Lee's fur business.'

'Curiouser and curiouser,' she said into her brandy glass.

'I know. It seems I'll have to travel with the really big fur shipments. There's one leaving Sunday for the States. He wanted to know if I could go. I didn't know what to say. I said I'd have to think if there was time to make all my personal arrangements. He didn't look too pleased. Anyway, I rang Morrison who said I had to go whether I liked it or not.'

Her face was anxious.

'Is it dangerous, Steve?' she asked. 'Must you do it?'

He surprised himself by laughing.

'I suppose the answer to both of those questions is yes, Em,' he said. 'I'm a bit too young for the soft life I've been living. And thinking about it, I'm not too pleased with myself for being shit scared when I thought my nice comfortable rug was going to be pulled from under my feet by the ICAC. To tell you the truth, I'm still shit scared, but at least it's about something positive.'

She was silent, biting her lip, and then she came across the room to him, knelt and buried her head in his lap.

'I don't want anything to happen to you,' she said, her voice muffled.

'Nothing's going to happen to me,' he said. 'I'm not the type anything much happens to.'

She sat back on her heels and looked up at him. He thought how lucky he was to have her and traced the line of her chin with his finger. She sighed softly.

'What does the inspector man want you to do?'

'I don't know really. Neither does he, I suspect. Just keep my eyes and ears open. He was very interested when I told him I'd be working with Jimmy Lee, not Kwan personally. He said it completely confirmed something they had been wondering about. It seems Mr Lee is higher in the Triad tables than Kwan and that they're working together.' He leaned down, pulled her up on to his lap and pushed his face in her thick dark hair. 'Em,' he said into her ear. 'I'll be away quite some time.'

He felt her shoulder tighten under his hand.

'How long?'

'I don't know exactly. The furs go by sea, in one of Kwan Ching's cargo boats. They land at San Francisco and then go by road to Los Angeles. I have to stay with them until they're delivered and then I fly back.'

'It'll take at least two weeks,' she said sadly.

'Will you be faithful?' He asked it abruptly. He hadn't meant to, but his old insecurities were knocking like the pain in his head.

'I think I might manage it for two weeks,' she said lightly.

'What happens if it's three?'

She made a little hiss of exasperation.

'Steve! Stop it. I love you, remember. And I'll be faithful. I'm only afraid you won't be safe.'

'If you're faithful, I'll be safe,' he said, and it seemed to him that her commitment could be a talisman to keep him in one piece throughout whatever happened.

She lay quietly in his arms as if she understood the way his mind was working, then she turned her head and kissed him gently, nibbling at his lower lip and taking his hand to slide it under the silk of her kimono where her small breast curved.

He cupped his hand around the soft swell, hesitated, and said: 'Em, I've got the most God-awful headache.'

She shook with sudden laughter.

'That's supposed to be my line,' she told him as she got up to get him an aspirin.

By ten thirty at night the house of the Sos was in deep darkness. Poppy lay on the hard bed, staring at the ceiling, wide awake. It was still, but not silent. Outside she could hear the soft rustling of a light wind in the trees and occasionally the call of a night bird, screeching its way across the sky.

She was restless and she knew what she wanted. She wanted a man, but for the first time in her life a specific one: Paul So, and he was asleep in another room just a few yards down the corridor.

Angrily she heaved herself over on to her side, burrowing her face into the small hard pillow. She still had to move with care – the burns on her body had not completely healed and were sore to the touch. Lovemaking would be difficult, but not impossible.

She wondered if he were lying there in the darkness thinking of her. She willed him to be wanting her, and she gently stroked at her own breasts until the heat generating inside her was becoming too much to bear.

Since the fracas with Jade the day before he had been different with her; no less caring and concerned, but sad somehow. After Jade had flounced off he had helped her to her feet in an impersonal way that she found hurtful.

'Well, I'm glad she's not my sister,' she had said defiantly, standing in the garden while the wind caught at their hair. 'I don't care.'

He had shaken his head slowly.

'Poppy, Poppy,' he had said, 'we are all brothers and sisters.'

After that he had not mentioned the incident again. But it was on his mind. She knew it. And she knew that he disapproved of the way she had behaved.

'But it was Jade,' she whispered into the darkness, while her hands caressed where she longed for him to caress her. 'It was Jade who started it. Honestly, Paul, it's not fair to be angry with me. I was not to blame.'

She would say that, she decided, and then she would lean her head on his shoulder and press herself to him. If he wanted her and if he were to make love to her, she would be forgiven. He would have to forgive her then.

She felt as if she were on fire at the thought of him touching her, and her own fingers strengthened their stroking. But that was not what she wanted at all. She wanted his fingers, not her own. She shut her eyes and imagined him doing what she was doing. She imagined him gently lowering himself on to her so as not to cause her pain. Then she tried to picture what he would look like naked beside her. Would he be erect immediately, or would she have to coax him into life? That would be better, she decided. The others had all been so very ready. It would be better to find that he was slower and she could worship him with her hands and with her mouth until majestically he would rise and ride her, almost as if the favour were his.

The rolling waves of desire she was experiencing were almost unbearable.

'Love me, Paul. Love me,' she whispered into the dark. 'Yes, oh yes – that's so good. Don't stop.'

She would beg him, a woman humbled by him and hungry for him. She would open herself to him, be his vessel. And that way he could not refuse her.

Suddenly she slipped out of the bed and, wearing the voluminous cotton nightgown that Mrs So had found for her, she crept barefoot across the room. The door creaked as it opened, and there was nothing she could do about that except hold her breath so as not to add to the noise. Leaving it open behind her, she made her way on tiptoe along the narrow corridor, her feet cold on the stone floor. Outside Paul's door she stopped. The impulse was to knock, but that too might wake Mrs So or even Pao and his wife.

So she opened it, as little as possible, and slipped like a small grey ghost into his room. He had not woken and she could hear his slow, sleeping breath as she stood and with infinite care closed the door behind her. It creaked and he grumbled in his sleep and turned.

Softly she moved towards his bed, feeling the depth and warmth of a Chinese carpet under her feet. The silk masked any sound she was making, but it was hard not to breathe faster as she neared the bed. She was standing above him now and could just see his head, dark on the white pillow. She was not certain what to do. If she just woke him, he would send her back to her room. She must arouse him first, she decided, so he could not resist.

Gently she pulled the nightgown off her shoulders and let it slip to the ground. Then carefully she took her feet from its folds and swiftly slid under the sheets, pressing herself close to him where he lay.

'What!' He sat up abruptly, almost tumbling her from the small bed. 'Poppy! What are you doing?'

She plucked at him, pulling him down and wrapping her arms around him.

'Paul. I'm miserable. I want to talk. It's easier in the dark. You're angry with me about Jade. But it was Jade who started it. Honestly, Paul, it's not fair to be angry with me. I was not to blame.'

The rehearsed words tumbled out and she buried her head into his chest, holding him tight to her, as he tried to pull away, hampered by the narrowness of the bed.

'I'm not angry with you, Poppy,' he said quietly. 'But I will be if you don't go back to your own room.'

'Let me stay, Paul.' She made her voice childlike. 'I want to be with you. I'm miserable. Please make me happy. And let me make you happy.'

He was wearing pyjamas, western pyjamas, and she let go of him to undo the buttons of his jacket so that she could place her head on his chest properly. She wanted to feel his skin on hers.

He was breathing heavily and then he groaned and wrapped his arms around her, holding her very close to him. She winced as he pressed into the burns and instinctively he released her.

'It will have to be gentle,' she whispered. And, her hands freer, she sought below where his pyjama trousers were tied around his waist.

'Oh, Paul – you do want me,' she said. 'Paul, I'm so glad.'

She was smothering his face with kisses.

276

She felt all the muscles of his back bunch as he pushed her away from him with strength she could not combat to hold her at a distance.

'Of course I want you,' he said, his voice not sounding right. 'I think of nothing else, Poppy. But it's not going to happen. Not like this.'

'But, Paul, it's impossible with you so near. How can I stay in that little room alone, cold, wanting you? I want to be in your arms. I want you to love me. Paul – I want you to fuck me. I need you. Before, it was anyone. Now it's just you. And you won't let me make you happy. Paul –' her voice was urgent '– Paul, I could do so much for you. Let me love you and kiss you. Let me touch you everywhere. Let me just please you. You don't have to touch me at all if you don't want to. I won't mind. If I can make you satisfied then you'll need me again, and that's what I want. It will be enough. Please, Paul. Let me do it. Please let me do it.'

While she strained to be close to him again, he had managed to swing his body over her and out of the bed so that he was standing. Then he bent down and bodily lifted her into his arms.

'You're going back to your own bed,' he said.

'I'll make a terrible noise and a scene,' she threatened, wriggling in his grasp. 'Paul, I want to stay.'

'You won't make a noise and you won't make a scene. I love you, Poppy. I love you very much, but there's still a lot to think about. For both of us. Now you'll go back to bed like a good girl, and tomorrow we'll talk properly. We should have talked before,' he added quietly.

She could see his head silhouetted and tipped downwards to look at her and the thought that he loved her quietened her. The heat was still there, but it had a different quality. She was at peace. He wanted her; she had felt that, but he loved her more than just fucking. It was a sobering thought, and she lay still in his arms while he walked across the room, and grunting quietly, managed to open the door without putting her down.

He carried her down the corridor and back into her own room where carefully, as if she were as precious as she felt he was, he put her down and pulled the bedclothes over her. Then he leaned to kiss her on the mouth.

'I think you're going to have to marry me, Poppy,' he said as he went.

To Sammy's exasperation, Mi was not at home when he finally got back to Wong Tia Sin. It had taken him a while to find a locksmith and he had needed to get some tools. He had an idea in mind that might save a lot of time.

He had had two cuttings of the keys made, one to give to Gary as a fail-safe. He had intended to ask Mi to take them to the Big Fat Hot Lips. He was certain Gary would turn up about midnight, but he might be a lot later than that himself. They could miss each other.

He had already scribbled a note to go with the keys. He put them all together in an envelope and left them stuffed between the back of the bed and the wall, just in case Mi came back. They left messages for each other there and money, if she needed it. It wasn't the finest hiding place, but he had no reason to think anyone would be searching his room.

He felt safe. The situation smelt safe. He was pretty certain that in no way was he rumbled. He was their decoy duck, and a sitting one, and they were content to have him. Anyway, they didn't figure he'd be around long once he got Stateside. It was to be goodbye to Broken Scissors for him, they thought.

Before going out again, he rang Mi at the club. He didn't want to hot-foot it over to Kowloon to talk to her before he went back to the factory. It would only waste time.

Once he found she wasn't coming back, he made the conversation brief.

'If our friend comes in, tell him I'll be late. After one o'clock,' he said. 'Tell him to hang on until I get there. Not to go away.'

'Yes, Sammy. I tell him,' she said.

'Good kid,' he said, then added, suddenly feeling a wave of affection: 'Hey – it's time you left that crummy joint. We don't need that kind of money any more.'

'Oh, Sammy,' she said. 'You very too kind.'

'And you can take time to learn to speak English,' he teased her before he put down the phone.

It was a complicated journey over to Castle Peak Road and, dressed as he was in his old patched jeans and matted sweater, public transport had to do it. He was using that same bag as he had used the day he first met Gary, turned to its filthy side. It held the tools he needed and he just hoped that some overzealous cop wouldn't stop him. He could be taken in for burglary.

Castle Peak Road was quiet with a light mist softening the street lamps. He padded along in his sneakers, turning down to the left of the Green Butterfly factory and into the narrow and quieter street at the back where the staff entrance was. He held his breath as he tried the first of the keys. Sometimes they did not work at all. But this key slid easily into the lock and turned. A small push, the door was open and he was inside in the darkness of the building.

He had brought a thin pencil torch with him which he used with care. He knew there was a nightwatchman on the premises, but that he never went to the basement. The basement was secure. No one, without keys, could possibly get in without blowing a hole in the side of the building where the goods entrance came out.

Hugging the walls, his hands sweating, he crept up the stairs to the front hall and the elevator. All was quiet. With deliberate slow and careful movements, though his impulse was to hurry, he opened the elevator just wide enough to slip inside. Then he shut the gate and pressed the button for the basement. It seemed to make a hell of a din as it groaned its way down and he worried that the nightwatchman might just hear the whirr of the operating machinery. But all was still as the cage jerked to a halt. He slid back the inner gate and put his hand through the iron mesh of the outer door to where the large padlock swung steely and grey in the thin torchlight.

He opened it with the second key, which was as smooth as the first. He sent up a mental thank-you to Loi Chow, the locksmith who had surpassed himself and without asking too many questions.

He shut the lift gate quietly, padlocked it again and then picked his way soft-footed across the huge basement to where the sealed packing cases were piled below the goods exit.

He settled himself behind one and crouched down so that even if the nightwatchman came down in the elevator he would not be easily seen. But the elevator remained still, and with only the narrow beam from the torch for light, he systematically set about breaking into one of the packing cases.

The heavy-duty cardboard boxes were secured by bands of metal forged on to each other. The easiest way would be to cut through the board and he had a saw which might just have done the job, but how would he put the box back together? Come the morning, it had to look as if it had not been tampered with, though he figured he'd have some time for more perfect repairs when he started the day's work. He had been alone most of the time in the basement throughout the day. There was no reason to believe that tomorrow would be any different.

He had a wire cutter with him, but it took nearly half an hour to get through the crucial metal band which ran over the opening to the packing case. Eventually it snapped, and he grimaced at the thought of the problems of trying to rejoin it with the soldering outfit that he had brought along.

The opening of the box was held together with great steel staples. Lack of light was hampering him and it took another twenty minutes to wrench these out. He had not reckoned on the staples being there, and when the band went back into position it would have to hide the fact that the staples were gone.

By sheer brute strength he managed to move two of the other metal bands sideways until he was able to open up the cardboard just sufficiently to pull out one of the coats.

He squatted down on the floor and spread it out, shining the torch down from a height to get a better look. It was a black and white checkered fur – much the same in design as the one he had seen that morning. But this one was lined with a synthetic black quilted lining.

The secret had to be something to do with this lining, he decided, but it looked perfectly normal and felt normal to the touch. Underneath the lining maybe? He took a knife from his bag and, holding the torch between his teeth, carefully cut at the stitches which held the quilting in place. It wasn't easy to do; the knife kept slipping. A razor blade would have been better. He swore softly and tried again.

He'd missed the stitching and the knife had made a small hole in one of the neat patches of quilting. As he moved the coat into a better light, he spotted it – a thin trickle of white powder coming from the small gash he had inadvertently made.

He squatted back on his heels and grinned into the darkness.

'That's it, is it?' he said. 'The clever bastards . . .'

Delicately he pricked each patch in the quilting until the fabric showed a small hole. Each hole he squeezed oozed the same white powder.

'Well, I'll be . . .' he started to say. And at that moment the elevator groaned and began to lurch its way upward.

It frightened the life out of him; he felt his stomach turn to water, but he was all right, he told himself. No one could get into the basement. No one had a key – unless Jimmy Lee himself was turning up in the middle of the night.

He settled himself behind the packing case and waited, his confidence evaporating when he realised that the lift was grumbling its way down again. He found he was holding his breath and that he was sweating. He shut his eyes and thought he would pray if he could think of who to pray to.

He heard the jerk as the lift stopped. The light was on, throwing a panel of light down the centre of the warehouse. He still sat tight. They couldn't get in. Or could they? He could hear the padlock rattling and whoever was opening it, or trying to open it, was not taking any care to be silent. Then he heard the gates crash back, and someone turned on the lights so that the warehouse was suddenly blazing. Crouched behind the boxes, he felt very exposed.

He sat tense, the hammer he had been using clenched in his hand. It would make some sort of weapon, and if there was only one out there he stood a chance. He thought there might only be one as he could hear no conversation, only a strange shuffling noise and an occasional bump as if something heavy was landing on the floor. Whoever it was was moving around a lot, but what they were doing he couldn't make out.

He made himself as small as possible in his hiding place and waited for the inevitable, debating whether to get up and face it. Could he bluff it out? Announce he was the warehouseman? Demand what the hell was going on?

Too late, he decided. He should have done that the moment he heard the lift come down. And anyway, it would sound too thin at midnight.

The strange heavy shuffling and patterings followed by thuds were getting nearer and now he could hear heavy breathing, as if someone were using a lot of energy. If whoever it was came past the box, he was done. They couldn't help but see him. There was nowhere to hide. Facing it was best. The decision made, he got to his feet, the hammer clenched in his hand.

And froze.

Confronting him was the huge, mangy head of a lion – a lion standing upright on its shaggy hind legs and with the sneakers of one of the two men inside the crude skin showing below the roughly painted pads.

Lion-dancers! What the hell were lion-dancers doing there at night? was his first thought. And then his second and last thought was that they were practising in secret, of course.

$$\approx 12 \approx$$

FRIDAY

Gary was telling himself that he'd probably fall off the barstool if he had one more drink and thanking heaven that Suzie watered them with blatant disregard for the weights and measures authorities. It was as well she did. If he had truly drunk all that he had seemed to drink, he would have been speechless, legless and witless.

He and Mi had been playing games magnificently. She had flirted, pouted and laughed with him as he made the odd clumsy-looking pass while shouting for more drinks. Suzie, this time with a pink carnation behind her ear, had lurched over occasionally, thrown him melting glances from under her caked mascara and enquired if he were happy, honey?

He was not happy. It was nearly four o'clock in the morning. The tarts had taken their business home and all the men left in the Big Fat Hot Lips, mostly sailors, were drunk.

It was easier for Mi, he decided grumpily. Whatever he was buying her was only water. She was disconcertingly sober.

'Gary,' she finally whispered to him on the pretext of nibbling his ear. 'I worried. Very.'

'I worried very, too,' Gary said back into her ear. 'Do you think he's gone straight home?'

'Prehaps,' Mi said. 'Prehaps we go find out, eh?'

'He won't be at your other – ' he coughed ' – your working pad?'

'He not got key.'

'Well, we better go home,' Gary said.

He knew he shouldn't set foot near Sammy's pad, but as it had no telephone, making contact was impossible. He decided it was a chance he had to take. He and Mi made great play of their leaving, Mi holding him up and he protesting she was asking too much money. Once in the street, he hailed a taxi that wasn't keen to go out to Wong Tai Sin, nor wanted to wait when they got there. The driver reluctantly agreed to sit outside the housing estate only when Gary refused to pay unless he did.

Sammy was not at home. The squalid room was bare and Gary wrinkled his nose at the smell and said: 'Christ, is this where you two live?'

'It home,' she said, resigned, and he pondered what people would do in the cause of duty, and what made Sammy run to a dangerous job that had him living like this. The guy deserved a medal, he thought.

'What we do now?' Mi asked. 'I frightened.'

'Nothing to be frightened about,' he said, trying to sound convincing. 'He's just been held up, I guess. He'll come home. Maybe he's been home and gone out again. Is there any way you could tell?'

Mi's face looked pinched and she was near to tears. 'He said two o'clock. It nearly five,' she wailed. 'Gary, you find him for me, eh?'

She went over to the narrow bed.

'Sometimes he leave message and things here,' she said. 'I look.'

She thrust her hand down the back of the bed and felt for a moment. Then came up with a brown envelope that jangled. She held it out to him.

'You open,' she commanded and he realised she was afraid of what the envelope might contain.

Inside, wrapped in a piece of paper, were three keys, two of them obviously belonging to heavy-duty padlocks. The keys to Green Butterfly Furs, Gary reasoned. But to which door and which padlocks? The paper was a brief note addressed to him. It said: 'The stuff goes out in a plain green van in unsealed packing cases through the goods entrance. It is picked up and brought back in sealed packing cases about two hours later. Follow that van!'

'These are for me, Mi,' he said. 'They may unlock where Sammy is. I'll check. Listen, I'm going now, but I want you to ring me first thing in the morning if he's not home. Ok? If he's not, tell me you miss me and want me to come over right away. If he is home, say you want to see me tonight.'

'I understand,' she said woodenly. 'But I too much frightened. Very.'

He gave her a hug and a kiss, wishing he could comfort her more.

She loved Sammy, that was obvious, and he wondered at how she could ply her trade and love him at the same time. Women were pretty weird, he decided.

The taxi driver had waited and was none too good-tempered, though his mood improved when Gary gave him a large tip once they were back Hong Kong side. He weighed the keys in his hand as he went up to his room debating whether or not to wake Jade and deciding against it. His mind was full of Sammy. What had he been up to? And what had happened? Could he possibly have been blown? And if he were blown, what had he found out that Gary did not know and now might never know? And if Sammy were blown, did that mean he, Gary, was blown too?

The message light was winking like a red eye in his room, and the instructions were to ring Jade no matter what time it was.

He dialled her room and the phone was answered instantly.

'Where have you been?' she asked plaintively.

'What you might call hanging around,' he said. 'How did your day go?'

'Fascinating. But where have you been?'

'Waiting for a guy who didn't turn up.'

She must have caught the note of anxiety in his voice, because she said: 'And you're worried about it?'

'Some. But what happened to you?'

'I found out about the *Brian Leigh*.'

'You did! And?'

'It was Grandfather and his friend Chan Koh Leung. They did it together. They were working for the British government . . .'

She was about to launch into the story and he knew his tired, worried mind wouldn't keep up with what she was saying. Besides, it still didn't sound like a part of his scenario. He said: 'Beautiful Jade, don't tell me on the phone. You shouldn't, and anyway I can't take it in. I have to sleep and I have to think. It's nearly six in the morning.'

'I'm sorry,' she said. 'Shall we meet tomorrow?'

'About midday?' he suggested. He wanted to give Mi time to telephone.

'As late as that?' she said. 'Grandfather was talking about going to Fanling early.'

'Does he want you to go with him?'

'Yes. But I don't want to.'

'If he wants you to, go,' he said authoritatively. He had a strong feeling that he was going to have things to do in the morning that didn't include Jade, like following plain green vans.

'I don't want to see Poppy. Not until this black eye has gone.'

'She might have a worse one,' he suggested.

She giggled. 'I suppose you don't feel like coming round and inspecting mine?'

He did. But he was going to have to sleep. Just in case.

'I'll inspect all of you later,' he said, and she laughed again.

'All right. Now go to sleep.'

'You too, sweetheart,' he said. 'I love you.'

'That's nice,' she sighed as she put the phone down.

He slept only fitfully, but at ten o'clock the phone rang. It was Mi and she was crying. She had completely forgotten the code in her distress and she said: 'Gary. Oh, Gary. Police come. They find Sammy dead. He in harbour. Someone bad has broke his neck.'

'The question is, what had he found out to make someone kill him?' Chief Superintendent Morrison was asking, tapping his unlit cigarette against his lower lip.

'I don't know,' Gary said dully. He was full of grief which he knew was unprofessional and that he should cast aside. But he could not help remember the squalid room where Sammy had spent his last days in an effort to stop kids back in LA getting hooked and killing themselves on junk; Sammy, killed in an effort to stop evil men getting rich on their deaths. Mi had sounded inconsolable on the phone. He knew her call could be putting him in danger, but he could not bring himself to stop her talking. She had sobbed and told him how Sammy's last words were that they didn't need that kind of money any more.

'He want me learn to speak English proper,' she had said. 'I will. For him.'

But her last chance of a decent life had almost certainly gone with Sammy.

He phoned Morrison from a call box and arranged to meet him at the Noonday Bar in the Excelsior Hotel. The bar would be safely and anonymously crowded with tourists watching the gun on the harbour being fired at midday in Hong Kong tradition.

They managed to get the two end seats at the corner of the curved bar, and ignoring the thick leather arm rest, Morrison sat bolt upright in an avenging posture complaining that Sammy must have been careless; that now they had a murder on their hands and an embarrassing one at that.

Gary lost his cool. He made it clear without actually saying so that he thought Morrison a pompous prick.

'Something went wrong,' Gary told him tersely. 'It would have been bad luck. Sammy wasn't careless. He was smart and streetwise and good at his job, and I reckon you ought to be worrying more about who did it than blaming his death on his own carelessness.'

The chief superintendent went red in the face then and asked if there had been any communication once Sammy had taken the job at the Green Butterfly factory.

'I spoke to him the night before last.'

'And we don't know where he went last night?'

Again Gary shook his head. The keys were heavy in his pocket. He ought to tell the Brits about them, but he wasn't going to. This, he felt, was something he wanted to sort out for himself. And though he could guess where Sammy had been, he wasn't going to tell Morrison, because it could have been that Sammy had moved too quickly. Not carelessly. Too quickly. If he had, there had to be a reason and the reason was probably that a shipment was leaving Hong Kong very soon now.

'As you've lost your oppo, I think you should contact our man inside,' Morrison was saying. 'Well, he's not quite inside, he starts working for Jimmy Lee on Saturday. He's a licensing officer called Stephen Norris. They've been wooing him.' He smiled thinly. 'We persuaded him to take the job. He's about to become the chief security officer for Green Butterfly Furs. They have a shipment going to the States on Sunday. Our man will be with the furs.'

'Sunday?' Gary asked, alert again.

'That's right. By sea. One of Kwan Ching's cargo boats to 'Frisco and then by road to LA. That's the plan.'

That was it, Gary thought. Sammy had had to move quickly if the shipment was going on Sunday.

'Did Sammy know this other guy was going?'

Morrison shook his head and signalled the barman for a refill of his glass of orange juice.

'Why weren't we told?'

'When would we have told you? We only knew ourselves last night. What difference does it make?'

'None, I suppose,' Gary said. But it did. If Sammy had known there might not have been any reason for him to move quickly.

'It's coming together, isn't it?' Gary said. 'The heroin goes out with the furs, supplied by Jimmy Lee. Or the furs are a blind. The stuff travels in a ship, supplied by Kwan Ching. We can pick them up in the States all right. Or alternatively you can raid the place now.'

'If you are right, and there is any heroin,' Morrison's tone said he doubted it very much, 'don't you think it would be better to break up the entire gang? Both your side and here. In one swoop. Find out where the stuff is coming from.' His tone was mocking. 'Perhaps we should just let them go a little further. In fact,' he said, his voice sharpening. 'as this is my manor, that's the way we shall do it. Let them continue, and if you are correct, we'll smoke the lot out.'

The maddening thing was that the man was right. He, Gary, was letting emotion get in the way. But how far to let them continue? It would be much, much better, he thought, if there were no more deaths. Most importantly, not Jade's death or the death of anyone like her grandfather.

He left the Excelsior, knowing that now he must get in touch with Washington and that in the end, in spite of it being Morrison's territory, he'd do what his own control wanted.

'I have to go down to the chapel. Do you want to come with me?'

Paul So had come out into the small sheltered garden of his home where Poppy was sitting, trying to read *Nicholas Nickleby*. The only books in the house in English were by Dickens. Dickens bored her.

'Please,' she said, putting the book down with relief.

'You are bored?' he asked.

'A little.'

He sighed.

'Come then. We'll walk and talk at the same time.'

He insisted that she put on a light coat of his mother's and she said: 'I'll have to go back to the hotel very soon. I need some clothes.'

'And sight of the bright lights?'

'And sight of the bright lights,' she agreed.

She had decided when she woke that morning and was lying warm and cosy while asleep still hovered, that she was going to be totally honest with Paul. Thinking further, she had realised that it was indeed her nature to be open. She did say what she felt; she had no secrets, but he was the first man who had made enough impact on her to examine how a relationship should be.

They walked the narrow pavement down to the chapel, holding hands.

'I'm sorry about last night,' she said suddenly.

He stroked her palm.

'So am I,' he said, his tone rueful. 'I found it exceedingly difficult to sleep after you'd gone.'

'And I slept right away. It was what you said that did it.'

'About marriage?'

She hesitated, staring out over the flat field that ran alongside the road.

'More like you loving me, I think. That was the important bit.'

'Well I do.'

'And I you. But marriage . . .' she sighed. 'I'm not religious, Paul. It would be hard for me to be a proper wife to a pastor. At least, I think so. I'm not sure what pastor's wives have to do.'

'Help aid the flock.'

She shook her head doubtfully.

'Can you imagine me into good works?'

'Not easily,' he said, 'but it might not be as difficult or as boring as you think.'

She was silent.

'You should have fallen for Jade,' she said. 'She's the unselfish one. I'm selfish and self-centred. Everyone says so.'

'Forget what everyone says. Do you believe you are?'

'Perhaps not. Not right inside me somewhere. I think perhaps I've never been very happy. Yet walking down this road with you, holding your hand, I am happy.'

'And how about the bright lights?' he teased.

'I only want them when you're not with me. And you couldn't be with me all the time.'

He laughed.

'Surprisingly I could be with you more doing this work than if I were an office worker. We could be together a great deal. But I must tell you, Poppy, my work is important to me. I will never give it up. And I would never divorce. We have to give each other time. I need that as much as you do.'

She nodded. 'I understand,' she said. 'But how do we get time?'

'That's the question,' he was saying when she stopped dead and made a sudden exclamation.

'Look there – ahead,' she said. 'I could swear that's Grandfather standing outside the church. No one else can be as tall as that.'

He peered ahead.

'Well, it's certainly Jade with him. And another man. Were you expecting your grandfather in Hong Kong?'

'No.' she said. 'Let's hurry.'

She broke into a little trot and waved. He lengthened his pace to keep up with her. The group standing under the trees outside the chapel did not move.

Poppy was with them fractionally before he was. She stopped dead in front of the tall, elderly man, looked up what was a considerable distance for her, and he heard her say: 'Good morning, Grandfather. What are you doing here?'

'Looking for you.'

'Well, you've found me.'

The old man grunted and said, pointing: 'And this is the Reverend So, eh?'

Paul put out his hand. 'I'm Paul So, sir,' he said.

'McKenzie McKenzie. You've been looking after her?'

'Trying to, sir.'

The man had such presence and authority that Paul found he was fidgeting, waiting for what would be said next. Ian McKenzie McKenzie was pulling his lower lip between two fingers and looking thoughtfully at Poppy. Jade, who was standing slightly back a little, had a large black eye, Paul saw.

'This is Michael Blake,' Ian McKenzie McKenzie suddenly said, bringing the other man into the group.

'Morning – or is it afternoon?' Blake said. He was much shorter and rounder than the old gentleman, but had considerable authority himself, Paul noted. Then he said: 'Silly hanging about on the pavement here, Ian.' He turned to Paul. 'Is there anywhere we can talk?'

'Well, in the chapel,' Paul said, 'or we could walk back to my home if you would prefer. It would be more comfortable.'

'Walked far enough coming from the station,' McKenzie McKenzie said. 'We'll talk in the chapel.'

Without any further conversation, he turned and stomped up the path to the doorway, his back as straight as a twenty-year-old's. He ducked as he went through the door and stood looking about the inside of the chapel while the others clustered behind him.

'Might well be in Glasgow,' he pronounced.

Somehow Paul did not want whatever discussion was about to take place to be conducted in his church. He said quickly: 'In the garden outside there is some seating. It is more comfortable and convenient than the pews in here.'

The old man gave him a sharp look, but Michael Blake seemed to have understood his anxiety and said: 'Good thinking. We'll go outside.' And it was he who led the way through to the garden, where they settled themselves around a rough table surrounded by wooden chairs and one small settle.

'The ladies from the congregation who help out have their tea out here,' Paul explained. He felt it was necessary to say something.

Ian McKenzie McKenzie nodded. He had seated himself so that he dominated the table. He was unmistakably the chairman of the board.

'Now then, Poppy,' he said. 'What have you been up to?'

Paul had not sat down. He was standing behind Poppy, his hand on her shoulder, and he felt her stiffen.

'She has been very badly treated, sir,' he said, speaking for her. 'A man she met – ' he paused, wanting to explain in the most gentle way ' – abused her and tried to make her into a heroin addict. She nearly died.'

'Why did this man do these things?' the grandfather asked Poppy, forcing her to speak.

'I don't know,' she said in a small voice.

'Who was he?'

'He was called Kwan Ching,' she said, her hands tightening in her lap. 'Jade and I had dinner with him and three other people the first night we were here.'

'And who were the other people?'

'The man you met with me at the races, Grandfather, Jimmy Lee,' Jade said. 'A Chinese girl called Emma who really saved Poppy, and her boyfriend, an English policeman. You know that the two Chinese men are both Triads.'

'Yes, I know,' her grandfather said tersely, 'but I want Poppy to speak for herself.' He turned to direct his question to her again. Paul squeezed Poppy's shoulder and her hand fluttered up as if she meant to hold his. 'Now, you've no idea why this man did these things?' he asked again. 'He gave you no clue?'

Poppy shook her head.

'None at all. He talked about you a great deal. He said he intended to follow exactly in your footsteps. He wanted to be as rich and as successful as you are.'

'And that was all?'

'That was all.'

'He was trying to find Poppy again, sir,' Paul said. 'That was why we thought it wise to keep her here, where she would be safe.'

'She'll be safe back in Hong Kong now I'm here.'

Paul noticed Michael Blake move slightly in his uncomfortable seat.

'Ian,' he said. 'She's better off right here and even better off in Scotland. You should take them both home.'

'Not until I find out why this young man tried to kill my granddaughter,' Ian said. his voice stubborn. 'And there are the other deaths to consider. I'll not be leaving here until I know what it's all about.'

'I think you know what it's all about, Ian,' Michael said, and his eyes never left the older man's face. McKenzie McKenzie held the look for a few seconds, and then he stared down at the table.

'There'll be no peace until it's resolved.'

'Leave it to the police,' Michael urged.

'No.' The syllable came out like a small explosion. 'How old is this Kwan Ching, Poppy?'

'About twenty-five maybe. I don't know. A year or so older than I am.'

'And Jimmy Lee is how old?' He was asking himself the question. 'Perhaps the same?'

'I think Kwan is a little older,' Jade volunteered.

'Very successful young men for their ages,' Ian said. 'I think I should be knowing them better. Perhaps we should buy you both a fur coat tomorrow. That would seem to be a good idea. Jade tells me that was the original reason these laddies came into your lives. Tomorrow we shall buy fur coats.'

'I don't want a fur coat, Grandfather,' Poppy said.

'Poppy is right.' Michael Blake's voice was stern. 'You have no right to involve the girls, Ian.'

'I want to be involved,' Jade said.

'For heaven's sake, Jade,' Michael Blake started to say, and then began sneezing.

'I think Poppy should stay with me, sir,' Paul said firmly. 'I don't think perhaps you understand Triad societies.'

'I'm told they're all wiped out these days,' the old man said, his voice sardonic.

'They'll never be wiped out. And they are dangerous.'

Michael Blake was groping for a handkerchief.

'Ian, go home,' he said. 'First thing tomorrow. You're nearly eighty years old, man. It's not the same any more.'

'Don't challenge me with age, Michael.' Ian McKenzie McKenzie's blue eye had turned a steely grey.

Poppy had shaken off Paul's hand and suddenly stood up.

'Grandfather,' she said. 'Couldn't we leave it to the police? And why do you say there will be no peace until it's resolved? Does that mean that Jade and I aren't safe here in Hong Kong?' For the first time, she looked at her sister. 'Is that why you want to be involved, Jade?'

'In a way.'

'You see, Grandfather,' Poppy went on. 'I'd like to stay here. I was wondering if you could find me a job.'

Her grandfather's face was a caricature of astonishment.

'A job! You, Poppy! You want a job?'

'Yes. I want a job. In Hong Kong. Or Fanling, if possible.'

'You want to stay here?' Her grandfather was finding it difficult to grasp.

'Yes. I want to be with Paul. To see if maybe we could be together all the time.'

Ian McKenzie McKenzie seemed lost for words.

'Let me get this straight,' he said. 'You want to marry this young preacher?' He sounded incredulous.

'I didn't say that. But yes. If it would work.'

'And you, laddie?'

'I love Poppy very much,' Paul told him, 'but we need time to see if she would be happy in my life.'

Ian McKenzie McKenzie was shaking his head.

'Well, I'll be—' he muttered. 'So you want a job, Poppy? But what can you do?'

'Not a lot,' she said cheerfully, 'but I don't see why I couldn't learn.'

292

'Can we find her a job, Michael?'

'I expect so.'

The old man sighed.

'Well, if you want to stay here, then it's got to be resolved,' he said. 'Because unless it is, neither you – or this nice young man you love will ever be safe. Not for one day, one hour or one minute.'

Gary had had a hell of a time hiring a van, and a nicely anonymous one at that. Another van, he had decided, would make more sense for following a plain green one through the factory district of Kowloon.

It was a black van he found in the end, rather too big for his needs, but running smoothly and in good shape. He set off for Kowloon side and Castle Peak Road and the premises of Green Butterfly Furs with that anticipatory surge of adrenalin which made the boring and the dangerous parts of working for the DEA worthwhile.

Of course, there was nowhere to park. He saw the staff entrance at the back of the building and further along the closed heavy wooden flap behind which he assumed, from Sammy's information, the furs came and went. The only way to wait and watch was to double-park – hardly inconspicuous – or to keep driving round the block or up and down the street. He double-parked for five minutes and was debating whether to move on when he got lucky. A plain green van skidded around the corner and double-parked itself outside the wooden flap. Two young Chinese emerged simultaneously from the front seats and ran around to the back of the van to unlock it.

Between them they manhandled a large heavy-duty cardboard box to the flap, then banged hard on the wood making a drumming sound, before going to the van for another box. Someone inside the building swung open the flap and the box was slid down a shute into the warehouse.

Working at high speed the two men delivered four boxes and then refilled the van with four others which were sent up from below. They were far too busy to notice Gary, lurking some yards down the road. The van loaded, they slammed the back doors shut, locked them and then drove off, raising dust in the windy street.

Gary's luck held. He was able to stay with them and as they were travelling along a main road, his presence seemed normal enough in the general crush of Kowloon traffic. He followed them up past Boundary Road and into the New Territories. Where the hell were they going? he wondered, as they drove in and out of Sha Tin and on further north, keeping to the main road.

It was at Tai Po they finally turned off and made their way through the acne-scars of new development and down to a small but busy harbour. With the same speed and efficiency they had shown at the factory, they loaded their cargo on to a flat-bottomed sampan which seemed to have been waiting for them. Watching, Gary saw a woman in a coolie hat navigate the sampan through the busy harbour with considerable skill. She headed for a small cargo vessel which was called *Hillfan*.

A crane on the deck of the ship neatly pulled the boxes on board and then lowered four more to take their place. Then the sampan woman manoevred her craft back to the harbour. The two men who had been sitting smoking then helped her unload and refilled the van.

Gary decided he could afford to lose the van and its drivers when they drove off. He wanted to see what happened next to the ship. But nothing happened until an hour and a half later when the green van returned and the routine was repeated. The vessel remained anchored and with little sign of life on board.

He debated what to do. Dusk was falling. He needed some back-up, and to his chagrin he realised he was going to have to tell Morrison where the furs were going. He was also going to have to get into that warehouse himself, with the keys that Sammy had so thoughtfully provided, and look into one of those boxes.

Michael Blake could not face Beryl, and so he filled in the time before meeting Arthur Watson-King with a drink or two at the Bull and Bear. He was feeling slightly high and gently philosophical when Arthur arrived.

'Don't like coming into Hong Kong at night,' the old man grumbled as he settled himself on a bar stool and signalled for a drink. 'Hope it's worth it.'

'At least you can park,' Michael said, adding fatuously: 'Every cloud has a silver lining.'

'What's up with you?' Arthur said.

'I think I'm in love,' Michael said. He sighed. 'Have you ever met my wife, Arthur?'

'Once.'

'What did you think?'

'Charming woman.'

'Liar.'

Arthur ignored that and said: 'So who are you in love with?'

'Jade McKenzie McKenzie. And she's about to get herself killed.'

'Oh, really.' Arthur's glass was being handed over, and he seemed more interested in a long gin and tonic than imminent mayhem.

'Yeah. The old man's here.'

'So I heard.'

'He wants a showdown with Jimmy Lee and Kwan Ching.'

'The Triad couple.'

'The very same. When I told him he was eighty and to go home, he accused me of challenging him with age.'

'You'll be out of a job, old boy, if you're not careful. So what else is new?'

'Well, I can tell you what happened to the *Brian Leigh*.'

'Know that already. Rascal, that Chan Koh Leung. When's the showdown?'

'Ian's talking about buying furs from Jimmy Lee tomorrow. And he says he'll sort out Kwan Ching later. I told him to leave it to the police.'

Arthur looked thoughtfully into his drink.

'He can't do that, can he? Too much dirty water. Well, he can't officially, that is. But the night has a thousand eyes if you know where to find 'em. Where's the showdown?'

'I don't know yet. I'll find out if I can.'

'You going?'

'I'd like to.'

'How good are you against a martial arts expert?'

'You've got to be joking.'

'Then if you go, get a gun. I'd leave it to the professionals if I were you, though.'

Mike chuckled softly.

'Don't challenge me with age,' he said.

Arthur sighed. 'Well, there's life in most of us old dogs yet.' He stared thoughtfully into space and then said: 'Just hang on a minute, will you. I have to call a pompous ass of a policeman. If he was a decent kind of chap, we'd have found him in here. But would you believe, he doesn't drink.'

And with an expression of deep disgust, Arthur ambled off his bar stool and disappeared into the crowd. Michael ordered another drink, and imagined himself incapacitating Jimmy Lee with a brilliant and brutal karate chop. He couldn't quite bring himself to imagine killing the man. Putting him out of action would do, he decided, and Jade would fall into his arms and love him for ever.

He was sneezing when Arthur Watson-King came back.

'I told you to watch that cold, old chap.' he said.

'It was the most astonishing thing ever.' Jade's voice was sleepy, her head was cradled on his shoulder and he was gently stroking her breast. 'Can you imagine, Poppy marrying a pastor!' She gave a little giggle. 'I can't take it in and neither could Grandfather. It's astonishing, isn't it?'

'You forget. I've never met Poppy, honey.'

'Of course not. Well, she wants to stay there in Fanling for the moment. It's as if she feels safe with her pastor. He is a nice man, but I simply can't imagine it working. And, incidentally, she hasn't got a black eye.'

'Did she mention yours?'

'Nope. Not a word.'

She curled herself tighter into him.

'Tomorrow Grandfather and I are seeing Jimmy Lee.'

He sat bolt upright.

'Where?'

'He's coming here. Bringing some fur coats for me to choose from. Grandfather's supposed to be buying me a present. I made the arrangement. I wouldn't let Grandfather talk to Jimmy. It must be safe here in the hotel. He can't do anything awful in the Clipper Room of the Mandarin, can he? He's coming at nine thirty. Could you be sort of nearby – just in case?'

Gary had planned to go to the Green Butterfly factory in the morning and bold as brass let himself in with Sammy's keys in broad daylight. On the way back from Tai Po, he had driven back past the factory and noted their working hours. The Green Butterfly factory did not work on Saturdays. He should have a clear run, except for the inevitable watchman, but he'd have to take his chances on that.

'Yes, I'll be around,' he said, thinking that at least he'd know where Jimmy Lee was.

'Nothing can go wrong, can it?' she was asking urgently. 'Grandfather was reluctant about the hotel, but he finally agreed. He didn't want me to be with him, but I said he could hardly pretend to be buying me a coat if I wasn't there to try it on. What do you think it's all about, Gary?'

'I honestly don't know,' he said, thinking he wished he did. 'I don't know yet where your grandfather comes into the story. Maybe he doesn't at all. It may be that Kwan Ching did what he did to Poppy just because he's a sadist.' He wasn't even convincing himself, let alone her, he thought, and decided to stop her questions with kisses and caresses until her eager body, voice and hands were urging him to take her. And in the sweetness of what followed, they both forgot Jimmy Lee.

Later, when she was sleeping soundly and softly, he slid back to his own room, leaving her to sleep alone.

$$\approx 13 \approx$$

SATURDAY

Michael Blake had slept badly. As usual, he had been relegated to the spare bed, though these days he didn't mind so much. It was easier to fantasise without listening to Beryl's heavy breathing and her odd occasional snore. He would have bet his last Hong Kong dollar that Jade never snored.

Jade was on his mind, but not for sexual reasons. It was her safety and that of her grandfather that was exercising him. Arthur Watson-King was all very well as a fail-safe, but he played the cards so close to his chest that it was impossible to know if points had been taken.

At a quarter to nine he made the decision to ring Ian and announced that he, Michael, would be with them through thick and thin today, regardless.

He punched out the number of the Mandarin and was promptly answered and put through to Ian McKenzie McKenzie's room. There was no reply. He asked the operator to try the breakfast rooms and then the lobby. Eventually reception told him that Mr McKenzie McKenzie's key had been handed in and that he had gone out about ten minutes previously.

He then asked to be put through to Jade. She answered quickly, sounding fogged with sleep.

'Jade?'

'Yes.'

'It's Michael. Do you know where your grandfather has gone?'

'Gone?' She sounded more alert. 'No. Isn't he in his room?'

'Reception say he's gone out.'

'My God! What time is it?'

'Nearly nine.'

'Oh, Michael,' her voice was a wail of distress. 'I'm supposed to be meeting him in the lobby at nine thirty. Jimmy Lee is coming . . .'

'I know. But your grandfather has gone out.' He said it patiently. 'Listen, I'm coming straight over. I'll be there by nine thirty. Ok?'

'Right. I'll be in the lobby.'

He phoned Arthur, who sounded sleepy and cross, then showered, shaved and dressed in record time, his brain working all the while. Ian might just have gone for a walk. He might be in the gents at the hotel. He might have popped into McKenzie McKenzie House for some reason. He could, on the other hand, have decided to take matters into his own hands completely. The old bugger was stubborn enough, and if he wasn't at the hotel at nine thirty, then what?

He decided to take a taxi rather than get his car from the underground garage of his apartment block, but was still caught in a traffic jam at Admiralty where rebuilding was going on. It was nine thirty-seven exactly when he reached the Mandarin and hurried into the lobby, without waiting for his change from the taxi driver.

There was no sign of Ian. There was no sign of Jade, nor indeed of Jimmy Lee. He checked Jade's room. There was no reply. Her key was not at reception. She was not in the breakfast room, but Gary Smith was. On the same errand: looking for Jade.

Together they went back down to the lobby and started asking questions. It was one of the porters outside who came up with the information that Miss McKenzie McKenzie had left with two men just a few minutes ago.

'Europeans?' Gary asked.

'No, Chinese,' the porter said. 'They go car.'

The two men looked at each other.

'Let's go back inside and sit down and think this out,' Michael said. Gary Smith had a sort of wild look, as if he might dash off and do something disastrous. 'We must look at it professionally.'

He put strong emphasis on the word 'professionally' and it seemed to work. Gary took a deep breath, nodded and walked ahead through the revolving doors, suddenly all one piece again.

'But I don't think we ought to waste much time,' Michael added. He knew exactly how Gary felt. He could have rushed off and done something idiotic himself. 'Any theories? I can tell you that Ian left the hotel before a quarter to nine, and he left alone.'

'And Jade left at half-past with two men. It suggests that by now they are all together somewhere.'

'Where?'

'My guess,' Gary said, groping for a cigarette and handing one to Michael, 'is the Green Butterfly Fur Company's factory.'

'Why there?'

'Jimmy Lee's the head of a Triad society. Kwan Ching's the Incense Master. They hold initiations there. It's the society's headquarters.'

'In that case,' Michael said, 'I would imagine that is exactly where they are. Shall we go?' He heard himself making the suggestion as if he were asking someone to go in to dinner. Too casual by far. Overplaying the stiff upper lip, he told himself.

Gary was tapping his fingers on the upholstered arm of the chair, the cigarette hanging from his mouth.

'Yes, we'll go. But since you mention being professional, we're going to need some back-up. I have to make a phone call.'

'Who to?' Michael asked.

'A pompous prick of a policeman.'

'Ah.' In spite of his anxiety, Michael had to smile. 'I last heard him referred to as a pompous ass. Let us hope that, pompous or not, he is efficient.'

Gary seemed to be an unconscionably long time phoning, and his face was worried when he came back. 'I've had to leave messages,' he said. 'Would you believe, I couldn't get one bloody European policeman. All taking the day off because it's Saturday, I suppose. I didn't want to say too much to a Chinese.'

'Some of the Chinese are more reliable than the Europeans,' Michael said gently, but it didn't seem the moment to make an issue of it.

The cab they took, fortunately, had a driver whose English was almost non-existent and who kept his transistor playing a wailing, tinkling music as loudly as it would go.

It was beginning to dawn on Michael that they seemed to be rushing into this adventure in a rather foolhardy fashion.

'Shouldn't we work out what to do when we get there?' he asked mildly. 'How do we get inside the place?'

'I have the keys,' Gary said, and launched into a brief explanation of how and why. 'The problem is, I have no idea of the geography. The initiations are held in the warehouse, in the basement. That's where Sammy worked. And that's where I suspect they'll be. According to Sammy, it's the most impregnable place in the building.'

There was a hold-up in the tunnel across to Kowloon and Michael muttered they would have been quicker taking the Star Ferry and getting a taxi from the Ocean Terminal in Kowloon.

'I don't think either of us is thinking that clearly,' he said. Then he heard himself say abruptly: 'She's important to you?'

'Very,' Gary said, his jaw set, and Michael felt that sour wave sweep over him again, wishing the man didn't look so all-American, so Clark Kent, and then, being charitable, he told himself that Gary could hardly help the way the Lord had made him.

The taxi dropped them where Gary asked – on the corner of Camp Street – and then they casually walked one block until they reached the factory.

'The key has got to belong to the staff entrance,' Gary said, eyeing the impressive front door of the building. 'Sammy wouldn't have had the key to that.'

'Staff entrances,' Mike said, 'are traditionally around the back.'

'Right,' Gary agreed. 'Come on.'

The staff entrance was there, the street was quiet, and Gary muttered: 'Only one way to do these things. With confidence.'

He strode to the door and pushed a key in the lock. Before he attempted to turn it, the door opened.

'Christ!' Mike said.

'Don't like the feel of that,' Gary whispered. 'Go very easy.'

They slid inside and found themselves in a small lobby with a cubbyhole to the side. It was empty. There was only one flight of stairs and they went upwards. Gary leading and Mike close behind, they crept up the stone stairs, and Mike had the ridiculous feeling that Gary Smith not only looked like Superman, but he was Superman. He didn't appear remotely frightened, while he, Mike, was scared witless.

But his feet did their duty and took him up the stairs, where they found themselves in a deserted main hall. The front door was closed and there was no lighting.

'So how do we get to the basement?' Mike whispered.

Without speaking, Gary pointed to the big elevator. With infinite care, he was sliding open the iron gates, holding his breath as they protested. Yet Mike had the definite impression that the place was totally deserted. He would have sworn that there was no one there but them. He found the thought comforting.

The groans and grumbles of the lift as it descended made them nervous. Instinctively both flattened themselves against the side walls. It had struck Mike with some force that if the place were not deserted, if there was someone in the basement and if the gates were mesh, they would both be sitting targets as they lumbered into view. It seemed that Gary had the same thought.

When they juddered to a stop they saw the gates were mesh and the warehouse lights were full on, but after a breathless moment, it was clear that there was no one there. Also the padlock which held the outer gates was swinging loose. At the far end away from the lift were several dozen large packing cases, and the room, which was bitterly cold, was flung with pelts of different animals. Facing the lift in the centre of the basement was a heavy wooden table covered with a piece of red paper decorated with Chinese characters. There was a slight smell of smoke in the air, but nothing else. Where was beautiful Jade? Where had they taken her? he wondered frantically.

Cat-footed, Gary came out of the elevator and moved into the warehouse. It cheered Mike to note that Gary held his hand near to his breast in a manner that denoted something a little more useful than the Schaeffer pen, cigarette lighter and nail file which were the nearest things to weapons he personally had on him.

'They've only just gone,' Gary said. 'Fuck it, we've just missed them.' He stood taut and wary, but his face was sad.

Gary's evidence for recent departure was some warm pipe tobacco ashes on the table and floor below, and a cigarette butt on the floor that still smoked gently.

'Ian and someone else?' Mike said. They were still whispering. 'Any sign of Jade having been here?' He believed he could still smell the gentlest drift of the perfume she wore, but decided it must be imagination.

'No,' Gary said. 'But she must have been.'

'Now where?' Mike asked. 'Lee's home? Kwan Ching's? The Green Butterfly shop?'

'No.' Gary was thinking. 'No, I don't think so. But maybe—'

Before he could complete the sentence, the lift behind them jerked, groaned and, creaking, started to journey upwards.

'Maybe they're coming back,' Gary said. He gave a fast look around the area, then said: 'Quick, get behind those packing cases.'

Moving quickly, they swung two cases around to make a barrier with the wall behind them, and then crouched. Gary had a small but lethal-looking gun in his hand, which he poised on the top of the box. Neither of them spoke, hearing only the grumbling and the whirr of machinery as the elevator changed direction and started to descend.

'You all right?' Gary whispered.

'Fine,' Mike said, lying through his teeth. His windpipe felt as if someone was squeezing it, and his breath sounded like a steam engine.

'Good,' Gary grunted.

They heard the lift stop again and the sound of the doors being opened. There was the shuffle of diffident footsteps moving into the room, a pair of footsteps with no confidence in them, then nothing more.

Slowly Gary started to stand up. Mesmerised, Mike stood with him.

Standing in the middle of the basement, a perplexed look on his face, was a European male, about five-feet-ten, with curly brown hair, wearing a dark suit and holding a briefcase in his hand.

When he saw first Gary and then Mike's head appear, he nearly jumped out of his skin. Then he said in the aggrieved voice of a startled man: 'Who the hell are you?'

'Who are you?'

Ian McKenzie McKenzie stood like an ancient cedar, straight and

302

menacing above the small lolling figure of the Chinese.

'I am Jimmy Lee.'

The old man banged his hand down on the big wooden table, disturbing the red paper that covered it.

'I said who are you?'

'Don't you know?'

'I would not be asking the question if I knew the answer.'

'I think you do. But there will be no explanations yet. Not until your granddaughters are with us. This is, after all, a family affair.'

Jimmy Lee lifted himself from the wooden chair where he had been sitting and added: 'I'm sorry, but I'm afraid you are going to have to wait a little while. I shall leave you alone. I have things to do. I will return when Jade arrives. I shall take these with me.'

On the red paper, just out of Ian's reach, were two gleaming blades from a pair of broken scissors.

'We shall need them later, you see,' Jimmy Lee explained, his voice gentle.

He went to the lift, his walk so casual as to be insolent, while Ian wondered whether to kill the little bastard now or later. He'd have done it there and then, but if Jade *were* on the way to this freezing cellar, he must wait. And he himself wanted the truth of what it was all about. He wanted to know if he had guessed the answer correctly.

One of the advantages of being very old, he thought as he lit his pipe, was that death could only eventually be a blessing; and that one became calmer. He had never been fatalistic as a young man, but now he found himself increasingly so. He had put himself in this situation by phoning Jimmy Lee and changing the rendezvous with the intention that Jade should not be involved. If Jade were on the way, and if Poppy were on the way too, that must be fate or God taking a hand. He only hoped that in his case the sins of the fathers would not be visited on the children.

So he sat, an old man in a cold cellar, keeping his mind clear and his pipe lit and waiting for either death or life.

He did not have to wait very long. It was about ten when he heard the lift descend. He continued to sit, smoking, long legs crossed, his eyes on the ceiling.

Jimmy Lee came back into the cellar with another man. Both held a blade of the scissors.

'Move,' Jimmy said.

As if he were going up to bed, Ian rose slowly, almost sleepily, to his feet and carefully banged out his pipe on the edge of the table.

'Move, I said,' Jimmy Lee shouted, dropping the cigarette he was smoking and missing when he attempted to stamp it out.

Silent, Ian moved towards the lift, and the three of them travelled together to the ground floor, one small man each side of the tall one.

'Where are we going?' he asked.

'On,' the man he did not know said.

'On?'

'On.' The man regarded the blade he held with pleasure, stroking his thumb along the length of it. Melodramatic little bastard, Ian told himself.

There was some kind of large Japanese car outside and in it was Jade, not looking frightened, he was pleased to note. She was, in fact, looking rather angry and superior, her delicate nostrils flared as if she could smell something very nasty indeed. Perhaps she could. She was flanked by two flashily dressed Chinese, one of whom climbed out and motioned Ian to get in where he had been sitting.

Ian pushed his long body into the car and settled himself next to the granddaughter.

'Morning, Jade,' he said. 'I find you in bad company.'

'Not of my choosing,' she said spiritedly. 'These men hijacked me.'

'Damn bad manners,' he grumbled.

The Chinese had got back into the car and it was crowded on the back seat. Jimmy Lee and the man with him were in the front, the second man in the driver's seat.

'Who is the chauffeur?' Ian asked. The man's face flushed with fury.

'That's Kwan Ching. You might have heard me speak of him,' Jade said. 'He's not usually a chauffeur. He's in shipping, but maybe times are bad.'

That's my girl, Ian thought and squeezed her hand.

They drove from Castle Peak Road into Nathan Road. Ian wondered as they headed down this most crowded of thoroughfares if anything would happen if he and Jade screamed for help. No one would hear it above the noise the Chinese made.

At Jordan they turned right, past the jade market, and headed for Yau Ma Tei and the typhoon shelter where thousands of boat people lived in damp poverty. They stopped on the waterfront, and with the broken scissor blades digging gently into their ribs he and Jade were marched across the pavement on to a small jetty where a large junk waited.

'Come aboard,' Jimmy Lee said. 'I know you like boating, Jade. It does interesting things to you.'

He saw her lips tighten and her head go higher.

'And I was so disappointed,' she sighed.

His lips tightened then.

'You won't be next time,' he warned.

'And where are we going now?' Ian felt it wise to end the conversation, such as it was.

'To sea,' Kwan Ching said. 'Stop asking questions.'

On board, Kwan Ching said in Cantonese: 'Where's the other girl?'

'She should be there,' Jimmy Lee said. 'It seemed pointless to bring her into Kowloon. They're taking her direct from Fanling.'

'They've got her?'

'I don't know. But they will.'

He turned to Ian.

'Is your Cantonese still as good? Did you understand all that? It was kind of you to lead us to Poppy yesterday. We had been looking for her for a long time.'

'The Cantonese is pretty rusty,' Ian lied, lighting his pipe. 'It's a wee while since I've heard it spoken.'

They were shepherded into the cabin and the door locked. Once they were alone, Jade collapsed in a chair and said: 'Are you all right, Grandfather? What happened?'

'I just changed the arrangements a mite. But I'd no expectation that they'd take you – or Poppy.'

'Grandfather, you must tell me now. What is it all about?'

He sighed deeply.

'It's nothing I'm proud of, lassie.'

The boat was leaving the jetty, moving fast through the lanes of the moored hulks which were home to the boat people. Behind, the skyscrapers of housing estates receded, and then the door of the cabin was unlocked.

'I think we'll keep you two apart,' Kwan Ching said. He was stroking the blade again. 'There's a cabin below with a nice comfortable bed in it, Jade. We'll take you down there, eh? Come along now.'

This time she went white and shrank back in her chair. Ian was thinking fast, but there was nothing he could do. Then he suddenly felt despair at what might happen to her, and sunk his head in his hands.

He only heard Jade's footsteps, firm and defiant, as she left the cabin.

It was quiet on board for a while, and then he heard a shout of rage.

'You fool,' Kwan Ching was bellowing in Cantonese. 'There's a lock on the inside of the door and she's bolted it.'

'How could I know?' Jimmy was shouting back. 'I only hired the thing yesterday. You'll have to wait for your fun until we get to Ping Chau.'

Ping Chau? It was one of the furthest islands, near China and on the edge of Mirs Bay. What the hell were they going to Ping Chau for? It had been deserted for years, its inhabitants labouring in the restaurants of Soho or San Francisco. Still Jade, it seemed, was safe for the moment.

He thought he might as well have a little sleep. At his age he slept a deal better by day than by night and there was no sense in missing an opportunity for a gentle doze.

Gary's face had broken into an involuntary grin at the Englishman's 'Who the hell are you?'

'You wouldn't be Steve Norris, would you?' he asked.

'I am.'

'I'm Gary Smith. I sell private jets.'

'Oh, yes,' Stephen Norris's face was wooden. 'I've heard of you.'

'I'm Michael Blake.' Mike added. 'And now you can put that thing away, Gary. It makes me nervous.'

Gary laughed and put the gun back in its small holster. The sight of Steve Norris, briefcase and all, had cheered him. Reinforcements, even slightly overweight ones, were never a bad thing.

'Are you on your own here?'

'Yes. They went off. Jimmy Lee said something unexpected had happened and to lock the place up.' He jangled a bunch of keys in his hand. 'He particularly wanted the basement locked. I'd just come down to have a sniff around. They won't be back until later tonight.'

'Who are they?'

'Him and Kwan Ching.'

306

'And do you know where they've gone?'

'To the other factory, they said. I don't know where it is, though.'

'I think I do,' Gary said softly. 'I think it's a factory ship. Listen. We have a problem on our hands, Steve. We may need your help.'

He explained concisely what had happened so far that morning and Steve Norris listened, propping his behind on the edge of the wooden table.

'What do you want me to do?' he asked finally

'Come with us. I reckon they've taken Jade and Ian McKenzie McKenzie out to that ship in Tai Po Hoi Harbour. We need a police launch and some help from your lot.'

'There's a police launch already watching the ship,' Steve said. 'Morrison told me late last night. But it doesn't sound right to me. You can't be sure that's where they've gone. We can't just board a ship, brandishing pistols. I'll have to talk to Morrison. The important thing is surely the heroin. Getting those two out of trouble could blow the whole operation.'

His voice said, by its tone, that Gary ought to be thinking the same way.

'On the other hand,' Mike put in quietly, 'we can't leave a girl and an old man to be murdered and not do anything about it.'

'They're probably dead already,' Steve said brutally. 'Still, I suppose you're right. Those damn McKenzie McKenzie girls have caused nothing but trouble since they arrived in the place. I'll go back up to the office and phone Morrison and ask if I can come with you . . .'

'Any weapons on you?' Gary asked.

'Something,' Steve said curtly. 'But Morrison's going to ask what's in this basement, and I'll never get another opportunity like this. While I'm phoning, you two start looking.'

'The heroin will be in the sealed cases,' Gary said.

'Well, get into one of them,' Steve said. 'I'll be back.'

'Cheerful cove, isn't he?' Mike said as the lift disappeared. 'Where do we start looking?'

Gary had been prowling, checking each box for one that might just open easily.

'Jesus,' he said suddenly. 'Come here, Mike. This one's been got at. Maybe Sammy did find something before—' He couldn't bring himself to end the sentence.

The wire bands around the box had been pulled away, and a black and white checkered fur coat was stuffed without care into the top of the case. Impatiently, Gary pulled it out, and as he did so, a faint cloud of white powder floated from it. 'It would be the lining,' he muttered. 'Something to do with the lining.'

He spread the coat out and realised that Sammy *had* found something before he died. The quilted lining was punctured with small holes, and through each hole ran the tiniest trickle of white.

'Sewn into the quilting,' he said. 'The crafty sons of bitches. That is a factory ship in the harbour at Tai Po. A garment factory ship. Brilliant!' There was admiration in his voice, as from one pro to another. 'Now all we need to know is where they get the opium from.'

'And find Jade?' Mike suggested.

'And find Jade,' he agreed.

Gary carefully took a sample of the heroin, putting it in a small flat tin which sat neatly at the bottom of his back trouser pocket. Mike, on the other hand, helped himself to a claw hammer which had been hidden by the box until they had moved it.

'Might give a clue or two,' Gary said. 'Prove to that pompous prick that there is heroin. Right under his nose.'

Steve was coming back into the warehouse. 'Find anything?' he asked.

'Yep,' Gary said. 'Lookee here.'

He handed over the coat and pointed out the holes where the heroin ran. Steve gave a whistle.

'Neat,' he said.

'Very neat. Now what?'

'We go to Tai Po and make contact with the launch there. Then we check back. Ok? I've got a car outside. But I'd better lock up, like I was told. Just in case I get through this day alive and without being blown.'

Steven Norris drove well. They threaded their way through the heavy traffic up into the New Territories, not losing any time, but it still wasn't fast enough for Gary. His momentary euphoria at having been proved right about the heroin had gone. He was worried sick about Jade, and Steve's unsentimental remark that she was probably dead already kept repeating itself in his brain like a bad song.

'Do you think we'll be in time?' Mike suddenly asked from the back seat. His voice was more than anxious and it occurred to Gary suddenly that maybe Jade was important there too.

'Why are you coming with us?' he asked abruptly.

Mike shrugged.

'Because I want to.'

'It's dangerous. Have you got any kind of weapon?'

'I can squirt ink in their eye from my Shaeffer fountain pen,' Mike said, his voice dead serious.

Gary resolved he'd better lose him before things got rough. Amateurs were always a problem.

They made their rendezvous with the launch, which he was pleased to see had been made to look like any pleasure boat. The police skipper, a taciturn man, said: 'Nothing much happened today. No deliveries. Except a girl. Chinese. They took her on board about quarter of an hour ago.'

'What did she look like?' Gary asked, feeling sweat come out on his forehead.

'Look like? Chinese. They all look the same. Small, dark, slit-eyed.'

'Goodlooking?'

'Wasn't that close.'

'Was there a very tall elderly European man with her?' Mike asked.

'No. She was alone except for two Chinese fellows who seemed to be hustling her. They arrived in the green van we were supposed to watch out for. But I'll tell you something. That ship out there hasn't been out of harbour for six weeks. I reckon she's getting up steam now. She's going somewhere later.'

Mike was fidgeting.

'Listen, Gary – they could be doing anything on board there. Why can't the police board her? They might be torturing Jade. They might kill her. We've got to stop it.'

'No way,' the launch captain said. 'My instructions are to lie low and see where that ship goes. If we move too early we'll fuck up the whole operation.'

Gary didn't say anything. His problem was that he knew the man was talking sense. If they boarded the *Hillfan*, they'd catch Jimmy Lee and Kwan Ching, but the American end would be in jeopardy and whoever was supplying the stuff would melt into the wood-work. It would negate Sammy's work, his own work, and the work of hundreds of other agents around.

He had to think of a way of saving Jade and saving the operation at the same time. But for the time being, it was going to be follow that ship and pray it wasn't too late.

After five hours in the cabin with the bolt securely drawn and heavy enough to resist anything but an all-out attack on the wood of the door, all Jade was really suffering was hunger. She had been offered food, but that would have meant opening the door, so she had declined. Kwan Ching had shouted in graphic detail what he intended to do to her and her sister once the opportunity arose, but she shut her ears and tried not to be frightened.

Five hours was a long time – too long to remain continually terrified. She had no doubts that Jimmy Lee and Kwan Ching had murder and worse on their minds, but found she was worrying about the method more than the possible eventuality. She also had a sense of everything being her own fault. She had listened to no one, interfered in things that did not concern her, upset a lot of people and now was suffering the consequences.

She cried for a little while. She slept for a little while. She created fantasies, and the most powerful of these was that Gary would save them. In fact, the more she thought about it, the more convinced she was that Gary would save them. Somewhere out there he would be moving heaven and earth. And maybe Mike would be trying as well.

It was gone five o'clock in the evening when she heard her grandfather's voice outside.

'Jade. We are going ashore,' he said. 'They are threatening to sink the junk if you don't come out, leaving you on it.'

She had been dozing again, and sat up, her hand to her mouth.

'Grandfather – what shall I do?'

'I can't tell you that, Jade,' he said, and he sounded calm. 'It must be your decision.'

She thought briefly. Where there was life there was hope, and there would be no life or hope locked in a cabin on a sinking junk.

'I'll come out,' she said.

As she opened the door, there was no sign of Kwan or Jimmy, just the men who had picked her up at the hotel and, as they had had in the morning, each with a knife to prick at her ribs.

It was dusk up on deck and she could see the faint outline of land close by, still lit red from the last of the sun. They were coming into a small jetty and she could see the dark shapes of unlit buildings a little way inland. There was no sign of any life and she shivered; the place seemed deserted, the atmosphere sinister even from the deck of the junk.

Ashore, they did not walk for very long, both she and her grandfather flanked by two men. It was a deserted village, eerie in the red light from the departing sun. The small procession that they made eventually halted, dark and silent, outside one of the houses just inside the village. Kwan Ching, who had been walking ahead, knocked softly on the wooden door.

Equally softly it was opened, and they were thrust into a dark room. She heard the door close behind them. A pale yellow light from an oil lamp flickered and increased in strength, and she saw Poppy, sitting on a hard-backed wooden chair, with a Chinese standing each side of her.

When Poppy recognised Kwan Ching, her hands went over her mouth and she began to whimper. Jade hurried forward and knelt in front of her. 'It's all right,' she said. 'We're all together now.'

But Poppy's eyes had become round and they never left Kwan Ching.

'Please don't let him come near me,' she said, clinging to Jade's hand until it hurt. 'Please.'

Jade felt a sense of desperation at the thought of trying to stop any of them doing anything they wanted to, but she forced herself to sound reassuring.

'It's all right, Poppy,' she said. 'Really it is.'

The six men in the room were talking rapidly in Cantonese. Jimmy Lee seemed to be the authority figure, and eventually the men who had snatched Jade from the hotel bowed and slipped out through the door. Those who had brought Poppy followed, after another brief conversation.

'Now we are all together,' Jimmy said, his voice satisfied. 'Now we can get down to business.'

Jade had been looking around the bare, stony room. Her grandfather had placed himself before the empty hearth, as if he expected a fire to be there for the purpose of warming his coat tails. She sat on one of the four upright chairs that the room possessed and the only other furniture was a small wooden table set in the centre of the room covered with red paper and Chinese characters.

She noticed that someone had left a soft bag on the floor, and from this Kwan Ching was taking two robes, one of which he handed to

Jimmy Lee. Both men solemnly donned them over the Western trousers and sweaters they were wearing, moving without haste. Then a sword was taken from the bag and laid on the table, its blade glinting wickedly in the soft wavering light from the lamp.

Resplendent in their mandarin robes, Jimmy Lee and Kwan Ching moved to stand behind the table. His hand on the handle of the sword, Jimmy Lee said: 'White Paper Fan, 415 of the Triad Broken Scissors Society, stand forward.'

To Jade's astonishment, her grandfather, as Scottish as Balmoral in his tweed trousers and Shetland cardigan, stepped one pace away from the hearth.

'Now what are you on about, laddie?' he asked.

'You have betrayed your brethren. You shall be killed by myriads of swords,' Jimmy Lee said. 'We are here to try you. I, the Hill Chief, and Kwan Ching, the Incense Master, shall be your judge and your jury.'

Jade found that she was digging her nails into the palm of her hand, but her grandfather merely looked faintly uninterested.

'I have no brethren to betray,' he said.

'That is true,' Jimmy said. 'You have no brethren because they were slain, and at your orders.'

Ian McKenzie McKenzie shook his head pityingly as if he were dealing with lunatics. The obvious contempt enraged Kwan Ching. Moving like a cat he came from behind the table.

'Take that expression from your face, you murderous pig,' he said. 'We know. We know the truth. Because I was there. I was there when it happened. It was bad luck for you that they missed me. I have been able to wage vengeance. I have been their avenger and tonight it will be finished.'

The room went very quiet and then her grandfather asked: 'Where were you?'

'At the house of Ip Bak Fook on 7th January 1959.' Kwan was pacing as he spoke. 'The house of my grandfather and grandmother. Your men killed my mother and my grandfather. They killed their friend, Wan Yu, and they very nearly killed my grandmother and me. I was four years old, left with a scissor wound in my lung. My grandmother's throat was cut, but she too survived and never did she let me forget what had happened, nor fail to remind me of my duty. I wish she were alive to see this night.'

Jade sat rigid, remembering the newspaper cutting and at last understanding the significance of the deaths of 7th January.

'Why would Grandfather do anything like that?' Poppy asked suddenly.

'Because of the gold, and the ship that he sunk. Your grandfather was the White Paper Fan of the Triad society. He joined as a boy. It was the same society to which Jimmy's grandfather, Ip Bak Fook, belonged. He –' he pointed a contemptuous finger at Ian – 'and our grandfather were the two White Paper Fans. Our grandfather was a moneylender. Together they advised on administration and finance for the society. But their friendship did not stop Ian McKenzie McKenzie's hired assassins killing him that night.' He stood, his arms folded in the sleeves of his robe, his voice like that of an orator, and addressed himself to Ian. 'And there were others, Ian McKenzie McKenzie. Not one man from the crew of the *Brian Leigh* lived to tell the tale of what had happened and what you had done. You were not brave enough to wield the scissors yourself. You sent assassins to kill with the weapon of our own society and to make it appear that it was Triad murdering Triad.

'Your treachery stretched to the assassins themselves. They died at the hands of British justice; your son-in-law wearing the black cap and pronouncing the death sentence; with the connivance of his translator in the court.

'But most of those who plotted with you are dead now. More deaths will come. We have made our own justice. And tonight you and your family will die by the broken scissors as you killed my family and all those other men who sailed on the *Brian Leigh*.'

Poppy was crying, her hands covering her face; appalled, Jade found she could hardly breathe.

'Is it true, Grandfather?' she whispered.

He shrugged. 'I told you, lassie, you can't make omelettes without breaking eggs.' He had not for one moment lost the look of the laird at his own fireplace, but the lines on his face seemed to have deepened and his skin was grey. He moved closer to the table where Kwan and Jimmy Lee stood.

'Jade and Poppy are not my family,' he said. 'They have no part in all this.'

'Nor had my mother, or my grandmother. Nor had I,' Kwan said.

'And nor, indeed, had my mother and sisters,' Jimmy Lee said. 'You would not remember my father, Ian McKenzie McKenzie. He was too unimportant for you to note. But he was one of the crew of the *Brian Leigh* and the second son of Ip Bak Fook. My father also died on 7th January 1959, when your assassins came to our boat at Aberdeen and killed him with the scissors, weighted his body and dropped him into the harbour.

'My mother joined him there of her own free will soon after. I was three years old and lucky. A distant relative took me in and made me his son. Sons were always valuable. But what happened to the rest of my family, I have never known.'

'You were responsible for much misery, Ian McKenzie McKenzie,' Kwan Ching said. 'Now it is time for the traditional Triad retribution. First you shall die, and afterwards we shall enjoy your granddaughters before they too die. Poppy knows already what it is to be loved by Kwan Ching.'

Ceremoniously, both Chinese took the one half of a blade of scissors from under the deep sleeves of their silk robes and, at funereal pace, they moved from behind the table and towards Ian McKenzie McKenzie.

'Your hour has come, old man,' Kwan said, his eyes glinting. 'It is the time.'

It was then that Poppy began to scream.

The constant rocking of the launch as they sat waiting for the *Hillfan* to sail was beginning to make Gary feel faintly queasy. Mike and Steve were both pale green.

'You'll be pleased to hear, gentlemen, that they are weighing anchor.' The skipper, who appeared to be enjoying his passengers' discomfort, nodded towards the *Hillfan* and turned on his own engine.

They kept at a respectable distance from the ship as she moved with surprising speed into the channel that led to the open sea. With the normal movement of the launch, the sick feeling began to abate and the colour return to Mike's and Steve's faces.

'Where could she be going?' Gary asked the skipper.

'China, maybe. Any one of the islands.' He shrugged.

'Are there many islands?'

'Dozens.'

Even he began to show some interest when the *Hillfan* continued to steam due north-east once she was in the open sea. Dusk was falling, and he muttered something about being too obvious and slowed down the launch.

'When it's dark, we'll catch up,' he said, 'but she's not going to China and there's only one more island out there – Ping Chau.'

'Ping Chau?' Steve said. 'It's been deserted for years.'

'Yeah,' the skipper said. 'But the villages are still there, aren't they?'

It was just outside Ping Chau that the *Hillfan* dropped anchor again. Using binoculars, even in the fading light they could just see a boat, containing three figures, being lowered.

'Can't you get nearer?' Gary asked impatiently.

The skipper did not bother to answer.

'We'd be too obvious, Gary,' Steve said soothingly.

'All right, I know,' he said, irritable.

He was straining through the binoculars, watching the three distant figures land, trying to decide if one of them could be Jade. The old man was certainly not there; his height would be unmistakable. Though he would have sworn that one of the figures was that of a girl, it didn't look like Jade. The walk and height were not right.

'I think that's Poppy they've got,' Steve said suddenly. 'It looks remarkably like her, even from here.'

The three figures vanished, walking inland to what looked like a small village; then the *Hillfan* pulled up anchor and, with one small farewell hoot, steamed away, this time sailing due south.

'She's going back to Hong Kong,' the skipper muttered.

'Now what?' Mike asked.

'We stay here,' said the skipper. 'I'll just use the radio.' And he disappeared below.

The sky was red and a full moon was floating by the time Gary spotted the fast-moving junk coming from the south heading for the small jetty where the dinghy had been left.

Only silhouettes were visible, and one of those coming from the junk and on to the jetty was unmistakably Ian McKenzie McKenzie. There were four other figures of similar height, and one smaller one.

'That's Ian and that's Jade, I'd swear it,' Mike said.

'I'd swear it, too,' Gary said, still staring through the binoculars.

'Certain?' the skipper asked and headed back for his radio.

'Makes sense,' Steve said. 'They picked Poppy up from Fanling and took her to the nearest port, Tai Po. That junk has had to sail all the way round the coast from Kowloon. And the rendezvous is

Ping Chau. Great place to store heroin. Even process it when you come to think about it.'

'Sod the heroin,' Mike said. 'I'm bloody going on that island and see what's happening to those two girls and that old man.'

'Don't be fucking stupid,' Steve said. 'What can you do? You'll get yourself killed.'

'And I won't have to live with the thought that I sat on a boat with a pair of bleeding binoculars watching while it all happened, will I?' Mike said fiercely. 'You can't stop me, and I'm going even if I have to swim.'

Gary had already moved to where the dinghy was hanging from the stern. He had never been in any doubt that he was going on the island.

'We'll go together,' Gary said. 'Amateurs!' He snorted.

'Good man,' Mike said, and moved to help him lower the dinghy.

'You'll ruin the whole operation,' Steve protested. 'We were told to observe. Nothing more.' But his voice lacked conviction.

Gary was experiencing the highest high he had ever felt. He was going to do something positive, and Jade was still alive. The bad tune had gone from his head. There was still a chance.

'Come and join us?' he suggested, and Steve barely hesitated before saying: 'What the hell? Why not? All the trouble that bloody Poppy caused me. Stupid if it was for nothing.'

The three of them had the dinghy in the sea, the motor going and were pulling away from the launch when they heard the yell of protest from the skipper, then silence.

'We did that smartly, didn't we?' Mike said. 'Ah well, many hands make light work.'

'And what are we going to do when we get there?' Steve asked.

'Play it by ear,' Gary said. 'What have you got?'

There was a pause and then Steve groaned.

'Fuck!' he said. 'Nothing. I had a pistol in that briefcase.'

The *put-putting* of the motor sounded very loud.

'I've got a hammer,' Mike said, producing it from the band of his trousers.

'And what about the Schaeffer?' Gary asked.

'I've got that, too,' Mike said.

'And I've got a gun,' said Gary. He had kept the binoculars slung around his neck and he stared through them to the land.

'Cut the engine,' he whispered. 'Something's happening.'

316

They watched as four men, silhouetted against the moonlit jetty, scrambled aboard the moored junk.

'We can't land there now,' Gary said. 'But by my reckoning, that leaves two men, the girls and old Ian.'

'By mine too,' said Mike.

'Better odds,' Steve suggested.

'Much better odds,' Gary agreed. 'Unless there are some we don't know about?'

They waded ashore on to a soft beach a hundred yards or so from the jetty. On the still night, they could hear laughter and the click of mah-jong tiles from the moored junk.

'Move it,' Gary whispered, and they ran light-footed over the sand on to a rough road which led to the houses.

The three of them melted into the deserted village. Gary noted with approval that Mike, the amateur and the eldest, was doing rather well. The breathless one was Steve.

Now something positive was happening, his mind was clear. There were three of them against two Triads. He thought that was a fair assumption. They ought to be able to hold their own as long as they found them in time. He pushed away the thought that they might be too late. He tried not to have distracting thoughts of Jade. He had to keep a cool, clear head.

The street of the village was dark and they were moving with extreme caution, clinging to the stone walls of the deserted houses. The moon threw weird shadows, and a nightbird flapped its wings with a rustling creak that made them all stop and listen.

Speed, Gary knew, was essential, but care was important too. There might be more of the little yellow bastards around, he thought. It would not help if they found themselves ambushed, so he continued to lead, moving in the dark patches, his ears tuned and his eyes looking for a light.

They would have passed by the house which appeared as dark as all the others if it had not been for the bloodcurdling scream that stopped them all in their tracks.

'In there,' Mike said, pointing to the dark shape of the house. 'Now what?'

'We go in,' Gary said. 'Fast.'

Running on the balls of his feet, he flung himself towards the door of the house, the gun in his hand. He crashed his full weight on the old wood, and it gave, sprung open, catapulting him into the room with his own momentum and leaving him off balance. He was aware of Jade's terrified face and the continuous screaming of Poppy.

It was Mike who saw clearly what happened. The two men in the red robes turned as Gary burst in, their faces both surprised and livid, and Ian McKenzie McKenzie, who had been standing facing them from a distance of perhaps six feet, quickly slid both hands under his sweater and into the band of his trousers, producing two throwing knives which seemed to leave his hands in the moment they appeared. One caught Kwan Ching full in the middle of the back. He made a gurgling sound and fell.

But the knife aimed at Jimmy Lee flew wide and the Chinese moved with the agility of a man trained in the martial arts to place himself behind Ian McKenzie McKenzie and plunged the blade of the broken scissors full into the back of the old man's neck.

'Getting old,' Ian said distinctly, as blood gushed from his mouth, and he slowly toppled forward like a felled oak.

Jade had darted to the table and grabbed the sword.

'I'll kill you! I'll kill you!' she was shouting at Jimmy Lee who moved towards her, the bloodied scissor blade in his hand. She was directly in Gary's line of fire.

'Get out of it, Jade,' he shouted.

Steven moved in to snatch at her. A vicious stroke from Jimmy Lee caught him in the shoulder, but Jade was out of the way; Gary took careful aim, shot the blade from the Triad's hand, and then sent another quickly into his left arm.

Jimmy Lee screamed as the bullets hit. The steel clattered to the stone floor, while he stood, both arms useless, blood running down his fingers. Stephen kicked the blade away from where it lay and appropriated it for himself.

'I think their reinforcements are coming up,' Mike said. He had positioned himself to the side of the door and as the first of the men from the junk darted in, knife in hand, the hammer landed with deadly effect on the back of his head. Gary caught the second man with a bullet placed neatly in the shoulder. The third and the fourth hesitated in the doorway, taking in Jimmy Lee's bloody hand and arm, the gun, the sword which Jade held like a rapier, the screaming girl and their two inert companions and fled, straight into the arms of three burly Hong Kong plainclothes detectives.

'You took your time getting here,' Steve grumbled, recognising his own kind. Poppy was still screaming, a long, high-pitched ear-tearing sound that caused Jimmy Lee to hiss 'Shut up!' at her. To everyone's relief, she did.

'You've had a right old caper here,' one policeman said, looking around the room. 'Morrison's going to go mad. You were supposed to be observing.'

'Oh, fuck off!' Mike said. 'Don't be bloody silly.'

He was, Gary saw, standing stock still and staring at Ian's body. He was crying behind the thick glasses that had stayed on all through the encounter.

'You all right, mate?' one of the detectives asked Steve whose shoulder was oozing copious amounts of blood.

'Of course I'm not bloody all right,' Steven said. 'Do I look all right?'

But he would be all right, Gary thought. He was more fascinated by Poppy. Slowly, as if she were about to creep up on someone, she had risen from her chair and with the utmost delicacy was walking tiptoed across the floor to where Kwan Ching's body lay on the stone floor.

Slowly, like a gymnast, she squatted and with one questioning finger, touched him. She paused, half stood, bent again and the touch become a prod. The body remained inert.

Then she looked up.

'He's dead,' she said. And her voice was a trumpet call of triumph. 'He's dead.'

Gary put away the gun and moved to where Jade was kneeling by her grandfather's body, the sword slack in her hand. Gently he took it from her and lifted her to her feet.

'Are you all right?' he asked. 'It's all over now. It's finished.'

She was dry-eyed and shocked, but she nodded, a doll's head wobbling on a slender neck.

'Grandfather's dead, isn't he?'

'I'm afraid so. We were just too late.' He hesitated, seeking for words to comfort her. 'But he went the way he lived. He would have hated to live too long. Jade, remember, he never grew old.'

'That's true,' she said, still staring down at the body and the wound in the old man's neck. As if the words were squeezed out, reluctant and sad, she said: 'But perhaps it was justice if Kwan was telling the truth.'

'That we will never know,' he said.

She was quiet and then she looked up at him, her eyes suddenly alive again.

'Oh yes, we will,' she said.

Once it was all over the end of the affair became confused in Jade's mind. Her memory of events resembled a half-remembered nightmare that went on for too long before waking. It seemed to her that almost immediately the Hong Kong police from the launch were joined by other more sinister men who sidled into the cottage with the air of undertakers. It was they who removed the bodies from the stone floor, taking them away as if they had been sacks of rubbish. Jade watched with anguish as her grandfather disappeared into the darkness. Outside she could hear the barking of dogs. Poppy sobbed like a small child.

They had then walked in the moonlight to the jetty where the junk that Jimmy Lee had hired was anchored. One of the harder, second group of men had said: 'Might as well use this.'

Kwan Ching's body and that of the other dead man Steve had hit with the hammer were put on board and the junk was towed out to sea and left. Later on the way back to the mainland there had been a terrific explosion and a ball of fire that flared and died on the horizon leaving dark smoke across the moon.

Her grandfather's body had been placed on the large cruiser that the second group of mysterious men had arrived on. Gary, Mike and Steve went with them as they pulled away into Mirs Bay.

She and Poppy had been taken back to Hong Kong in the police launch by one silent man who grunted with satisfaction when the explosion lit the sky. All he said as he dropped them at the Queen's jetty was: 'Don't talk about this to anyone.'

But Poppy had fled to a phone to talk to Paul So. She had been sitting alone in the garden of his home, reading, when the two men had grabbed her. 'Paul will think I've just walked out,' she said. 'I'm not leaving him worried sick for one moment longer no matter what anyone says. He'll come and fetch me. I want to be back with him.'

It was gone one in the morning when Gary arrived at the hotel. Jade had been trying to doze, but remained totally wide-awake, her mind full of pictures of her grandfather's body.

Gary rang from downstairs. 'I thought banging on your door

would be the last straw in a terrifying day,' he said. 'But I'm on my way up.'

When she opened the door she flung herself into his arms and he held her close. He was rocking and soothing her, saying as he had said on the island: 'It's all over now. Relax. It's finished.'

She drew a deep breath.

'But is it?' she said. 'What will happen about Grandfather?'

'There will be a big and impressive funeral here in a few days' time. It will be said that your grandfather died of a heart attack in the home of a man called Arthur Watson-King who lives in the New Territories. They were old friends.'

Jade sighed. 'A cover-up?'

'It will all be covered up in the end,' Gary said. 'We discovered from one of the men who kidnapped Poppy that he and his partner were responsible for Sammy's death. They were a pair of lion-dancers who interrupted Sammy when he was looking for the heroin.

'One of them bit the dust when Mike hit him with the hammer. He's now been conveniently blown up with Kwan Ching on the junk that Jimmy Lee hired. Poetic justic for what happened to the *Brian Leigh*, wouldn't you say?'

'And the other three men and Jimmy Lee?'

'They are to be charged with heroin smuggling.'

'Not murder?'

'No, not murder. Jade, you must forget the murders. It is best. The British are adamant there is no mention of them. What your grandfather did to get the gold back was totally condoned by the authorities, you know.'

She was silent and then said: 'That makes it almost worse. What did Grandfather get out of it, except to have to live with the knowledge of what he had done? There must have been more.'

'I think your grandfather was given a lot of amnesty for things past, and blind eyes were shut while his business grew bigger.'

She shook her head despairingly and asked: 'So what happens now?'

'I have to go back to Washington to report to my people.'

The sense of loneliness flooded back.

'Oh, no, Gary – when?'

'Tomorrow. There's going to be a hell of a row because we had intended to follow the shipment through to the US. We wanted to see who received it so we could smoke out whoever is running the American end of the operation. It might still be possible. We may take a chance on letting go the cargo that Jimmy Lee intended to send on Sunday and see what happens. There's going to have to be a lot of elaborate subterfuge to get away with it as Kwan Ching is dead. The Brits are working it out now. Once the cargo gets Stateside there will be a lot of quiet arrests around here. The tracker dogs that the undercover Brits brought out to the Island found about two million pounds' worth of raw opium; Sammy's guess that it came in with the rabbit furs was right. My guess that it could have been coming from the Yunnan Province in Southern China was right too. The *Hillfan* not only steamed to pick the opium up from the Island, she acted as a factory ship with the opium being processed into heroin. Other workers sewed it straight into the quilted linings of Jimmy Lee's fun furs with a machine that had been specially made for the purpose.'

'I don't care about the heroin,' she said fiercely. 'I care about all the people who have died.'

'Don't you think there will be many more who will die from the heroin?' he asked her, his voice sharp. 'The amount of junk that Jimmy Lee and Kwan Ching have been producing could finish off more people than you could visualise. It could kill graveyards full of people.'

She sat, her head dropped.

'Will you be in trouble if the American end goes wrong?'

'I don't think so. We Americans are quite gallant. They will appreciate we couldn't leave two beautiful girls to die.'

'They would have killed us,' she said slowly. 'Very nastily. Ah, well,' she sighed, then added: 'Poppy's gone back to Fanling with Paul.'

'Best place for her. And for the next few days until after the funeral, Mike will be looking after you. You won't be alone.'

'Is Steven all right?' she asked, remembering his bloodied shoulder and how he had pulled her out of danger.

'Still moaning and groaning, but he'll probably get some commendation, so he might even finish up happy.'

There was a small silence, and then Gary asked:

'Jade, what are you going to do after the funeral? Will you stay here?'

'No, I won't live here,' she said slowly. 'I don't belong here, I realise that. What I am going to do, Gary, is to go to Venice and see Miss Tibbets. I want to know my father's part in this story. I don't believe he had anything to do with it, in spite of what Kwan Ching said. But I want to be sure. Somehow I think that Miss Tibbets has the final answers. Also', she added, 'she is the only one left to ask.'

He went to the mini-fridge and he took out half a bottle of champagne.

'Then,' he said, 'we shall drink to our meeting in Venice. I'm not going to let you go Jade. Not ever.'

≈ *14* ≈

VENICE

Jade stayed on in Hong Kong for the funeral, which Mike arranged. The old man's ashes were scattered at sea from one of his own ships and she cried out her grief that day, as she and Poppy, the chief mourners, shook a bewildering number of hands and murmured thanks for condolences to dozens of faces they had never seen before.

Her grandfather, she discovered, in spite of all that had gone on in the past, was a popular man. Then came the shock when Mike gently pointed out that the vast empire, even the soaring green-marble McKenzie McKenzie building that was too old-fashioned for the ever-changing city, now belonged to her and Poppy.

'And, of course, the shareholders,' he added.

She decided to think about the implications after she had been to Venice. Mike explained that the business virtually ran itself, with batteries of lawyers, hordes of employees and a brilliant board of directors. But a figurehead always helped, he said.

He saw her off at Kai Tak airport, shaking her awkwardly by the hand. He looked as if he wanted to kiss her and it suddenly dawned on her how he felt. Touched, she leaned forward impulsively to kiss him and he flushed, took off his glasses, leaving his brown eyes vulnerable, and started to sneeze. Then they both laughed.

'Hayfever?' she asked.

'No, you,' he confessed.

'I'll be back,' she promised. 'Soon.'

'Good,' he said simply, gave a little wave and turned and walked away, a small authoritative man looking as if he had somewhere important to go.

The journey was arduous, and she crept off the plane at Venice airport absolutely exhausted. In the small arrival hall, she was waiting for her luggage when a voice said: 'Carry your bags, ma'am?'

She felt her tiredness lift as she spun to see Gary, a grin a mile wide on his face.

'I don't believe it. How marvellous!' she said as he wrapped his arms around her.

'You really must stop getting yourself picked up at airports,' he said, bending to kiss her.

The journey across the half-frozen lagoon by water-taxi was sheer magic. A crisp rime of frost had turned the tall reeds into silver bayonets, and long-legged birds paced majestically in the shallows, while busy ducks scuttled away as the boat chugged quietly through the water. She lay in her fur coat, curled into his arms, her head on his shoulder. The boatman ignored them, looking ahead and whistling gently to himself, as the domes and minarets of Venice appeared mistily on the horizon.

'What happened when you got back to Washington?' she asked.

'Not a lot. We cleared out the warehouse in Echo Park, caught all the small fry and a couple of the big boys. There will be a lot less heroin around LA until they get organised again. And, of course, they will get organised again,' he said bitterly.

'Were they the same gang?'

'Yep. More Broken Scissors Triads. Mostly working as waiters. Several of them had come originally from Ping Chau. They knew the island and knew it would be a safe place to hide the raw material. We never discovered exactly where it was coming from in Yunnan, but maybe the Brits back in Hong Kong will do that. Not that it will help. It's the one province the Chinese government has never been able to control when it comes to growing the poppy.'

'Umm.' She nestled closer into him. It was cold after Hong Kong. 'Now what?'

'I'm on vacation.'

324

'How long for?'

'A month.'

'Lovely,' she sighed. 'You can help me find Miss Tibbets.'

He stroked her hair.

'Don't be disappointed if you can't find her,' he said. 'She must be an old lady. She might well be dead, you know.'

'Oh, no,' she said, her voice confident. 'The way Grandfather said she was in Venice was so positive that I'm certain I'll find her. My only worry is how.'

'If she's here, that's no problem.' he said. 'Either she'll be in the telephone book or the British consul will tell you where to find her.'

'Are you sure?'

'Certain.'

'Oh, good,' she said.

They checked into the Gritti Palace with a room overlooking the Grand Canal. Immediately the boy who had brought up their bags left, Jade started hunting for the telephone directory.

Gary was right. It was amazingly simple. There was Eleanor Tibbets in among the Ts and living on the Fondamente.

Suddenly, faced with the reality, contacting her didn't seem such a good idea. Jade sat on the bed, her head bowed, looking at the name which seemed to have jumped out of the page. Was Poppy right? Would it be better to leave well alone? She remembered Emma's words: 'Why don't you just concentrate on who you are *now*?'

'Do you think I should get in touch with her, Gary?' she asked, her voice doubtful.

He was hanging his suits in the wardrobe and turned to consider the question.

'Not if you don't want to,' he said gently. 'But I think maybe you'll always wish you had.'

'That's a fat lot of help,' she said crossly, staring at the name again. Then her hand went out slowly to pick up the phone.

'*Pronto?*' It was a definite English voice speaking.

'Miss Tibbets?'

'Speaking. Who is that?' The voice was deep, assertive.

'My name is Jade McKenzie McKenzie Martin.'

There was a long silence and Jade found herself floundering. 'Miss Tibbets, I'd like to come and see you. Talk to you.'

'What about?' The tone was now just verging on rudeness.

'My father, my grandfather, myself and my sister Poppy.'

Another silence and then Miss Tibbets said: 'Is Poppy well?'

'She is well.'

'Umm. That is pleasing. Very well then. When do you wish to come?'

'Whenever would be convenient to you.'

'This afternoon at three o'clock. We shall have tea. Presumably if you have the telephone number, you have my address.'

'If you still live on the Fondamente,' Jade said.

'I do. Very well then. Three o'clock.'

The phone went down with a sharp click.

'Well?' Gary asked.

Jade laughed.

'She sounds formidable.' She mimicked: 'This afternoon at three o'clock. We shall have tea.' No wonder my father wrote her such a grovelling and humble letter.'

'Well, don't you grovel and be humble,' he said. 'And in the meantime, we shall enjoy Venice.'

'In bed, please,' she said. 'Love and sleep are what I need if I'm to have my wits about me this afternoon.'

'Love, sleep and food, in that order,' he said. 'We have nearly four hours. Will that do?'

'You're in charge,' she said happily.

She was nervous as the water-taxi dropped her at the quay near Miss Tibbets' home. The house was tall, overlooking the Laguna and across to Santa Michel. Diffidently she rang the bell which pealed long and loud somewhere inside; the door was almost immediately opened by a young Chinese girl.

'Do come in,' she said in perfect English. 'Miss Tibbets is expecting you.'

The girl led her up a curved staircase to the first floor of the house and into a large drawing room full of fine pieces of antique furniture. The walls were covered with huge blow-ups of Chinese children of all ages, incongruous in the setting. Seated on a hard-backed long settle by an open fireplace where a log fire burned was Miss Tibbets.

She was more than seventy-five, her face freckled and lined. She had a sharp beaky nose and bright blue eyes. She was upright, her hands, freckled like her face, folded in her lap.

'Hallo, Miss Tibbets,' Jade said, conscious of the sound of her high heels as she crossed the polished wood floor, her hand outstretched.

The old lady touched fingertips, regarding Jade with the steady, disconcerting gaze of a child.

'What a pretty girl you have grown to be,' she said, but without warmth. 'Sit down.' She indicated a tall-backed Florentine chair at the other side of the fireplace.

'You will have to speak clearly,' she said when Jade was seated. 'I am a little deaf now.'

There was an uncomfortable lull; the only sound in the room was the gentle crackle of the fire.

'Tell me,' said Miss Tibbets, 'how is your grandfather?'

The tension, the long journey and the cold attitude of Miss Tibbets were suddenly too much. Tears spurted, and as Jade groped in her handbag for a handkerchief, she said: 'Didn't you know? He's dead. I don't understand how you don't know. It's been on every radio, in every newspaper. He died of a heart attack last week. In Hong Kong.'

Miss Tibbets' back stiffened even more and the old hands clasped and unclasped in her lap.

'Dead?' she said. 'Ian dead?'

She rose and Jade realised just how old she was. Her body creaked upright, she grasped for a stick that had been concealed at the side of the chair and walked, tapping her way, across the room to the window. There she stood, straight-backed, looking out, and Jade realised that she was hiding tears.

Impulsively Jade followed her. Standing a pace or two away, she said: 'Miss Tibbets, I'm so sorry. I didn't mean to shock you. I truly thought you'd know.'

The old lady turned and slowly shook her head.

'I rarely take any interest in what goes on in the outside world these days,' she said, the bright blue eyes glistening. 'Since I lost my children . . .'

She sighed and held out her hand.

'Help me back to my chair, my dear,' she said.

The atmosphere had changed, softened. She leaned on Jade's arm and sank back on to the high settle, careful of her old bones.

'You loved your grandfather?' she asked abruptly.

'Very much,' Jade said.

'I loved him too,' Miss Tibbets said quietly, as if she were talking to herself. 'He was a buccaneer. Sometimes a bad man; more often good. He had such spirit and courage when he was young.' She nodded slowly, her head trembling on her thin neck. 'He was the only man I ever cared about, but he never really cared for me.' She shook her head. 'It was all so long ago. There is no one left who would be interested any more. No one left to remember.'

'I understand, and he did too,' Jade said, remembering the day at Macao. 'He said that great age could be a burden.'

'It is, my dear, it is. My babies have all gone into the world. Quite rightly,' she said with a touch of the asperity she had first shown. 'The young owe the old nothing.'

'He said that too,' Jade told her.

'He loved you?' The bright blue eyes were demanding truth.

'He did,' Jade said. 'But not at first. We weren't really his grandchildren, were we? But in the end I think he felt that we were.'

'No, you were not his grandchildren. He did not really want you in the beginning. Not at all. And I parted with you both most reluctantly. Your father never knew about the deal. He never understood fully what was going on. But perhaps he understood enough to leave Hong Kong for ever. How is he?' she asked abruptly.

'He is dead, too—' Jade hesitated, wondering whether to explain how and why, but Miss Tibbets seemed to require no more information. She merely shook her head sadly as one used to news of departure.

'He deserved better than your silly, flibberty-gibbet mother. But they all would do anything for her. Your grandfather spoiled her. She was the apple of his eye.' Her voice was acid. 'She was like her mother. The girl your grandfather married was silly and stupid too. Not worthy of him. No one was worthy of him. It was wicked of me, and I have prayed for forgiveness many times, but I was glad – glad, when she died.'

Jade was losing track.

'When who died?' she asked.

The old lady looked at her and said impatiently: 'Ian's wife. She was called Sylvia. She died when your mother was born. I hoped that perhaps Ian would turn to me, but he never did. He devoted himself to the baby, and Margaret grew up to be as pretty and stupid as her mother had been.' She shook her head. 'Why do men who are strong love women who are so weak? Why are men such fools—?'

She paused and gave a harsh little barking laugh. 'And why am I telling you all of this?'

Jade had been standing listening, but something made her drop to her knees in front of the old lady. It seemed to her that perhaps if she were at child level, Miss Tibbets would continue to talk.

'Please, Miss Tibbets,' she said, 'won't you tell me what happened? Do you know where Poppy and I came from? Are we sisters? Kirsty – do you remember Kirsty, my mother's maid?' Miss Tibbets nodded and pursed her lips. 'Kirsty said she thought we really were sisters, and that the newspaper cutting about the baby by the harbour was not true; that you only took children from the New Territories.'

'I did it for your grandfather. He wanted to make your mother happy.' The old lady sounded distracted, and Jade leaned forward to hold her hand.

'Would it help if I told you what I know already?'

The blue eyes, still young in the old face, were suddenly sharp.

'What do you know?'

'That at about the time we were adopted, Grandfather got a lot of gold back for the British government. He hijacked a ship and had all the crew killed.'

'You know that? How?'

'Miss Tibbets, it would take so long to explain, but the sons of some of the men my grandfather had killed are still alive. And they planned revenge. They were Triads. In the same society that Grandfather once belonged to.'

'You shouldn't know these things,' Miss Tibbets said fiercely. 'No one should know those things about your grandfather. He was only doing his duty.'

'I understand that.'

'I wonder if you do. It was hard for him. His heart was not in it, and it was the children that concerned him. You and Poppy mostly.'

'Poppy and I?–' Jade gently jogged her on.

'Yes. You are not sisters. You are cousins. You were the only girl child of one of the seamen who had been –' she hesitated 'disposed of. Your brother was sent to a relative who was pleased to have another son. Your grandfather had his men bring you to me. It was true that I normally only took children from the New Territories, but you were from the boat people.

'It was a few weeks later when another of the wives of the seamen

329

who had been –' she could not bring herself to describe what had happened' – threw herself into the harbour, leaving Poppy. It was not easy, but your grandfather managed to get her back from the authorities and brought her to me. Her brother was found a home with a comparatively rich furrier. Your grandfather insisted that Poppy's brother should believe the man was a relative, and I believe the boy has done well.'

Jade, with the fire blazing at her back, was shivering. She was realising that Jimmy Lee must be Poppy's brother, and Kwan Ching, dead and in a thousand pieces in Mirs Bay, had been hers.

'But what was to be done with you girls? The Chinese did not want you. Your grandfather would not agree to leave you both with me. He felt you deserved more, and most important, he wanted to make his daughter happy' She paused and said, surprising Jade: 'You don't have a cigarette, do you?'

'Sorry, I don't.'

'Ah well – in that box over there.'

She pointed across the room and Jade, anxious not to break the flow of the story, hurried to bring one and light it. The old lady held it awkwardly and took deep, uneasy puffs, blowing out smoke. Then she said: 'Margaret could not have children. It was a cause of great unhappiness to her and your father. She longed for babies; she was obsessive about babies and she wanted mine. But I was not prepared to let my babies go to her – silly, stupid woman that she was.

'But when your grandfather asked me, and he had brought you both to me, what was I to do? I could refuse him nothing,' she said sadly. 'I never refused him. Ever.'

Had they been lovers? Jade wondered.

'And so?' she prompted.

'And so,' said Miss Tibbets, acid again, 'I permitted him to talk me into letting you go. But it wasn't to be straightforward. Oh, no. Ralph was to contact me, ask me, beg me to let his Margaret have two of my children. Your grandfather never forgave Ralph for marrying your mother. He would not have made anything simple for him.

'So Ralph had to pay.' She sniffed. 'I suppose I should not have taken his money, but you see, I was not popular in Hong Kong. I did not have the finances to run my home, so I had to—' She paused, and gave a gentle little cackling laugh. 'I had to beg. I really rather

330

enjoyed it. It was hard for the rich expatriates to refuse to give to orphan children. They knew they exploited the Chinese. And the Chinese rich knew they exploited the Chinese poor, so they paid up too. But I was not popular. Not at all.

'They were always trying to send me back to England,' she said, her tone confidential. 'But I wouldn't go. Oh, no. And then when the letters came from Ralph, I made sure he paid. It pleased your grandfather a great deal.'

She nodded to herself and asked, inconsequentially: 'Do you want tea?'

'After the end of the story,' Jade said, anxious not to have anything stop Miss Tibbets talking.

'The end of the story? Well, the end of the story was that the assassins who had killed your real parents and all the others who had been involved in the *Brian Leigh* came to trial. The great irony was that your poor father – he was a good man; he deserved better than Margaret – had to conduct not only the enquiry into the loss of the ship, but the murder case as well.

'He may have suspected; he was no fool, your father. He must have known very well that it was all something to do with Ian's skullduggery, but he tried the cases with honesty. He pronounced the ship loss a fortuity because, in his reckoning, that was what the evidence told him. Your grandfather was delighted. It was exactly the decision he wanted. And he was delighted, too, when your father donned the black cap for the assassins. It all went Ian's way. But then things always went your grandfather's way. Your poor father suspected he had been manipulated, but he was not sure how. It seemed better to him to step down from the bench. His wife had the two little girls she yearned for, but at what price? And then your grandfather suggested he ran the British end of McKenzie McKenzie. It was Margaret who was the thorn in the flesh. It was she, with everyone dancing attendance on her whims and fancies, who caused it all.' She stopped and said: 'Give me another cigarette. And tell me – how is Margaret?'

'Her mind has gone,' Jade said. 'She is senile.'

The old woman snorted.

'She never had a mind to lose.'

Jade was silent.

'And Poppy. Tell me about Poppy.'

'She wants to stay in Hong Kong. She is in love with a Baptist minister.'

'A nonsense. She will never fit into an Asiatic world. It is too late for that. Just as this European world is too late for me. I would like to go home, but there is nowhere to go. Your grandfather gave me this house three years ago. He said I would be safe here. But my life was spent in South East Asia. What am I doing in this place of palaces?'

'I don't know where to go either,' Jade said on impulse.

'Go anywhere but Asia. Marry a white man. And for all your life you will be different, interesting, an object of curiosity.'

Jade was not sure whether Miss Tibbets was being serious or sardonic.

'Do you really mean that?'

The old woman sighed.

'How should I know? I don't know about anything any more. I'm nearly eighty years old, I've nothing left. My dear girl – do what you want; live how you want.' She chuckled again. 'I always did. And I don't regret a thing. How they used to duck and weave when they saw me coming in Hong Kong. Money is the thing that kills. You and Poppy will always have too much of it. Your tragedy will be never to know whether you are loved for yourself. I never married. I stayed alone and made my own life. And I don't regret that either. The one thing I regret is that I sold you and your cousin. It was not worthy.' She got to her feet with sudden energy.

'And now,' she said, 'it is definitely time for my tea.'

When Jade left Gary at the Gritti Palace, she promised to return immediately after she had seen Miss Tibbets, but as she walked down the steps of the tall house on the Fondamente, she needed time to think.

She wandered along the broad pavement and found a café that overlooked the broad lagoon and sat, her coffee cooling on the table before her, while she watched the big steamers making their way to the open sea.

Then she meandered through the cobbled back streets patterned with pretty gardens to the Grand Canal.

She had not told Miss Tibbets the truth about the young man her grandfather had sent to the furrier. She had not mentioned Kwan Ching at all. She had given the old lady no details of their revenge and the people who had died. There seemed no point.

For her the jigsaw was now all of a piece. And if she wanted, it would not be difficult, she realised, to find her real relatives. Her mother might even still be alive. Kwan Ching would have known the answer, but it was too late to ask him.

It struck her that the great irony was that Kwan and Jimmy Lee had wanted revenge for their families, without ever knowing that she and Poppy were their family. Kwan Ching had tortured his cousin; Jimmy Lee had made love to his on a deserted beach and planned a complicated death for her later.

But Emma had been right. What point was there in finding her real family? It was best to begin from when she had been adopted; to assume her life started then.

She took the little gondola ferry across the Grand Canal amidst black-clad women with shopping baskets spilling fresh vegetables, and then began to walk back to the Gritti, not hurrying. She had to make a decision.

She had still not fully made up her mind when she took the lift to the third floor where Gary waited. When she came in the door, he was stretched on the bed. The window was open to the balcony and a breeze billowed the sheer curtains. He stood up immediately and moved towards her, taking her hands in his.

'You've been a long time,' he said. 'I missed you. How did it go?'

She put her handbag down on the dressing table, stalling for time. She kicked off her shoes and sat down on an armchair.

'Poppy and I are cousins,' she said abruptly. 'Kwan Ching was my brother and Jimmy Lee is Poppy's. Grandfather arranged all our lives after the massacre. He put Jimmy and Kwan into Chinese homes, and he put Jade and me with Miss Tibbets for my father to adopt. My mother desperately wanted children, but couldn't have any. My grandfather played God. And, according to Miss Tibbets, he adored my mother, my father adored her and neither of them gave a damn what they did if she was happy.' She was quiet for a moment, while Gary waited. 'My God, all the implications are quite terrible. So many people dead, revenge, my father hardly able to live with himself, and Grandfather buccaneering on, as pleased as Punch that his daughter had two babies who weren't hers and never really could be. Gary, it's quite terrible. The only people in the whole story who have come out on top are Poppy and I. And come to think of it, we're pretty screwed up.'

He was sitting on the dressing table, a cigarette in his hand.

'For a start you are not screwed up. Not you,' he said. 'And why shouldn't you have come well out of it? You were babies; innocent, hardly to blame for anything that happened. Now come on, take it easy. Come back to the States with me; start a new life, sweetheart. Forget it all.'

She was silent. Then, very slowly, she shook her head.

'Not yet, Gary.' she said. 'I can't keep starting new lives. I think I've got to finish the old one. I need some time. The other night when I got so smashed and I was going on about leading my own life, and no more albatrosses and all that jazz – it sounded great at the time, but the trouble is, I'd only be going against my own nature. I think perhaps I was born to be one of those boring people who need some sort of responsibility, and it seems to me now that I have a lot of responsibilities. My mother: who is going to look after her now Father and Grandfather are gone? I have Poppy, who always has been my problem, right from when we were babies. She is never going to make it with Paul So. Someone will need to pick up the pieces.'

'Jade—' he started to say.

'No, please listen. There is another responsibility. That vast empire that Grandfather built up. Mike said it needed a figurehead and muttered something about the shareholders. That's a responsibility, too, isn't it? That business was built on such rotten foundations; piracy, murder – and maybe Grandfather was into heroin like you thought. He was totally amoral, wasn't he? So perhaps I could do something about the foundations, make them respectable, shore them up a bit with some good works.' She spoke mockingly. 'But it would be possible. There's all the money in the world, isn't there?'

He started to pace around the room. He ran his fingers through his blond hair and it was standing on end.

'Jade. You can't go through life wet-nursing your mother, your sister and the shareholders of McKenzie McKenzie. What about me? I happen to love you. I happen to want to spend the rest of my life with you. I actually would like to marry you.'

She bit her lip.

'I know,' she said. 'And I'm not saying no. I'm just asking for time if you'll give it to me. And I won't be wet-nursing anyone. Like I said, there's all the money in the world. I shall bring Mother back to Hong Kong. Kirsty will come, I know she will, and they'll have every bit of help that they could possibly need. As for Poppy, well, that's a bridge to cross when we get to it. I just want a little while to understand the McKenzie McKenzie business and try to set up something good from all those profits. Mike will help me.'

'Don't you know Mike's in love with you?' he said angrily.

'Yes,' she said simply. 'That's why he'll help me.'

'And what about me in all this?' he asked. 'Where do I fit in?'

She stood up and walked to wrap her arms around his waist and bury her head in his chest.

'I don't know yet,' she said, her voice muffled. 'I love you. But must we marry? Can we be modern and have an affair – live together when we can for a while until I know?'

'I'm not a modern man, Jade,' he said. 'I want to marry the girl I love. I'd like to have babies. I want the sort of life my father and mother had. And I don't want to play second string to my wife.'

'I know, I know, I know.' She hugged him tighter, aware that his arms were not around her. 'But will you wait?'

'Yes, I'll wait.' He was silent and still unresponsive. 'But not for very long, Jade.'

'It won't be for very long,' she said. 'I promise.'

Fiction

☐	**Castle Raven**	Laura Black	£1.75p
☐	**Options**	Freda Bright	£1.50p
☐	**Dupe**	Liza Cody	£1.25p
☐	**Chances**	Jackie Collins	£2.50p
☐	**Brain**	Robin Cook	£1.75p
☐	**The Entity**	Frank De Felitta	£1.95p
☐	**The Dead of Jericho**	Colin Dexter	£1.50p
☐	**Whip Hand**	Dick Francis	£1.75p
☐	**Secrets**	Unity Hall	£1.75p
☐	**Solo**	Jack Higgins	£1.75p
☐	**The Rich are Different**	Susan Howatch	£2.95p
☐	**The Master Sniper**	Stephen Hunter	£1.50p
☐	**Moviola**	Garson Kanin	£1.50p
☐	**Smiley's People**	John le Carré	£1.95p
☐	**The Master Mariner Book 1: Running Proud**	Nicholas Montsarrat	£1.50p
☐	**Platinum Logic**	Tony Parsons	£1.75p
☐	**Fools Die**	Mario Puzo	£1.95p
☐	**The Boys in the Mailroom**	Iris Rainer	£1.50p
☐	**The Throwback**	Tom Sharpe	£1.75p
☐	**Wild Justice**	Wilbur Smith	£1.95p
☐	**That Old Gang of Mine**	Leslie Thomas	£1.50p
☐	**Caldo Largo**	Earl Thompson	£1.75p
☐	**Ben Retallick**	E. V. Thompson	£1.75p

All these books are available at your local bookshop or newsagent, or can be ordered direct from the publisher. Indicate the number of copies required and fill in the form below   10

....

Name_____
(Block letters please)

Address_____

_____

Send to CS Department, Pan Books Ltd, PO Box 40, Basingstoke, Hants
Please enclose remittance to the value of the cover price plus:
35p for the first book plus 15p per copy for each additional book ordered
to a maximum charge of £1.25 to cover postage and packing
Applicable only in the UK

While every effort is made to keep prices low, it is sometimes
necessary to increase prices at short notice. Pan Books reserve
the right to show on covers and charge new retail prices which
may differ from those advertised in the text or elsewhere